THE
DEVIL'S
BACKBONE

THE DEVIL'S BACKBONE

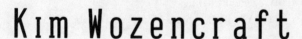

Kim Wozencraft

ST. MARTIN'S PRESS

New York

www.stmartins.com

Design by Kathryn Parise

Library of Congress Cataloging-in-Publication Data

Wozencraft, Kim.
The Devil's Backbone / Kim Wozencraft.—1st ed.
p. cm.
ISBN-13: 978-0-312-29063-4
ISBN-10: 0-312-29063-2
1. Sisters—Fiction 2. Women detectives—Texas—
Fiction 3. Stripteasers—Fiction. 4. Austin (Tex.)—
Fiction. I. Title

PS3573.O98D485 2006
813'.54—dc22

2006043423

First Edition: September 2006

10 9 8 7 6 5 4 3 2 1

For Lloyd Harrell

aka

Crimefighter

ACKNOWLEDGMENTS

Thanks and more thanks to my marvelous agent, Betsy Lerner, of Dunow, Carlson, and Lerner Literary Agency in New York, and to my exceptional editor, Jennifer Enderlin. You went above and beyond this time around. Thanks to Rich Green for excellent suggestions at the manuscript stage. Blair Breard and Cindy Sweeney were kind enough to read and comment on early drafts. I am grateful to Donald J. Davidson, whose close reading and exemplary copyediting led to many improvements. Thanks also to William H. Schaap, Esq., for being in my corner.

To my mother and sisters, thank you for your love and support and kindness.

And to my friends: Blair Breard, Robert Leaver, Martha Frankel, Lynn McCarty, David Nyzio, Cindy and Patrick Sweeney, Melissa Story, Deborah Hitts, Hanna Roth, and Richard Boes—thank you so much for being there.

ACKNOWLEDGMENTS

I must make one posthumous acknowledgment. Howard Swindle (1945–2004), a Pulitzer Prize–winning journalist at the *Dallas Morning News*, encouraged me at a critical time in my life to return to writing and pursue it with passion, and for that encouragement, as well as for his friendship, I am most grateful.

And thank you especially to my children: Maxx, Dash, and Sasha. I cherish you.

THE
DEVIL'S
BACKBONE

ONE

She tried to open her eyes. Slowly.

No go. They felt full of sand. She pressed her palms against her eyelids until tears came, trying to rinse away the grit. Slowly again, trying to force the lids up. A glint of light, and then glare was everywhere. Morning sky. Sun already well into its arc. She closed them again. She was on her back, that much she could feel. She reached out a hand, eyes still closed, brain throbbing against her skull in time to her pounding heart. Earth. She was on the ground somewhere. Where? Not that it mattered.

She rolled onto her side and felt grass against her face, smelled green grass. She hoped she wasn't on someone's front lawn, prone there, being stared at by some guy in a bathrobe out to get his morning paper. Her heart pounded. Her head pounded. A flock of grackles screamed aggressively from someplace close. She heard the beat of wings and the bird yells receded. She lay there, waiting, wondering how long it would be before she could get to her feet.

Last night was lost to her. No memory of it whatsoever. A black hole in her brain. Maybe it would suck up some of the others, eat up molecules of the memories she just couldn't handle these days. The ones that wouldn't leave her alone.

Wheels against pavement, the sound of footsteps approaching. Shit. She forced her eyes open, her head pounded, she rolled onto all fours. Her stomach tightened; she fought the urge to vomit. Where the fuck was she?

Black shoes, navy socks, a man's muscular calves. She forced herself to look up.

Cop. She looked past him to where he'd parked his bicycle.

Park police. Austin PD.

Shit. A piece of last night crept into her brain. She'd driven here, somehow, to the park. She loathed this place. The road had been undulating, like a black ribbon floating on water. She'd tried to focus on the white stripe at the edge. She'd made it to the parking lot. Turned off the ignition. She didn't remember after that.

"You okay miss?" His voice resonant.

She nodded her lie.

She brought herself to her feet.

"You should do radio," she said.

He smiled, but didn't seem flattered. "Got some ID?"

She looked past him. There was a parking lot. Her car was in it. Her blue Mustang. Maybe her bag was there. She pointed toward the car.

"I think, maybe in there."

He turned and looked at the car, alone in the small lot.

"Can you make it over there?"

She nodded and took a step. She heard blood pulsing through her ears. *Whoosh, whoosh, whoosh.* The rhythm of heartbeat.

At the car, she handed him her driver's license.

"Katherine Metcalf."

She nodded, though it seemed odd to be addressed by her given name. She'd gone by Kit for as long as she could remember. The nickname her father had given her. Her neck hurt. The throbbing in her brain was working its way down her spinal cord.

He studied her license a moment. Then pulled his hand-held from his belt. Keyed it and said some things. Somewhere behind the whooshing in her ears she heard him give her name, date of birth, and license number. He stood holding his radio and looking at her.

"Are you drunk?" he said.

Kit shook her head no. "Was," she said. Stupid. Volunteer nothing. She couldn't think for the pounding in her head. "I'm okay now," she said.

His radio spit static and she heard "Subject clear, no warrants," and he said something back and tucked the radio onto his belt.

"You don't look so well," he said. "How'd you wind up here?"

"I was out with friends." What the hell. Make it up as you go along. "I realized—on my way home—I shouldn't be driving. I pulled in here."

"Good move," he said. He eyed her carefully, gauging. "But you don't need to be spending the night passed out in a public park."

"I know," Kit said. "Believe me. I know."

Maybe there was something in her eyes when she said that. Or maybe he just felt like being nice.

"Tell me you don't make a habit of this."

"No," she said. "Honest. I don't. I just, I don't know. Big party. It got away from me."

"Go home," he said. "Sleep it off."

She thanked him. Got in her car. Her hands shook as she tried to fit the key into the ignition. The cop walked back over to his bicycle, stood watching her.

She started the car. She brushed her brown hair back from her face. She drove slowly and carefully. Headed toward her apartment downtown.

Headed toward the bottle of vodka in the freezer.

"Hair of the dog," she whispered. Do not pass go. Do not collect two hundred dollars. Get thee home.

She had to be at work by four.

What time was it, anyway?

⌗

The Grey Goose had helped. Taken the edge off. Kit had been cautious, swallowing it like medicine, in controlled doses at specific times. She was better now, or something approaching better. Not looped, but no longer hungover. Mellowed out. The way she needed to be to function at this fucking job.

She gyrated across the hardwood dance floor, and a face behind a window caught her attention. She'd seen him around. She danced over closer to his window. Her hair fell freely, in waves to her shoulders. She wore a black micromini, in that nanofabric stuff. Her breasts were hidden beneath a black tube top that she had yet to remove and let

4

drop to the floor. Timing was everything. She felt loose now. Loose as a goose? For the time being anyway.

He was watching her dance. He'd shown up for the first time a few weeks ago, and had quickly become a regular, coming in two, three, often four times a week. With his sandy hair and keen blue eyes, he was hard not to notice. It was his demeanor, though, that caught her attention. The dancers had nicknamed him Sweet.

Cheryl, her black curls highlighted psycho pink and pulled into a cacophony of ponytails, was at the other end of the small stage. If you could even call it a stage: a twenty-by-thirty-foot rectangular dance floor bathed in red light with a disco ball hanging dead center and floor-to-ceiling, chrome-plated poles placed four feet out on either side of it.

Kit let her eyes connect to Sweet's, only for an instant, and then moved across the stage to dance next to Cheryl. He was interesting, that one.

"I wish the damn glass was tinted," Cheryl said, "so we wouldn't have to see these jerks jerking off." Kit nodded emphatic agreement, in time to the music. It was Cheryl who had brought Kit, her insides twisted with nerves, on-stage for her first shift—what had it been, eight months ago? Who could keep track? Who *wanted* to keep track? Cheryl had showed her the ropes, made silent jokes with her eyes when Kit first noticed that the men in the booths were masturbating as they watched the women dance. It was nothing new to Cheryl. She'd been dancing for years, in many different clubs—some of them hard-core—moving from one place to the next whenever she tired of the boss.

"I'm so bored," Cheryl said. "Do you think I'm A.D.D.?"

Kit grabbed a pole and let herself spin slowly around it.

"No," she said, "you're just easily distracted."

Cheryl slid into a split. She'd been a gymnast in high school, and could bend her body into all kinds of shapes. She wasn't particularly muscular, the way some gymnasts got, but she was strong and had good balance. She pulled herself up into a handstand and did an inverted split, came out of it into a slow-motion cartwheel. In charge of her body.

"You don't look so great," Cheryl said.

"Rough night," Kit said.

"You? I'm shocked."

"I'm sure."

A dancer Kit hadn't yet met was in the middle, beneath the disco ball, bending and sliding, snakelike, to the funk/hip-hop/seventies-disco fusion of the Brushing Teeth Baby Buttheads blasting from the speakers. Kit synced her movements to the bass as she eased back over in front of Sweet's window. Sweet, always courteous, his blue eyes full of good intentions, and on top of it the guy was a good tipper.

She whirled around and dropped into a crouch, her back to him, then slowly straightened, peering at him from between her legs, giving him a teasing money shot. She slipped around, bringing her right leg over in a hook kick and shooting it back up into an inside-out axe kick. Sometimes, while she was dancing, she brought her karate into the routine. That was the joke: These moves she was making, so erotic to the men watching her dance, could break their bones. Amusing. Okay. That frightened her. More and more often her thoughts seemed like guerrilla fighters, lurking behind bushes, waiting in ambush. Bring on the black hole, brain. Bring it on and suck up the madness. Disintegrate it.

She whipped around into a back kick, and around again, and crouched in front of Sweet, anticipating his smile. He obliged.

Because I am . . . the music blasted . . . *because I am. A raw believer.*

Back across the stage and—ugh—there he was. Not that one. Please. Back for more. The Tarantula. His face looked like one: the way his beard covered so much of it, and his head was a mass of black hair that aspired to dreadlocks but couldn't quite cut it. It was his eyes, though, that made her want to keep her distance. Like marbles or something. Clear and cold, with that gray tint. She couldn't see his mouth; his mustache hid it.

The music segued into a Stones song and Kit shook off the willies and shook her body and shook her head and did it all to the beat thumping out of Blaze's industrial-strength sound system. She moved to the music and looked at the screwed-tight face of the guy in the booth in front of her, clean-cut, this one, but there it was, he was close and getting closer, wanking away in his little black closet, and was this the most fucked-up job ever in the whole entire world or did it even really matter whether there were guys watching her dance and yanking on their penises, trying to, trying to . . . c'mon, baby, c'mon.

. . . *andsexandsex. Lookatme!* The music pulsed, pumped, pulled her across the stage, past all the little windows and all the little faces, and there was the Tarantula again, his eyes almost slits now, his arm pumping hard and fast, go, Johnny, go. Go. Isn't that special. Kit spun around so she wouldn't have to see it. Cheryl turned her head so the guy wouldn't see her wink at Kit, and Kit did a spin so he wouldn't see her smirking reply to Cheryl. She bent over and shook her ass at him: *Look at me!*

I'm in tatters.

Kit moved around the stage taking broad steps now, funky, in time to the music, needing to see anything besides the expression of pseudobliss on the face of the ejaculator. That was the thing: there they sat in their little black booths, jerking themselves off, and when they finished, they would look at you like they'd just fucked you, and *wasn't it the best sex you ever had, baby?*

She tossed her head, spun, whipping her hair in circles around her head, smiling all the time, oooh, there it was, here was his moment, the Tarantula's head tilted back, his mouth went slack, his arm slowed, then stopped.

Kit wondered if he was happy.

When was break time? Maybe she could sneak in a shot of vodka. Ezra, the bartender, was good about that.

She moved her hips to the music, caressed herself, and looked at the pairs of eyes, the longing in all those eyes, behind the little square windows in the little black booths. Maybe selling Austin real estate hadn't been such a bad gig after all; even dealing with hopeful first-time homebuyers might be preferable to this. But she couldn't make this kind of money anywhere but here. For what it was, Blaze's was the best.

She saw the Tarantula slip a folded bill through the slot beneath the window, watched paper money fall onto the pile of bills in the Plexiglas cube that caught the tips. She couldn't make out the denomination, but would bet the Tarantula's bill had a portrait of Ulysses Grant, who'd helped the United States steal a big chunk of Texas from Mexico.

She danced and tried not to keep looking over at the hole in the floor of the stage, back in the corner behind her, from which her relief would emerge any minute now: a fresh dancer, another nearly naked body climbing the ladder from the dressing room below to spend her four hours up here in the glow of red lights and lusting male eyes, knocking down the kind of bucks that secretaries and administrative assistants only dreamed of making. And much of it in tax-free cash.

Cash. Cash. Cash. That was what she told herself this job was about. That was what kept her coming in through that back door five times a week to pull her shifts. She held no illusions—as Cheryl and some of the other dancers did—about using her *career* at Blaze's as a launchpad to fire herself into legitimate show business. But there were moments when she was onstage, when some guy was sitting there in his booth and Kit could see that he wanted desperately to touch her, he needed it like he needed air, he was going to die soon if he couldn't run a hand over the curve of her hip and press his lips to her neck, there were those moments when a look caught her off guard and she knew she liked the job not for the money, but for the power. Dipshit in the booth could want until he dropped dead: He wasn't going to touch her. She was the one calling the shots. She was the one enticing and inviting and showing him what he could never have. Even with those she thought she might have been interested in—if interest was even a possibility lately—had she met them in different circumstances, even with them, maybe even especially with them, she drew sustenance from their helplessness to control the situation. She could dance right up to the window, she could writhe like she had to have them this instant, she could run a hand across her body the way they were dying to, and she could turn and flit across the stage to another window and do the same thing to the guy in that booth. And the next one. And the next.

She could have them all wanting her, all needing her, and not one of them could do a single damn thing about it.

That was it.

She could make them feel, if not exactly as she had that night—the night that would not go away—at least something of the way she had felt. She could make them feel powerless to control what was happening to them. Powerless. As she had been. She could make them helpless.

She could take their breath away.

Why had she driven to that goddamn park? Unconscious. Blacked out. Why had she gone *there*. How twisted was that?

"Cheryl," she said, still moving to the Stones, "are you bored?"

"More than," Cheryl said, smiling to a cute young guy with freckles who, judging from the look of awe and astonishment on his face, might be on his inaugural trip to Blaze's. "Come with. Let's wow this newbie."

Kit ponied her way closer to Cheryl and followed Cheryl's lead as they danced their way through the swim, the funky chicken, the shark, the snark, and then Kit did some moves as Cheryl maintained a basic groove, axe kicks over Cheryl's head, spinning hook kicks with Cheryl slipping her hands out of the way at the last possible second, they went on, dancing together, and the kid so into it he forgot to take his thing out and play with himself, or else he was too shy.

"He's sweet," Cheryl said to Kit, "don't you think?"

Kit flashed a smile at the kid. "We've got a Sweet."

Sweet kept his hands on the window ledge, where the dancers could see that, unlike most of the other men in the booths, he wasn't jerking off. Kit had him pegged as a savior, one of those guys who would come to the club and watch and wait and watch, make himself a regular, and then finally try to catch one of the dancers in the hallway and talk her into changing her ways. Tell her she was too good for this, this was beneath her, she was beautiful and deserved something better in life. Right.

"He looks like Friedrich Nietzsche." Kit danced past Cheryl.

"Huh?" Cheryl raised a blond, perfectly shaped eyebrow.

"This philosopher guy," Kit said. "I had to read his garbage for a class."

"Whatever." Cheryl slowly pulled off the long white gloves she wore, flung them across stage, ran her hands across her eyes like Catwoman, showing off long purple nails.

Fred looked from one to the other of them, his hands creeping down toward his crotch. It was new music.

From the Stones to Outkast. Fred was getting into it. Groovin' now, movin' to the music. Kit and Cheryl pranced around the stage in a slow oval path until they were back in front of him.

"Know what Fred said?" Kit tossed her head dramatically, put her lips into a sex-kitten pout. She knew how to make fun of herself.

"Your philosopher Fred?" Cheryl went into a shimmy.

"He's the one who said God is dead." Kit did a spinning crescent kick, which looked good to Fred if you could judge from his smile. He was into her moves.

Cheryl spun past, her impeccably plucked eyebrows now

raised, like a couple of question marks lying head to head on their sides.

"I don't believe that for a minute," she said. "God is not dead. Things could not possibly be as fucked up as they are on this planet unless somewhere, somehow, there is a man sitting up there in heaven in charge of it all."

"And," Kit added, "he said woman was God's *second* mistake. Fred did. I read it in that class and it's stuck in my brain."

"Like a splinter, sounds like."

"You gonna tell me? Is that the ultimate put-down? Even when it comes to mistakes, women take second place? Ask me, Fred had his head up his ass." She could do this. She could have a perfectly normal conversation.

Cheryl had her hands in fists and was pumping them up and down, doing that sixties classic, the jerk.

"Customers love this retro stuff," she said. "I'm sure of it."

"He said when God created woman, boredom ceased, but so did a lot of other stuff." Kit grabbed a pole again and let her body slide around it. She glanced toward Sweet's window. The booth was empty.

"I wish boredom ceased." Cheryl reached behind her back and slipped loose her hot-pink bra, dangled it, smiling at the windows, and let it drop to the floor. "I'm like, chronically bored."

"I mean, women were the second mistake?" Kit unzipped her mini and shimmied out of it. "Should we take that as a compliment? Should I ask you how you *feel* about that or should I ask you what you *think* about that?"

"Kit," Cheryl said, "lighten up already. All we have to do is get up here on stage and move to the tunes and let these jerk-offs jerk off. They're paying. We're playing. You tell me who's mistaken."

⊞

It was almost midnight when Kit followed Cheryl down the ladder into the dressing room. Ezra had helped her through the shift, pouring a double and slipping it to her discreetly when she'd approached him while on break.

Cheryl changed quickly and sat down on one of the upholstered stools in front of the long mirror that lined one wall.

Kit stood at her locker, staring at her street clothes hanging limp on their hooks. When she looked over, she saw Cheryl gazing at her in the mirror.

"I'm meeting Rick," Cheryl said. "Wanna have a drink with us?"

All Kit had to do was say sure. Say yes. Get out, socialize a little. She wouldn't, she knew. She'd go home to her apartment, pour a cranberry and vodka, and climb into bed with a book. She didn't want to go out for drinks. She wanted to go *in* for drinks. She didn't want to yammer the night away, saying nothing. She didn't want to be the third wheel, tagging with Cheryl and Rick, who thought Cheryl worked evenings as a keyboarder at a law firm.

"Did you tell him yet?"

Cheryl paused in her application of blush to shake her head firmly. No.

"It's not serious, Kit. And no matter how much they claim it doesn't matter, it always winds up mattering. They get possessive. Don't want other guys seeing their girlfriend nearly naked. I told you. Don't tell them. It never works out."

"I don't even have someone worth lying to," Kit said.

13

"Besides," Cheryl said, "it's not like I'm serious about this guy. Who needs the bullshit? And whatever happened to Rusty? He was cute. For a cowboy."

"He asked me to marry him," Kit said, slipping into her skirt, this one the color of apricot, and rather less revealing than her stage skirt. She pulled on a T in a slightly lighter shade and ran a brush through her hair.

"If he was looking for domestic help, he should've put an ad in the paper." Cheryl popped her mascara brush back into its tube and screwed it tight. "Did I tell you I bought a new car?"

"What'd you get?"

"It's a Z. Fast and furious, babe."

"You're going to get hurt, the way you drive."

"I'm a good driver."

"No. *I'm* a good driver. You're a speed demon."

"Come on, Kit," Cheryl pleaded teasingly. "Go out with us. Just one drink."

"Famous last words," Kit said. "Some other time."

"That's what you always say."

Kit left Cheryl primping in front of the mirror, readying herself for her date, and walked down the hall toward the back door of the club, wondering if she would ever get herself together enough to go on one herself. If she even wanted to. She knew she could do it. She'd been with Rusty. She could be with someone else. Maybe. But not the way she was now.

She walked across the parking lot toward the back row, where employees were required to park, scanning the lot carefully, looking for anything amiss, anything unusual. She didn't want to. She hated it: always looking, always expecting, but it was not a matter of choice. It was damn near automatic.

What she wanted was to walk calmly to her car and get in and hit the iPod and drive home and not have some kind of freaking mental meltdown on the way. She forced her thoughts to the subject of Rusty, tried to use him to push away fear: his crooked smile, the way he used to look at her with a mix of affection and desire that pulled at her, connected her to him. She saw him leaning against the wide barn door, squinting against the sun, waiting as she approached for an afternoon ride. He was a good man. She wished, sometimes, that she had been able to commit to him. And then she would bring herself quickly to her senses—remembering her mother's marriage, the career sacrifices, the way her mother catered to her father's needs, always, while rarely attending to her own. Kit just wasn't up for that, not even on a good day.

She didn't know what she *was* up for. She walked across the lot, trying to press down the mild panic—now *there* was an oxymoron—which these days stayed with her almost every waking moment. Every sober moment. And those were getting few and far between. Lately she was trying to laugh at it, scare it away with her teeth bared. But not grimacing. Smiling. Like nice people—or people who wanted you to think they were nice—managed to do. It was easier when she drank. Easy to smile then.

She spotted Cheryl's new Nissan, the Z gleaming sleek gunmetal gray under the pinkish glow of the vapor lights, thought about veering over to take a look. As usual, Cheryl had ignored the parking rule. Her car was in the middle of the lot. Cheryl seemed to have it all together. She was never without a date; she was never without ample cash. She was never without a smile. Kit hadn't ever seen her in even a slightly bad mood. The car suited her. Hell with it. She'd look another time. Right now she was going home. Maybe she could get enough alcohol into her system to fall into a deep and dreamless sleep. That was what she wanted. No, needed.

She keyed the lock to open the Mustang. It was a good car. A sixty-six. Vintage. Kit didn't mind the trouble involved in finding parts when they were needed, which wasn't often. Still, a new car might not be the worst thing for her right now. Make some changes in her life. Even superficial change might help right now.

She turned and walked back toward Cheryl's car, easing between a row of vehicles, her eyes on the Z. She thought she heard something, over near Cheryl's car. She stopped. Listened. Traffic sounds from out on the boulevard, cars accelerating off a green light at the intersection in front of the club. She walked again.

But then, as she neared the shiny new vehicle, she heard something. Definitely heard something. Movement, from behind Cheryl's car. She froze, felt her insides go liquid. Silence. It was nothing. It was just her stupid apprehension, playing tricks on her again, leading her to expect the worst. She stepped toward the car.

A grunt, a gasp, and a figure burst from behind the front fender—*whoosh!*—bulky, crouched low, hurtling toward her. Kit heard her bag hit the ground with a thud; her keys clinked against pavement. Fear washed through her, engulfing her as the form hurtled toward her. She heard a voice in her head, a screaming voice, a voice screaming—*Run!*—and it wasn't even a voice in there, it was something else— *Run!*—but she couldn't move. Another grunt as he charged forward and the whites of his eyes as he neared. He slammed into her, knocking her onto the blacktop. She sprawled on the pavement. A jolt, a shiver-charge electric struck her from within, sending heat, a burning red rage exploding inside her belly, shocking clean down to her fingertips.

She scrambled to her feet as he pulled himself up, faced her, his features mashed and twisted beneath black stocking, And then everything went sluggish: She watched him raise his arms to tackle her, to grab her body and throw it back to the ground, but he was moving so slowly now, she had all the time in the world to shift her weight and she heard him growl *Better back off, bitch*, and as he lurched toward her, she felt herself move. Her legs tensed beneath her, knees flexed; she shifted her feet. He lunged, his arms flung apart to grab her. His chest was wide open. She kicked hard, throwing her hip into it, throwing her whole body into it, throwing everything she had into it, all the rage and anger and hurt; she smashed with the ball of her foot, nailing his solar plexus. He gasped, knocked back by the force of her kick; she stepped right and hit him square in the jaw with a roundhouse kick, sending him sideways, spilling onto the pavement, his mouth open, seeking air, his lips twisted like writhing worms beneath the black hosiery pulled over his face. Blood seeped purple from his nose and Kit moved to hit him again, but he scrambled away, scuttling across the blacktop crablike, pulling himself sideways away from her. She stood watching, stunned, almost outside herself, as he dragged himself fully to his feet and staggered into the darkness of the vacant lot behind Blaze's, bent over and clutching his chest.

She grabbed her bag, scraped her nails against pavement as she scooped up her keys, and ran back toward the club, slipping between cars, her bag slamming against someone's side-view mirror and almost taking her down. She tripped up the stairs and felt her keys in her hand, where was the key, where was the key, her hands wouldn't work, her fingertips were numb against the metal of the keys. She could smell them, the odor of metal lodging at the back of her throat, she could smell her keys but she couldn't grip the right one, they were a jumble of small shiny objects hanging from her key ring, tangled together like a nail puzzle. She gave up and banged against the back door, the fleshy side of her fist striking the hollow metal door. She banged and banged, glanced over her shoulder across the lot, waiting for him to return, waiting for him to come at her. She heard the thud of the exit bar bang the door from inside, pressed herself against the brick wall to let it open. She shoved past Cheryl into the building, nearly knocking her to the ground; she turned to grab the door and yank it shut.

Cheryl stood staring at her, holding a tube of lipstick, her top lip shining with freshly applied peach shimmer, the bottom one still ordinary flesh tone. Her lips made an almost perfect O as she took Kit's arms, questioning silently.

Kit heard herself gasping and felt air cutting into her windpipe.

"Out there." She gulped air. "A man."

Cheryl started to open the door but Kit grabbed her, shaking her head no.

"He might," she said, but couldn't finish the sentence. She felt her lungs seize up, and she was trying to breathe, air was all around her, the disco beat thumping through it from somewhere far away in the club. She stood, looking at Cheryl, trying to tell her what was wrong, but she could only stand there, waiting to see if her body was going to start functioning again or if she was going to fall to the ground unconscious.

"Kit?" Cheryl stared at her, her brow etched with fright, her lips pulled tight now and stretched across her face in a grim line. "Kit?"

Kit stood, her own mouth open, and felt a tiny bit of air seep down toward her lungs, felt her ribs give way, barely, and then wider, and her throat seemed to open and she sucked down some air. She held on to it, afraid to let it go, afraid she wouldn't be able to get another breath, and then it escaped on its own. She tried again, inhaled.

Cheryl held on to Kit's arms, her chin dipping and rising in cadence to Kit's breaths, as if keeping time for her.

"A man," Kit whispered finally. "Out there."

"Who?" Cheryl's voice squeaked out the question, and Kit could see Cheryl was afraid of the answer.

"No clue," Kit said. "Not the first idea."

And then there was movement at the end of the hallway, and Blaze's smoke-hardened voice, deep and scratchy, saying *What's-this, what's-this*, and the rubber thud of her boot heels striking linoleum as she marched toward them.

Later, in Blaze's office, Kit sat watching her boss's lips move, but the words flowed around Kit's head, slipping past her ears without registering. Blaze was insisting on calling in a doctor to see Kit, that much Kit was gathering. She sat shaking her head no. No, she did not want a doctor; no, she did not want to go to the emergency room.

She didn't want anything. She slumped there, remembering.

That night.

Blaze sat behind her desk in her Jones New York suit, a cream number probably calculated to make her brilliant red hair an even more conspicuous feature than it was on its own. Curly verging on frizz, shoulder-length, big and magnificent, Blaze's hair and lips were all Kit could focus on. Except for the lips, also brilliant red, Blaze's face was a blur. The room around them was a blur.

"Blaze," Kit said. "Please. I do not want to call the police. Please."

It hadn't happened. The words rattled around in Kit's head. It hadn't happened. This time, she had defended herself. There had been a dirty little battle out there in the parking lot, and she had won. She hoped she had broken the fucker's jaw, and knew there was a good chance she had. So what was this fear, this lump of dread, that seemed to be churning in her stomach like some indigestible chunk of meat?

"Kit." Blaze was still talking to her. Kit closed her eyes, pressing the lids tight together, held them shut. Opened them. She brought Blaze's face into focus: the perfect pale skin, the pert nose, the gorgeous cheekbones. Blaze was a looker, but not one who traded on her looks. It was her eyes that told the world she was all business. Hazel and fierce, the deep green around the pupils connecting jaggedly to the burnt sienna around the rims, like cat's-eyes. "Kit." Blaze's voice dropped lower, confidential in tone. "I'll accept that you want to avoid medical attention, though I still think you should be seen. But darlin', I *have* to call the police. No choice. Word of this gets out, there'll be a bunch of Baptists bangin' on the front door trying to get my license. It won't do. Now you're gonna have to stay here until the cops can drag their asses out of Starbucks and get over here to take a report. You want a drink?"

Kit nodded yes and heard a hallelujah chorus in her head as Blaze turned to the credenza behind her desk and reached for a bottle of Don Julio. "I'd offer champagne but this is hardly the occasion." She chuckled, and Kit heard a laugh coming from her own mouth. "Or maybe it is," Blaze added. "Sounds like you kicked his ass."

Kit took the offered crystal shot glass, eyed it gratefully.

"It'll help you relax, dear. Drink up."

Kit took a sip, anticipating the burn down the back of her throat, wanting it. It went down more smoothly than she'd expected.

"Whoa," she said, her voice coming out slightly husky.

"No," Blaze said, "giddyap," and threw the liquid into her mouth like an Old West gunslinger in a saloon, slamming the shot glass down on her desk with authority. She leaned toward Kit. "Any ideas? Any of the customers pissed off at you or anything like that?"

"No," Kit said. She felt calm wash through her with the liquor. "My business here stays on the stage. I don't do parties, I don't date customers. There's no reason for anyone to be mad at me."

"A rapist, maybe?" Blaze looked, for an instant, almost vulnerable.

Kit closed her eyes. Shook her head no. No. She didn't know. She was dizzy. Still needing air. Needing it more than ever.

"Robbery?"

Kit opened her eyes again. Blaze shifted in her chair,

glanced at the TAG Heuer on her slender wrist. The diamonds circling the watch face glittered brightly under the halogen mini flood trained to illuminate the black marble surface of her desk.

"You were next to Cheryl's car?"

"He was hiding behind it."

Blaze sat back, running an index finger along the edge of her crystal glass.

"And you don't have the first idea who it might have been."

Kit shook her head no. Again.

"Well, look," Blaze said, "the cops get here they might start asking a few extra questions. I'd like it if you'd help them stay on the topic."

"Which is?"

"What happened to you tonight."

"What else would I tell them?"

"You remember that little speed-freaky customer? The one with the fried red hair, wiry guy, all jittery? I think his name was Weatherby."

"Doesn't ring any bells."

"The cops were in here a few weeks ago, asking me did I know him, et cetera, et cetera."

"I'm not following."

"I didn't know him, or only as far as I recognized him from a photo they had. He was in here pretty regularly."

"And?"

"They were from homicide. Said the guy'd been murdered."

"So what's that got to do with me?" Kit felt confusion swirling slowly into her brain, washing her thoughts around, sucking them into a tiny vortex one right after the other.

"Nothing, I'm sure. But you know how the cops are. They might need a little help staying focused on the matter at hand."

"What did you tell them?"

"Just the truth. He was a regular. Other than that, I don't know a damn thing about his business. Or why anybody might want him dead." Blaze poured another shot of tequila, offered the bottle to Kit.

Kit nodded yes. Liquid gold, it was, going down. Relief.

"But, for God's sake," Blaze said, "the guy was so *obviously* into meth. No need to call in Sherlock on that case, or else Jimmy Dean can't make sausage worth a shit."

Kit wanted to say something, but her voice wouldn't cooperate. She sat mute, wondering at her social ineptitude. She bobbed her head up and down, hoping it looked like she agreed, even though she didn't remember ever seeing the speed-freak guy. Like that meant anything.

"Anyway, just give 'em the best description you can," Blaze said. "Not that I think they have a snowball's chance in hell of finding the bastard. But we'll keep our fingers crossed. Did Cheryl say anything to you?"

"Cheryl? No. Why?"

"You said he was behind her car."

"And?"

"That's my point. I mean, there's no reason for anybody to be after any of my dancers. It was just some kind of random thing, is what it looks like to me. Some nut job."

Kit sat staring, feeling a kind of numbness set in, like it had before. But this time was different. Beneath the numb, way down in there, she could feel the beating of her heart, as though she had one hand on her chest and was feeling it through her fingertips. She could feel it pulse through her arm and spread throughout her body, circling back on itself in the center of her chest.

"Right," she said. "Random attack. Lucky me."

By the time Kit left Blaze's office and wandered down the hall to the dressing room, it was empty. The last shift had gone home. The club was silent. Kit hadn't realized how long she'd been in there with Blaze. And the cops. They'd taken forever to get there. She had answered their rote questions as obliquely as possible while Blaze looked on, strangely quiet. Then they'd left, offering assurances of increased patrol activity in the area. Big deal.

Kit took her robe from her locker and stepped over to the couch, stood staring at it. She was scared to stay here. But she was even more afraid not to. She lay down on the couch and draped the robe over herself. Slipped off her shoes, let them drop to the carpet.

Fatigue. Bodily. But her brain wouldn't cooperate. Things were buzzing, there inside her skull. She just wanted some sleep. She would take even ten minutes of the stuff. Anything.

She thought briefly about calling her father. Or her sister. Not an option. She refused to involve them.

The fluorescent light in the dressing room burned at her eyes, even through closed eyelids. She wanted to turn them off, but couldn't. She could not make herself get up and turn out the lights. She was too tired to move, and too scared to be in the dark. Fuck it. Sooner or later her brain would have to give in and let her get some sleep.

Sooner or later.

She was somewhere on the edge of unconsciousness,

drifting uneasily into it, when a soft tap on the door brought her instantly upright. Her entire body pulsed to the beat of her pounding heart, hangover style. Shit. But whoever it was, they'd knocked.

"What?" she said.

The door opened. Ezra, the bartender and bouncer, showed his shaved head from behind the door.

"I'm locking up," he said softly. "Want me to walk you out?"

"I think I'll just stay here," Kit said.

He looked troubled for a moment, his gray eyes staring into her bloodshot ones.

"Sure?" he asked finally. "You're welcome at my place. Alex won't mind."

Kit considered, or tried to, for a moment. She'd met Ezra's partner, and was sure Ezra was right. He wouldn't mind. Alex was a very nice man. It wasn't that she feared intruding.

"Thanks," Kit said. "I'll be okay."

"All right then." Ezra stepped far enough into the room to reveal his well-toned body, muscled-up arms and chest beneath a skintight black T. "If you change your mind, call me." He pulled the door closed behind him.

Kit lay back down on the couch, tried to make herself relax. It wasn't happening. She lay there awhile, and then got up and headed down the hallway. To the bar. A couple more shots should do the trick.

And it didn't matter to her if an entire battalion of marines arrived to escort her to her car. She was not going back out there.

TWO

A flash in the rearview caught Jenny's eye and she glanced up, expecting the glint to have come from the hellish afternoon sunshine reflecting off someone's chromed bumper. It hadn't.

The white flare was followed by red and blue, the three colors strobing in the mirror from the marked squad car that had fallen in behind her. How had she missed seeing *that*?

"Shit," she muttered. She sighed and eased off the gas, hit the signal arm, and heard the *clink-clink-clink* of the turn indicator. She eased to a stop on the gravel-covered shoulder and pressed the button to roll down her window. Heat and noise blasted in with each passing vehicle. She eyed the rearview and watched the cop put on his hat, grab his ticket book, and step out of the car.

She remembered those days, sitting on the side of the

highway, waiting for some asshole to come barreling by fast enough to set off the alarm on the radar. She did not miss working patrol division.

As the officer approached, she saw him discretely unsnap the strap that held his gun in its holster. Procedure. Just in case. She didn't know how fast she'd been going, but it wasn't like she'd busted radar doing one-ten or something. She was simply late for work.

Damn. Who could say what it was, why she had such a hard time getting out of her apartment. No matter how early she set her alarm, how conscientious she was about making sure in advance that all she'd have to do was shower, dress, grab her snack, and head out the door, it seemed that the last five minutes before her departure time somehow ran amok on her and became fifteen or twenty. She'd been pulled over for speeding more than once.

She heard the crunch of the officer's shoes on gravel and looked up. He had on aviators. Bad sign. No doubt he wished he was on a motorcycle instead of stuck driving one of those dog-ass Fords the department insisted on buying year after year.

"License and registration, please," he drawled.

Like any good detective, Jenny kept her driver's license tucked behind her police ID. Now she opened her badge case and slipped her index finger beneath the ID to pull it out, making sure the pair of eyes behind the aviators got a solid look at the badge as she did.

He cleared his throat.

"You're with the department?"

Jenny nodded and displayed her badge case. "C.I.D."

He gave a little laugh and scuffed a shoe against the gravel.

" 'Scuse me then," he said. "Have a nice day now." He turned and walked back to his squad, shaking his head slowly.

She rolled up her window and blasted the air conditioner full on. It was hotter than the hinges of hell's gates out there. She felt bad for him, having to work in it. And glad he hadn't felt like giving her any grief. They all aspired to make detective, the patrol officers, and didn't want to make any enemies in C.I.D. All was well.

She checked her side mirror, waited for a particularly slow rubbernecker to pass, and then pulled back out onto the freeway. The patrol car was a tiny dot in her rearview when she kicked her speed up to eighty. She was going to have to make some serious time to get to work with anything even remotely related to punctuality. But she would pay attention now, keep an eye out for lurking squad cars.

Her plan was to stay at her desk doing paperwork and making phone calls from three until six, and then comp the remaining five hours of her shift. She was going shopping this evening. Headed to the mall to fill out the bridal registration forms. Make lists of gifts she and Luke wanted at their wedding. Luke had said he would meet her there if he could, but he was on a case and didn't know if he'd get free in time.

She had worked enough extra hours lately to take plenty of compensatory time. Most of those hours she'd spent investigating the sad fate of a guy named Jake Weatherby, yet another life-wasting speed freak, and getting nowhere. Unless something big broke on that case this afternoon, something that would lead her to the person or persons who'd released Weatherby from his tortured life by puncturing his heart with a nine-mil slug, she'd be out of the office by six but still getting paid until eleven.

It wasn't until she parked in the lot at the department that she discovered she'd left her Tupperware container of baby carrots and grapes at home on the kitchen counter. Even with all the last-minute rushing around and careful ticking off of items on her mental checklist—turn up the thermostat to keep the air conditioner from kicking on, make sure the windows were locked, check the stove and toaster, etc., go back and check the thermostat again—she'd left it. She wondered if it were an indication that she felt, somewhere deep down, guilty about her priorities. She was a good cop. She worked hard, she was conscientious, and she didn't cheat on her hours. But lately, wedding plans had taken over her life. Not that it was going to be some kind of grandiose affair, but she wanted it to be perfect. She wanted to love every minute of the ceremony, even the nerves before she walked down that aisle. Everything would be just right. Even down to the flowers. What she wanted most of all was for her father to be happy for her. She'd become obsessed with which boutonniere to select for him. White, she thought. Definitely something white.

She scanned her ID card and went straight to the employee lounge, where she stood wishing there was something that contained even an iota of nutrition in any of the garishly packaged snack bags that hung suspended in rows behind the Plexiglas shield of the vending machine in front of her. The room was empty but for her. Evening shift had hit the streets; day-shift cops were headed home, or wherever. Her eyes glazed over as she tried to decide between a bag of X-treme Doritos that no doubt had an extreme amount of artificial flavoring in them and just plain old-fashioned Fritos corn chips, which she knew had an extreme amount of salt in them.

She went for the salt. At least her internal organs were acquainted with the substance. She was struggling with the package when she heard someone enter behind her, humming the wedding march. She turned to see Leila Jane, her drop-dead figure evident even beneath the dark blue patrol uniform, her shoulder-length blond hair pulled into a neat French braid at the back of her head.

"Dinner?" Leila asked.

Jenny, still struggling to rip open the package of chips, shook her head no.

"I don't know why they think they have to seal these things up to endure the rigors of interplanetary travel or something," she said. Just then the bag popped open, scattering Fritos across the beige linoleum of the lounge floor. "Damn!"

"Nervous?" Leila Jane flashed her impeccable pearly whites, evidence of extensive orthodontic attention in her juvenile years, and unclipped her tie, reclipping it to her left pants pocket.

Jenny stooped to pick up the scattered Fritos. Why Leila, whose father would happily have funded a year or two in Europe for her, chose to spend forty hours a week in a patrol uniform with a gun belt strapped around her slender waist, was a mystery. But Jenny was glad Leila was a cop, and especially glad they were roommates, residing in a bungalow on the horse ranch Leila's dad owned just outside of town. The view through her bedroom window was of pastures, and the beautiful creatures they contained.

She tossed the handful of chips into the trash.

"Not nervous," Jenny said. "Just forgetful and uncoordinated." She dug into the nearly empty bag of Fritos. "I left my snack sitting on the kitchen counter, in case you want it when you get home."

"What is it, tofu du jour? Barbecued soybeans? How can you eat that crap?"

"Grapes and carrots," Jenny said, trying not to sound defensive. "You remember, Leila, don't you? From when you were a kid? Real food? Good for you?"

"Oh, you mean like Coco Puffs? Lucky Charms?"

"Speaking of luck, I got pulled over on the way in." Jenny crunched a mouthful of Fritos.

"Were you speeding? Was he cute? Single? Anyone I know?"

"I didn't notice. He was nice, though."

"How could you not notice?"

Jenny offered a chip to Leila. Leila shook her head no, made a face.

"I want you to be my maid of honor," Jenny said. It popped out, just like that, the decision made even as she was speaking the words.

Leila's face broke into a smile and she reached for Jenny, hugged her tight.

"Of course," Leila drawled. "Of course, of course!" She stepped back suddenly, looked earnestly at Jenny.

"What about your sister?"

Jenny shook her head.

"She'd hate me for even asking her," she said. "She'd do it, I'm sure, but not because she wanted to."

"But shouldn't you at least *ask* her? First?"

"Why stress her?" Jenny said. "She'll go as far as bridesmaid, but I'm telling you, she would *not* be comfortable as maid of honor. I've given it a lot of thought, Leila. You do it. She'll be relieved."

"Okay then." Leila was beaming. She leaned toward Jenny, whispered conspiratorially. "Are we having a bachelorette party?"

"I thought that was mandatory."

Leila clenched a fist to her chest, shot two fingers out, forming a sideways V symbol.

"Peace out, girl," she said. "I am now officially on party detail." She grabbed her tie from her pocket and twirled it around her head as she headed out the door and down the hall, laying down one of those lip-farty beats and half dancing as she went.

Jenny headed the opposite direction, toward C.I.D., hoping none of the higher-ups happened to be watching the surveillance cameras at the moment. They'd throw a shit fit if they saw Leila bopping down the halls like that in uniform. She smiled to herself. Leila could always tell them to kiss her ass and take off for Europe and spend a little of Daddy's money.

The office was nearly empty, too. Jenny wound through the large room full of shoulder-high cubicles to her own, in the far back corner of the room. Her desk was reasonably neat, its surface clear but for the in-out box, the square black telephone, and the outdated PC with its cheap keyboard. The city couldn't actually afford to keep up with the latest technology, though the mayor was good at blah-blahing to the public on the subject.

She sat down, crumpled the empty Frito bag a little harder

than she needed to and tossed it in the wastebasket, wishing she hadn't eaten the things. Dusted her palms together to knock off the salt. What had she been thinking?

She pulled the sheaf of new cases from her in box. The first two were convenience store robberies, which fell into the Blind Luck category because that was what most likely would be needed to solve them. The third report was of an elderly woman who'd been tied up in her home by three men, beaten, robbed. As Jenny read she felt a familiar anger churning inside her. Assholes. But the complainant thought she recognized one of the assailants; he'd been at the house earlier in the week cleaning out the gutters. Wouldn't it be sweet, really sweet, if the woman were right in her ID? This one she wanted. What kind of sick prick would beat up an old woman for a TV set and some silverware? She imagined the lovely sound of steel ratcheting as she secured handcuffs around the gutter man's wrists.

Her reverie was interrupted when a fresh report sailed over her shoulder and landed on the desk before her. She lifted herself in her chair, peering over the edge of her cubicle; Sergeant Batista's head and shoulders were visible across the room. The guy moved fast, for sure.

"Take a look," he called back to her. "I'll see you in a few."

Jenny plopped back down into her chair. This was not good. She wanted to leave early tonight. She needed to leave early tonight. She did not need Sergeant Batista's personal interest in one of her cases.

Then she saw the name of the victim. And the location of the call.

What the hell was this? She scanned the rest of the report quickly, looking for listed injuries. There were none. Lovely.

But Kit? Dancing in a damn strip club? This just plain sucked. Jenny felt a stab of guilt. She'd been all wrapped up making wedding plans, trying to decide whether to press her sister into service as her maid of honor, and she didn't even know Kit had taken a job at Austin's premier gentleman's club. And not as a bartender, either. Exasperation needled at her spine. What in hell did Kit think she was doing? Her occupation was listed in the report as *dancer*. Call it what you want. Jenny sighed. It was what it was.

And what it was since Jake Weatherby got wasted was the target of an investigation into a pornography ring, one whose boss evidently played rough.

In the sergeant's office, a windowless rectangle done in the same government functional style as the rest of the offices in the building, she paced.

"I'm telling you, she won't talk to me about this," Jenny said.

"She's your sister."

"Yeah. And if she wanted me to know about it, she would've called me. There's no way. I didn't even know she was working there."

Batista picked up his copy of the report, scanned it. "Says here she, quote, fended off the attack, unquote."

"When we were kids," Jenny said, "one day these two boys, we were playing allie, allie, in free, and Kit got into an argument with them on the other team about whether she'd made it in to base, which was a swing set in the back yard. She couldn't have been more than, like, seven or eight. So they're giving her grief about it, saying they'd got her before she tagged base. I'm still hiding, but I hear them shouting and come out from behind the hedge. One of them has her from behind, her arms pinned to her sides, and the other one kicks her in the stomach. It knocks the air out of her, she's doubled over trying to get a breath. The one's behind her, holding her up—all of a sudden she flips him right over her back, onto the ground in front of her. Wham! She's on him like a wildcat, punching his face and screaming, I mean screaming, calling him a coward, and then the other one pulls her off and she whirls around and smacks him right across the face, screaming at him—*Kick me again and I'll kill you!* She was seriously pissed. She took off like a jackrabbit and left them standing there all beat up."

Batista was grinning, enjoying the story.

"I caught up with her in the woods at the end of the block," Jenny said. "She was bent over and breathing hard, but when she saw me, she stood up and got this huge smile on her face. I wanted to go home and tell the grownups what the boys had done, but she wouldn't do it. Made me pinkie swear I wouldn't tell."

"You saying she has issues with authority?"

"I'm telling you that she won't talk to the cops about what went down at Blaze's. Not even to a cop who's her sister. She'd consider it ratting."

"She filed a report."

"Look again. The owner filed the report. Kit's listed as the victim."

The sergeant glanced at his copy and tossed it back onto his desk, stroking his mustache.

"You'd do better to give the case to someone else," Jenny said.

"I already have." Batista brushed a hand across close-cropped black hair. "But I thought you should know about it.

The Weatherby thing and all. The club." He kicked back in his chair, crossed his feet on one corner of the desk. "I mean, I'd be concerned if a relative of mine were working there."

"In some cultures it's considered very rude to show someone the soles of your shoes," Jenny said.

"Good thing I've got boots on, then. You didn't answer my question."

"You didn't ask a question. But to answer it, I am concerned, Sergeant. Very concerned. I know my sister. She'll talk to me when she's ready to talk to me. Not a moment sooner. And as for the Weatherby case, not much there."

Batista leaned forward to pluck a toothpick from a ceramic, boot-shaped holder on his desk. He put it in his mouth and began chewing on it.

"Essentially zilch," Jenny added. "All we have is a twenty-six-year-old speed freak who liked to hang at Blaze's and somehow managed to die from a bullet instead of an O.D."

"And how's our man under?"

"Seeing lots of tits, I guess," Jenny said. "But nobody's talking to him. Not yet."

"Does it bother you?"

"What."

"Him seeing all those tits."

"Should it?"

"You'd have to answer that yourself."

Jenny rolled her copy of the report into a tube, stood up clutching it.

"I guess after this," she held the report up, tapping it against the palm of her hand. "I'm kind of glad he's there."

THREE

In the dressing room, Cheryl popped a frozen burrito into the microwave and hit some buttons. She turned to Kit.

"Want one?"

"Leafy greens." Kit shook her head no, morosely pulling a container of salad from her lunch box. "Can't get enough of them." She slumped onto the couch.

"You're in a mood," Cheryl said.

True enough. She was in a mood, the same one she'd been in forever, it seemed. Only intensified now to a degree that scared her. That sorry son of a bitch. She hoped she'd hurt him good. She hoped his jaw was wired shut and his sternum had a huge blue bruise, right over the place where his heart—in theory—was located. Bastard. She pulled a thermos from her lunch box, poured red liquid into the little plastic cup. Cranberry juice and Grey Goose. Mmm-mmm good. Fuck it. She wasn't drunk. She wouldn't get drunk. Just take this goddamn edge off.

He hadn't come back that night. The night she spent half sleeping on the same couch where she was seated now, talking to Cheryl as if she had everything under control. But she didn't. It frightened her, the thought that he might come back. But more than that, what scared her was that she wanted him to. She wanted another shot at him. Only this time she'd be ready. Seriously ready, not just out there in the night dealing with her usual abnormal sense of impending attack, but actually armed with the knowledge that he was out there waiting for another chance at her.

Sick. It was sick, this desire she had to fight him again. It was twisting her up inside. Something in there was ready to explode. She had to control it. That was all she knew. She had to.

She looked up.

Cheryl had sat down next to her, was staring at her.

"I wanted to wait for you," she said. "Blaze told me to go on and leave, that she would make sure you were okay. She practically shooed me out the door."

"Sweet of you," Kit said.

"Are you okay?"

"I guess. Yeah." Kit stabbed at her salad. She filled her mouth with a forkful of arugula, hoping Cheryl wouldn't persist with questions so she wouldn't have to persist with her lies.

"Cops find anything?"

"I waited all night by the phone," Kit said, honey-dipped sarcasm coating her words, "but they never called."

Cheryl got up and pulled her dinner out of the microwave, rejoined Kit on the couch. "Did you call them, ask what's going on?"

Kit shook her head no.

"Maybe they were trying to steal my car? Do you think?"

"Why are you asking all these questions, Cheryl? I got mugged. The cops'll never find him. End of story."

Cheryl nibbled at the end of her burrito, chewed thoughtfully. "It's just that you said he came out from behind my car."

"What, you think he was after you?"

"Me? What on earth for?" Cheryl took a larger bite, wiped her mouth with a paper napkin and placed the napkin carefully on her bare right thigh.

"You do parties, am I right? Maybe someone wasn't happy?" Kit didn't even know why she was pursuing the thing.

"No way," Cheryl said. "They know the rules going in. No touching. Believe me, Kit, I haven't pissed anyone off."

"Blaze seemed to think it might have been something like that. Some customer pissed off about after-hours work that wasn't entirely satisfactory."

"Blaze said that?"

"Not exactly. But her questions. She was speculating."

"Would someone please tell me," Cheryl said, "what is so bad about dancing up close and personal at bachelor parties and football thingies and birthday parties? There are ground rules. I've never had a bad situation arise. At any private gig whatsoever." She let out an exasperated sigh. "Did she mention me?"

"Blaze? No. Why?"

"I have a feeling she knows, you know. That I'm not adverse to picking up a little work on the side. But, Jesus, it's not like there's anything wrong with it. It doesn't cost her a dime. Her and her fucking policies."

"I believe that's *no*-fucking policies."

"Yeah, well, I don't. Ever."

"Ever?" Kit heard herself asking the question calmly. Conversing with Cheryl. Her voice sounded normal enough.

Cheryl snickered. "You know. Not ever as part of the job. My sex life is separate from my work life, is what I mean."

"Blaze is just worried about her license," Kit said. "About the Baptists coming after her."

"I don't think it was even a customer," Cheryl said.

"Why not?"

"I just don't."

"Oh. Okay." It was just that simple. Cheryl didn't think it, therefore it couldn't possibly be true. Kit wished she had that kind of certainty. But she knew better. It was a setup for a fall, thinking that way.

"No, really," Cheryl said. "I mean, I just don't believe it was a customer. That's all I'm saying."

"I know," Kit said. "I said okay." Why was she talking about this. She didn't want to talk about this.

She did want to talk about this.

"What about the Tarantula guy?" Baiting Cheryl now, she guessed, or something like it. Wishing she could let it go.

"No way," Cheryl said, her voice squeaking disbelief. "No way it was him."

"He gives me the creeps."

"Kit," Cheryl said, "I know him. It wasn't him, no way no how. He's just here scouting for talent."

"Coulda fooled me."

"Yeah, well, I guess he doesn't mind getting his rocks off now and then."

"What kind of talent? Wait. Let me guess. He's gonna help you go legit?"

"You'll have to define that term." Cheryl flashed an uneasy grin.

"As in, what is he, some kind of producer?"

"Internet porn. Major league." Cheryl took another bite of her burrito and sat chewing, nodding as if to punctuate her statement. "I've worked for him."

"Does Blaze know?"

"Why? You gonna tell on me?"

"Of course," Kit said. "The class tattletale."

Cheryl grinned, questioningly, as though she wanted to be reassured that Kit was making a joke.

"What happens when you go legit?" Kit asked. "That stuff could come back and bite you in the butt, don't you think?"

"Hey. Lots of actresses got their start in porn. It's no big deal. Ned's cash is green and clean. I'm telling you, he's not a bad guy."

"He gives me the creeps."

"He wouldn't if you got to know him a little."

"I'll pass."

"He told me once he likes your look. It's the easiest gig you can imagine. Go to the studio, pose for a couple of hours, walk out with a fistful of money."

"Yeah. And then one night your cousin in Des Moines is online and clicks his mouse, only to find you splayed across his computer screen in your birthday suit."

"Well, if my cousin in Des Moines wants to look at naked ladies, why should he cop an attitude if I happen to make a few extra dollars being a naked lady? That makes him a bit of a hypocrite, don't you think?"

Kit finished her salad and put the lunch box back in her locker. The alcohol was working. She was calmer now. She sat down at the long makeup mirror to touch up before she had to go back onstage.

"Anyway," Cheryl said, "you should think about it. I could set you up to make a few extra dollars. And you could come see my house, too. Did I tell you I bought a house? A fixer-upper, great way to invest cash. Spruce it up and everything and then put it on the market. Trade up."

"Sounds like you have a plan."

"Hey, I'm not so naïve as to think I'll be able to flaunt my bod once things start sagging and the wrinkles set in." Cheryl sat down next to Kit, leaned close to the mirror to inspect herself. "Oh, God," she said dramatically, smoothing a finger across her brow, "there's one now. The end is in sight."

Kit followed Cheryl up the steel ladder that led from the dressing room to the opening in the stage floor, thinking it was nice of Cheryl to try to cheer her up. They emerged into the soft red light of the stage. The guy in booth eleven looked about eleven. A youngster, his mouth agape at the bodies. Kit thought he should probably be at Disneyland instead of a strip joint. But he had to be old enough. The bouncers were scrupulous about checking IDs at the door.

She found herself hovering in front of the kid's window, even though the young ones were usually sloppy tippers. It didn't matter right now. This skinny little pipsqueak had not been out in the parking lot the other night. She felt relatively safe dancing for him. Suddenly her theories about empowering herself by making the customers want her and having them in a position where they could do nothing about it seemed seriously flawed.

She struggled through the rest of the shift, trying to distract herself from who might be in the booths by thinking about ways to bail out of this business altogether. She'd had enough. More than. Even if she didn't have a plan what to do after, if she worked hard for the next year and didn't spend, she could save enough cash to get the hell out of here. Do something different. Maybe even something worthwhile. Clean up this messy little excuse for a life. Worthwhile or not, she had to get out of here. She could go anywhere. Spain. Rome. Quito. Fuck it. Go back to school, take a master's in art history or something. Maybe she could even find someplace that wasn't on Al-Queda's map. Someplace where she could learn how to walk down the street without expecting to be assaulted.

Prancing around in her black fantasy underwear, getting ready to slip out of her bra and reveal the silver pasties covering her nipples—just what pervert thought these laws up, anyway?—and jiggle her breasts for the kid from Disneyland, she felt it strongly now. She could not keep going the way she was going. Something would break. Something would snap. She could not name the thing inside her, but she hoped she still had sufficient wits about her to fear it. She would scrape together enough cash to go somewhere far away for a good long while. But right now a year felt like forever.

Maybe she should do the private party thing. Or the Web thing. She just didn't know if she'd be able to go through with it when it got right down to posing for the pictures. It would be like letting other people own her somehow. They could hit a button on their keyboard and have her image there whenever they wanted.

But she could wear a wig, and things could be done with makeup. She could turn herself into someone she wasn't for the photographer, and then wash the war paint from her face and toss the wig in the trash and get on a plane to somewhere.

⚃

The Dojang in the Woods was low slung and built of cedar and stone, with large plate glass windows that let in plenty of light. Kit entered and bowed to the black belt manning the front desk as she headed for the dressing room, thankful for the aura of tranquillity that suffused the building. She was digging in her bag as she walked, looking for mints, and almost bumped headlong into Master Lee. Startled, she stepped back and bowed, managing this somehow despite the adrenaline coursing into her bloodstream.

"You have your sparring gear?" Master Lee's hair shone almost blue black. Kit focused on it, waiting to calm.

"Yes, sir," she answered respectfully. Maybe she didn't need the mints. It had been several hours now, since her lunchtime toddy. But Master Lee was eyeing her. She didn't know why. She met his eyes, going for normal. She needed his respect. He was like a tether to the kinder reality she hoped might be out there somewhere in the world.

She had seen him launch himself skyward and do the splits in midair, breaking five boards held on opposite sides. His spinning back kicks were legendary. He was not a large man; Kit was about his size, but he had such control of his body that he could take down much larger men, seemingly without effort.

"I'd like you to try *da soo in dae ryun* today."

"Sir," Kit said as she bowed before continuing toward the locker room. Sparring against two people. She hadn't even realized today was sparring class. So much the better. Real attackers. Adversaries she could see.

In the ladies' locker room, tying her red belt around the waist of her heavy white cotton *dobak*, the traditional Korean martial arts uniform, she concentrated hard on clearing her mind. No mind. Put completely out of her head all the pettiness, thoughts of Blaze and the fucked-up job and the right hooks her memory was constantly blindsiding her with. She put all the thoughts out, left them sitting there in her locker as she closed the beige metal door and clicked shut her combination lock. She would be eligible to test for her black belt in the fall, after more than three years of training. She was thankful she had this one tangible goal in her life. Something to hang on to in the midst of all this messiness that happened to be her existence on planet Earth.

When she got to the training room, most of the class members were already on the mats, warming up for class. One of her favorite workout partners was there, stretching.

A sculptor from Austin proper, Janet McCarty worked mostly with metal and gave her all every minute of every class. She nodded hello and motioned for Kit to join her.

Kit was pounding roundhouse kicks into the pad Janet held for her when Master Lee entered and shouted, *"Cha ryut!"* She leapt to attention with the rest of the students.

Master Lee bowed, and the class returned the courtesy.

"Put your gear on," he said.

Kit hustled with the others to their bags, lined against the back wall of the studio, and began pulling on the padded foam gear that shielded fists, feet, and skulls. She took her place in line, kneeling on one knee.

Master Lee motioned her onto the mats and then scanned the line. He called out Janet, and then Ray, a muscled-up, chunky guy Kit didn't really know, but about her height. The three faced each other in a rough triangle, and on Master Lee's command, bowed to each other.

"Fight stance!" Master Lee barked out.

Kit moved into position, body slightly sideways to her opponents, right hand tucked against her ribs, left hand raised in front of her. Though she knew that sparring was about scoring points, not about trying to hurt an opponent, her stomach was fluttering. *Him cho chung.* Control of power. Literally, "my energy centered."

"Shijak," barked Master Lee, and they were on her. She backed away, then approached Janet, shifting around, trying to line Ray up behind. That was the key, to keep her opponents in line, and in front of her. She moved fast, dodging and slipping across the mats. Janet popped out a snap front kick and followed with a combination. The backfist connected; Kit quickly bowed acknowledgment of the point as

she retreated, circling, trying to get them lined up again. She was already breathing hard, moving quickly, keeping them in front of her. It felt good.

Suddenly Ray scuttled around to her left and she was backed in a corner. The only way out was right through the two of them. She crouched to execute a double kick, planning to burst through as she did, but Ray jumped in and landed a roundhouse to her head.

A hard roundhouse, knocking her headgear loose—and something else. Loose. Her brain exploded, filled with white-hot light and shimmering crystals, and she instinctively grabbed Ray's leg and dumped him to the floor, his back smacking hard against the mats, knocking a gush of air from his lungs. He lay stunned; she had his leg pinned against her side, her brain roiling with the same chemicals that had filled it that awful night, flooding her with rage. Her vision went red and orange and red again as she raised her foot to stomp his exposed belly. She saw fear in his eyes and she gulped for air and pulled herself back, releasing his leg and leaving the mat quickly, positioning herself at a window, shaking her head like she was trying to physically shake out the memory, breathing, blowing out hard short breaths, trying to exhale her anger—*and what the fuck was this, and when would it stop?*

And then Master Lee was at her shoulder, whispering something she couldn't hear, but the smile on his face told her it was a joke; he was trying to help her recover her wits. She tried to smile back, but her mouth wouldn't cooperate. He stepped back to give her some room, and she stood breathing and blinking her eyes, staring out the window at the stubby oaks and trying to push back tears that were threatening to leak over the rims of her eyes. Why was she *crying*, for God's sake. It wasn't about this; it wasn't about an illegal blow in sparring class. She wouldn't. She just *wouldn't*, that was all. She blinked rapidly, bit down on her tongue, hard. There.

When she finally turned around and walked back to the mat, Ray was down on one knee, as though frozen in the act of genuflection, his back to her. The expected posture in such situations. He stood and turned to face her, bowed and apologized earnestly. Kit could tell he felt bad about having gotten carried away.

Master Lee instructed them to sit down and called out a couple of other students to spar.

Kit sat down and Janet slipped in next to her. Ray opted for a place away from them.

It was there with her now, throbbing inside her skull. She brought her knees up, folded her arms across them, and rested her forehead on her arms. She shouldn't be sitting like this; she should be maintaining the legs-crossed-hands-on-knees position of sitting attention. Maybe Master Lee wouldn't mind, being as she'd gotten clocked.

It.

As though the blow to her head had knocked it loose and now it was there blocking all thought, seeping into the crevices of her brain.

Freshman year at the University of Texas, and she'd been moving through the semester in the fog of loss, her mother gone last year forever. Kit was pulling a 3.9 with her crazy-ass declared major in philosophy, pretending to look for some answers. How many angels can fit on the head of a pin? *Dinner and a movie*, he'd suggested, this guy she didn't know except for the hours they'd logged in Contemporary Moral Problems, centered that semester on abortion, capital punishment, and free speech. He was clean-cut, wore khakis and sport shirts, not Kit's usual type, if she could be said to have one. But he was engaging in class, a thinker, and when he asked her out, she decided to give it a shot. She couldn't imagine why he'd be interested in her, as burnt-out as she was then, arriving for class at the last minute, disheveled, often hungover, her brown waves yanked into something that vaguely resembled a ponytail, and who knew what she'd grabbed to wear from the pile of clothes on her bedroom chair—she certainly didn't. *Dinner and a movie*, but as the credits rolled on *Leaving Las Vegas*, he suggested they drive over to Barton Lake and enjoy the night sky. She should have gone home, but the film had left her feeling especially melancholy and she didn't want to go home to the house where her mother had died. Should have. She'd shrugged okay, and felt an increasing sense of foreboding as he wheeled the car to a secluded spot in the huge park. She should have told him she wanted to leave right then. Should have. She didn't know how to tell him. She accepted his kiss.

He pressed her to accept more, and she didn't want to, but he got insistent. And when she struggled against him he got angry, and, suddenly, he was ripping at her and pawing at her and she was trying to push him away and couldn't. She couldn't. He was stronger, he was intent on getting what he wanted, and what he wanted was sex, consensual or not, and he took it, pressing a hand over her mouth, stifling her yells, and she had punched and slapped and kicked at him ineffectually, consumed with her helplessness to fight him off. When he finished, she bolted from the car and ran into the night, gasping, crying, retching, hating herself, loathing her stupidity, feeling bruised and beaten and wretched.

She'd run first, run to get away from him, run as though he were chasing her, but he wasn't. She heard his car start, heard the sound of his tires on gravel, heard the engine sound fade into the night.

She walked then. How far she didn't know. She walked and walked and walked, feeling her hands trying to pull her clothing back into place. She stopped at some point, hid behind some bushes, crouched there with tears streaming down her face and drool sliding off her chin, vomited until there was nothing left to come up. She pulled her torn underwear from beneath her skirt and left it in the dirt under the bushes, stomping at it, grinding it into the ground, crying and crying and crying.

She hadn't told a soul.

She had thought about telling her father, thought about the satisfaction of knowing Wade would track the guy down and most probably torture him for a good long time before putting a gun to his head and blowing a .45-caliber hole in his skull. She had wanted to. Sometimes she still did.

Janet nudged her. "You okay?" she whispered.

Kit raised her head slowly, trying to come back to herself. She nodded yes, though there was a throbbing pain where the blow had landed, square on the right side of her head, just above the ear. She was dizzy.

"Feeling a little light-headed," she said.

"Look at the bright side," Janet said quietly. "Maybe you'll spend the rest of the day punch-drunk."

It didn't sound half bad.

In the locker room, women sat drying themselves with towels, folding their uniforms and tucking them into gym bags, gossiping. Kit slowly pulled off her sweat-soaked dobak, the perspiration gone cold now, the uniform damp with it, trying to get her bearings. Things seemed to be slightly out of sync, the women's movements happening at less than normal speed.

Laura, a thirty-something mother of two who'd gone back to college last September, sat quietly on a bench next to her locker. She saw Kit looking at her and brightened momentarily before emitting a huge sigh.

"I hate my husband," she said simply.

"I hate my husband, too," said Janet, brushing her black hair in front of the mirrors above the sinks.

"Do you know why I hate my husband?" Laura said, addressing the room at large. "This morning he's sitting at the kitchen table, reading the paper. I've just packed school lunches, made breakfast for everyone, gotten the boys onto their school bus, cleaned up after making the lunches and breakfasts, and now I'm sweeping the floor. And he's sitting there reading the paper. Hasn't lifted a finger all morning. I get to where he's sitting, and I'm standing there with the broom, and he keeps reading the paper. I ask him to move his feet. And he says he doesn't want to move his feet."

"Maybe you should have asked him to bend over so you could shove the broom up his ass." Janet deftly applied a thick black line across the curve of one eyelid and stepped back to appraise it in the mirror. "Know why I hate my husband?"

Kit and Laura looked at her, waiting.

"He hasn't learned to multitask. If he could just learn to multitask, I could fall in love with him all over again. Like, if he could do *anything*, anything else at all, while he talks on the goddamn phone, things between us would be totally peachy. He's always on the phone. Constantly."

"Try handing him a broom next time he's yakking," Laura said. "Maybe he could learn to sweep the floor and talk on the phone at the same time."

"Or fold clothes from the dryer and talk on the phone," someone chimed in.

"Or do the dishes."

"It'll never happen," Janet said, lining her other eye. "We almost got divorced last time I asked him to help fold the laundry. No, I've made up my mind. When my kids get to college, I'm headed for Paris. Solo. And I don't mean Paris, Texas."

Kit pulled on her clothes and listened to them banter. Usually she enjoyed it when the married ones got going in the locker room. Most of the women at Blaze's were still single; stripping and marriage didn't mix well. But when she heard these women talking, it reinforced her sense that she'd made the right decision last year when she'd said no to Rusty's proposal.

The sun was hovering just below the tree line, glittering through the tiny rounded leaves of the live oaks, when Kit stepped out of the dojang. The heat hit her before the door closed behind her. It actually felt good, kind of like taking a sauna after the workout. And it was bringing out the scent of cedar. She followed a stone path around the side of the building, sat down on a plain wooden bench at the edge of the small stream that ran there. On the other side of the stream was a rock garden, very spare, very Zen. She focused on a rounded river stone resting on a bed of small, dark pebbles. She liked to come here after her training, not to think, but to not-think.

Often she had difficulty stilling her mind, emptying it of questions still unanswered, question unanswerable—some of them popping into memory from the philosophy courses she'd taken. How silly had that been, to major in philosophy? She'd loved it, maybe in part because it had made her father apoplectic when she told him what she had chosen as her major. She had replied to his anger with a Zen saying, not that she knew a bunch of them, but still. *The one who is good at shooting*, she'd said, *does not hit the center of the target.* Wade had looked at her as though he thought his oldest daughter might recently have been brainwashed by aliens.

She sat now, gazing at the rocks, and but could not still her mind. Her brain was bruised from that damn kick. She could imagine thousands of blood cells rushing to the scene of the accident, trying to knit things back together.

And then came the Question. *Give me a break already.* She couldn't stand this. The answers, in order of importance: Breathing. Drinking water. Eating food. Sheltering myself from the weather. Paying rent and taxes on time.

The answer was simple: She didn't have a clue what she was doing with her life, aside from exploiting this talent she seemed to have for getting the shit kicked out of her on a relatively regular basis.

Footsteps on the stone walkway caught her ear. A moment later Janet sat down next to her on the bench.

"How's your head?" she asked.

Kit shrugged. "It hurts. Feels like my skull is full of cotton."

"I wasn't talking about that," Janet said.

"Oh. You mean like—"

Janet nodded.

Kit shrugged again.

"What happened? When he kicked you?"

Kit didn't know what to say. She didn't feel she knew Janet well enough to open wide and say ah.

Janet went into her bag and came out with a business card. She offered it to Kit.

Kit took it, glanced at the name, and then let her hand fall into her lap.

"She's very good," Janet said. "She's good at handling trauma."

Kit felt uneasy that Janet had discerned so much from the incident on the mats.

"Relax," Janet said. "I've been there myself." She laughed. "Why do you think I'm working my ass off in this class?"

Janet stood, made a move as if to put a hand on Kit's shoulder, but seemed to think better of it.

"Just take her for a test drive," she said. "See if it works for you. And don't forget to put some ice on that noggin. Soon."

Kit nodded her thanks and stuffed the card in the back pocket of her jeans. She listened to Janet's footsteps fade toward the parking lot, heard the engine of Janet's Jaguar rumble to a start.

Therapy. Right. That's what she needed. Like she didn't have enough free-floating anxiety. Now she was supposed to go sit in some shrink's office and try to dig up more of the stuff.

She waited until she heard Janet's car pulling off the gravel drive and onto the main road before she stood up and walked to her Mustang.

She took her place behind the wheel and sat. The car's interior was hot enough that she felt a fresh wave of perspiration seeping out through the pores of her skin. She made no move to start the engine. She let the sweat bead, form little rivulets, trickle down her face slowly.

Maybe if she sat there long enough, if she sweated hard enough, she could rinse out this dreaded something inside her, let her rage wash out through her skin. Because, however big this mess was in her head, however painful it would be to deal with, she had to clean it out. Get rid of it.

If she failed, it would devour her. And then there would be, truly, nothing left to lose.

She reached into her bag, dug out her lunch box. Opened the thermos and finished off the last of her cocktail in one long swallow. The burn felt good. The warmth flooding through her felt good.

She sat, waiting to feel normal, or as close as she could get to it.

FOUR

The Gypsy Wolf Cantina de Lamar looked like a dump. The wide wooden plank walls of the exterior seemed to have been nailed up by carpenters who'd gotten into the tequila before ever lifting a hammer. Jenny pulled around back to park, wondering if Luke had checked the place out personally or gotten a recommendation from one of his friends.

It may have looked like it should be condemned from the outside, but the cumin and cilantro aromas that greeted Jenny when she stepped inside told her the food would be excellent. She smoothed her blouse, gave the greeter a nervous smile, and said she was meeting someone. Was there a reservation for Saner, party of four?

Luke was already at a booth in the back corner of the restaurant. On the walls next to him were papier-maché masks of wolves and hammered tin masks of wolves. There were images of wolves on the ceiling, of wolf packs laid into the ceramic tile tabletops, there were carved wooden wolf heads hanging between the racks of inverted, martini-style margarita glasses above the bar. Luke had one of those glasses before him on the table, the bubble-blown pale green glass with a dark green rim still mostly full as he perused the menu.

He stood as Jenny approached, slipped a hand around to the small of her back, and kissed her full on the lips, pulling her close before quickly releasing her.

"You look great," he said. "I've been thinking about you all day. Couldn't keep my mind on anything else."

Jenny saw a bruise just in front of his left ear, showing through the trimmed three-day growth of beard on his face. She reached to touch it.

"What's this? Are you okay?"

Luke took her hand from his face, laughed at himself.

"I told you I couldn't keep my mind off you. I went out with L.T. on an arrest. Couple of sorry-ass armed robbers. Didn't seem to want to come with us. One of 'em landed a right hook." He touched the bruise gently. "That'll teach me not to let my mind wander."

"Damn, Luke. What if he'd pulled a pistol on you?"

"I know. I know. You don't have to tell me."

Jenny sat down and he slid into the booth across from her. He had on a light brown linen jacket with the palest blue cotton T beneath it, and Levi's. His hair was brushed straight back, but refused to be tamed, falling in slight curls at the sides of his broad forehead. It matched almost perfectly the color of his jacket. Beneath the jacket, Jenny knew, was a shoulder rig holding a Baretta .380. Light. Compact.

Point-and-shoot lethal. Luke laughed at the detectives who felt it necessary to bulk up with Glocks under their jackets, said it was only a matter of knowing how to aim.

"So you got them?"

"Plus I behaved myself completely. Once they were in cuffs." He took a sip of margarita. "This is kinda cool, you know, meeting your dad."

"Come on," Jenny said. "Tell me what you really think."

"I'm feeling a little, ah, tense," he said. He motioned for the waitress and ordered a margarita for Jenny before leaning across the table and taking her hand in his. He looked around the restaurant.

"You make me feel like howling," he whispered. "Just wait till the next full moon. We'll go out in the woods somewhere." He raised her hand to his lips and kissed her fingertips ever so gently, sending a charge right down her center. Jenny had never met a man who made her feel the way he did. It had so stunned her that it had taken her more than awhile to even begin to trust it. And him. She hadn't thought there'd be any way it could last. But it sure seemed to have. More than a year now since they'd begun dating, and still, every time she saw him, it happened again.

"Don't be like that in front of my dad," Jenny said. "This'll be hard for him."

"C'mon," Luke said. "I'm quite the catch, don't you think?"

"He'll say we're rushing things. That we shouldn't be in a hurry."

"I love you Jenny. I want you to be my wife. We're ready."

"Just, you know, play it cool in the romance department."

"What, he'll get jealous?"

"Probably. On some level. Don't most dads?"

"Yeah." Luke sipped his margarita and sighed. "I guess they do. Think I will?"

Jenny looked at him.

"When our little girl decides to get married."

"I'm not even pregnant yet."

"I know." He took her hand again. "But you can bet that gorgeous ass of yours you're gonna be. And soon, if I have any say in the matter."

Jenny felt her face blush hot. The thought of it thrilled her and scared her at once. A baby. Their baby.

"So how were things at the office, dear?" Luke shifted gears, gave her one of his grins.

"Kit got attacked."

The grin disappeared. "Kit? As in, your sister?"

Jenny nodded. "In the parking lot. At Blaze's."

"Holy shit."

Boot heels struck smartly against the floorboards of the restaurant. Jenny recognized the cadence of the step, and the look on Luke's face confirmed she was right.

"We'll talk later," she said quickly. "When we're alone. She wouldn't want my father to know. She probably doesn't even want me to know."

"But what happened? Is she okay?"

"She mugged her mugger, it sounds like. I've brought the report. I'll show you later."

"At Blaze's?"

Jenny hushed him with a discreet finger to her lips.

"Later. Please." She turned to watch her father approach. Thirteen years a Texas Ranger, and Wade exuded authority right down to the ring he wore on his right hand: a cluster of tiny diamonds in the shape of a revolver. Mom had given it to him when he was inducted into the Rangers. He'd thought it too much at first, but had worn it every day of his life since.

Jenny turned and slipped out of the booth to greet her father, her heart fluttering with nerves. What was she scared of? She was a grown woman. She had a right to get married.

Wade was in his usual off-duty outfit, khakis done in a military press, razor-sharp creases running down the front of each pant leg, a khaki shirt with a bolo tie sporting a silver state of Texas at the collar, his summer Stetson, and brown lizard-skin boots custom-made in El Paso. He arrived at the table and leaned to kiss Jenny's cheek before he straightened and extended a hand to Luke.

"Wade Metcalf," he said, his deep drawl causing a couple at the next table over to turn and take notice.

"Luke Saner, Mr. Metcalf. It's a pleasure. Your reputation precedes you."

Wade nodded his acknowledgment of the compliment, glanced over his shoulder at the door, and then stood eyeing the table.

"I guess you've got it covered," he said.

"Don't worry, sir, I got your back," Luke said, then added quickly, "but if you'd prefer to face the door—"

"No, no. It's fine." Wade put a hand on Jenny's shoulder and slid in next to her. "By the way," he said, "no need to call me sir." Luke nodded okay.

"What can I get you, sir?" The waitress was at the ready, hip cocked, hands tucked into the back pockets of her jeans.

"What's that y'all are drinking?" Wade motioned at the glasses. "Margaritas?"

"Patron," Luke said.

"I'll have one of those." Wade flashed a smile at the waitress, all charm. She gave a little bounce onto her toes and whirled around to head for the bar.

"Perky little thing, isn't she?" Wade's eyes followed her. He pulled his attention back to the table and picked up a menu. "I'm half-starved," he said. "Y'all 'bout ready to order?"

"Maybe we should wait for Kit," Jenny said, her hand tapping the table nervously.

"Oh." Wade's tone was flat. "She's coming?"

"I thought I told you." Jenny met Wade's eyes as he tried to discern whether she was fibbing.

"Maybe you did," Wade said. "Maybe I forgot."

A silence descended. Luke sipped his margarita, Jenny hers. Wade turned to look for the waitress.

"My dad sends his regards," Luke said. "I told him we were having dinner tonight."

"And how're things in Blanco?" Wade asked.

Jenny was relieved that Luke had found something to say. Luke's dad was the sheriff of neighboring Blanco County, part of Wade's territory. Though Jenny wasn't sure how often the men ran into each other, she knew Wade had helped out on a case or two over there. She hoped they got along.

"Fine, I guess," Luke said. "He's heading out to some big sheriff's convention in California. Los Angeles. I think he left this afternoon."

"I guess we'd better hope he doesn't go Hollywood on us."

"My dad?" Luke laughed. "Somehow I doubt it."

"Me, too," Wade said. He leaned back and shifted around in the booth, hanging one arm over the back of it. He looked relaxed, Jenny thought, but she knew he had just positioned himself for a quick exit. "Yeah," he was saying, "I always managed to enjoy myself at those things. Conventions. Seminars. Whatever the hell they call them. Not sure I ever learned anything, though."

Luke's mouth curled into a one-sided grin. Jenny thought she might melt. Wade looked around again for the waitress.

"There she is," he said as his drink was placed in front of him.

He took his glass and raised it.

"Well, goddamnit, here's to the future Mr. and Mrs. Luke Saner. Congratulations." He took a long swallow and smiled at the shocked faces of Jenny and Luke. "Hell," he said, "y'all think I'm a damn moron? Come on, drink up. I'm happy for you."

Jenny and Luke raised their glasses and tapped Wade's. The three of them drank. Jenny's thoughts were swirling, but mostly she felt relief. Thank goodness he'd spared them the torment of going through dinner wondering how to break the news. She took another swallow of her drink, a gulp actually, and turned to Wade.

"Daddy," she said, her voice pitched high with suspicion, "did Kit tell you?"

Wade practically guffawed, then lowered his voice and looked at Jenny seriously.

"What do you think, little girl?"

Jenny looked at him for a long moment, and realized that there was no way Kit would have told him.

Wade put his arm around her shoulder, pulled her close, and looked hard at Luke.

"You don't have to tell me, sir," Luke said. "I'll just say this for myself. I'm honest, I work hard. I may not be a Ranger, but I'm a damn good cop, and I love your daughter."

"Well, now, that's a mouthful," Wade said. "I just hope y'all are gonna find time to get out and have some fun, in amongst all that hard work and honesty."

Luke grinned and nodded. "Oh yeah. We plan to do that."

"What happened there?" Wade said, motioning to Luke's bruised jaw.

"Went out to arrest a couple of armed robbers today. One of 'em got a shot in before we were finished."

"Hope you hit him back."

"I did what was necessary to effect the arrest."

Wade smiled. "They trained you good, son." He turned to Jenny. "Anything new on that Weatherby murder?"

"We're stumped," she said. "Why? You keeping secrets?"

"Naw," Wade drawled, "Not that I could say." He eyed her playfully, sipped his margarita. "Anyway, it's not my case. Just curious."

"Wanting to solve it yourself?" Jenny laughed.

"Aw, little girl, that's no fair. When have I ever stolen a case away from you?"

"Never, Dad," Jenny said. "But you do like to keep your nose in my business, now, don't you? Admit it."

"Just trying to help out," Wade said. "That's my job, isn't it?"

"I'll keep you posted," Jenny said.

Luke's eyes moved to the front door of the cantina and quickly back to Jenny. She couldn't be sure, but she thought she'd seen something like alarm flash through them.

She turned. Spotted her sister standing just inside the door. She waved a hand.

"There's Kit."

Wade glanced over his shoulder and turned quickly back to Luke.

"Goddammit, I love her," Wade said. "But I will never as long as I live understand her. She'd have made a hell of a fine cop. Could've done it easy. Know what she majored in?"

Luke shook his head no.

"Fucking *philosophy*. What the hell use is that?"

Jenny saw that cornered look in Luke's eyes. A brief glimpse of *oh-shit-what-do-I-do-now*. Only for an instant, but long enough that she was sure Wade had seen it, too.

What Luke did was raise his glass in a toast, which seemed to catch Wade by surprise. Wade lifted his glass.

"To the love of knowledge," Luke said. "To the seekers of truth everywhere." He kept his glass raised but leaned across the table to kiss Jenny on the forehead. "And to the love of my wife-to-be. I cherish you."

Jenny swigged back a portion of her drink and watched Wade sip his carefully while he eyed Luke for signs of insincerity. Evidently there were none. Her father followed his sip with a healthy belt and a smile for his future son-in-law. Jenny turned again. Kit was still frozen at the entrance to the restaurant. Jenny waved. There was an urgency in the motion of her hand that seemed to stir Kit to action.

❖

Kit saw Jenny waving. Shit. She did not want to be here. She was here. *Press on, sweetheart.* She walked slowly into the restaurant, veered toward them. Walked slowly some more. Dreading this. Why had she come here? She walked some more, and still wasn't there, her eyes on the back of her father's thick head. Her thickheaded father.

For Jenny. She was here for Jenny. She loved her little sister. Wanted to protect her and take care of her and at the same time wanted nothing to do with her because what the hell did Jenny know about anything? Jenny was part of it, part of the goddamn machine that sucked in human beings and chewed on them for most of their lives and then stuck a Happy Retirement card in their hands and spat them out on the front lawn of the old folks home. Jenny had jumped in there and become, not just part of it, but part of the enforcement arm of it, and how disgusting was that? She put people in jail. She believed, or pretended to, all the bullshit.

Kit walked along the bar, eyeing all the pretty bottles lined up in front of the mirrored wall, gleaming beneath halogen lighting. It was time for a change. She could barely taste the vodka anymore. Tequila might help her through this whatever-it-was she was walking toward. Family outing.

Jenny's getting married. Jenny's getting married. Drink up. Jenny, Dad's favorite little girl. Kit wanted desperately, as she walked toward the table, for her little sister to be entering into something real. A real relationship, not some bullshit marriage. The real thing. True love. True and lasting love. If such a thing existed.

She wondered if they'd already told Wade.

And then she saw the man sitting across the table from Jenny and froze. She stood staring, realizing at the same time that she should not be standing there staring. She could not help it. She stood, trying to make sure of what—of whom—she was seeing.

It was Sweet.

No.

It couldn't be, but yes. Yes, it was, she was sure of it. Holy shit. Holy motherfucking shit. Holy cow named Mary from Toledo, Ohio. It was Sweet.

She made herself walk. Toward the table. Getting closer now, and closer. And yes. It *was* Sweet. The guy who came to club and rested his hands on the window ledge and watched her dance and take off what scant clothing she'd had on in the first place.

"Kit," Jenny said. "Meet my fiancé."

Holy fucking cheese enchilada.

"Luke Saner." He stood and shook Kit's hand. If it hadn't been for the shock of recognition and the fact that this was her sister's fiancé she was exchanging electrons with, she might have liked the feeling she got from it.

"What are we drinking?" Kit said. She tried not to stare at him.

"Let's get right down to business," Wade said, and maybe that was concern in his voice, not that Kit could tell.

She thought she saw something in Sweet's eyes, a flash of fear maybe, or an invitation to conspiracy; she wasn't sure. He had to know she recognized him. He had to know who she was. Or maybe *what* was more descriptive. What she was. He was acting like he didn't recognize her. And the act was convincing. Somewhere at the edge of her vision, her father's arm was signaling for a waitress. He seemed to want relief as badly as she did. Way to go, Dad!

And then she saw the bruise. Left cheek. Her vision went gray, black, white, and back to normal in a matter of seconds, in a matter of eons. She saw the twisted lips of her attacker, beneath that black stocking. What the fuck was this?

She shook her head quickly, bringing herself back to now. It wasn't jiving; this couldn't be the man. But the bruise was in the right place. He was a patron at the club. She couldn't make the thought fit into her brain. She heard a late-night infomercial announcer speaking in her head: *Do you suffer from . . . cognitive dissonance?* She couldn't focus.

"Nice to meet you," Luke was saying. "Jenny's told me a lot about you."

Yeah, Kit thought, how many million times have those words been said, and gosh, Luke, you know all kinds of things about me, don't you, Sweet? But he probably didn't know how well thought of he was at the club. He probably didn't know they called him Sweet. Unless maybe Cheryl had gone out with him or something.

"Kit." Wade had stood up. He placed a hand lightly on Kit's shoulder, kissed her cheek.

This was too weird. Dad was being totally civilized tonight. "Hey, Dad," she said. "Shot anyone lately?" She gave him what she hoped was her sweetest smile, the one that reeked of syrup and sarcasm.

"Always the comedian," Wade said. "Sit down, girl, get yourself a drink, and take the bite out of that tongue of yours."

"I'm afraid even alcohol can't do that," Kit said. But she smiled at him, trying to be anything but what she was. Trying to be normal, maybe even her father's idea of normal. She squeezed into the booth, sitting next to Sweet. Or Luke. Whoever the fuck he was. She waited for things to come back into focus.

"Not to be rude," she said, "but what happened to your face?"

"Aw," Wade said, "let him alone."

She could have gone off on him, had to fight not to; instead she flashed a glare. He was such an asshole, her father, talking to her like she was a goddamn four-year-old or something.

"I'm curious," Kit said, directing her comment at Luke. Her voice was as cool as shade.

"He got into it with a couple of armed robbers," Wade said.

"How refreshing," Kit said. A drink had materialized in front of her. She took a deep swallow, savored the scent of alcohol on her breath as she exhaled. The burn of it in her nose and throat.

All three of them looked at her expectantly, but as though they had no idea what, exactly, to expect.

"I mean, that you were actually trying to arrest real criminals," Kit said. "I find that refreshing."

Luke turned to her. "One of 'em popped me when I wasn't looking. I should've been paying closer attention." He nodded at Jenny. "Truth is, I was daydreaming about your sister there."

"Oh God." Kit laughed. "But, hey, milk it for all it's worth, is what I say."

"Maybe it's the truth." Luke leaned back to appraise Kit. "Why do you assume it's a line?"

"Maybe I've heard enough of them to last three lifetimes," Kit said. She was not liking this guy. He was better behind glass, where she didn't have to listen to him spout crap.

"Well, darlin'," Wade said, "you're a good-lookin' woman. You'd best get used to that."

Kit sat, silenced. Had she just heard a compliment from her father? Had that just happened?

"Thank you, Daddy," Kit said. "Does that mean I'm required to put up with an extra portion of horseshit? Because I'm a *good-looking woman*?" She raised her glass to her lips. It was empty. Scanned the cantina. "Is there a waitress working this table, or what?"

Wade turned to take a look around, and almost instantly the waitress appeared.

"Another round," he said, sounding like he was asking for aspirin. The waitress nodded and left, maneuvering her way toward the bar.

Kit nodded thanks to her father. Jenny caught her eye.

"Dad beat us to the punch," Jenny said. "Figured it out before I could work up the nerve to tell him."

"That right?" Kit saw Wade watching her. "I know," she said. "I'm the oldest, I was supposed to go first. What can I say?"

"You tell me," Wade said.

"I'm still looking for Mr. Right, but I'll settle for Prince Charming if he comes with decent health insurance."

"I'd be happy if it was just someone with a job," Wade said.

"In my own time." Kit sighed. "My own sweet time."

"Darlin', I gave up worrying about you a long time ago. A man can't have two full-time jobs." He sipped his drink, his eyes on her from above the rim of the glass. There was a coldness there that frightened her, though she doubted that at the moment it was directed at her. Just part of Wade's demeanor. He could be one mean son of a bitch when he thought he had to be.

She wondered briefly what might happen if she announced that dear sweet Luke was a regular at Blaze's. Wouldn't that be fun to watch.

She shifted her gaze to her little sister. How on earth was she going to tell Jenny that her fiancé was a fucking jerk and that there was no way in hell Jenny should marry the guy?

And then she let herself get to the real question: was it was possible he had been the one who came out from behind Cheryl's car? Though the bruise was in the right place, it wasn't all that serious. But maybe that second kick hadn't landed as hard as she'd thought. She couldn't really say; she'd been in the fight zone by then. Now, sitting right next to him, she wasn't picking up any kind of vibe that might indicate he'd been there. But the key to being a successful psychopath was to possess a level of detachment that let you smile at someone, charm them into liking you, trusting you, and then lure them off to the murder site.

When the food came, Kit could barely touch hers. She felt all twisted up inside, like there was a rope running through her middle and people at either end were turning it in opposite directions. She kept flashing back to the attack, brutal bits and pieces of it striking at her brain, as if she were in a boxing ring and taking blow after blow to the head: a flash of bright white light followed by the darkness of night and the rush of the assailant toward her.

What the hell. Take another drink. Drown the flashbacks in tequila. Drown them.

She couldn't do this. She couldn't bear sitting there, haunted by forty seconds of terror. She grabbed her bag and excused herself from the table, leaving Wade and Jenny and Luke staring after her.

"What's got her?" Wade asked as his eyes followed Kit walking toward the back of the cantina, where the bathrooms were. He looked at Jenny as though she should know.

Jenny shrugged, concern in her eyes.

"Kit's complicated, Daddy, you know that."

"As well as anyone," Wade said. "She's drinking a lot. Even for her."

"Maybe she just had to go to the bathroom," Luke ventured.

Jenny and Wade gave him a look. Wrong.

⚏

In the small hallway at the back of the restaurant, Kit stood in front of the wall-mounted pay phone and pulled out her cell phone. She looked once more at the business card Janet had given her. Eeenie, meenie, miney, moe. To call or not to call. One of Kit's friends in high school had been going through therapy during senior year, and as the semester progressed Kit watched her grow more and more depressed. Finally, Kit asked her about it, why her therapy wasn't helping.

"It will," her friend had said, and laughed a small laugh. "I look at it this way: You go in there a reasonably okay person who maybe has a problem or two that she wants to deal with. But the therapist isn't happy until he has you lying on the floor in a puddle of your own tears, helpless to deal with yourself. That's progress, don't you think?"

Kit hadn't known. Seventeen, and that was the year her mother died. When the school counselor suggested she try some therapy, she had quickly refused. Not interested. Don't even want to think about it. Jenny had been fifteen that year, and they'd nursed their mom through the end stages of breast cancer.

Her mother, in bed, tufts of brown fuzz sprouting from her scalp, looking already ghostly gone, would stare at something Kit could not imagine, and did not want to. That last afternoon, with the curtains drawn against the daylight and the room stale with the odor of illness, the odor of sickness, the odor of death waiting in the wings, Kit sat at the edge of the bed and held her mother's hand and listened as her mother whispered, "I'm sorry."

It made no sense. She heard the words but could not fathom why her mother had uttered them.

"For what?" she'd asked, but in that brief moment between her mother's utterance and Kit's realization that she didn't understand it—at all—her mother had lapsed back into the morphine zone, her eyes gone blank and almost closed.

"For what?" Kit tried again. She felt her mother's hand tighten helplessly around her own, felt, not strength, but weakness, the weakened grip of the dying. She remembered turning to see her father in the doorway, dressed for work, his Stetson already on his head.

Her mother waited until later that night, late in the night, to die, though by that time Kit was sure it wasn't a case of her mother holding on to life, it just happened to be how long it took for the cancer to fully wreak its havoc.

Maybe she should have gotten help back then. Maybe talking to a professional would have benefited her. But she had never believed in professionals. What the hell did they know? Sometimes it still hit, though: the thought that if she hadn't been walking around in a cloud of unexpressed grief she wouldn't have accepted that date, and it wouldn't have happened.

A deep voice jolted her from her thoughts.

"Excuse me?" A man was next to her, motioning at the pay phone. "Are you . . ." He pointed at the phone.

"Oh," Kit said. "No. Please, go ahead." She stepped back to give him access to the phone. Politely. Oh so politely. She knew how to be polite. Sometimes people deserved it.

A small shudder ran through her. How had he gotten so close to her without her noticing? She stepped away farther and stared at the number pad on her cell phone.

What the hell. If it got too bad, she'd bail on it, that was all. Wherever it took her, it couldn't possibly be worse than where she was right now.

Staring at the card, she had to blink a few times to clear the tears sufficiently so she could read the number. The man on the phone had his back to her and was yelling into the pay phone, asking someone where the hell they were.

"You have reached the office of Dr. Emily Wolfe," the message said. The voice held compassion, or something like it. The voice sounded gentle. Did they take courses in that? *Your Voicemail: A Tether to the Truly Fucked-up Client Base in the World at Large and How to Exploit It.*

The compassionate voice continued. "Please leave your name and phone number, even if you think I already have it, and I will return your call as soon as I can."

Kit left her cell number and clicked her phone shut. There. One small step for—whatever. She sniffed a few times to clear her nose and dabbed at her eyes with her sleeve. She hated this. Tears. She would not let Wade see them. But they wouldn't stop.

Fuck it. She pushed open the ladies' room door and headed for the paper towel dispenser. She grabbed a few and dampened them under a faucet, pressed them against her face. When she pulled the paper towels away, Jenny was staring at her.

"In here," Jenny said, and moved to the last stall in the bathroom, the large one for patrons with disabilities. She held the door open, waiting for Kit. "Please," she said.

"What," Kit said, "you brought some cocaine from the evidence locker?"

"Maybe you should try stand-up." Jenny laughed, giving Kit an I-can't-believe-you look. She closed the door quickly behind them, slid the lock bar into place.

"Tell me everything," Jenny said.

Kit stared at her, wondering if Jenny already knew about Sweet. Or Luke. Whatever, whoever he was. Was she looking for confirmation?

"I mean it," Jenny said.

"How long have you known him and when did he ask you to marry him?"

"Kit. I'm serious. Talk to me."

"And why are you getting married, anyway? And why to a cop?"

"It doesn't fucking matter, does it? We're in love."

"It's kind of Nietzschean, in its way."

Jenny's mouth dropped open in total disbelief.

"What's that supposed to mean?"

"Whatever doesn't kill you makes you stronger." Kit stepped next to the wall, leaned back against the brushed steel bar bolted to the wall. "Oh, look," she said, "a toilet. I can just lean over and puke if I want to."

Jenny's face went red with anger.

"Kit," she said, controlling her voice, "I know about it."

"Then will you please enlighten me? Because I have to tell you I don't know what the fuck is going on here." And it was true, she didn't. But she damn sure was not going to be the bearer of bad news the very same night Jenny announced her engagement. And if Jenny already knew Luke liked to hang at Blaze's, it hardly made sense for Kit to weigh in with her own opinion on the matter. What would she tell her, anyway? That her fiancé was highly respected by all the women who took off their clothes in front of him?

"I got the report," Jenny said quietly. "I know you were attacked."

Kit almost slid down the wall, whether from relief or embarrassment or too many goddamn margaritas she wasn't sure.

"I don't want to talk about it," she said.

"I knew that before I came in here," Jenny replied. "But I need to know you're okay, and I have to tell you, you are *not* acting okay."

"I'm okay."

"Prove it."

"A little sloshed maybe. Prove it how?"

"How the hell am I supposed to know? Are you eating? Are you taking care of yourself? I hope that crack about cocaine was actually a joke."

"Of course it was." Kit felt the familiar sense of shame rinse over her, like some kind of fabric softener that worked on human muscles. She could barely stay standing. "I'm okay," she managed. "I just called a therapist, Jenny. I'm taking care of myself. Okay?"

"What happened?"

"Probably just what you read in your report. Did it say I kicked his ass? Because I think I did. I know I landed a kick to his jaw." Kit eyed her sister. Jenny didn't seem to make any connection between Kit's kick and Luke's jaw. It was a kind of relief, as much as anything could be at the moment.

"Good for you," Jenny said. "Now all we need is to find out who the hell it was and why he did it."

"Maybe there's no reason."

"Maybe." Jenny dug in her bag. "But I'm not so sure. Here."

Kit stared at the gun Jenny held out to her.

"Take it," Jenny said firmly. "And keep it with you."

Kit reached for the weapon. It was a Walther PPK. An older one, but in mint condition from the looks of it.

"It's loaded," Jenny said. "but nothing's in the chamber. The safety's right here." She pointed to the little lever on the body of the gun, above the trigger guard. "You remember, right?"

Kit felt the weapon heavy in her hand. It occurred to her briefly that her sister might be issuing a suicide tool. No. She would not go there. She would not.

"I don't think I should ha—"

"Kit," Jenny interrupted. Her voice was almost pleading. "I don't want you getting hurt. You need to be able to defend yourself."

Kit opened her Crumpler and slid the weapon into the large side pocket within.

"It was just some guy," she said. "Some fuckup looking for money or sex."

"Or both," Jenny said. "Doesn't matter. He's some kind

of fucking psycho, and I'm sure he's one very pissed-off psycho right now. Pissed off at you."

"You've got a point," Kit said. Her lips felt thick. "But he might not even be able to recognize me. I think I took him by surprise."

"Fine and good," Jenny said. "But if he comes back, this way you're equipped to deal. Look, you outshot me every time Dad took us to the range. Keep it with you. For my peace of mind, if not your own."

"Peace of mind," Kit slurred. "What a concept." Kit chuckled to herself and closed her bag. Jenny was not going to back down on this one.

Jenny unlocked the door and led the way out of the stall. She stopped suddenly and turned to face Kit.

"And I hope that at some point," she said, "you'll feel like telling me what went down. I need the details."

"What for?"

"So I can find the asshole and throw his butt in jail."

"What about the rest of him?" Kit said.

"That, too." Jenny said. But she was smiling now.

Kit pasted a smile on her own face, thankful that she hadn't told Jenny about Luke. She didn't need to deal with any more bullshit tonight. She couldn't. Her bag felt unusually heavy on her shoulder.

As she followed Jenny toward her father and whoever-the-hell the guy was sitting across the table from them, the guy Jenny was planning to marry, the announcer's voice droned in her head: *It's time once again for our Bulgarian proverb of the day: If you wish to drown, do not torture yourself with shallow water.*

And now back to our regularly scheduled program.

She approached the table, saw Luke talking earnestly to her father and Wade listening intently. Wade saw her nearing; he made a small motion with his hand. Luke stopped midsentence, turning to watch her and Jenny approach.

Secrets. About her?

But as she slid into the booth next to Luke, Wade was saying, ". . . enough about business. Let's talk about this wedding coming up."

Kit looked at her food, glanced up to see the looks pass between Jenny and her father and Luke, looked back down at her food. She would have to move it around on the plate. Take a bite or two. Make an effort to convince them she wasn't losing her mind.

She wasn't. She wouldn't. At least Jenny seemed to believe she was sufficiently functional.

She stuck her fork into the rice, lifted it, and sprinkled the grains over the frijoles before mixing them in. The man sitting next to her could pretend not to know her, but he knew her. He came to Blaze's and watched her dance. Often. Had he told Wade what she looked like in pasties? Was that what they'd been talking about? He was sitting there, right next to her. He had a bruise on his jaw.

And she had a gun in her bag.

FIVE

Walking across a parking lot. Broad daylight in the middle of a glaring afternoon. People on the street. Kit walked, looking carefully at each parked car she passed, not so much imagining as expecting attackers to be lurking behind them.

Her heart was jumping around in her chest, arrhythmic, seeming to pound sideways against her ribs, making her blood rush so fast that her hearing was muffled, as though she'd just shot up forty-seven stories in a very fast elevator and her ears hadn't adjusted to the change in air pressure.

She felt keenly each step forward, the asphalt hot against the beaded rubber soles of her shoes. In army-green cotton DaNangs and a pair of black leather Pumas that conformed almost exactly to her feet, she walked, avoiding eye contact, thinking only *I am going to get some help now. I am going to get some help now.*

Maybe.

The sun shone overhead from almost the center of the sky; the sun is a star. And she'd seen how many stars there were in the night sky when you got out of town into the countryside, all those suns out there, and were there planets orbiting them and were there creatures, was there life on those planets, and what the fuck did it matter if she had a hard time walking across a parking lot without expecting to get raped or murdered? What did it really matter in the larger scheme of things? And just what was the larger scheme? Who even came up with the concept? How many angels can you fit on the head of a pin? *Who cares?*

She found the plain glass door with simple black letter-ing centered on the glass: Hill Country Awareness Center. She didn't need awareness. She had too much of it; that was the problem.

She entered and followed the hall around a quick right turn to a dead end. A directory, black with changeable white plastic letters behind glass, hung on the wall in front of her. DR. EMILY WOLFE M.D. 2ND FLOOR. Listed in black and white. Black. White. Black. White. Black-white-black-white-black-white. The words clanged in her head, clanging. Clanging. *Stop!* Think of anything. Think of anything else, even think of your father. Think of Wade. Remember the time he showed up at the annual Ranger picnic with a lion? And a lion tamer? Jenny was four then and loved it, begged Daddy to let her bring it home. Kit felt sorry for the lion, wishing he would turn suddenly and flee into the countryside. The lion tamer had a scar on his neck, and Kit hoped it had come from a lion.

Able to think in sentences once more, Kit looked again

at the directory on the wall. To the left was a along stairway leading up to the second floor of the building, and to the right, an elevator.

She decided to climb. Just keep burning energy; leave less for the gray matter to consume, and maybe, like a computer, it would automatically force itself into a sleep state in order to conserve battery power and avoid a loss of data.

She took the stairs methodically, at a reasonable pace, counting as she went. Twenty-one of them. Frank Sinatra . . . *when I was twenty-one, it was a . . .* It was a what. Kit remembered twenty-one as being not a very good year. Not at all. Senior year at UT and strung out on one controlled substance after another. Living off campus with a drug dealer named Ralph. Pulling a 3.8, existing in two worlds: the party life with Ralph, the paper chase of academia. She'd written some pretty impressive papers while coked out of her mind, but then philosophy lent itself to such endeavors.

She saw him sometimes on campus. The guy, the just-a-movie-and-dinner guy. The rapist. When her eyes met his, they held indictment, prosecution, conviction, and punishment in a single glance. She thought about killing him, sometimes. Fantasized about how she would do it. Always it was slowly. Always he begged her for mercy, apologized a hundred times and a hundred times more. He wept and drooled, he crawled on the floor while she walked behind him, holding her father's .45 automatic aimed at the back of his brainless fucking skull.

She realized she was standing on the landing at the top of the staircase, looking out a small window. Looking at the parking lot she'd crossed a few minutes earlier. Or was it a few hours? She didn't know how long she'd been there. She made a U-turn and walked down the hall to another hall that led right. A small sign with an arrow: DR. EMILY WOLFE.

Air hung stale in the hallway. She forced herself through it toward a door at the end.

When she opened it, she smelled green. She stood in the doorway and scanned the room. There was a ficus tree in one corner. A hanging basket of ivy in another. On the square glass-and-oak coffee table in the middle of the room, flanked by two overstuffed couches in a southwestern print, were several potted plants and a floating candle in a large bowl of water. Rounded river rocks filled the bottom of the bowl. A tabletop fountain gurgled softly atop a corner table. Kit recognized Chopin's Prelude no.4 in E Minor playing softly from a boom box on another table. The music alone could make her weep. Functioning as the sound track to her mood, it was almost overwhelming.

She entered, closed the door softly behind her. There was another door directly opposite her. Closed. Kit took a seat on the couch nearest the door, put down her bag, began looking through the magazines on the table. Doing the ordinary thing. Doing what normal people did. *Texas Monthly*, *Organic Style*, *Sojourner Truth*, *Utne Reader*.

She left the magazines and sat back on the couch. The room was soft and comfortable. The room was gentle. There were no windows. The lighting was dim, but not dingy. It was like a cocoon in here. She closed her eyes. She wondered if she could feel safe here. No one knew where she was. That was a start. Toward feeling safe.

But apprehension intruded. Prickled at her skin like heat rash. She'd never been counseled before, had never seen a shrink. All she had to go on was what she'd seen on TV or at the movies, what she'd read in books and magazines: one step removed from reality, shaped for a purpose.

She heard laughter behind the door and a black Labrador emerged, trailing a red leash, and then a woman came out holding the lead. The dog approached Kit and licked her hand. She patted him, wondering if Janet had given her the wrong business card and sent her to a dog psychologist. Maybe that was what she needed. A dog psychologist. Someone who could show her how to cope with her urge to growl and bite.

"Icky, stop that." It was the dog's owner, speaking affectionately to her pet. And then to Kit, "I'm sorry."

"It's fine," Kit said. "I like dogs." Was that her voice, sounding so normal and sociable? She thought of the pet she and Jenny had grown up with, a German shepherd Wade had given them for Christmas when she was eight and Jenny six. She had fallen in love with Ranger immediately. And he with her. They spent summers running in the woods, Kit imagining they were on the frontier. She made shelters from small trees and vines where she curled next to Ranger and hid from outlaws. Ranger was her protector; she feared nothing when he was at her side.

They'd had to put him down a scant few months after her mother died. It had been pain on top of pain, mourning on top of mourning. But he had been suffering terribly from hip dysplasia. To keep him alive for their needs would have been cruelly selfish.

She patted the dog again, then raised her face to the woman. "Did you call him Icky?"

The woman laughed again. She seemed to be in a good mood for having just finished a session with a shrink.

"Yes," she said. "That's his name." She knelt and Icky turned to her, slurping her face. "And Mommy wuvs her wittle Icky Ickums, doesn't Mommy? Yes. Oh, he's my wittle fweety-pie."

A figure emerged from the doorway. Dr. Wolfe was of average height, solidly built, almost chunky, with coppery skin. She had dark brown eyes, liquid but keen, high cheekbones, and a broad forehead. Her hair was darkest brown, almost black, parted in the middle, straight. It hung to the middle of her back. Native American. Kit wondered from what nation.

"Please." Dr. Wolfe waved Kit into her office. She smiled, showing even white teeth. Kit patted Icky goodbye and followed Dr. Wolfe into her office.

Like the waiting room, the office was simply furnished. Next to the door was a maple desk, tidy, with a calendar open in the center, a small lamp and a corded telephone that looked to be from the eighties, square and industrial. Along the far wall, a couch with a woven blanket draped, centered, over its back and a couple of throw pillows in the same earth tones. Kit sat down, and Dr. Wolfe sat in the chair that faced the couch. Between them was a rectangular coffee table, also oak and glass. On it was a box of tissues, the box in tones of muted mauve. Kit wondered what sort of person wound up designing tissue boxes. She'd never seen one she liked. They were all, every last one of them she had ever in her own life seen, just plain ugly. Maybe it was on purpose. Maybe they were trying to make you cry so you'd have to buy another box.

Dr. Wolfe sat waiting, a quiet smile on her face.

Kit had no idea how to proceed.

"You sounded distraught the other night," the doctor said. "I'm glad you're here."

"I was attacked," Kit said. "Not for the first time. The first time I dealt with it myself, but this time, I . . ."

She felt an ache deep in her throat, the ache that told her she was about to cry. Dr. Wolfe waited silently.

Kit couldn't talk. If she said another word the dam would burst. She tried to swallow the ache, gulp the pain away.

Dr. Wolfe leaned toward her.

"Kit. It's all right. Talk to me."

"I was a freshman in college. My mother died when I was seventeen." Kit heard the words coming out of her, the details of the rape. The smallness, the dirtiness, the stupid lack of judgment on her part, the utter helplessness she'd felt. She'd gone oddly calm once she began talking, or maybe it was numbness, she couldn't actually tell what she was feeling. It was as though she were sitting next to herself, listening to herself tell the doctor her pathetic little history, ready to offer a second opinion if called upon by Dr. Wolf. She reached for a tissue not because she any longer feared she would cry, but because she needed to touch something, something real and physical in this room, to reassure herself that she was here. She talked, heard her voice go out in monotone, leaden, told the woman sitting across from her how close she'd come to suicide. She talked ever so calmly about the incident—wasn't that what her father and Jenny called these kinds of things, these crimes? *Incidents?*

"I'm so sorry you went through that," Dr. Wolfe said, and Kit could tell that she meant it. Just that, just that *acknowledgment,* lightened the weight in Kit's chest. She felt heartened somehow.

"Thank you." Her voice sounded small.

"You say you dealt with it yourself? How did you do that? What did you do for yourself?"

Kit sat, silent.

Finally Dr. Wolfe said, "You're a survivor, aren't you." The question delivered as a statement.

"So far," Kit said. "I guess." She heard her mother's voice in her head, singing: "Que será, será." Whatever will be. And who knew? She didn't know if she was a survivor; she only knew she had managed, thus far, to survive.

"Let me ask you, Kit, and I hope you feel comfortable enough to be honest with me. Are you suicidal now? Do you think about taking your life?"

"I don't think so," Kit said. "I don't think I would go there." It occurred to her how easily she could accomplish it. The gun was in her bag. On the floor. Next to her leg.

"That's good," Dr. Wolfe said. "You're obviously a woman of some intelligence, not to mention fortitude."

"I feel like I'm losing it," Kit said, almost before she realized what she was saying. The words just seemed to slip out, as if some truth had been hiding in her brain, waiting for the right person to tell itself to.

"You're not," Dr. Wolfe said. "You're not crazy. I can tell you that right now. You've suffered a horrible trauma, Kit. I can't believe you weathered it without help, and now another one on top of the first one. No one can deal with these things alone. It's kind of a miracle that you're even here. You must be extraordinarily strong."

She looked at Kit with her dark brown eyes alert and tuned in. Kit had never talked to anyone who seemed to be so genuinely interested in what she had to say. She was having difficulty believing that Dr. Wolf was really as absorbed as she seemed to be.

"But you don't have to do it all alone," Dr. Wolfe said. "It's okay to seek help."

Kit sat, not knowing what to say. It's okay to seek help. Okay. It's okay. So I'm here, seeking. Can you help me? Is there a cure?

"Can you tell me about the more recent attack?"

"It was after work," Kit began, and heard herself saying things like, "I wanted more than just to get away. I wanted to kill him, right then and there, I wanted to watch him die, and I hated myself for wanting that but it didn't stop me from wanting it." She did not like what she was hearing, these vicious emotions coming out in words, out into the open, where they could no longer be her secrets. But even going over it, recalling the details and telling them to the doctor, Kit felt oddly calm. Or maybe disconnected was a better description. She didn't know. She wanted a drink.

"But again, you've survived it," Dr. Wolfe was saying. "More than that. You managed to fend off the attack. That's no small accomplishment." She gave Kit a smile, almost like she was proud of Kit for beating the attacker.

"It haunts me," Kit said. "Hits me at the oddest moments, out of the nowhere. I can be walking along and everything is, well, as okay as things get for me, and suddenly it's like I've been broadsided. I'm right back in it, reliving it, over and over and over again. I feel so totally . . . helpless."

"Even though you are hardly that."

"Even though. It's funny. I handled myself so well the other night, like I was on autopilot or something, but now I'm at the mercy of memories. And sometimes it's like the memories are more horrible than the reality of what happened. They really *are*, if you consider that the attacks are over and done with—until it happens again—but the memories of the attacks linger on. I'm being assaulted by them."

"Until it happens again?"

Kit nodded, afraid to explain further. What she needed to say might sound crazy. Insane. About the faces of the phantom attackers, the ones who came at her again and again. The rapist was there, though infrequently, and always he met his end with a bullet. Sometimes she fired the gun. Sometimes Wade made an appearance to pull the trigger. But it was Luke she couldn't talk about. How could she tell Dr. Wolfe that, sometimes, the attacker pulled off the black hosiery that had mashed his features and twisted his lips, he pulled it off and tossed it skyward, and it floated there, ghostlike, entrancing, and when Kit managed to pull her eyes from it and back to the face of her assailant, the face that she saw belonged to Luke Saner. She wanted to believe this was her mind's way of telling her who'd come after her that night, but the rational part of her did not want to believe it even *could* have been him. If it was, if it were, if, if, if. Cheerleaders, the chant of cheerleaders, if, if, if.

"Kit?" The doctor was looking at her patiently. "You said, until it happens again. You expect another attack?"

"Sometimes."

"Not uncommon in someone suffering from post-traumatic stress syndrome."

"So they have it catalogued. They have a name for it."

"I don't put a whole lot of stock in the American Psychiatric Association," Dr. Wolfe said. She pointed to a large book with a plain blue jacket on the corner of her desk and wrinkled her nose. "If you go by the *Diagnostic and Statistical Manual of Mental Disorders*, even happiness could be characterized as a mental disorder. I do, however, know a bit about trauma, and I know that though the damage can never really be undone, you can learn to live with it. You can teach yourself how to cope with it."

Kit nodded, but she had doubts about her ability to learn to live with the violence that seemed lodged in her brain, the recollection of it, the reality of it.

"You work? Able to hold a job?"

"I've knocked around some," Kit said. "It doesn't take much to hold the job that I have now."

"Which is?"

"Ever heard of Blaze's?"

"More than once. From other clients." There was no judgment in her tone.

"From Blaze's?"

"Various establishments. You'd be surprised at the number of women in the quote unquote adult entertainment business who wound up there after being abused, assaulted, raped." There was a sadness in Dr. Wolfe's voice. "It makes sense, though. What better way to regain power over your own body than to flaunt it in front of men who can't touch you."

"Unless they can catch you in the parking lot."

"Do you have any suspicions? As to who it was? Any ideas?"

Luke's face again. Kit shook her head no.

"He was hiding behind my friend Cheryl's car. He had black hosiery pulled over his face. Completely grotesque."

"Could it be that she was his intended victim? Do you know her well?"

Kit shook her head no. That she had referred to Cheryl as a friend but had to admit, to herself anyway, that she didn't really know Cheryl very well, left her feeling silly. Or worse, stupid.

"Who knows?" she said. "Maybe it was first come, first served."

"Could well have been. Most likely was."

Kit shrugged.

"What about your family life, Kit?"

"I hate my father, and he hates me back. Or maybe it's the other way around, I'm not sure. He and my younger sister get along great. He's a Texas Ranger, as in, like, an icon for law and order if ever there was one. He's very well respected on the force. My sister Jenny is a cop, too. Austin PD. Detective."

"Your mother?"

"Dead. Breast cancer. I was seventeen."

"That must have been very difficult."

Kit nodded. Difficult. A completely inadequate description.

"Does your father know where you work?"

"He thinks I bartend, if he even thinks about me at all. He's probably just glad I'm not dealing drugs or something like that."

"Does your sister know?"

"She didn't. Until recently. She got the report that I'd been attacked after work, so she found out. But that's about all. We didn't talk about it much."

Kit glanced furtively at her bag; looked up to see Dr. Wolfe's eyes on her. There was something in there, and Dr.

Wolfe knew it, but her look made it clear to Kit that she was not going to press the issue.

"Are you on good terms with them?" The doctor shifted in her chair and straightened her skirt.

"I guess." Kit smiled. "Jenny and I go to dinner at my father's house pretty regularly. I'm not sure why, exactly, some kind of attempt to keep the family in touch, or something like that."

"A tradition."

"You could call it that."

"Why do you expect another attack?"

Kit looked sharply at Dr. Wolfe, wondering at the sudden change of subject. Dr. Wolfe looked back at her, eyes filled with a kind of concern. If the question was a non sequitur, the doctor seemed fine with that. Maybe it had even been intentional. Kit thought only attorneys used that tactic.

"I'm not sure," Kit said. "I just know I do. Maybe because it's a reality for me. It's happened twice."

Dr. Wolfe nodded and sat quietly, waiting for Kit to continue.

Kit didn't know how to continue, where to go from there. She wanted some tip from the doctor, a quick fix for the flashbacks that hit her seemingly from nowhere. She wanted it all just to go away. She lived in dread of what was inside her own head, the bits and pieces of violent memory, waiting in there like hand grenades whose pins were pulled at random, creating explosions of fear in her mind. She knew the fear of attack—she lived with that, suffered in its grip—but now it seemed mixed up with something else, something dark in there that she could neither fully fathom nor begin to explain, something she was only just becoming aware of. Maybe it was the actual telling, the talking to Dr. Wolfe; maybe that had made room in her mind for thoughts and memories previously hidden under a layer of immediacy. She felt her insides go liquid as she wondered if it was some kind of evil, the kind mentioned in Genesis—and how long ago had *that* been written?—the evil that lurked inside every living human heart, waiting, biding its time, craving expression. Whatever it was, she was scared of it.

"He didn't cry." Her words, but where had they come from?

Dr. Wolfe raised her dark eyebrows; her eyes invited Kit to continue.

"At my mother's funeral. My father didn't so much as shed a single tear."

"He's stoic."

"More than stoic. It was like he wasn't moved. Like he was so used to living with his emotions shut down that he couldn't find them. Even such a powerful one as . . . She was his wife. She loved him, really and truly loved him."

"Did that make you think he didn't love her? The fact that he wouldn't, or maybe couldn't, cry."

Kit had to think about it. She didn't want to think about it. About him. She didn't want to think anything about him. She wanted him to disappear from her life. Painfully. As painfully as her mother had.

"Maybe he cried in private," Dr. Wolfe ventured. "Maybe he was only afraid of showing his emotions, not actually cut off from them."

"It didn't seem that way. It seemed like he was just ready

to get on with things. Put her body in the ground and get on with business."

"Do you love your father, Kit?"

Her thoughts went all scrambled, whirling inside her skull. Did she love her father? What kind of question was that? Did she love her father?

"He still hurts me. So I guess that means I love him. Somehow. But it doesn't feel like I love him. It feels like I hate him."

"Hurts you how?"

"With constant, unmitigated disapproval."

"Of your job?"

"Of my whole life. It's like I've never done anything even close to right. Not in his eyes." Kit stared at the floor, eyes downcast. "If I'd gone into law enforcement, maybe I'd have had a shot." She looked up at the doctor. "But then I'd have had to live hating myself." She didn't add: more than I already do.

She and Dr. Wolfe sat looking at each other, the unspoken sentences hanging between them. Kit knew what the doctor wanted to ask. *Do you hate yourself? Do you think, somehow, that you deserve these bad things that have happened to you?*

"What was he like when you were small, Kit? When you were a little girl?"

It was darkness again, there in the center of her mind.

"I don't remember. I don't remember much about him before I was in fifth grade, really. I can see him from then. I can see him on the riding mower, out in the front yard, on a Saturday afternoon. And at some of the picnics. I can see him at the grill, cooking steaks and drinking beer with his Ranger pals. Before that, it's only glimpses, like little pieces.

Standing in the doorway while my mother read to us, waiting to kiss us goodnight. But it's all broken up somehow, not like a whole picture."

"Was he involved in your school life? Did he come to plays or dance recitals or athletic events you were in?"

"Once." Kit said. "I was on a softball team, a church league, and the coach was sick and was calling around to team members asking if any of their parents could stand in for him at practice. We had a big game coming up, the district championship, and the coach wanted us to practice. I begged him to come. My father. And he surprised me by saying yes."

"That must have made you happy."

"It did. Until we started practice. And my dad was out in the field, not really knowing what to do, but we kind of knew anyway, the team did. We were doing batting practice, with runners on the bases. And someone hit a ball to my father, and he picked it up off the ground, and there was a runner on third heading for home, and everyone in the field was shouting, 'Throw it home, Throw it home!' And so my father did. But when he threw, the ball plunked to the ground about three feet in front of him." Kit shook her head slowly. "I thought I would die of embarrassment."

"Because he blew the play?"

"He didn't know how to throw a ball. You know how guys insult each other saying, 'Oh, he throws like a girl.' My father threw like a girl. And all the girls on the team threw like ballplayers. I wanted to crawl in a hole."

"But saying he threw like a girl, that's only saying he threw like someone who'd never been trained how to throw a ball, isn't it?"

Kit nodded yes.

"Did you expect your father to know how to do everything? Apparently he didn't play ball growing up."

"Very apparently."

"But he'd still volunteered to help out the team. Wasn't that worth anything in your eyes?"

"Of course. But it was still, I don't know, I was embarrassed, that's all. That's what I felt."

"Did you say anything to him? After?"

"I didn't have to. He was as embarrassed as I was, I could tell. We didn't say a word all the way home, even after we'd dropped off the girls who were riding with us."

"So on some level you expected your father to be omnipotent, to be able to handle any situation, regardless of his level of experience?"

"Not after that."

"Perhaps he became more human, more fallible, in your eyes?"

Kit smiled. "I guess I would say yes."

Dr. Wolfe shifted in her chair, crossing one leg over the other.

"And your mother? Do you have early memories of her?"

"Oh yes. I remember her from when I was pretty small. I can see her clearly. The day I climbed up the back stairs to the apartment we were living in, it was in Fort Worth, these wooden steps that led up to the kitchen door, and I went running up them and shook loose a nest of yellow jackets and got stung about eight times. I remember lying on the couch all afternoon and her coming to check on me and dab Milk of Magnesia on the stings to take down the swelling. A neighbor had told her it worked."

"Did it?"

"It helped. I was still pretty miserable, with a fever from so many stings and all."

"And how old were you then?"

"It was before kindergarten. I must have been about four. I can remember her taking me to my first day of kindergarten, too. Clearly."

"That must be a comfort, being able to recall her so well now that she's gone."

"Yes," Kit said. She hadn't thought about it much, but now that the doctor mentioned it, it was.

"We have to stop now, but I'd like to see you again in a couple of days, if you can manage it."

Kit felt an odd sensation of connectedness when the doctor said that. Dr. Wolfe wanted to help her. Someone in the world wanted to help her. Actually help her.

"There have been great strides made in the treatment of trauma over the past several years. I'd like you to try to remember where you are and what you're doing when you suffer those flashbacks, when the traumatic memories hit. It's important. I know it won't be easy for you, but it will help us in the treatment."

Kit stood reluctantly, not ready to go back out into the world. This place felt like a sanctuary.

"There's also the option of medication," Dr. Wolfe said. "But I try to refrain from it whenever possible. We can explore our options as we progress."

Kit nodded.

"You'll make it," Dr. Wolfe said. "I sense that about you. Just try to remember. Things *will* get better."

As they stood to walk to the door, Dr. Wolfe put a hand

on Kit's shoulder. Kit shuddered, only slightly, but they both felt it. It was always like that. Whenever someone touched her unexpectedly, her body recoiled slightly. It had been that way since the rape. She had to know in advance if someone was going to make physical contact, otherwise her body reacted in fear. She did not know how to even begin to stop that from happening. It was a subtle reaction, but unsettling every time it happened.

As she stood waiting for the elevator, she hoped vehemently that Dr. Wolfe was right. She wanted to believe that things would get better.

But as the elevator descended toward ground level, Kit felt her fears returning. She had hoped somehow to carry with her a little bit of the sense of safety she'd felt in Dr. Wolfe's office. It wasn't happening.

She stood at the glass doorway, knowing there would be a blast of heat when she opened it. Another murderously hot summer afternoon. She dug in her bag for her sunglasses. Her hand hit something hard and metal. It was not her glasses case.

Okay, so open the door and walk outside. You can protect yourself. You're armed. She remembered something Wade had told her, one afternoon after they'd been out on the shooting range. Jenny had asked him what it was like to kick down a door and run into a building, knowing that there were people in there with guns, people who wanted to hurt you.

Wade had laughed, kind of wistfully, and he'd said that you had to rush in there with the same attitude that the bad guys had. You had to believe in your heart that you didn't have one single goddamn thing in the world to lose.

She pushed open the door and stepped out into the heat, realizing with a shock that she hadn't mentioned anything at all to Dr. Wolfe about Jenny and Luke being engaged. About Luke's bruise, about her fear and disbelief at the possibility that—no. No and no and no. It wasn't, and it couldn't be. That was all. That was why it hadn't come up. She could not, did not, believe that Sweet had been the one. It was only a sick game that her mind was playing on her. One of many.

She heard the soft slow whoosh and muted thump of the steel and glass door closing behind her. She took a step. And another. She was walking down the sidewalk. On the sunny side of the street, only both sides of the street were sunny. Sunshine was everywhere, baking, grilling, broiling all it touched. Creating before her eyes a fresh hell, burning the top of her head as if her hair were on fire. What was inside her skull? What was it, in there, lurking among the neurons, waiting to knock her to her knees with fear? Was that what she needed to save her sanity? To be knocked to her knees?

Maybe if it happened, if she found herself flung down into the correct position, she could manage to fold her hands in front of her heart.

And pray.

SIX

Kit climbed down the ladder, clinging to the metal railing carefully, shaking with fatigue. Her skin was moist with perspiration; she wondered if even her sweat smelled like booze. She didn't care. She'd almost called in sick, after her session, but she'd walked to her car and driven to work and slugged down a shot of vodka from the bottle under her front seat and trudged into Blaze's and got up onstage and danced. And now it was three and she was done for the day. The afternoon loomed.

She sat on the soft pseudosuede of the couch in the dressing room and peeled an orange, focusing on its crisp citrus essence as the scent wafted up. She'd got a good one, ripe and juicy, and it was cool going down, delicious. She was trying to enjoy it.

She finished the orange and sat quietly, hearing the pulse of the music through the ceiling. She should get dressed, get out of here. But that meant she'd have to go outside, to the parking lot. She thought back to the session with Dr. Wolfe. Maybe the attack had been random. Maybe it had been meant for Cheryl. Maybe, maybe, maybe. She still had to get from here to her car and try not to fall apart in the process. But it was daytime. It was a sunny day.

That didn't change anything.

The door to the dressing room opened and Kit started, dropping her orange peels on the carpet.

"Take it easy, girl. It's only me." Cheryl walked over and slumped next to Kit on the couch. Kit picked up the orange peels and only then noticed the pasty color of Cheryl's skin, the slump of her shoulders.

Cheryl sighed a huge sigh.

"I'm never drinking again," she said. "Ever."

Kit stared. "What got you?"

"The nectar of the gods," Cheryl said.

"Said the Aztecs. They also killed young virgins in sacrificial rites."

"I hardly qualify," Cheryl said. "But I do genuinely and totally feel like I got sacrificed." She turned to face Kit, green eyes pleading. "Can you cover for me?"

"No," Kit said. "I'm done for the day. I have to go home." Should she finish the sentence: I have to go home and drink the rest of the afternoon away. You think you've got a hangover?

"Please? Just this once? I'll cover two shifts for you, you say when. I promise."

Kit sat, not wanting to say no, but needing to say no.

"And I'll split my tips with you. For both shifts."

"Cheryl."

"If I don't get home and get prone really fast, I might actually just die, Kit. That's how bad I feel."

"You could have called in sick."

"And gotten fired. I've done that once too many times." Cheryl moaned quietly. "Fuckin' tequila."

Kit felt bad for her. What the hell. She could just as easily drink here as at home. There was a bottle in her locker. And she wouldn't have to go back out there. She wouldn't have to make that terrifying trip to her car.

"All right," she said. "But you don't have to split your tips."

"One more thing." Cheryl seemed to be trying to smile. It came out weak.

Kit waited.

"I'm in the cage."

"Cheryl."

"Kit. *Please*." Cheryl gazed at her with seriously bloodshot eyes. "I'm not functional. I'll get in there and vomit."

"I might, too," Kit said. "Go on home. I'll do it."

Cheryl pulled herself to her feet, as though her body were something she had to drag around behind her.

"Thank you," she mouthed silently.

"Feel better," Kit said.

Kit watched her move slowly toward the door, open the door slowly, and slowly ease through it.

"Shit," she whispered.

She hated the cage. The tips were better than good—you could make three times what you did working the stage—but the thing induced in her an undeniable claustrophobia. She'd only been half kidding when she told Cheryl she might puke.

And she didn't like it that the customer could talk to her, and expected her to talk back, through an intercom system. It was too private. Too damn intimate.

She went to the mirror to touch up her makeup. She was doing a blue thing today, kind of punky, her hair crimped into tight waves and streaked electric blue, her eyelids painted the same color, and blue nail polish on fingers and toes, wearing a blue satin thong, black spaghetti-strap sandals to show off the nail polish, and glittery blue pasties on her nipples beneath a sheer blue waist-length cape with glittering silver trim. She'd even taken time to put on outrageously long false eyelashes. She was a superhero . . . a comic book character. She was making fun of herself, and, by extension, everyone else in the place. She wondered if anyone got it.

She listened for a moment. No sounds of anyone approaching. She quickly slipped the bottle from her locker and threw back a slug. Sweet relief. And another.

<hr/>

The cage was what it was: a cage. With bars, even, on three sides. Maybe Blaze was going for jailhouse chic. The front was the same Plexiglas that formed the windows of the regular booths. A small speaker and mic hung from the right front corner of the cage. Talk to me. Tell me what you like. I'll do anything to please you. This job was such bullshit. Kit climbed into the cage, feeling like a lab rat: tossed into a situation where she had to use her wits to survive and wondering if her wits were up to the stupid task at hand.

Just dance. No. Just sit here curled up in one corner of your cage until someone shows up to get their jollies. She plumped the pink satin pillow in a rear corner of the cage, curled herself against it, feeling the alcohol work its magic. Calming now. Getting steadied. She lay there, snuggling against the pillow like it was a long lost lover, trying to tune out the thump of the bass from the stage down the hall, feeling like she was lost in the woods and everywhere she looked she saw the same damn view. Trees everywhere, not a forest in sight. There had to be a way out, but she couldn't see it, couldn't get her sense of direction.

She told herself to relax. The maintenance dose was working. She felt the tension melt out of her shoulders and was surprised at how much had been in there. Just relax. Close your eyes. And relax.

She heard the door open. A customer entered; she heard the stool squeak as he sat down on it. Okay. Don't relax. Forget about relaxing. She opened her eyes.

She saw who it was and squeezed her eyes shut and opened them again. Trying to make sure she wasn't imagining.

Luke. Sweet. Whoever he was. Sitting there, like any other customer, sitting there waiting to get his rocks off, get his thrills, wang-dang-doodle himself until he shot his wad onto the concrete floor beneath him, breathing heavy, satiate himself with a heaping platter of female flesh, engage in intercourse both sexual and not. Waiting for Kit to stand up and do what he told her. To do.

She stood. Looked at him. Saw it all in her head. *Here comes the bride* . . . Organ music. She could see Luke at the front of the church, looking down the aisle as Wade escorted a beautiful, glowing Jenny, Luke there waiting for the bride's father to hand over the goods. Her sister, standing next to him at the altar, all in her flowing gown and veil and clutching a bouquet of white roses and baby's breath. A pastor and choir. Till death do us part. Promises, promises.

And Jenny, all in white, thinking this moment was the beginning of dreams coming true.

Sweet sat there as he always did when he came to watch the dancers. Hands on the window ledge, but instead of his usual slight smile of appreciation, his face looked frozen with apprehension. Even in the darkness of the closet, Kit could see the remnant of the bruise still on his jaw.

"Kit," he started, his voice coming through the speaker in the cage, "I—"

She whirled and hit the button to bring the music into the cage, into Luke's booth, and went into it immediately. She was gonna let him have it. She was gonna show him what he'd be missing once he was a married man. She stretched, raising her arms high overhead, knowing that it trimmed her figure, showed off her breasts. She turned to give him a profile, accentuate her feminine outline. She arched her back.

"Kit—" he tried again.

Kit reached quickly and turned up the music volume. Fuck you, Luke Saner.

He slumped away from the microphone in the booth. He stared. But it was as if he weren't actually seeing her.

She was gonna scare him away from his engagement to her sister. She had to. For Jenny's sake.

She danced, having to focus on the music just to keep some kind of time to it. Suddenly it was as if her body was on a two-second delay; always before it was just a matter of listening and moving, it was automatic, but now, with Luke watching her, she couldn't get with the rhythm. Was it his eyes? Were they doing this to her? She focused, every movement an effort, and wondered what it looked like, this animated rag doll bopping around in the cage in her svelte blue superhero outfit, her comic book perversion version of Wonder Woman. Or was she UnderWoman, prancing around in blue underwear under the gaze of the male of the species, under duress, under the pretext of just doing her job, under the guise of being a willing participant in this craziness. She danced, and looked at Luke, and looked at him again, so cool he was, so in charge, he paid his money and took his chances, and today he'd drawn her, Kit—*the winner!*—and she danced and danced some more, or she guessed that was what she was doing. It didn't really feel like dancing, it felt like she was underwater, moving through thick liquid; the effort of simply making her arms and legs respond was breaking her out in a sweat. Her ears filled with a noise like whitewater, like a raging river, and she couldn't hear the music. Her vision went yellow, a million minuscule yellow bugs flying around her head, swarming around her in the cage. Her limbs went limp; she slumped to the floor.

She sat there unable to move. Feeling ridiculous suddenly in her see-through blue cape with the shiny blue danglies covering her nipples, reminding her somehow of the tassels that streamed from the handles of her bicycle when she was seven, and the pom-poms she'd shaken and twirled the year she did drill team in tenth grade. Go, team, go! She'd been fooling herself, thinking she could get up on stage and take it all off and that because the customers couldn't reach her, couldn't touch her or take anything from her, it would empower her. Maybe it had, for a while, or maybe that was just another delusion.

She looked at Luke, sitting there with his hands on the window ledge, only his eyes indicating an awareness that something wasn't right with her. But he wasn't sure, she could tell. He thought maybe this was part of the dance. He expected her to spring to her feet and continue.

Kit looked at him, tried to move. Her limbs wouldn't budge. She had no strength. She sat, waiting for Luke to say something, waiting for her body to come back to her. She could hear the music again, the BeeGees. Staying Alive. *Ah-hah-hah-hah*. She managed, finally, to drag herself up. Stood in the middle of the cramped booth. Looked at her sister's fiancé. *Ah. Hah. Hah.*

She directed her words toward the microphone in the corner of the cage.

"Go get your money back," she said. "Ask for a refund. I can't do this right now." She opened the frameless Plexiglass door and ducked out.

In the dressing room, Kit used her cell to call Dr. Wolfe. She got the machine. She hung up. What could Dr. Wolfe do but reassure her that she wasn't losing her mind, whether she was or not? She dressed and went down the hall to Blaze's office.

Blaze, dressed casually in Levi's and a western shirt, with blue-gray ostrich-skin boots on, was bent over some paperwork. She motioned Kit to a chair.

"What's up?" Blaze asked.

"I was covering for Cheryl in the cage," Kit said. "She's sick, and—"

"Again?" Blaze cut in.

"She's really sick," Kit said. "Stomach bug."

Blaze snorted and carefully placed her Montblanc on the desk.

"And?"

"I can't cut it today, Blaze. I'm sorry."

"So who's gonna work the cage?"

"Can you get someone?"

"Just like that?" Blaze looked at her with dismay.

"I'm really sorry, okay, Blaze? Really. I'm just, that attack, things are too weird right now. I thought I was okay but I'm not. I have a call in to my therapist."

"You're seeing a therapist?"

Kit nodded. "I had to."

"No, no, it's okay. That's good," Blaze said. She nodded slowly, knowingly, as though she'd seen this kind of thing before. "Go ahead then. I'll find someone."

Kit stood to go. She was at the door when Blaze spoke. "Kit."

Kit turned. This office was so orderly. So kept. A place for everything, and everything in its place.

"Don't think I don't understand," Blaze said. "You've been through something. You're going through something. Whatever. But please let Cheryl know that I have to be able to depend on you girls."

"I will," Kit said, knowing the warning wasn't meant only for Cheryl.

✦

In her car, she checked the parking lot for observers. Empty cars. No one coming or going. She pulled out the bottle and swallowed down some vodka. Hot vodka, from being in the hot car on a hot afternoon. She grimaced. Nasty.

But so damn good.

She was pulling out of the parking lot when her cell phone beeped, signaling a new voice mail. She dialed up. The message was from her father.

"Kit," he was saying, "come to the house as soon as you get this message." Click.

What was his problem and who did he think he was, ordering her around like she was a recalcitrant teenager or something? It wasn't like he was ever around and willing to listen to her, willing to be there for her. It wasn't like he'd ever once called her before. She hadn't realized he even had the number. Let him call Jenny. Let her go hold his hand. He'd probably tried her first, and when she wasn't available, decided to settle for his *other* daughter. Hell with him. She would make the six P.M. class at the dojang and sweat out the toxins and then call. If she even felt like it by then. She pulled a tiny turquoise Listerine Pocket Pak from her purse. Slipped two of the filmy strips out and placed them on her tongue. Let's take communion. Oral care strips. Right. Her eyes watered as her tongue felt the antiseptic burn. Fix your breath, you fucking addict. You reek. She was dizzy, feeling ragged from the cage, from Luke's appearance there. She'd thought she was going to pass out. Yeah. Let Dad wait. She'd go burn off some steam. Then maybe she could deal with him without letting him make her crazy.

Traffic was light, and ain't life grand! Kit wheeled into the parking lot at the dojang and realized she had a few minutes. She took inventory: Was she sober enough even to take class? She walked around back to sit by the stream. Shallow water gurgled softly over the limestone stream bed, worn smooth and wavy by all those years of being caressed by water. Kit breathed deeply, slowly, focusing on the stream, searching for calm.

But she couldn't stop the image of Luke from popping into her brain. Luke at the restaurant. Luke at Blaze's. She was sure he'd never mentioned to Jenny that he patronized a strip club. She wondered what other sins of omission the guy was guilty of. She wondered how big a liar he actually was.

She took out her cell phone and dialed information, got the number for the Austin Police Department. Arrests were a matter of public record. After being passed around through a couple of departments, she reached someone who seemed willing to answer her questions. She told the woman on the line she was a reporter looking into the arrest a few days ago of a pair wanted for armed robbery. The woman told her to hold for a moment, and when she came back on line, Kit could hear the sounds of a computer keyboard clicking away. And then some mouse clicks.

"I'm sorry," the woman said, "I'm not showing anything in our records. You're sure it was Tuesday? This past Tuesday."

"Yes," Kit said. "And I believe one of the arrestees assaulted one of the officers? Anything on that?"

"Oh," the woman said. "Oh yeah. Here it is. Not to mention that I heard about that one personally. What paper did you say you were with?"

Kit clicked shut her phone and dropped it into her gym bag. Okay. So maybe Luke hadn't lied about that. But he hadn't told Jenny where he liked to spend his off hours, and that made him still a liar. Or at least deceitful. She would confront him, that was all. What she wasn't sure of was whether she should let Jenny in on things first. But if she did, Jenny would forever remember, on some level, that Kit had been the one bearing the bad news. She would associate Kit with Luke's malfeasance. What was that Sophocles thing? Kill the messenger who bears bad news? Jenny would despise her.

Kit sat there, watching the stream and trying not to let herself get angry, or angrier than she already was, at Luke. Some people just weren't happy unless they were constantly stirring up shit. Or maybe he was walking around unconscious— God knows, there were enough folks in the world doing that. Maybe he was just selfish and thoughtless. She hated to think of Jenny falling in love with a creep.

As she walked around to the front of the dojang, she focused on emptying her mind of all the petty bullshit distractions of— Of what? Of living? No. Not of living. Living was one thing.

All she was doing lately was surviving.

At the front of the building, she stopped abruptly.

The door threatened. She could not make herself open it. She could not pass through.

She didn't know how long she stood there. The sound of her cell phone ringing from inside her bag jarred her back to where she was, staring at the heavy wooden doors.

She turned and walked to her car, moving slowly, exhausted. She did not know why. The caliche parking lot was mostly in shade from the trees surrounding it. If she'd had to park in the sun, the interior of her car would have been just about sufficiently preheated to bake a cake.

Even with the shade, the Mustang was already hot. Inside, Kit cranked the air to full and dug into her bag for her phone. She did not want to think what it might be stashed next to. It scared her, knowing the gun was in there. Jenny had thought to help her protect herself. Instead she was only reinforcing the fear.

There was another message from Wade. The same as the last one: You need to come home as soon as you can. This one sounded more urgent than the last.

⧉

He was on the back porch. In his rocker. Kit saw from his eyes that he was drunk. And she couldn't be sure, but it looked like he might have been crying.

She slipped through the screen door and went to him, sat down in a patio chair across from him. He just stared at her. Didn't say a word. Just stared.

"Daddy?" Her voice sounded childlike, even to her. Not just childlike. Scared childlike. And she was. He was scaring her. She thought of the afternoon she and Jenny had driven their mother to tears with their bad behavior, who finally sent them to their rooms. *Wait until your father gets home.* Kit spent close to two hours in total dread of what might happen. Her mother had never been that angry.

Her father, either. When he arrived, Kit crept out into the hallway to listen as her mother burst into tears while listing the perfectly awful things Kit and Jenny had done that day: ignoring her, refusing to pick up their rooms, taking the garden hose and filling the flower bed out back until it was nothing but mud, jumping in and pretending it was a swimming pool, running into the kitchen tracking mud and

111

water all over the wide pine floorboards. When Karen finished, Kit heard Wade heave a great sigh, and then he came into her bedroom and told her to drop her drawers and bend over the bed. She'd never been so frightened. Her knees trembled as she lay bent over on her unmade bed, her blue jeans and panties down around her ankles, and she heard her father take off his belt and then he hit her with it and the pain made her cry out, and with it the degradation made her burst into tears, and she cried out, "Daddy, I'm sorry, I won't ever do it again, not ever, Daddy, Daddy! Please!" Sobbing, tears pouring from her eyes, and he hit her again, and a third time, and she was wailing by then, the pain enough on its own to make her sob, but more than that it was the humiliation that made her cry.

She had her pants up before he closed the door and she stood rubbing her butt and crying silently, listening for cries from Jenny's room down the hall.

None came.

There was the sound of Wade's deep voice, lecturing.

Kit waited, anticipating the sound of leather slapping against skin.

Instead, she heard a giggle. Jenny was laughing. And then Wade was, too. Laughing. Her sister had skated once again. It was always like that. Kit bore the brunt of his anger; Jenny was always forgiven on the grounds that she must have been acting under Kit's influence.

Kit looked at her father. He rocked slowly, looking past her, looking into some horrible place. And then it hit her.

Jenny.

"Daddy?" She barely got the words out.

"She's dead," Wade whispered. "She's been murdered."

Kit felt herself go weightless, like her body had suddenly metamorphosed into pure white light. She wasn't there. She wasn't there at all. And then a crash inside her skull and a heaviness descending, pulling her earthward, pulling her down into the ground. She could only stare at him. His eyes connected to hers and something passed between them, a pain so fierce that Kit thought it would knock her over. She rocked back in her chair and then felt herself go limp and a million questions were flying around in her head, *whys* and *hows* and *are you sures*, flying in circles, doing loop the loops around and between each other, banging into the bones of her skull.

"She was at the mall," Wade said. "Last night. She went to meet with the bridal registry consultant, or whatever the hell you call it. She went to register for gifts. She picked out dinnerware, goddammit. She chose silverware and crystal and all that other crap that people get at their weddings." He polished off his drink, grabbed the bottle of Wild Turkey on the table next to his rocker and poured another. He held the bottle out to Kit. She took it and took a swig straight out of it. And then another.

"What happened, Daddy? Where is she?"

"A ranch hand found her body," Wade said. "This afternoon. Down a well over in Blanco County. Over on the Devil's Backbone."

"Oh my God." Kit heard the words come out, but it didn't feel like she'd spoken them. They sounded like they'd come from somewhere else, someone else.

"They're doing an autopsy. But they told me already it was a gunshot wound." He took another drink and carefully put his glass down and let his head fall into his wide palms. "Bastard shot her in the heart."

Kit grabbed the bottle again, swigged hard, returned the bottle to the table.

"Found her car still at the mall. Locked. Untouched." He shook his head slowly. "Doesn't make a lick of sense. There's no reason." His voice was husky. He was fighting back tears.

Kit felt her own, trailing down her cheeks slowly, dripping onto her thighs. She rubbed them off and dried her hands on her shorts, but more came and she didn't try to stop them. She felt like she'd be crying for the rest of her life. Like this pain would never stop, never even ease up. Someone had taken her sister from her. Forever.

SEVEN

Kit sat. She breathed. She was breathing and not smelling the sickly sweet scent of too many flowers in too small a space, like at the funeral home. The lights were soft. The couch was soft. She was sitting on a soft couch in a peaceful room. She felt like hell. Head throbbing, heart fluttering, hands shaking, stomach churning. She didn't want a drink. She did need a drink. That was all she knew.

The door opened and Dr. Wolf emerged, her forehead etched with concern.

"Kit," she said, "please come in."

Kit stood and followed Dr. Wolfe. She took her place on the couch. She saw the box of tissues on the table, ugly as ever. Dr. Wolfe sat across from her, letting her long skirt fall over her legs. She placed her hands in her lap, ready to listen.

Kit did not know what to say. She was empty, and her body was surrounded by a bubble of something soft, like an invisible cloud had enveloped her and she was floating inside it, not really here on the planet. Just hovering.

She saw Dr. Wolfe's lips move. It took a moment for the voice to reach her, muted by the bubble of softness around her.

". . . your message yesterday evening," the doctor was saying, "you sounded . . ." The doctor's lips stopped. Kit waited for the rest of the sentence, but it never reached her ears.

"Suicidal," Kit whispered, and then the bubble vanished, and she was there in the office and heard a cardinal calling to its mate outside the window. It was probably brilliant red. She was certain of that.

"Are you?"

Am I what?

Oh. That.

"I told you." Kit heard her words travel through the air toward Dr. Wolfe's ears.

"Jenny's dead" went the words.

Kit felt her lips moving. She was speaking to Dr. Wolfe. "Someone killed my sister. I really don't know. I don't know how to go on."

She felt it coming on hard, and knew it was pointless, but still she tried to choke back the tears. To no avail. She reached for a tissue, blotted at her eyes.

"I'm so sorry, Kit. I am so, so sorry."

"I don't know why," Kit said. She ran down the details of Jenny's death, what little she knew of it, the words coming out of her mechanically, and inside, even as she was reciting them, there was only numbness.

She told the doctor about Luke, about his coming to the club and about seeing him at dinner and realizing her sister was about to marry a man who was two different people, about her confusion over whether and how to tell Jenny what was up with him, about wondering if it had been Luke who attacked her that night, about Rusty, about all of it.

Dr. Wolfe sat, quietly listening. Kit finished, silence descending as she waited for Dr. Wolfe to say something that would make it all okay, something that would make sense of the situation. The doctor looked at her, waiting for more.

"My father."

"Yes?"

"I don't know."

"You were about to say something."

"I don't know. That's all I can think."

"What's he doing? How is he coping?"

"He's coping by investigating. He's in lawman mode."

"Does he have any idea? Are there suspects? The paper said no leads."

"I think he suspects everyone right now."

"You?"

It took a moment for Kit to understand the question.

"Does he suspect me?" Kit said the words, but still the concept was out of reach. She couldn't get her brain wrapped around it. "Does he suspect me?"

"Yes. Has he said anything that would make you think he considers you a suspect?"

Kit tried to think through it, to replay the moments she'd spent with her father since Jenny's death. She struggled to think as confusion and fear bounced hand in hand through her brain, as though her gray matter were one of those huge blow-up castles that children loved to bounce in, flinging themselves against the walls to be hurled back to the center of the thing and scramble to their feet so they could do it again, all the while laughing and shrieking. There had been conversations, that much she knew. She saw her father's face, her father's eyes, her father's hands. But what had Wade said? Something that would make her think he suspected her? Now was the moment she should tell Dr. Wolfe. What happened to her, sometimes, the tricks her mind played. How there were holes in her memory, big ones that held hours, how some days she woke up without a memory of where she'd been the night before. Different holes from those created by alcohol. Very different. It didn't happen often. It happened rarely. But it *had* happened, and each time it did, she was terrified by it.

She should tell Dr. Wolfe.

The night Jenny died. The night they'd gone to dinner at the Gypsy Wolf. Kit had gone home to her apartment, her brain trying to comprehend that her sister's fiancé might have been the man who attacked her. She'd tried to read, thinking to distract herself, but the margaritas had left her too woozy to concentrate. She drifted off almost immediately; the last thing she remembered was hearing the book drop to the floor.

When she woke up, she was standing, fully dressed and apparently functional, at the corner coffee shop, holding a cup of coffee in her had and staring at the cashier—who was looking at her impatiently. The space in between was blank. Maybe it was only the time it took her to wake up that morning and dress and walk to the coffee shop that was missing. Maybe it was that she'd been sleepwalking that morning. But she didn't know. She had no way of knowing, and no way to find out.

She should tell the doctor.

No, she should *not* tell the doctor.

"I hadn't even considered the possibility," she said finally. "It never occurred to me that he would."

"Does it now?"

"Me?" She shook her head. No. "He doesn't suspect me. No way." Kit couldn't even grasp the possibility. She looked at Dr. Wolfe, felt the skin on her face trembling. It seemed almost like Dr. Wolfe was the one who suspected her.

"You told me that she was his favorite. That you felt inadequate as a daughter, that you considered him inadequate as a father."

"What are you saying? I don't understand what you're saying."

"I'm not saying anything, Kit. I'm asking questions to try to help you."

It did not seem like help. It seemed like accusation.

"You said you hated him, Kit. Do you hate him?"

Kit sat, unable to speak. The clouds came on, rolling in like a sudden thunderstorm, swirling in her brain, and then her father's face, smiling and not smiling at the same time, his smile conniving and sincere, his eyes full of love and self-loathing, his eyes confusing her, his lips forming words she couldn't hear.

"We both loved Jenny," Kit finally managed. "I know that much. That much I know for sure. He loved her and I loved her. She was a good person, Dr. Wolfe. She was a loving and sincere person."

"What about your father? Is he a loving and sincere person?"

"He's a beast." Her own words stunned her. She didn't know where they came from. She hadn't meant to say it. But it occurred to her now that she meant it. She meant what she'd just said. *He's a beast.*

"Do you hate him?"

"I don't know." She was being honest. She didn't know. She knew she didn't want to hate him. But she thought probably she did. On some level. She despised him.

Dr. Wolfe sat, not prodding, just waiting for Kit to come to terms with an answer.

"I think I do," Kit said. "I think that's probably an accurate statement."

"A lot of people think Carl Jung was a wacko," Dr. Wolfe said softly. "A little too spiritual to be thought of as a real shrink." She smiled, more to herself than to Kit. "But one thing he said that I agree with very much was this: The opposite of love is not hate."

Kit saw her father's face, staring down at her little girl face from his full adult height. Her father the lawman, her father the good guy, who took bad guys off the street and put them in cages where they belonged. Her father the hero.

"The opposite of love," Dr. Wolfe said, "is indifference."

Kit felt vaguely upset with herself, but resolute that things should head in a different direction. Love, hate, indifference. None of it mattered right now. It hadn't really jelled in her mind, until this moment. She'd been feeling, underneath all the not-feeling, hiding under the self-inflicted numbness, a desire for vengeance. But she knew now that vengeance would not free her from the over-whelming sadness, would not bring Jenny back, would not do anything but bring more violence into her life. That, she did not want. Not vengeance. But she did want, more than anything now, to find the person who'd done it. And face him. Just face him. See him. Make him understand that she knew. She knew he was responsible. That was all.

"Kit," Dr. Wolfe said finally, "do you feel capable of go-ing on?"

Kit shrugged. She didn't know. She felt as if she were slogging through clouds, as if the clouds in her brain had escaped somehow and surrounded her. As though she were stranded in a miasma of confusion, a confusion of gray, swollen sadness swelling up from the very earth beneath her feet. She could sit there and see the desk and the chair and the walls and the box of tissues on the coffee table, she could see the doctor who was there trying to help her; she could see everything in the room, but she couldn't get a grip on how to keep breathing. She wanted to be consumed by the cloud, by the gray; she wanted the air against her skin to become acid and eat her alive, quickly and efficiently, simply consume the very molecules of her physical exis-tence and leave nothing behind but air. She wanted to evap-orate into nonexistence.

Cease breathing.

Disappear.

Leave no trace.

"Do you want me to place you somewhere? For a while? Where you can be looked after and feel safe?"

Kit stared at her. Safe from what?

The unspoken words: from herself.

She shook her head no.

"I am okay," she said firmly, trying to persuade not just the doctor, but herself. "I can get through this. I will get through this." She wondered if she believed herself.

"I'm concerned. You seem thoroughly overwhelmed."

"Putting me in the loony bin is not going to help."

Dr. Wolfe smiled. "I'm talking about a hospital, Kit. You would be cared for. You could rest. You could gather your strength."

"I promise you. If I start to feel like I'm losing the battle, I will tell you."

"You mentioned suicide. Earlier. When you first came in."

"I know. But I won't give in."

Dr. Wolfe looked at her closely. Kit could see her evaluating, looking for some outward indication of Kit's ability to persevere, trying to calculate risk. As though there would be some manifestation of suicidal intent that she could read on the surface of Kit's skin, or in her eyes.

"I'm staying at Jenny's old place," Kit volunteered. "I'm not alone. Jenny's roommate is there."

Dr. Wolfe sighed, stood, and went to her desk. She picked up a small white tablet of paper. Her prescription pad. She returned to her chair and placed the pad on her thigh, scribbled something on it.

"I want you to fill this," she said. "And take the medication. I'm thinking strictly short-term here, no more than two or three weeks. But you've been through too much. This will level you out, just for a while, until you can get back to a frame of mind where we can accomplish something."

Kit took the slip of paper Dr. Wolfe offered. She heard

in her head a television announcer's voice, that low, almost whispered tone that followed the heavy red meat of the advertisement, the words stepping on each other's heels, tumbling out so quickly you expected a gasp for air just any second: *side-effects-may-include-drowsiness-dizziness-nausea-vomiting-rash-jaundice-confusion-dyspepsia-and-memory-loss.* Memory loss. That's what she needed. Forget the symptomatic relief, just give me the desired side effect. She nodded as she slipped the paper into her bag. Thought back to those times in college when she would have delighted at copping a script for legit drugs. Now she wondered if she'd even take the stuff.

"I want you to come back day after tomorrow," Dr. Wolfe said. "And I'd like you to call me sometime tomorrow afternoon. Just check in. Let me know how you're doing. That sound all right with you?"

"Yes," Kit said. "That sounds all right."

"Kit," she said, "I'm here for you. You don't have to go through this alone. I'm here."

Dr. Wolfe stood and leaned toward Kit, opening her arms. Kit felt herself surrounded in a warm, generous hug. God, how long had it been since she'd felt something like this? Something like simple affection.

She stepped back and folded the prescription in half, and in half again, and in half again, and realized Dr. Wolfe was watching her, waiting to see if she would fold it yet again. She tucked it into her pocket and felt her lips attempting to smile.

"I'll get through it," she said.

Dr. Wolfe nodded yes.

"Call me if you need me, Kit."

"I will," Kit said.

She walked out the door and through the waiting room. The woman with the dog was there. Icky perked up when he saw Kit, lifting his head and letting his jaw fall open into a pant.

"Stay, Icky," the woman said, smiling brightly at Kit.

Whacked. Totally whacked. But harmlessly so, or it seemed that way.

Kit closed the door behind her and stood in the hallway, trying to gather herself for the journey down the stairs. She made herself promise that she would call Dr. Wolfe if . . .

If what?

If she felt like driving her Mustang into a bridge abutment at a hundred and ten m.p.h.? That was the thing. You just never knew when someone would twist off. Including your very own self.

Kit held the railing on the way down. The staircase was long and steep.

EIGHT

T he coffin was obscene. Titanium, maybe, in a metallic palest-of-pale blue finish. Ugly as a tissue box. It looked like it had been finished in nail polish aimed for the preteen market. It was sleek and rounded, with fixed, color-coordinated hardware and a fully adjustable bed. White crepe interior, the brochure had said. Sunray head panel.

Kit didn't know why Wade had chosen such niceties, if that's what they could be called. The coffin was closed this afternoon, the kind of afternoon that wilted flowers with dry, baking heat. Closed to protect those at the funeral from the sight of what was left of Jenny's ravaged body. What could it have looked like, after being thrown down into an empty well. How many bones had broken? How bad were the bruises? How much blood had soaked her clothing, pouring from the wound in her chest?

Kit stared at the coffin, fearing to contemplate what the final moments of her sister's life had been. And the moments after, maybe hours after, when the murderer had lifted Jenny's lifeless body and cast it into the gaping black hole in the ground. What had it sounded like when her body hit the bottom? How far down had she gone before striking the earth?

Kit stared. The coffin should have been wood. It should have been plain and simple and wood. It should have been something that could return to the earth, slowly and gently, not a damn time capsule imprisoning her sister's remains for future archeologists.

She sat next to her father, choking back sobs, feeling the weight of Wade's arm on her shoulder, the muscles in it tense with a dangerous rage. His eyes were bloodshot from whiskey. She didn't want to think about what her eyes looked like. She'd had vodka for breakfast, with a Listerine chaser. Stood there in front of the mirror above the sink, in a bathroom in her father's house, and when she happened to catch herself in the mirror and saw herself sucking down the liquor, disgust hit her right in the stomach. But it didn't prevent her taking another pull, straight from the bottle. She stashed it under the sink, behind a stack of toilet paper rolls. Swigged some Listerine, foul-tasting stuff, burning her mouth worse than the booze, and spat it into the sink. Dysfuckingfunctional. Headed to her sister's funeral.

She stared at herself in the mirror and it hit her again, out of the darkness in her mind. Relentless. Over and over: the image of a bullet blowing a hole in Jenny's heart.

The blood of it.

She bent and retrieved the bottle from beneath the sink. One more hit. One more before the funeral. And then more

Listerine. A voice in her head said, *What the fuck are you doing?*

She had no reply.

She thought about emptying the rest of the bottle into the sink. Instead, she put it back into the cabinet.

She would need it later.

And she needed it now. Wade's arm rested across her shoulders. The preacher's voice droned on.

Wade hadn't cried. Last night. Late. Kit didn't know how he could not. Stoic, was it? She sat, numb, hearing the preacher's tenor voice float out in consoling tones across the pews, slipping into the ears of the gathered lawmen and women, the smattering of Jenny's old high school and college friends, the secretaries and administrators from the police department.

They seemed not to know how to act, the lawmen, the gathered Rangers and Austin officers and detectives. Not because they were at a cop's funeral, it seemed to Kit, but rather because of the circumstances of Jenny's death.

It had not been a heroic death, raised out of the ordinary by supreme self-sacrifice. Jenny had not died in the line of duty, in some blazing gun battle or daring rescue attempt. It was a small and miserable death, from out of nowhere, with no suspect and no motive and no opportunity for lauding the courage of the deceased. Those present could not approach Wade and offer consolation with words like honor or valor or justice.

Kit could hear the preacher's voice, but his words swirled past, nothing more than verbal vapor, floating to the rear of the room, slipping down onto the plush lavender carpet and beneath the heavy oaken double doors at the rear. She smelled roses; the room stank of roses and cologne and aftershave and the collective breath of those gathered to put Jenny's body into the ground.

Her eyes stung. She closed them and wondered what her sister was wearing, there in her coffin. Wade most likely had delivered Jenny's police uniform to the undertaker. Kit hadn't asked. She hadn't asked him anything. Not today, not last night. Luke had dared to show his face at her father's door, arriving shortly after Wade came home with the brochure. Last night Luke had dared to hug her. He had dared to let her see his tears. Kit wondered if they were real. If anything about her sister's fiancé was real. Wade opened the brochure and showed them the coffin he'd selected. Luke approved, apologizing to Wade for breaking down and telling him that he would do everything he could to help Wade find Jenny's killer. Kit had stared at the photo of the coffin in the brochure and nodded blankly and handed it back to Wade. They had names. At least he hadn't picked the one featuring Monet's *Water Lilies* or *The Last Supper* or the one they called *Fairway to Heaven*, which had a big piece of golf course painted on it.

Wasn't civilization just grand?

Amen. Kit opened her eyes and saw people raising their heads from the bowed position as they said it: Amen. The preacher had been praying. Amen. Everyone had been praying. Amen.

She heard Leila Jane crying now, sobbing in the row behind her. She turned and saw a man next to Leila, her father maybe, pull Leila close and let her cry on his shoulder. She felt Wade's arm tighten against her own shoulder, felt his body shudder. She wanted to cry; she felt like she was crying, but there were no tears left inside her. She was crying, she was sobbing inside, but her eyes remained dry. So dry that Kit felt they might simply turn to dust, disintegrate in their sockets. She closed them again and leaned forward, pressing her eyes against her hands, feeling the damp sweatiness of her palms against her eyelids. She pressed against the darkness until circles of light appeared on the backs of her eyelids, expanding outward like miniature universes, like stars exploding, and then everything was white and then a blackness pushed through the white and grew, eating away the light until she was in darkness again.

Amen, they said. Amen.

So be it.

People were standing up, moving toward the center aisle, moving toward the doors at the back of the room. Kit felt Wade's hand on her elbow, urging her upright, guiding her toward the exit.

She was in a car, a limousine, Wade still next to her, Luke sitting across from them. Luke looked haggard in the semigloom of the limo, his eyes glazed with pain. The bruise on his jaw had gone yellow, almost disappeared. The seats were black leather, the carpet black, the entire interior of the limo black, black, black. The sunlight muted by tinted windows. The driver up there somewhere, starting the engine, pulling out behind the hearse. The engine hummed. Cool, conditioned air flowed from strategically placed vents, fighting against the heat of all that sunshine.

"Daddy," Kit said. And then she could find no words.

Wade took her hand in both of his, held it on his thigh, patting it, trying to soothe, but Kit could feel his distance, could tell that his mind was somewhere far away, seeing vengeance, playing out one scene after another of what he would do to the person who took Jenny away from him.

The graveyard was an oasis of green, the lawn stretching crisp and brilliant, the grass manicured, weed free. Kept.

The somber driver held the door for them, closing it with a quiet efficiency after they exited the vehicle. He didn't have a face. Kit couldn't see his face. She tried to focus, to gain an image of his eyes or mouth. She could see his suit, and his white shirt, and his dark tie. That was all.

She was sitting again, now in a padded gray metal folding chair, between Wade and Luke, and she looked at Luke and felt naked. Knowing that he'd seen her up on stage, she felt like she was sitting at her sister's interment without any clothes on. She heard the pulsing music that pounded the stage at Blaze's, the bass, *ba-boom*, *ba-boom*, *ba-boom*, and then realized she was hearing the sound of her own heart, beating in her chest, her pulse filling her ears.

She watched as the preacher tossed a handful of dirt onto the top of that spotless, gleaming coffin and knew he was saying *From dust you came*, but she couldn't hear anything but her heartbeat. She wondered if she was about to faint.

She saw uniforms, two rows of police in dark blue, baking in the heat, standing at attention on the other side of the coffin. A contingent from the police department, paying respects to her sister.

She sat in the chair and felt the heat from the sun and saw the blue of the cloudless sky and smelled the green from the grass on the ground beneath her, the ground that held so many bodies, the deceased, the dearly departed, those who had passed on, gone to their reward, left the land of the living. The dead.

Jenny. There in the coffin. Her sister.

She saw her mother's white granite headstone. Jenny's body would lie next to their mother's. Karen Ann Metcalf. Loving wife and mother. 1955–1995. What would Jenny's headstone say? She wondered what words Wade had chosen.

⊞

When they got back to Wade's house, she didn't have to sneak into the bathroom to drink. Women bustled in the kitchen, Ranger wives, making sure the dining room table was covered with food. The kitchen bar held beverages. Kit made a drink, an actual vodka and cranberry, ignoring the stares. She took a civilized sip and walked to the living room, which was filling with people she didn't know. And then she noticed Rusty and took a real swallow.

He was practically wedged into a corner, clutching his dress Stetson, his discomfort evident from the intense focus in his pale green eyes, as though he were in the woods somewhere with a rifle in his hand, hunting for prey. He saw her looking and approached cautiously.

His black western shirt was pressed free of wrinkles, his boots polished spotless. He had on a bolero tie of braided black leather with gleaming silver tips.

"I'm sorry for your loss, Kit," he said. His voice held a tremor. He tossed his hat on Wade's easy chair and placed his hands on Kit's shoulders. "She was a good woman." She felt him start to pull her toward him, start to embrace her, but he stopped suddenly and let his hands drop back to his sides, leaning down just slightly to bring his eyes to the level of hers. "I won't ask if you're okay," he said.

Kit stood, looking into his eyes, almost the color of sage, wondering at the distance that had grown between them since she'd said no to his proposal.

"I'm not," she said. "But what's new?" He half-smiled, and she looked past him to the corner of the room where Leila Jane was talking to Wade. Wade seemed engrossed, hanging on every word Leila spoke. Kit couldn't imagine what Leila was saying. She saw Wade pull her to him and hug her. She saw his lips form the words *Thank you*.

"I'll see you around, Kit," Rusty was saying.

"I'm sorry—," Kit started. She hadn't meant to be rude to him.

He waved off her apology and picked up his Stetson and said he had to get back to the ranch. She should come by. They could go for a ride. She wondered if this was an offer of friendship, or an attempt at reconciliation. There was no way to tell.

He stood there, holding his hat, waiting for Kit to say something.

"It's so hard to believe," he said finally. "I mean, I saw her just the other day."

Rusty stayed in a cabin on Leila's father's ranch, a few hundred yards from the bungalow Jenny and Leila shared. Part of his pay for running the ranch. Kit stood watching him look at her, wishing she could find some response, remembering the way she'd felt toward him for all those months, how close they'd gotten. The weekends at his place.

His cabin had been a respite, a place of peace and quiet. The bedroom held only a brass bed, tarnished—not at some factory, but by time—a small cherrywood dresser, and a plain wooden chair. There was a stone fireplace in the living room, a deep, comfortable couch, slip-covered in pale blue denim, and matching easy chair. No television. An acoustic guitar sat in one corner. The main windows overlooked the pasture. In the kitchen was a butcher block table. A radio on the wooden countertop was the only intrusion from the outside world.

She'd awakened next to him, brushed a tiny piece of straw from his curls. He rolled over and kissed her neck. His eyes bespoke contentment.

He went to the barn to saddle the horses. Kit met him there with coffee. He kept looking at her, mischief in his eyes.

"What?" she asked, and he only smiled and looked away.

When they finished the coffee and mounted up, Rusty urged Pepper, a gray gelding with a smattering of black spots across his hindquarters, into a brisk trot. Kit followed on Salt, the big, feisty Appaloosa that Rusty had saddled for her.

When the horses were sufficiently warmed up, Rusty gave her another look, this one playful.

"Ready to ride?" And then, before she could respond, he slapped Pepper lightly with the reins and dug in his heels and shouted, "H'yah now! Giddyap!" and Pepper leapt into a gallop.

Kit grabbed her saddle horn as Salt took off. She didn't have to do anything but hang on. Wind in her face and her hair flying behind her, she gripped tight with her legs and felt the immense strength of the horse beneath her as they galloped across the pasture, Kit loving the sound of the beating hooves against earth, grass glowing almost iridescent in the morning sunlight, and, for as far as the eye could see, beautiful blue sky.

She found her balance, then captured the rhythm of the gallop, and was able to let go of the saddle horn and lean over until her face was practically resting against Salt's warm, muscular neck, his mane whipping back against her cheek. Her thoughts left her and she rode, hearing Salt's breath as the animal ran and wishing the moment would go on forever.

They'd galloped a good long way before Rusty reined in Pepper, keeping him at a brisk walk as he headed toward a stand of oaks. Once there, he dismounted and tied Pepper to a tree branch, then held Salt's head while Kit climbed down. He tied up Salt and took Kit's hand, led her to a soft patch of grass under a nearby oak, and sat down. Still looking. Those glances at her that she couldn't fathom.

"Rusty," she said finally, "what is it? Why do you keep looking at me like that?"

He dug into his pocket and pulled out a ring. With a diamond on it.

"Because," he said. "Will you marry me?"

Kit was speechless. She felt like she'd been hit in the head with a blunt object, knocking the capacity for thought clean out of her brain. It was as though the particles composing her body had suddenly taken on the atomic weight of uranium, and she at once lacked the strength even to blink.

He wanted her to marry him.

The word came out of her mouth before she realized it.

Why?

He'd said it right back, incredulous at her asking.

Why?

There's no need, she'd said. We don't need that.

But it was what he wanted.

It was not what she wanted. She had watched her mother be Mrs. Wade Metcalf, watched her mother try to fit in with all the other Ranger wives who put up with all the macho Ranger bullshit, and though Rusty was anything but a Ranger, she was not going to marry a cowboy, or anyone else for that matter, and be cast in the role of wife. Wife? No thank you. She was not going to spend her life taking care of his needs, taking care of his desires, fulfilling his idea of what a wife should be, losing whatever tattered concept of self she might still possess.

She told him she couldn't, and he tossed the ring on the ground and mounted up and whipped Pepper efficiently, growling "H'yah!" so angrily that Pepper started, whirled in a circle before Rusty could straighten him out with the reins, and then Pepper took off, the whites of his eyes showing large. Salt stamped his concern, pounding his hooves against the earth, but did not try to jerk his reins loose from the tree.

Kit sat, watching Rusty astride the horse, Pepper galloping breakneck, growing smaller and smaller as the distance between them increased.

She had ridden Salt back to the barn at a slow walk, trying to leave ample time for Rusty to give Pepper a cooldown walk, and hoping maybe Rusty would cool down as well.

She'd left the ring next to the telephone on the little shelf that held it just inside the barn door. She unsaddled Salt and led the horse to its stall, certain that Rusty would come to look after him as soon as she was gone.

She got in her car and drove away, feeling as though something inside her had evaporated.

Rusty had made her feel safe again with a man. He'd been kind and gentle and supportive and patient. And fun. They'd had fun. He'd been everything Kit was looking for in a relationship. As much as she could handle, first time out, after what had happened. What had happened? Why couldn't she just say it? What was so difficult? Just say it: As much as she could handle after having been raped.

At some point after Kit drove away, Rusty had, in fact, cooled down. He had cooled down so much that he hadn't spoken to her since the day he asked her to marry him.

Kit watched him now as he maneuvered his way through the crowded living room, slipping between people who held plates of food and spoke at a volume barely above a whisper. He almost bumped into Leila as she turned away from Wade. Kit watched Wade's eyes follow Rusty out the door, and then Wade was coming over.

"Your old beau?" he said quietly.

Kit nodded yes.

"Rusty?"

She nodded again.

"Rusty what."

"Rupley," Kit said.

"What'd he say?"

"Condolences, Dad," Kit said. "He offered condolences." She felt impatient at Wade's sudden interest in what used to be her love life.

Wade leaned close to whisper.

"When this place clears out, we have to talk. I want to know everything about him."

Kit's head jerked back; she eyed her father.

"Rusty?"

Wade nodded.

"It's simple," Kit said. "He wanted to get married. I didn't."

"I'm not concerned about that," Wade said.

"Oh," Kit said. "Of course not."

Wade ignored the jab.

"What are you concerned about then?"

"Your sister's murder." Wade stared past her, taking in the people in his living room, looking as though he wondered what they were all doing there.

It took Kit a moment.

"You're crazy," she said. "I cannot imagine why you would look twice at Rusty."

"I'm looking twice at everybody," Wade said, still speaking so quietly that others in the room couldn't hear.

"There's no reason," Kit said. "Why on earth would he do it?"

"Why on earth would anybody?" Wade's voice was low and full of menace. She'd seen her father angry, she'd seen him hell-bent to do justice, but she'd never seen the kind of intensity his eyes held just then.

"What possible motive would he have to—" She couldn't say the words. To kill Jenny. It wasn't a robbery. Nothing had been taken. They'd found her shopping bags and purse in the car. Untouched. As though she'd gotten into the car and been ready to leave the mall parking lot when someone, somehow, had talked her out of the car. And then abducted her. Kit swallowed more drink and closed her eyes, squeezing them tight shut against the scenario.

"Kit." A pair of big arms enveloped her and pulled her toward a bear of a man. "Kit, darlin'." The deepest voice, and Kit recognized the aftershave. Burt Simmons. Her father's running buddy. "I'm so sorry, sweetheart. I am so, so sorry." He was holding her close, stroking her hair and pressing her head to his chest. She let him hold her, standing almost limp against him, flashing on the time he'd taught her to two-step at one of those many picnics. What had she been, nine? Ten? And big Burt Simmons with his wavy brown hair and shining green eyes had pulled her out onto the hard-packed earth with the band playing some Waylon Jennings number, and Burt had shown her the steps and twirled her around and smiled so proudly at Wade when Kit got the hang of it and was actually dancing with him. It was hard to believe some of the things she'd heard about Burt. Hard to believe that such a nice man could be so deadly when he was on the job.

She remembered the night, not so long after the picnic where Burt taught her the two-step, when Wade had come home with a look in his eyes that sent Kit and Jenny tiptoeing to Kit's bedroom, but the gravity in Wade's voice as he sat in the kitchen with their mother and told her of the day's events had drawn them back out, sock-footed, slipping silently down the hall to crouch outside the kitchen and listen. There had been some kind of standoff, a bunch of religious nuts holed up in a compound outside San Marcos. To hear Wade tell it, Burt had done his duty flawlessly, drilling a .308-caliber hole in the head of the asshole fool in charge of things from better than a hundred yards. Dropped him dead right through the kitchen window while the guy stood opposite his wife, who was holding their six-month-old baby. Mother and child were untouched, Wade said. Kit had sat listening to Wade tell it and feeling a deep uneasiness stirring up inside. She couldn't fathom why Burt had to kill a man who was only standing there talking to his wife. She and Jenny had shared a look of incomprehension, both knowing that there was something wrong with the story, neither knowing how to go about finding out what it was. They had crept back to Kit's room and put in a cassette, Robert Palmer's "Addicted to Love," and Kit kept hearing "lights are on, but you're not home," and wondering what the man's eyes looked like, after he'd been shot in the head, if he'd stood there staring at his wife before dropping to the floor dead. She'd wondered how long it took to die after a bullet ripped through your brain.

Burt. She was glad his wife had left him. He was probably not much fun to live with. She wished his ex-wife was here. She wished Sugar had come and brought her famous Mud-In-Your-Eye pie. Chocolate heaven it was.

"I'm here if you need *anything*," Burt was saying. "Anything. Whatever it might be." He released Kit and she stepped back to see that Burt was talking as much to Wade as he was to her.

"I know that," Wade said. "And I'm gonna hold you to it."

Kit knew what they were saying. When the time came, Wade would call on Burt to help him take care of Jenny's killer. There would be no arrest. There would be no day in court. The Rangers would handle this case.

Kit excused herself and slipped out of the crowded room, down the hallway to Jenny's old bedroom. Closing the door behind her, she could still hear the muffled hum of conversation coming from the living room. Somber tones, quiet, sad voices.

Wade hadn't done anything to the bedrooms after Kit

and Jenny moved out to begin their lives as adults. On their own out there in the big old world. Jenny had taken her desk, so there was a blank spot beneath the window that looked out over the three acres that was the backyard. Split rail fencing delineated the boundaries. On the other side of it lay someone else's ranchette. Kit wondered if the same people lived there as had when she was growing up. A childless couple whose names she couldn't remember. The neighborhood hadn't been particularly close-knit. People left in the morning to drop their children at school and head out to work, came back in the evenings to their televisions and loungers. The houses, on five-acre lots, were spread out enough that the concept of next-door neighbor was not fully functional.

She walked to the closet. A quilt was folded on the shelf above the wooden clothes bar that held three or four empty hangers at one end, next to one of Jenny's nightgowns and the bathrobe that she'd kept there for those occasions when she decided to sleep over after Sunday dinner.

Kit walked back to the bed, still made up with the pale green spread Jenny had as a teenager, the matching dust ruffle skirted beneath it. A charcoal sketch Jenny had done in high school was framed on the wall above the bed. She'd won first place at the annual art contest with it. It was an Appaloosa mare, her foal standing next to her. The lines were clean and precise. Jenny had always loved drawing, painting, sculpting even. The vase she'd done that same year, elegantly shaped, tranquil, sat on the nightstand next to the bed.

Kit sat. This was what was left of her sister's life. An almost empty room. A drawing of the horse she never owned. A vase full of air.

She heard herself sigh. And sigh again. Her breath could only leave her in sighs, as though by doing so she could empty herself of the sadness. But it seemed to her that nothing she could do, now or in the times to come, would ever take away the loss she was feeling. She could only wait, and try to get through the days, and wait more, and hope that, at some point, she would feel something, anything, other than this sadness.

The knob on the door turned, and the door opened slightly, slowly. Kit saw Leila Jane's head peek through the opening, and then the door opened the rest of the way and Leila was in the room, her blue eyes swollen and puffy from crying.

Leila looked at her, and Kit knew she was waiting to see if she should stay or leave Kit to herself. She nodded that it was okay for Leila to come in.

Leila closed the door behind her, came and sat next to Kit on the bed. The room had no smell to it; the vacant air held only an absence of life, absence of human activity. Kit noticed a dead cricket on the carpet, close up against the baseboard at the edge of the closet door.

"I can't believe it," Leila said quietly. "I keep trying to believe it, accept it, whatever, but I can't."

"I know," Kit said.

"Are you staying here?" Leila said. "Did you have plans to stay here for a while?"

Kit half-laughed, half-snorted. "I stayed last night. That's all I can take."

"I don't want to stay alone there," Leila said. "Without her. Not after this."

"Leila, no one is after you."

"Not that," Leila said, twirling a blond tendril around her finger, twisting it tight, then untwisting, then twisting again. "I just need someone in the house, and I think you shouldn't be alone right now, either."

Leila was probably right. But Kit wanted nothing more than to be alone. She didn't want to deal with any humans right now.

"Why don't you come and stay? Just for a while. Until . . . I don't know . . . just for a while."

"What did you tell my father? Out there?"

"Out there?"

"Yes. In the living room. You seemed to have his attention, no small feat in my book."

"Just, I was sorry, you know. And feeling pretty torn up. Kind of lost. Will you come stay?"

"I don't know."

"Rusty won't bother you, Kit. He's over it."

"My father says Rusty's—How'd he put it? Rusty is *on his list*."

"Because things didn't work out?"

"God only knows. It's not like Wade gives a shit about my love life."

Leila Jane got quiet, staring out the window thoughtfully. Kit stared after her, the brilliant afternoon casting an almost blinding whiteness through the window.

"He said something once, right after you broke up with him."

"I didn't break up with him, Leila. I didn't want to end the relationship. I just didn't want to marry him."

"He was so angry."

"He said what," Kit said flatly, not sure she wanted to hear.

"I'd told him that he should just leave you alone, forget about you, move on. Just accept the fact that it hadn't worked out and get on with his life." Leila eyed Kit, hesitated. "He said he planned to do that. He said he wasn't going to bother you at all. As far as he was concerned it *was* done."

"Yeah?"

"But then he got this look on his face and he said to me, he said, you know, Leila Jane, if you really want to hurt someone, you don't have to hurt them at all. What you have to do is take something away from them. Something they love."

"God." Kit couldn't imagine Rusty saying such a thing. So venomous. She felt a chill deep in her bones, like the marrow had flash frozen, and then it was gone.

"Did he say he hated me?"

"No. He said he wished things had worked out differently, but that he knew better than to pursue a woman who didn't love him anymore, if she even ever had."

Leila shifted on the bed; her eyes met Kit's.

"But I don't think he meant it. It was only anger talking."

"Leila," Kit said, "did you and Rusty ever . . ."

"Date?" Leila said quickly. "We talked about it. But no. We didn't. I think he was afraid of my father."

"How quaint."

"Did you want to?"

"Go out with him? I don't know. Not really, I guess. Maybe I was just feeling lonely or something." Leila sighed deeply. "Kit?" she said, almost whispering, "Does your father really think Rusty could've, I don't know, been involved? You know?"

"Leila, what did you tell Wade? For real."

"I told him what Rusty said." Leila stared at the floor. "I thought he should know."

Kit didn't say anything.

"I was supposed to go out tonight," Leila said, tears welling in her eyes. "Jenny set up a double date. Her and Luke and me and some friend of Luke's."

Kit opened her arms and Leila fell against her shoulder, sobbing now, and though Kit had thought there were no more tears left inside her, here they came.

"She was such a sweet, wonderful person," Leila said. "She was so thoughtful."

"Leila," Kit said, "I'll come stay. For a while." She sat, holding Jenny's best friend in her arms, holding Leila while Leila sobbed, and her head fell onto Leila's shoulder and they held each other and cried.

And then somewhere from inside the muddle of tears and pain, the agony of loss clouding her brain, something broke loose and opened, filling her with a hateful desire and a fearsome dread of that desire at once.

She did want vengeance. She wanted to find the person who'd killed her sister and make him suffer what she was suffering. Make him suffer more than she was suffering. And even as she was wanting it she was hating herself for doing so. She should not want this.

She wanted it. The way she wanted that guy, the rapist, the way she wanted him to suffer. The way she wanted whoever had attacked her in the parking lot that night to suffer. She wanted all of them to suffer. All the stupid, violent, unthinking brutes who brought pain into the world, all of them. They should get their turn on the receiving end.

She eased away from Leila, went down the hall to the

bathroom. She stared at the tissue box atop the toilet tank. The box had fake postage stamps all over it in various horrid shades of brown and red, the colors of blood-soaked dirt. She grabbed a fistful of tissues and wiped at her face. Blew her nose, tossed the tissues in the trash.

She looked at herself in the mirror. A wreck.

She bent and retrieved the bottle from beneath the sink, held it up to her image in the mirror. It was about a quarter full.

"Cheers, sweetheart," she whispered. "Enjoy it." She guzzled until she choked, leaned over the sink thinking the stuff was coming right back up, but she held it; she stood there choking it back, forcing the fire down her throat.

She raised herself and held up the bottle. Almost empty. If she took another swallow she would puke. She poured the rest down the sink. Fuck it. Just the hell with it. She was not going down. She was not. Not behind this shit.

She turned and grabbed more tissues. Leila Jane needed tissues.

She walked unsteadily down the hall, but who would blame her for staggering? Her sister had been murdered.

Leila Jane was still on the bed, sniffling, trying to stop her tears.

Kit sat and handed her the tissues.

"Will you be around tomorrow?" she asked.

"Yeah." Leila Jane snuffled, blew her nose. "I'm not going back to work until Monday."

"Okay," Kit said. "I'll bring my things over tomorrow afternoon."

Leila nodded, dabbing at her eyes with tissues.

"Kit," Leila said, "are you okay? I mean . . ." She didn't

seem to know what to say. She blurted out, "You smell like, I don't know."

Kit stood.

"Vodka," she said gently. "I smell like vodka. I'm going to get a drink of water now." She went to the door, turned to face Leila.

"Stay as long as you like."

Leila nodded, smiling her thanks, and lay back on the bed. Kit left her there, staring at the ceiling, and closed the door softly.

#

Wade was in the kitchen, watching as two women Kit didn't recognize pulled more food from the refrigerator and refilled two large platters with potato salad and macaroni salad and tuna fish salad and ham salad. She poured a large glass of water and drank it. Carefully. Not going too fast, but trying to get it into her system in time to catch up to the booze. She placed the glass in the sink, caught her father's eye and motioned him onto the back porch.

"I don't think you should take what Leila said about Rusty too seriously," Kit said. "You're on the wrong track if you think he had anything to do with this." So calm, she sounded. Like a damn cop, almost. She could have been amused at herself.

"You should put a cold cloth on your face. Your eyes are all swollen."

"Dad. It's a funeral."

Wade glared at her.

"Can't you keep your goddam sarcastic tongue in check? Ever?"

"I'm sorry," Kit said.

"How much have you had to drink?"

"Is this a contest?" Kit glared at him. "Because I know you'll win. But to answer your question, I've had a lot to drink. I've had enough to drink, thank you very much."

Wade stared at her. He shifted his gaze out to the horizon.

"I'd be talking to him anyway," he said. "He lives right down the road from them. He knew her. I gather he saw her almost daily, out riding and all. I need to know what he knows."

"Daddy," Kit said. "Just don't take what Leila told you too seriously. I know Rusty better than any of you. He's not capable of murder."

"Little girl," Wade said, his tone approaching something like affection, "don't fool yourself. Everyone is capable of murder. It's part of being human."

"I don't believe that," Kit said.

"I didn't used to," Wade said. "But I've been policin' too long to be able to fool myself anymore into thinking otherwise."

Kit nodded. Argument was pointless. Her father had his reality and she had hers. He stood with his thumbs tucked in behind his belt buckle, that silver star, and stared out across the backyard, looking past her. He sighed a huge sigh, a sigh that shuddered on its way out, and for a moment Kit thought he was going to break down. He caught himself and flashed a brief smile at her.

"It'll all be okay," he said quietly, almost as though talking to himself. He pressed his hands against his face, as though he could press back his emotions and avoid having to deal with them. Something seemed different, and then

Kit realized he wasn't wearing his ring, the revolver-shaped diamond pinkie ring that her mother had given him the day of his promotion to the Rangers.

"Dad," she said. "Your ring?"

Wade took his hands away from his face, held them before him, looking at them as though he were inspecting a just-finished manicure.

"I can't bear to wear it," he said. "Every time I look at it I think of your mother, and I think of Jenny. I think of how the two most important women in my life are gone forever. I can't bear to be reminded."

Kit stood wondering if that made her the third most important woman in his life, or if she was even important to him at all. He seemed to realize then what he'd just said, and pulled her to him.

"You know what I mean," he said.

"Yeah," Kit said. "I know what you mean." She stepped back.

"Kit," Wade said. "You and I, we've never been close, not since you got to be a teenager anyway. But it's just you and me now. You and me." He pulled her to him again. "We've got our differences, to be sure. But you have to know that I love you." He looked into her eyes, and his hands slid down her arms and across her hips, and she stepped back again, almost losing her balance. Something went through her, a vague discomfort, an awareness of her father's relentless strength and of the fact that he was a man and she was a woman. She hadn't liked the way he let his hands trail across her body just then, following its contours too closely, too familiarly. She felt intruded upon. She felt dizzy. Yellow played at the edges of her vision. She stepped back farther and shook her head and squeezed her eyes shut, trying to shake it out of there, and then she heard her father's voice asking her if she was all right, and she opened her eyes to the burning sunlight of day.

"No problem," she said. "What did you do with your ring, Daddy?"

"Pawned it," he said. "Just this morning."

"You *what?*"

Wade didn't respond to her tone.

"I thought I'd just put it away somewhere here in the house," he said. "But I couldn't stand the thought of it being anywhere close. I don't want to be haunted."

"It's a *thing*, Daddy. An object. It can't haunt you."

"Memories, Kit. It reminded me of too much."

"So you just got rid of it?" Kit said. "You couldn't even wait and ask if I wanted it?"

"Now just why in hell would you want it?"

"For the same reasons you didn't, I guess."

"It was mine to do with as I saw fit."

"And I never entered into the picture."

Wade said nothing.

"You may just wind up sorry, Daddy. Wait and see. You might wake up one morning and decide you want it back. But it'll be gone."

"Maybe you should take up writing an advice column for the paper."

"Thanks, Pop. Guess that's what I get for trying to talk to you. Silly me." Kit tried to calm herself. Not happening.

"Take it easy," he said. "What's done is done."

"No shit." Kit stared at him, wanting to ask him where he'd pawned it so she could go and retrieve it, but she knew he wouldn't tell her. He'd made up his mind. The fat lady was belting one out.

"I'll be back later," she said.

Wade looked startled. "Where you going?"

"For a drive," Kit said. "I need to think."

"I don't think you should be driving." He sat down in his chair on the porch. The one he'd been sitting in when he told her Jenny was dead.

Kit mumbled that she was okay and walked around the side of the house. The gate creaked as she opened it and again as she shut it. She walked out curbside. The street was lined with cars the entire length of the block. Funeral-goers. Here to console the family, to share in the grieving.

Kit got into her Mustang. She drove down the street, away from friends and family. Away from the scene in Wade's living room. She could see clearly, read the street signs. The streets weren't moving around on her. She was okay to drive. She was just fine to drive.

She woke up at dusk, opened her eyes, and realized, slowly, where she was. She didn't remember driving here. She didn't remember parking her car and getting out of it and walking around the back of the building to this place. This tiny garden behind the dojang. She wondered if she'd been seen by any students, passed out there on the bench. She guessed not. Of if she had, they'd chosen to leave her be.

The stream gurgled, water flowing past. She pulled herself upright on the wooden bench. Feeling better now. No longer wasted, not yet hungover.

She sat there forever, time slipping past like the water at her feet.

She stirred finally. Straightened. Tried to focus her thoughts. On anything.

Water.

Water slipping past like time.

Water. Element.

The five elements.

Water. Wood. Fire. Earth. Metal.

Five elements.

Mutual creation.

Mutual destruction.

Mutual creation, mutual destruction. The five elements.

Wood made fire, fire made earth, earth made metal, metal made water, water made wood.

Who would have wanted to? Who would have done that: put a bullet in her sister's heart? Who. And why. What possible reason?

Drifting. She was drifting.

Focus.

She would need her wits about her. She was tired of living in a haze.

Focus.

Mutual creation. Mutual destruction.

Wood feared earth; earth feared water; water feared fire; fire feared metal; metal feared wood.

What did she fear? What was this awful thing, this unnamed thing, this ungraspable thing that she feared?

Inside her skull.

Inside her.

NINE

Leila Jane was at the kitchen counter, grimly squeezing lemons into a measuring cup. Kit took a seat at the bar.

"Hey," Leila said.

"Hey," Kit replied.

"Where you been?"

"Had an appointment. My shrink."

Leila's head popped up. She tossed a lemon rind into the sink.

"You're seeing a shrink?"

"Just lately," Kit said.

"Is he helping?"

"She." Kit shrugged. "Who knows?" The session had gone nowhere. She'd sat on the couch and talked about the funeral and cried. Dr. Wolfe had been patient and supportive, seeming to understand that it was not the right time to press things. She had wondered about Kit's decision to go back to work so quickly, but accepted Kit's reasoning that staying occupied was best right now, even if occupied meant working at Blaze's.

Leila returned to her task, grinding a lemon onto the reamer, her lips pulled into a tight line, mashing and twisting like she was trying to squeeze the very life out of the thing.

"There's no word," she said. "Around the department. About, you know." She left the words unspoken. "No leads," she added.

"I want to talk to Rusty," Kit said.

Leila released the lemon from the reamer. The noisy little motor stopped.

"Try to find out what he knows, if anything." She didn't tell Leila that she wanted to warn Rusty that her father would be coming to see him. That her father considered him a suspect.

"I'm sure he was just being weird," Leila said. "I probably shouldn't have told your dad."

"Don't do a number on yourself, Leila. But let's go talk to him."

"Suit yourself," Leila said. "He barely had anything to do with her, you know, since you broke things off."

"Will you come with me?"

"He's usually in the barn about now." Leila tossed another rind in the sink, wiped her hands on a dish towel.

Kit followed her down the concrete porch steps and across the chalky gravel road toward the barn. The day would be hot, was already hot. Like the day before was and the day after would no doubt be. She realized with relief that her head had stopped pounding. The sun felt good on

Kit's bare arms. She wondered what she would say to Rusty.

She caught a whiff of oat as they entered the barn, and then the clean scent of hay, riding on the fecund odor of dry earth and horse dung. Rusty kept it pretty much spotless, or as spotless as a barn could be. She heard the stomp of a hoof against earth. One of the horses let out a snort.

"Hey, Pepper," Leila called. "Relax. We're not here to ride." She listened a moment, then called out. "Rusty?"

No response. Again, slightly louder. "Rusty?" She glanced at Kit and shrugged.

"Guess we'd better try the cabin. Though I can't imagine."

They walked out the back barn door into the sunshine and down a dirt path toward a modest cottage a hundred yards or so away. By the time they got to the small wooden porch, Kit's skin was covered in a fine sweat; perspiration beaded along her hairline and above her lips. It felt good, as though her body was taking the opportunity to cleanse itself. Maybe it was. She felt as if she could evaporate into the summer air. She touched her face, to make sure she were really there. The only thing she could feel inside herself was her heart, beating steadily. It was as if her internal organs had disappeared, except for the blood-pumping muscle in the center of her chest that worked on, thumping mechanically, circulating loneliness and loss throughout her body, sending memories of her sister into the cells of her very fingertips.

Rusty's Ford pickup was backed up to the porch, the navy paint pitted from years of wear. As Kit and Leila walked up, he stepped out onto the porch, carrying an old green canvas military duffel bag packed full to the point of bursting.

"Hey," Leila said. He dropped the bag onto the porch

and stood full height, eyeing them. "Holy shit," Leila said. "What happened to you?"

Rusty had a serious black eye; his right one, a deep blue and black bruise surrounded the eyeball. It was swollen half shut. Another bruise on his left cheekbone, and a cut across his forehead.

"Got thrown," he said. "And kicked. That gelding. Never woulda thought it."

"Where you going?" Leila asked, motioning toward his bag. "What's going on?"

"I got offered a job," he said. "Wyoming. An old friend of mine." He glared at Kit. "I figure this is as good a time as any to start fresh."

Kit just looked at him. He was lying. She knew he was lying, and he knew that she knew it.

"I came over to tell you my dad wanted to talk to you," she said. "About Jenny."

"He was here," Rusty said. "I couldn't help him. Wish I could've."

"Do you?" Kit tucked a hand in the back pocket of her jeans, cocked one hip out. Challenging.

"Yeah, Kit," Rusty said, "I do. I wish I knew something, *anything* about what happened to your sister. But I don't. I don't even know why anybody thinks I would."

Leila Jane took a step back from them, stuck her hands in the pockets of her jeans. Kit guessed she'd be uncomfortable, too, if she were Leila right at that moment.

"I'm just sorry for you," Rusty continued. "Sorry it happened, and like I said, sorry for your loss." He picked up his bag and stepped gingerly off the porch toward the truck, tossed the bag in the back. Turned to face Kit.

155

"And I'm sorry things didn't work out. Between us. It could have been good."

Now he wasn't lying. Kit felt bad. She hadn't wanted to hurt him.

Leila gave a short wave of her hand and turned away, calling over her shoulder as she headed back toward the barn. "I think I'll be going now. Stop by the house, Rusty. I need to talk to you."

Rusty nodded and leaned against his truck, first watching as Leila Jane walked briskly down the road toward the bungalow, then turning his gaze on Kit.

"I'm sorry, too. That it didn't work out," Kit said, shifting uncomfortably. "It couldn't work, Rusty. I'm not the kind of person you'd want to marry."

"Seems like that should be up to me."

"I'm sorry if I hurt you."

"You broke my fucking heart."

"Not because I wanted to. I did what I thought was right. For both of us."

He shrugged. "Whatever."

"You'll meet someone. You'll find someone."

"I found you. And then you ran away."

"I didn't want to get married. It would never have worked."

"Says you." He scuffed at the dirt with his boot. "And your old man, too."

"What," Kit said. "You two talked about me?"

"He just said he thought it was good we broke up. That I wasn't *right* for you. He loves you, Kit. Whatever you think about him, he loves you."

"I'm glad someone can tell."

"Oh, I can tell. He made it clear that he didn't think I was good enough. He said the one thing he wanted, now that Jenny and your mom were both gone, was to make sure you wound up with someone who could make you happy."

"I'm just sure he said that."

"Why should I lie?"

They stood looking at each other, and Kit could remember feeling drawn to him, but that wasn't what she was feeling right now. She looked into his eyes and tried to see if there was any possibility there, any way that her father should suspect him, and she couldn't see it, couldn't see any way. She couldn't see him intentionally harming anyone. That wasn't what he was about. This was a man who could take the wildest young colt and gentle it down, sweetly, connect to the animal and persuade it not just to take a saddle, but to like taking the saddle.

"He did that to you, didn't he?" Kit felt an odd ache as she said the words.

"I told you," Rusty said. "That gelding did it to me."

"You've never been thrown in your life," Kit said.

"Well, I have now," Rusty said. "Happens to every cowboy, sooner or later. I'd just been lucky, that's all."

"I don't believe you," Kit said.

"Why the hell not?" Rusty walked around to the driver side and opened the door. He leaned around the cab, facing her. "You threw me, too, Kit. You threw me but good." He got in and started the engine.

Kit watched as he pulled down the road, a cloud of white dust churning up behind the wheels of the truck as it disappeared around a curve in the drive and headed out toward the highway.

She guessed he'd forgotten about stopping to talk to Leila Jane. Or maybe now that her father wasn't his boss, he didn't feel the need.

She walked slowly back up the road to the bungalow.

When she got there, the lemon reamer was grinding away.

"That was fun," Leila said flatly. She tossed another rind in the sink.

"He didn't get thrown," Kit said.

Leila's expression questioned.

"My dad," Kit said. "I'm sure of it."

"Jesus." Leila stood there, holding a lemon half poised above the reamer and staring at Kit. "Are you positive?"

Kit nodded firmly.

"Man."

"You said it."

Leila grabbed a lemon half and pressed it onto the juicer.

"Luke called," she said. "He needs to talk to you. He said it was important and please call as soon as you could."

Kit thought about telling Leila. About letting her in on Luke's dirty little secret, about how Luke frequented Blaze's and liked to watch Kit take her clothes off. Yeah, Luke. Call you. Sure.

Leila stood staring at her.

"What," Kit said.

"Aren't you going to call him?"

"I will."

"No time like the present."

"I will, Leila. I need a moment."

Kit watched in silence as Leila mixed together the lemon juice and some sugar water and some tap water, stirring it into one of those glass pitchers that looked like the one on packages of Kool-Aid.

"Want a glass?" Leila held up the pitcher.

"Thanks," Kit said. She thought it might be nice to spice up the lemonade with a splash of vodka. Or maybe a cup and a half. And in the same instant saw herself spiraling into darkness. She would not give in. She would not cave to desires of escape. She would deal. With all of it.

"Maybe he has news."

"Not right now." Kit sipped the lemonade; it left her palate feeling clean and fresh, not like the stuff that came out of a package from the supermarket, full of dehydrated high-fructose corn syrup. Life is simple. Just add water . . . and pretend it's the real thing.

She wouldn't call Luke now. And she wouldn't call him later. If there was news, it would come to her soon enough. She wanted nothing to do with him.

She went upstairs to her room. Jenny's room. She sprawled across the bed.

When she woke up, it was dark. She went downstairs, calling for Leila.

No answer.

She locked the front door. She locked the back door. Leila seemed never to feel the need to lock up. She checked the windows and adjusted the thermostat. The house was warm after baking all day in the heat.

She sat on the couch and stared at the half glass of wine Leila Jane no doubt had left there before going wherever she'd gone.

Kit looked at the television. Thought about turning it on. For about two seconds. Her entire body seemed to be vibrating, like there was something inside her, some kind of electrical current zipping through her. Low-dose electrocution. She was going to shatter if she didn't do something. Her head would explode. The cops would come and rule it a suicide. Shotgun to the head. Only they wouldn't be able to find the weapon because it didn't exist anywhere but inside her own brain.

She dragged her bag off the floor by the couch. She took out the bottle of tranquilizers, the prescription meds Dr. Wolfe had given her. One every four to six hours, as needed.

As needed.

She spilled out a couple of tablets onto the palm of her hand. Fuck it. She tossed them back, grimaced at the taste, tried to work up enough saliva to swallow them. Her mouth was dry. Fuck it. It was only a half glass of wine. She grabbed the goblet and gulped, washing the tablets down.

She sat, wondering how long it would be before some kind of relief set in. And wondering why Rusty was beating such a hasty retreat. But maybe that was simply his way. That's what he'd done when she said no. Retreated. Completely and entirely. Going off now to Wyoming, to lick his wounds, the emotional as well as the physical ones.

She still could not fathom her father's interest in Rusty as a suspect. But then he was the cop, not she. Maybe he knew something she didn't. *Of course* he knew something, lots of things, that she didn't, about investigating murders, this one in particular. However she felt about Wade, he had a good reputation in the law enforcement community. There had to be a reason Wade had Rusty on his list of suspects. She wondered who else was on it, and if Luke Saner's name was there as well. One thing she did know about investigating murders was that almost always the killer knew the victim. Usually quite well. Strangers usually didn't kill strangers. Though there was always the chance that Jenny had fallen prey to some psychopathic serial killer, the odds were way against it. Jenny wouldn't have walked into that kind of trap. Usually the murderer was someone close. A friend. A relative. Someone with enough emotional investment in the victim to be driven—when something went awry—to murder.

She sat, staring at the blank screen of the television, waiting.

Maybe it was the wine—the plastic prescription bottle had a Day-Glo orange sticker affixed to it: Do not drink alcohol while taking this medication. Kit felt her body flood with warmth, she fell back onto the couch, and then there was darkness.

TEN

The door had been shattered. Dr. Wolfe's nameplate lay on the hallway floor. The doorknob dangled in the splintered wood. Kit peered inside. The waiting room was trashed. She listened, her heart fluttering with fear. She could see the interior door, the one that led from the waiting room to Dr. Wolfe's office, it, too, ajar, the lock also busted. Out of stillness came the sound of rustling papers.

"Dr. Wolfe?" Kit's voice trembled. She cleared her throat. "Emily?"

Dr. Wolfe appeared in the doorway, holding a file with papers sticking out of it at odd angles. A silver and turquoise bracelet dangled on her wrist.

"It's okay," she said flatly. "Whoever did this is long gone."

The coffee table in the waiting room lay on its side, surrounded by piles of potting soil dotted white with vermiculite. The ficus sprawled on the carpet, lay there as though gasping for air. A cast-iron plant, the ivy, a spider plant and all the others, too, were knocked out of their pots. They lay askew, their roots naked. Kit could almost hear them screaming for help.

She put down her bag and took up a pot, scooped handfuls of soil, taking a peace plant with its beautiful white spath and setting it carefully back inside before filling the pot with more soil. Maybe they would be all right. Maybe they would live. She took a paper cup at the water cooler and filled it, watered the plant, filled it again and again until the soil was muddy.

Dr. Wolfe stood watching as Kit took up a second plant and repeated the process, and then she joined Kit, repotting the plants, watering them. Together they righted the overturned table and placed the pots back on it. Large dark splotches of dirt remained scattered across the beige carpeting of the waiting room.

Kit stared at the damage.

"Let's go in," Dr. Wolfe said.

Kit followed her into the office and eased herself onto the couch. She'd awakened in the bed, awakened feeling like she had some kind of flu. She didn't remember getting from the couch to Jenny's room. Last night was a hole.

She sat on the couch, watching as Dr. Wolfe turned and pushed the door as closed as it would go. Files were scattered across the floor, papers strewn everywhere. The desk had been wiped clean; its contents lay in a pile on the floor next to it. The doctor uprighted her chair and and sat down.

"I wanted to call the police, but thought I should talk to you first." Dr. Wolfe crossed her legs and leaned forward, resting her arms on her knee.

"You think this is about me?"

"They have your file."

"And?"

"Yours was the only one they took." Dr. Wolfe waved an arm at the damage. "Do you have any idea who did this?"

Kit shook her head no, and then saw the way Dr. Wolfe was looking at her. Hoping for an answer.

"Are you going to call the police?"

"I'll have to." Dr. Wolfe looked at her grimly. "And I think I should."

"I think you should, too," Kit said. "And we probably shouldn't touch anything else. Maybe there are fingerprints. I'm sorry I touched things. I didn't know what else to do but try to straighten up. I wasn't thinking. It was stupid."

"Last night," Dr. Wolfe said, "did anyone, I don't know, did anyone call you or did you see anyone? Is anyone following you, Kit? Have you seen *anything* that might help us find who's done this?"

Kit felt herself rock back on the couch. She remembered knocking back the pills from the prescription, feeling weak for doing so, like why couldn't she cut it without chemical assistance. She remembered swallowing them down, gulping the half glass of wine Leila had left on the kitchen bar. And sitting there on the couch.

And then nothing.

She had no idea where she'd been or what she'd done. And this episode so close on the heels of the other one. She was losing her mind. That's what was happening. Losing it. This wasn't hangover-related. Not even close. She knew too well the interminable mornings after, when she would open her eyes and drag herself to awareness of her surroundings, suffering from amnesia, yes, but if she lay still and waited, bits and pieces of the previous night would dig into her brain, little splinters of memory, and gradually she could construct a picture of what had happened—where she'd been and gone and what she'd done after that sixth martini and last line of pretty white powder. A tenuous memory, yes, like a house of sticks ready to be blown down by the first big bad wolf that happened along, but memory nonetheless. This was different.

"I am here to help you," Dr. Wolfe said. "You have to believe that."

"I do," Kit said.

"Last night?"

"I took the medication," Kit said. "It knocked me out."

"Try to remember."

"I woke up this morning in my bed," Kit said. "Jenny's bed," she corrected.

Dr. Wolf leaned back in her chair, uncrossed her legs, let her hands fall to her lap.

"Kit," she said, "we need to determine who would want your file."

"I don't know. I've no idea."

"I didn't want to alarm you. But I think someone's been following me. I'm not sure. He drives a dark-colored pickup. I've only seen him at night. And it could be coincidence, but twice now he's been behind me when I pulled out of the lot."

Kit sat, thoughts roiling in her brain. Where was last night? Where was her recollection of last night? Someone had her file. Someone had wanted her file badly enough to risk breaking and entering. Had it been her? Did she just want out of it all, out of everything, out of life itself? Had she broken in, hoping to get caught, hoping to get shot? Where the fuck was her file? And what did it say? About her.

"Kit?" Dr. Wolfe's voice held concern. "Are you here? Are you with me?"

Kit nodded yes, slowly, bringing herself back to the room.

"Look, it's probably over. They got what they wanted. Now I have to do what I can to protect you, and the best way to do that is to figure out who took the file."

Kit said nothing. The silence hung in the air between them.

"I'm going to call the police and make a report of this. Do I have your permission to tell them it was your file that was stolen?"

"Do you need it?"

"I want it. I won't do anything to violate your privacy. But I think it's important that they know. It might help with their investigation."

"All right then," Kit said. "Tell them. Name names." What the hell. It wasn't like she didn't have several good excuses for being nuts.

"Thank you." Dr. Wolfe leaned toward her, placing a hand on her knee. "Kit," she said, "it's all right. It's done. If someone *was* following me, they have what they were after."

"But why would they want it? What use is it?"

"That I do not know. I'm treating you for trauma. There's nothing in there of much use to anyone besides you and me. We'll be fine. We'll press on."

"No," Kit said. "We can't. I won't put you in that position."

"You're not putting me in any position. We have work to do. You need help and I want to give it to you."

"That's admirable," Kit said. "I appreciate it, Dr. Wolfe, I really do." But she felt inside that she couldn't. She couldn't ask Dr. Wolfe to stick it out with her. Whoever took her file wanted more than the file. She felt it. She knew it. And she would not let Dr. Wolfe be part of it.

"I can't come back," she said. "I can't do this."

"You have to, Kit. Look, I'm a big girl, and if I felt it wasn't safe to continue, believe me, I would tell you. I know what I'm doing. I know how important it is that we continue treatment. You have to trust my judgment on this."

"I don't want to bring you into it."

"I'm already in it. And I want to be in it. I insist we continue."

Kit didn't answer.

"If it will make it easier for you, we can meet somewhere else. I'll ask one of my associates if I can borrow his office. Would that help?"

Kit stood, surveyed the wreckage of the office.

"I'm sorry for all the trouble," she said.

"We'll be all right," Dr. Wolfe said.

Kit took hold of the door by its edge, above the broken knob, and wedged it open. She stepped through. Silence followed her into the waiting room. The plants were still in their pots, looking wilted and weak. She couldn't have done this. Not even zoned out on that stupid prescription. But she wasn't at all sure why Dr. Wolfe believed her when she said she'd been at home last night. And worse, she wasn't sure she believed herself.

ELEVEN

Kit slipped out of her sheer pink negligee—*negligee, neglijah, life goes on, bra*—bra, bra, take it off, that bra, stretch it taut, shoot it into the air, no me, me, me fire it toward me! All those eyes—*oh baby, oh baby, oh baby yeah yeah yeah, do it like that.*

All those eyes and then she looked again and there in booth two was, was not a man, was a woman, and Kit looked again and it was a ghost. It was Jenny, Jenny's eyes asking Kit what on earth Kit was doing, Jenny's eyes pleading with her to stop. Jenny's blue eyes, pleading, and she'd seen that look before, she'd seen it, when had she seen it? and where? Jenny had Wade's blue eyes, Jenny's eyes begged Kit to— A slit of light as the door at the back of the booth opened and shut. The face disappeared from the window. Jenny disappeared.

Kit left the stage, struggled down the ladder, drained,

wrung out, feeling as if her brain were swelling, pushing against the bones of her skull, waiting to explode.

She turned from the ladder and there stood Blaze, posted in the center of the dressing room, hands planted on her hips, tapping one toe noiselessly against the carpeted floor. Kit moved toward her locker, wishing invisibility. Blaze snapped shut her cell phone and glared at no one in particular.

"Can you stay?" she said.

Kit realized Blaze was addressing her.

"Stay?"

"Here. Tonight. Can you pull a double?"

Kit shook her head no. Blaze raised her shoulders, flipped her palms upward.

"Why not?" Blaze's expression softened. "It might be the best thing for you," she added quietly. "Staying busy. So you don't have time to think about—things." Blaze had offered formal condolences earlier, when Kit arrived for work. She'd said Kit was smart to come back so soon, rather than sit home and dwell on things.

"I have an appointment," Kit said.

"It's almost eight," Blaze said. "What kind of appointment?"

Like it was her business.

"My therapist does evenings," Kit said.

Blaze opened her phone again, then slapped it shut and turned back to Kit.

"Cheryl's a no-show," she said. "Again. I could shoot that girl."

Kit cringed at the reference. Blaze didn't seem to notice.

"Isn't that kind of harsh?" Kit said quietly.

"Speaking figuratively, darlin'." Blaze grinned at Kit, then saw the look on Kit's face and fumbled the phone, caught it just before it hit the floor. When she stood upright again her eyes held unabashed anger. "Damn!" she said. "I really need someone to cover for her." She looked at Kit significantly.

"I'm sorry, Blaze, I can't. It's too late to cancel. You know how it is."

"Please," Blaze said. "I'll pay for the cancellation."

"It's not that," Kit said. Then, going for mercy, "It's not the money. I *need* to go."

"Never mind." Blaze said brusquely. She waved a hand in the air, as though brushing Kit off. "I'll find someone."

"You tried her cell?"

"Of course."

"I'm sorry," Kit said again, but Blaze was already dialing another number.

Kit dressed quickly. So what if she didn't really have any appointment. What she had was a murdered sister, and Blaze should've backed off. But Blaze wasn't good at taking just-plain-no-because-I-want-to-say-no, and Kit could not stay in that place another second. It was difficult enough working there in the first place, and even more so doing it sober. But she was. She was not drinking. She'd tossed the pills as well.

Outside the back door of the club, she stood a moment on the concrete porch, letting the leftover heat of the day bake her, feeling it rise up still from the pavement. She couldn't stop seeing the image of Jenny's face there in that booth window.

"Just maintain homeostasis," she whispered to herself. "That's all you have to do." She looked out across the lot, at cars shining in the pink-yellow glow of the street lamps.

Someone was standing next to her Mustang. Just standing there.

A man. Not even attempting to hide. Kit stood motionless, trying to make out his face. He had on a Stetson; his features were in shadow. She scanned the parking lot again, looking for a dark truck. Was it Rusty, waiting for her by her car? There were several pickups out there, among the numerous SUVs and occasional two-doors. None of them dark. She thought about easing back inside the building, finding Ezra and asking him to escort her. She stood looking and the cowboy removed his hat and looked toward her, running a hand through wavy, sand-colored locks.

Luke.

She walked toward him.

"Hey," he said.

He turned as she approached her car, smiled, and opened his arms, as though to console her, the way he'd dared to that evening at Wade's house, the night before the funeral. She started to let him, she wanted to let him, she wanted someone, even Luke, to hold her and ease the pain.

And then she felt something shift inside her, something warp, and her brain went red and her vision went black and she was on him, the first blow landing against his jaw, right where the bruise had been, hard, strong. She saw his head fling back, saw astonishment in his eyes. She drew up her knee and kicked, the blow to his chest, right where his heart should be, knocked him to the pavement, and she was stomping, stomping without aim, striking blows to his body that knocked air out of his lungs, gasps, grunts, air coming out his mouth and nose, and blood coming out of his nose, and he grabbed for her leg but couldn't get it. She kicked and stomped and felt her foot striking his body, fast, over and over, and then somehow he was rolling away, scrambling, crawling, and she lurched into her car and heard the engine start and the screeching of tires as she burned out of the parking lot.

Not seeing. Not seeing, just driving, fast and faster, careening out of the lot and onto the street. Horns blared and she pressed the accelerator and kept right on going. Past a blur of vehicles and garish backlit plastic signs as she gunned it down the avenue, possessed, driving the way her father taught her, fast and accurate, blasting toward nowhere.

She was out of Austin and into the dark of the countryside in minutes. The road rolled out before her, winding gently through the hills, past dark oaks and scrub pine jagged black against the dark blue sky. Traffic less than sparse now, headlights from an occasional car shimmering toward her, past her in a starry glare.

She drove, still fast, not knowing whether she was laughing or crying, laughing so hard she was crying. There was at least one thing her father taught her to do well: drive like a bat out of hell. She'd been twelve when he took her out to the parking lot at the high school one afternoon and showed her how to drive like a cop. Not defensive driving—offensive driving, how to use the vehicle as a tool, as a weapon. Now she drove.

She drove and tried not to think, but the thoughts crowded in, vying with each other for a place in her consciousness: Jenny, Luke, Wade, rape and murder, Outkast singing "Why are we here," murder and mayhem, that look, her father's eyes, she saw Wade's hands, Wade's large and capable hands, the ring on his finger, the gift from her mother, saw her mother in bed that afternoon, that afternoon she'd died and everything changed forever, saw herself under the shrubbery that night, crying like it would make a difference and burying her panties in the dirt, fucking scumbag, the smirk on his face every time she saw him on campus, and eyes behind windows in little black closets.

When she finally eased back on the accelerator, letting the car coast down to somewhere in the vicinity of the speed limit, she was way out of town, out of Travis County even. She became once again aware of her surroundings, cruising down ranch roads through the dark countryside of Texas Hill Country.

Luke.

What kind of person did that? She felt a wave of remorse wash over her, thick and syrupy, oozing through her, and then nausea. That wasn't her. He'd just been standing there, obviously wanting to talk. Was it contagious, the violence? Had she picked it up like a disease? Had it replicated inside her like some viral malady until it took over?

She didn't know where it had come from, and she didn't know why she had let her rage loose on Luke. He shouldn't have come there. He shouldn't ever have come there. Not, at least, from the time he'd asked Jenny to marry him. He shouldn't. That was all. *Yeah, yeah, yeah, and who are you to say, Miss Upstanding Moral Role Model of the Century?*

Drive on, girlfriend.

Maybe Jenny knew. Had known. Maybe Jenny hadn't minded where Luke spent his off-duty hours.

At some point, she looked out the passenger window and saw the Blanco River shimmering pale blue-white in the moonlight, its shallow waters slipping over the limestone bed. Her headlights flared on a sign at the edge of the highway: DEVIL'S BACKBONE.

She was there. She was close now to where she'd been headed without even realizing it. The place where Jenny's body had been discovered by a ranch hand on horseback, out tending fences. He'd noticed that the cover of an old dried-up well on the thousand-acre property had been moved. She wondered if Wade had talked to him yet, if Wade had seen fit to beat the shit out of him, too, under the guise of interrogation.

There were stories, lots of them, about this place. The Devil's Backbone, a humpbacked ridge, pushed its spine toward the sky at the edge of the Hill Country. People who lived here said there were ghosts. The spirits of Indians slaughtered by white men lingered still on this ridge, waiting for their time to return. She'd heard the stories as a child, stories about the voices of children and the sound of playful splashing in water. No children could be seen, but still the voices were there. Stories of bare-chested, scarred Indians on horseback, appearing and disappearing at the edge of the river. Stories of chill breezes in the middle of summer days, and the screams of massacres riding jagged on the icy air, cutting through the heat of afternoon, screams thick as blood. She thought about the other stories she had heard as a child, the stories told by her father and his Ranger pals as they sat on the back porch sipping whiskey and reminiscing about cases they'd worked, about the bloody history of their force.

One riot, one Ranger. They had it all under control. The governor's assassins. They'd played no small part in solving the Indian Problem.

She drove through the night, thinking to get out and look for the well, but had no idea where to start. It would be foolish to go out there now. She'd wind up lost and stumbling around in the dark, shrinking from the short, sharp barks of coyotes and the howling of wolves. She had no chance to find it. And even if she did, what then? Stand there screaming and cursing? Kneel there praying?

Fatigue washed over her in a wave. She felt herself slipping. Her head jerked up and she realized she'd been close to asleep as she steered the car down the quiet winding highway. Overhead, stars, millions and billions of them. Stars you couldn't see from town.

She cut west on a ranch road and followed it. She drove.

Luckenbach, Texas. Not much more than a small town square. A couple of cafés, shops, the post office. Four in the morning and it was still as a stone. Closed tight for the night, but she couldn't drive anymore. She eased the car to a stop in front of the post office, not much more than a wooden shack with a boardwalk porch under a shingled awning. She cracked her windows for air, reclined the seat as far back as it would go, and let her eyes close.

Sunlight in her eyes, slanting through the windshield. She was baking. The car was an oven. She was a muffin, baking. No. That was Jenny. Wade used to call her that, his little Muffin. If he'd ever had a nickname for Kit, she couldn't remember it now. Who cared?

She wiped sweat from her face, twisted the key to accessory, and rolled the windows all the way down. A slight breeze, already promising heat. Not much relief. Across the street she saw a place labeled simply The Bar. Closed. Thank you, Jesus.

Memories of last night, of what she'd done to Luke, tried to pry their way into consciousness. She pushed them back. Not going there this morning.

Her stomach growled. Hunger? The sensation was rare lately. She was hungry. She felt sticky all over. Her back hurt from sleeping almost sitting up. She needed to pee in the worst way.

She opened the car door, stepped out, and was about to close it when she realized she'd left the keys in the ignition. She grabbed them and dropped them into her bag. Wake up, Kit. She stretched, twisted her torso gently back and forth. Her body felt all kinked up. But it felt different today. It felt stronger, cleaner, maybe a little relieved at not having to fight off the assaults of alcohol on a daily basis.

She walked across the road toward the café. The hunger in her stomach felt reassuring, somehow.

The chalkboard on the wall listed menu items: steak and eggs, eggs and bacon, eggs fried, eggs scrambled, biscuits and gravy. Coffee, tea, iced tea, OJ. No sign of croissants here. She walked across the wide board floor, feeling the tiny cyclones of breeze as she passed beneath dark wood ceiling fans. She took a seat near the back, at a small round butcher block table with years of carvings in its surface. Lover's initials etched deep, couples contained forever inside the heart-shaped boundaries chiseled in hardwood.

She ordered buttermilk biscuits and a cup of coffee, and found herself having to concentrate to keep her hands from trembling when she lifted the coffee cup to her lips. Fatigue. Exhaustion. She was smooth wrung out. She did not want to admit that it might be withdrawal doing this to her.

At the next table a couple of sunburned cowboys, the real

thing by the looks of them, sat hunched over their plates eating huevos rancheros, silently savoring their breakfast of eggs and red chili sauce on tortillas. It smelled good, but Kit couldn't muster an appetite. Hungry as she was, it was all she could do to take a bite of biscuit.

She sat there, chewing, gave up and washed the thing down with a swallow of coffee. And sat some more. She felt like she was frozen in time, like she'd been there since who-knew-when and would be there forever.

A napkin fluttered to the floor between her table and that of the cowboys. The one with his back to her reached behind him, only halfway looking, to retrieve it. Kit glanced down.

She blinked her eyes shut, hard, and opened them. The cowboy's eyes held Kit's as he handed her the napkin, but as she reached to take it she saw something glitter on his hand. A diamond pinkie ring, glittering there on his finger. It was identical to Wade's, the one her mother had given him, with the stones set in the shape of a revolver. There couldn't be two of them in the world. She took the napkin.

"Thanks," she said. She turned back to her breakfast, chewed a lump of biscuit, unable to concentrate. She sipped her coffee, trying to wash the biscuit down.

The cowboys stood to leave, and before she could stop herself, she was at their table.

"Excuse me," she said.

He turned, the one wearing the ring. He reminded her of Rusty, a little, with his pale green eyes and sun-darkened face and the little crinkly lines around his eyes, premature aging from being out in the sun so much. Rusty used to laugh about it. Real cowboys don't wear sunscreen, he'd said. That was what hats were for.

Kit tried a smile.

"Great ring," she said. "Where'd you get it?"

"My girlfriend," he said. "For my birthday."

"Oh," Kit said. "Happy birthday."

He looked puzzled, then grinned at her.

"Thanks," he said. Then he sighed, and added, "We broke up."

Kit wasn't sure what to say. "Too bad," she said. "I guess."

"Maybe," he said. "Maybe not."

"Did she say where she got it?"

The cowboy glanced at her. If he'd been on the make, that last question backed him off.

"I'd like to get one," she said, adding hurriedly, "as a gift for a friend. It'd be just perfect."

"I wish I could help you," he drawled. "but I don't have the first idea where she picked it up. Maybe the Internet."

"I don't guess you'd consider selling it to me," she said. She wanted to tell him that his girlfriend got it at a pawn-shop, that it belonged to her father and that her mother had given it to him and it was needed, somehow, for what was left of her family.

He looked at the ring and looked at Kit and shook his head.

"Can't do that," he said. "She has a habit of breaking up with me. But she always comes back." He winked at her and let a hand slide down toward his crotch, hooking a thumb into his jeans pocket before turning to grin at his partner. The two of them shared a smile.

"Whatever," Kit said, feeling warmth spread up her neck and into her cheeks.

She sat back down and sipped at her coffee, watched them

ease out into the sunshine. Fucking clueless fucking cowboys. She paid her check and dragged her dead-tired body from the café, cringing as the screen door creaked shut behind her.

In her car, the air on now, the interior icy cold to help her stay awake, she watched the scenery roll by like a movie playing on the windshield. She drove across the Devil's Backbone, seeing the ring. Wanting it back. Wanting to hand it to her father and tell him never to let it go again, no matter what kind of pain it meant.

A flash, a glint of sunlight off the gleaming chrome bumper of an approaching car, there and then past her, and she saw the ring glittering on her father's finger as he took her little girl hands in his strong lawman's hands. Muffin, he'd called Jenny. She felt the car swerve and shook her head and brought herself back, pulled the steering wheel hard right, crossing back over the yellow stripes and into the proper lane. Her father's hands. She wondered if he would use them to strangle the person who had killed her sister. Or would he prefer to shoot them. He would get away with murder, she was sure of that. But Jenny was gone forever, and nothing her father might do would change that. She could not bear it. It was harder, in its way, than even the loss of her mother so many years ago. She felt the tears on her cheeks and let herself cry, freely, alone here in her car, let the ache in her heart expand fully into the confines of her skin, the emptiness of loss fill her wholly. She should not fight it. There was nothing to do but endure, capitulate to the pain. The only other option was oblivion.

When the tears were gone, she took out her cell phone to call Dr. Wolfe. No service. Too far out in the country. She drove.

TWELVE

The doors and locks were repaired, the furniture back in place. The carpet bore no stains. The plants were the only sign that something had gone amiss in the waiting room. They'd been pruned back to remove damaged stems. A few brown edges on a leaf here and there betrayed signs of shock. But they seemed to be surviving. Kit touched a cool green leaf. She had read somewhere that plants responded physically to human touch, and to music, to kind words, and even to kind thoughts sent their way. She hoped they were better at it than people.

Dr. Wolfe opened the inner office door. Kit stood and followed her inside, feeling a swell of apprehension wash over her. She would have to tell Dr. Wolfe about Luke. About what she'd done. She plunked herself down on the couch, her insides humming with tension, an anxiety that so completely filled her she felt as if her body had become one of those weird atomic acceleration contraptions and the atoms inside her were blasting toward each other at light speed, or however fast it was the scientists hurled them at one another, approaching the point where matter became energy. $E = mc^2$, wasn't that the formula? Just kick matter up to the speed of light times itself and presto, it becomes energy. She could transmogrify, go from the corporeal world into the world of energy, pure fuckin' energy. Or she could sit there and feel her body disintegrate, fall apart, break into pieces and smaller pieces and still smaller pieces. Once she got past the molecular stage, the sixty-five percent of her that was water would no longer be liquid. She could wind up as a pile of dust there on the office floor. She could be swept away.

Dr. Wolfe cleared her throat.

"I've gotten calls," she said.

Kit stared at her.

"Anonymous," Dr. Wolfe said. "Warning me to stop seeing you."

"What?" Kit had heard her, comprehended the words, but the question popped out anyway.

"The police tried to trace a location. Pay phones. Downtown." Dr. Wolfe crossed her copper brown legs and leaned toward Kit, brushing her long black hair out of her eyes, tucking it behind her ears. "Do you have any idea who it might be? Who's trying to scare me away from you?"

Kit thought of Luke. Thought of Rusty. Thought of the anonymous man who'd attacked her in the parking lot. Thought of herself. She still couldn't remember that night.

"Who knows you're seeing me?"

"Only Jenny's ex-roomate. Leila? The one I'm staying with now? She knows. And my boss at work, she knows I'm seeing a shrink."

"A shrink." Dr. Wolfe managed a smile.

Kit shrugged. "You know."

"I know."

"But they don't even know your name."

"You have caller ID?"

"Doesn't everyone?"

"Someone does know my name, obviously. And I'd like to find out who."

Kit heard a tremor in Dr. Wolfe's voice, and saw fear in her eyes. Though the doctor was trying to seem like this was nothing more than some kind of sick joke, her apprehension was obvious.

"I don't know what to do," Kit said. Her voice came out like that of a frightened five-year-old, a little girl trembling on her bed, scared of the monsters hiding under it, certain they were only waiting until Mommy and Daddy were asleep before they came out to eat her alive. Kit felt herself shudder, wrapped her arms around herself, hugging herself. She realized she was rocking. Lullaby and good night, there now, everything's going to be all right. There aren't any monsters, honey, it's all just in your head.

Only it wasn't. It wasn't all in her head. She rocked herself gently, back and forth, back and forth, her eyes closed tight against tears that wanted to come out, her lips trembling against any more physical expression of pain.

"Have you seen it anymore?" she asked. She kept her eyes closed, afraid of the answer.

"Seen?"

"The truck. The man following you?"

"No."

Kit shifted on the couch. There was no way to get comfortable, not even close.

"I beat him up," she said quickly.

Dr. Wolfe shrank back in her chair, her face clenched in apprehension.

"Who?" she asked. Incredulous.

Kit sat shaking her head no, at whom or what she wasn't sure, and then it welled up inside her and she was babbling, words spilling out of her mouth and tears spilling out of her eyes, the ring on the cowboy's finger, the ring that should be on her father's finger to remind him, and how could he just pawn it and forget it, how could he do that?

"Kit," Dr. Wolfe said. "Who did you attack?"

"Maybe you know why," Kit said, regretting her rude tone even as she spoke. "Maybe you can tell me why did my mother apologize for dying? Who apologizes for dying? And it's all just crazy, it's crazy, and Luke, I mean Luke who wanted to marry Jenny but likes to come look at *me* dancing naked on the stage even now that he knows she's . . . she *was* my sister! It's all so . . . I don't know. It's all just . . . so . . . fucked."

Kit felt a warmth in her chest, over her heart, realized she had one hand pressed there, pressed against her chest over her heart, and she could feel her hand move with the rising and falling of her breath, her breaths coming deep and ragged.

She didn't know how Dr. Wolfe could just sit there, watching her, waiting, her eyes with that steadiness, that keep-going-we're-not-done-yet look in them. Wanting Kit to go deeper, tell more?

"Was it for dying," Kit said, "or was she apologizing for something else while she happened to be dying? What was she sorry for?"

"What do you think she was sorry for, Kit?"

"I don't know."

"But what do you think? Why do you think she apologized?"

Thoughts swirled in her brain so fast she couldn't latch onto one. Thoughts swirled and twisted and swooped, thoughts scattered and regrouped, amassing like clouds building into a thunderstorm, billowing one atop the other, merging, blowing apart again, like an occluded front, hot meeting cold, the clash, the storm. The rain.

"Kit."

Dr. Wolfe was talking to her. She raised her eyes.

"Are you okay?" Softly.

Kit nodded, feeling as though she were choking. She nodded yes and tried to swallow.

"Who did you attack?"

"Luke."

"Why?"

"It just happened."

Dr. Wolfe leaned toward her, shaking her head no.

"Things like that don't just happen. What did he do?"

"He was just there."

"Where?"

"Waiting for me, after work." Kit wanted to curl up into a little ball on the couch. Just lie there, curled up and not thinking.

"Where after work?"

"In the parking lot. Like the other one. But by my car."

Dr. Wolfe leaned back in her chair.

"Did you—"

"I had thought, before, after the other attack . . ."

"You think it might have been him?"

"I don't know."

"Did you? Was that why you attacked him?"

"I don't know." She was telling the truth. She didn't know why.

"What did he do?"

"He comes there. To watch me."

"When you attacked him. What did he do?"

"He didn't fight back. And I got the hell out of there."

Dr. Wolfe sighed, a large sigh tinged with what sounded to Kit like helplessness.

"Do you think you can control yourself? Control your actions?"

Could she please avoid beating people up?

"Yes," Kit said.

"You're angry at Luke. Completely understandable. But you can't, you know, *act* on it the way you did."

"I know. I know that."

"Because you'll leave me no choice."

Kit felt her body stiffen, tried to hide it.

"We're going to have to stop now," Dr. Wolfe said softly. "But we'll need to meet again tomorrow. This is a lot to absorb."

"You got that right," Kit said. She felt a numbness creeping in. Dr. Wolfe couldn't help her. Dr. Wolfe needed time to think. Dr. Wolfe was cutting short their session. Was that allowed? Or fair?

"Kit," Dr. Wolfe said.

Kit's head jerked up.

Dr. Wolfe's voice was low and gentle, barely more than a whisper. "Kit?"

Kit opened her eyes. "Yes," she croaked.

"I want you to consider, seriously, checking in somewhere. Where you can feel safe. I could continue to see you there."

For the briefest moment the doctor's suggestion sounded like some kind of magical relief. But Dr. Wolfe was talking about someplace with a name like Nine West. A special wing. A psychiatric unit. One with doors that locked. At a hospital. A special wing at a hospital. Doors that locked and the only people with keys wore white uniforms and white lace-up shoes that squished almost noiselessly against pale green tile floors when they walked down the halls with their keys. She shook her head no, and kept shaking it. Adamantly.

"It wouldn't be like I was committing you, Kit. I'm not talking about that. You could check yourself in. Agree to stay for a certain amount of time, a week, ten days, two weeks. And after that time you'd be free to leave."

Yeah, right. Once they get you in there . . . Kit kept shaking her head. No.

No. No. No.

"You could feel safe there, Kit. We could both feel safe while I was seeing you. It's important to the therapeutic relationship that we both feel safe while we're pursuing it."

What was this bullshit?

"I'm sorry for what's happened," Kit said, surprised at the sound of her own voice. She was talking. She was even talking in normal tones. She sounded cogent. Her brain was serving up chemical cocktails, liquid fear on the rocks, the kind of stuff that could send a three-hundred-pound gorilla over the edge, make it jump around the room screeching and pounding its chest, but her voice was the essence of calm. "Dr. Wolfe," she said, "we talked about it before. If you'd prefer, if you'd be more comfortable, we can—I can—try to find someone else. A different doctor. You know."

"Is that what you want to do?"

"No," Kit said quickly. "No, not at all. As painful as this process is, I think you're wonderful, you've helped me a lot already. I think. I mean, it's still so, things are still so confused in my head, but I feel like if I continue with you, I might actually, I don't know, get somewhere." Had she made any sense? She needed to make sense.

Dr. Wolfe shifted in her chair. She was not happy with Kit's decision, that was clear. She eyed Kit carefully, and then sighed with resignation.

"All right then," Dr. Wolfe said. "We'll do the best we can under the circumstances." She stood, and Kit took the cue to rise. "But I hope you'll think over the options. You need to be someplace where you feel safe, and a hospital might be that place. I really think it would be best for you. I'm just asking you to consider it."

At the door, Kit glanced back. Dr. Wolfe was gathering her papers and placing them carefully in her satchel, the skin around her eyes crinkled with worry.

"Dr. Wolfe," Kit said, "do you want me to walk out with you?"

"No, no," the doctor said. "I'll be fine."

But Kit didn't get the feeling that Dr. Wolfe was at all sure she'd be fine. She found herself hoping, then, that she'd be the one to find out who was doing this. Before the cops did. Like they were even trying.

"Kit?" Dr. Wolfe's voice caught her, brought her back to where she stood in the doorway, staring at the doctor. "Are you sure you're all right?"

"I'll see you tomorrow," Kit said.

She walked down the corridor to the elevator, wondering if Dr. Wolfe thought she was bad luck. She didn't know how the doctor could think otherwise.

Shake it off, she told herself. *No one is going to attack. You're fine. You're just fine.*

She entered the elevator and turned to face the doors. Ground floor. Just push the button. She reached for it. The doors eased toward each other.

"Yeah," Kit muttered. "Everything's just totally fucking copacetic."

A hand came through the doors, slapped at the black rubber bumper strip. The doors jarred back open and a man in a business suit slipped through the opening. Kit jumped back, felt a stab of pain as one shoulder blade slammed against the rear wall of the elevator. She reached into her bag, felt the barrel, slipped her fingers around it, fumbling until she held the pistol grip firmly.

The man glanced over his shoulder at her, a sheepish smile on his face, started to say something. He saw the look on her face and turned quickly back around, punched the ground-floor button.

"Sorry," she heard him say, speaking to the doors in front of him. "Didn't mean to startle you."

Kit stared at the herringbone fabric of his light brown suit jacket. The center seam was stretched almost into a rip between his shoulders. He had a lousy haircut. He looked again, a nervous glimpse, and back to the front.

Kit pressed her back against the elevator wall, getting as far away from him as she could in the confined space. Stupid son of a bitch. Everyone always in such a rush. Like he had to make that elevator if it was the last thing he did.

As it almost had been.

Kit relaxed her grip on the gun, slid her hand out of her bag.

She wanted to say something to ease his alarm. She didn't know what.

The elevator doors opened and the man walked quickly away, not daring to look back.

Kit stepped out of the elevator, stood there. The doors whooshed shut behind her. She felt sweat trickling down her sides beneath her shirt, soaking into the elastic of her bra.

She wondered how her sister had done it. How Jenny had walked around day in and day out with a gun in her bag, or strapped into a shoulder holster.

She hadn't shot him. She hadn't made any fatal misjudgment. But being on this side of the deadly force equation had opened her eyes to just what a high-wire act the business of living actually is. How thin the wire is. How high it is above the hard cement sidewalk we think we're skipping down, holding ice cream cones and laughing, singing nursery rhymes and wondering if there really is a tooth fairy.

THIRTEEN

Bells going off, church bells, calling the believers to gather and pray. Kit opened her eyes to strange surroundings, lay there a moment before she was conscious enough to realize she was where she should be. In Jenny's room. The phone was ringing. She reached for the receiver, mumbled a hello.

"Kit." A woman's voice. Then it registered. Dr. Wolfe. "I woke you?"

"It's okay."

"I'll be using a colleague's office today. Is two good?" Dr. Wolfe's voice trembled with anxiety.

"Is everything—"

"I'd rather not go into it now."

Kit opened the nightstand drawer and retrieved a pen, scribbled down the address Dr. Wolfe gave.

"I'll see you this afternoon," the doctor said.

Kit hung up the phone and let her head fall back onto Jenny's pillow. It let out a soft *hoosh* as the air was knocked out of it. Feathers and down. Jenny had always liked soft, plump pillows. Kit stared at the ceiling, a return to sleep out of the question. She wondered what the name of the color was that Jenny had painted her room. It was almost white, but not quite, having just the palest tint of peach to it. The bed and nightstand and dresser were golden oak, the room overall a light, soft place to be. Kit had a picture, suddenly, of Jenny here with Luke. Of the two of them in this bed, making love, dreaming about babies and family.

Dr. Wolfe's brusque tone concerned her. Maybe Dr. Wolfe had decided not to let Kit exercise her own judgment any longer. *Only for a while.* Only so she could feel safe. So they both could feel safe.

She wondered if, when she showed up at this so-called colleague's office, there would be men in white suits waiting for her. She pictured her father's collection of 45s, the one she and Jenny got in so much trouble for getting into time after time, spinning song after song from the hundred or so discs in the collection, dancing around the living room, giggling, though Wade was forever forbidding them to play with his turntable.

What was that one song? The goofy, crazed voice intoning *"they're coming to take me away hahhah!"* And the weird atonal music screeching along beneath the voice. She could imagine the look on Dr. Wolfe's face, an expression somewhere between regret and the firm conviction that this was for the best.

Kit didn't have a clue what might be for the best. She sat up, punched the soft, plump pillow. Punched it hard.

"Now, now, Kit," she whispered, "we don't want to go and hyperventilate here, do we?" But she wasn't going to let anyone lock her up in some nut ward. Maybe she should just leave. Pull a Rusty and pack a bag and toss it in her car and get herself out of here. Out of Jenny's house. Out of Austin. Out of Texas. Out of the United States of America.

Go somewhere far away, where the consensus reality wasn't just so totally fucked that it made it difficult to god-damn breathe.

Dr. Wolfe sat in a chrome and black leather chair, a mini-malist contraption, looking deeply uncomfortable. Her colleague's office was in a shiny glass high-rise downtown. The room was bare but for the chair the doctor was in and an identical one Kit sat in, facing her, and a glass and chrome coffee table between them, resting on trim gray wall-to-wall. No desk, no bookshelves, no nothing, except for a smattering of large expressionist prints on the stark white walls, splashes of brilliant color in an otherwise black and white room.

Who on God's green earth could get in touch with her feelings in a place like this?

Kit could see that the doctor was deeply uneasy and trying to cover it.

"They came back," Dr. Wolfe said. "My office is in shambles. Again."

Dr. Wolfe sat looking at her, waiting.

"You don't think I—" Kit started, but couldn't continue. She was alone. Utterly and completely alone.

"I'm not making any presumptions," Dr. Wolfe said. "But

we both know it's about you. This is about you. Where were you last night, Kit?"

"You think I did it? Broke into your office?"

"What makes you say that?"

"The way you're looking at me."

"How am I looking at you?"

"Like it's my fault, somehow." She sat, and Dr. Wolfe sat, the two of them staring at each other.

There was nothing to say. Kit looked around the room, at windows, at the door. Looking for escape. She had to get out of here. She couldn't get out of here. If she left, she would wind up wandering the streets, babbling like a fool, unable to connect to consensus reality, unable to function. She would wind up on the sidewalk, her back pressed against a hard brick building, her eyes watching from ground level as people walked past, trying not to stare at her. Men in uniforms would come and scrape her off the pavement, take her to some asylum somewhere, and leave her there to die.

"I called the police," Dr. Wolfe said finally. "This time they brought in a fingerprint man."

"Prints are worthless without a suspect."

"They want to fingerprint my patients. For elimination purposes."

"All of your patients?"

"Any who don't have an alibi for last night."

Where was she? Last night? A mere eon ago? But she knew. Last night she had a memory of. She'd gone to the do-jang and tried to sweat out the memories, as though she could physically eliminate her toxic past, drain it through the pores of her skin. Afterward, she'd gone to Jenny's house and put salad in her mouth and chewed and swallowed, tried to wash down the food with iced tea. It had been a struggle. She'd felt like she was choking all through the meal. She'd been glad that Leila Jane was out for the evening. Now she wished Leila had been there. After dinner, she'd gone upstairs to bed, and at some point entered the world of dreams, wishing as she did that she could have good dreams, like she'd had early on in life, dreams of being able to fly, soar above the earth unburdened, flying just for the fun of it, because she could.

"Is there a problem?"

"In a word, yes," Kit said.

"Why?"

"I don't know exactly, except that I know I didn't do it and I guess I'd like you to take my word for it."

"Where were you last night? They don't need to print you if you have a firm alibi."

"I don't remember how old I was," Kit said. "When I stopped dreaming and started having nightmares."

Dr. Wolfe's face pulled tight.

"I don't have dreams anymore," Kit said. "I only have nightmares."

"Kit. Will you allow them to take you fingerprints?"

"You think I did it."

"I didn't say that. I'm asking you to let them take your prints."

"We're staying on the subject here?"

Dr. Wolfe nodded.

"I went to the dojang for a workout," Kit said. "That was after I left your office." *After I almost shot some guy in the elevator,* she did not say. "Then I went home and stayed there for the rest of the night. At Jenny's. I've been staying there—"

"You said that. You told me that."

Kit wondered if it was impatience she heard in Dr. Wolfe's tone.

"I forgot," she said. "Sorry."

Dr. Wolfe waited.

"I had salad for dinner and then I went to bed."

"And you didn't dream."

"Do you think I did that? To your office?"

"I think you were enraged when you left yesterday. We sometimes feel helpless to fully express our anger. It can come out in twisted ways."

"I didn't trash your office."

"So give them your fingerprints and that will be that."

"I was there yesterday. My fingerprints will be everywhere. Mostly on the tissue box, I'm sure."

"I'll make them aware of that."

"Do you think it was me?"

"No," Dr. Wolfe said. "I don't think it was you."

"Are you sure?"

"You sound like you have doubts yourself."

Kit sat, silent.

"I think you did just what you remember," Dr. Wolfe said. "Going home to sleep."

"Maybe it's someone else. A different patient they're after."

"The phone calls, Kit. They named you. They told me to stop seeing *you*. The question is: Who is it that wants that?"

Kit stood.

"I've put you at enough risk."

At the door, she turned to face Dr. Wolfe, who had risen from her chair. Kit noticed a pair of buckskin moccasins peeking from beneath the doctor's long brown skirt.

"Tell them okay," Kit said. "They can have my prints."

"We still have some time," Dr. Wolfe said.

Kit opened the door, shaking her head no.

"Kit," Dr. Wolfe said, "please call me."

❖

The adobe walls of the bungalow were bathed in sunshine when Kit pulled to a stop in the driveway. Another glorious sunny Texas afternoon. Hot as hell and only gonna get hotter. Before turning off the ignition, she rolled down the windows of the Mustang. She looked in the rearview, flashed a smile at herself. And then laughed at herself. Trying it on for size. She sat there, hearing the engine creak and pop from the heat. Metal stretching.

She wondered if she should go by her apartment, see that things were all right, but she didn't care enough about whether things were all right to go there and find out for sure. It didn't matter if the place had burned down. It simply didn't matter.

She got out of the Mustang and flung the door shut, wincing as she realized how hard she'd slammed it. She unlocked the front door of the bungalow and closed it and locked it again behind her. In the middle of the afternoon, she locked the front door. It saddened her, put a layer of sad on top of a layer of fear on top of a layer of grief. If she kept going this way, she would surely burn out her adrenals before she hit thirty.

She went upstairs to Jenny's room, stood staring at

nothing. Wondered if she'd remembered to lock the front door. Went back down and yes, she'd locked it. She walked around the downstairs, checking each window, checking the back door. She locked herself in for the day.

Back upstairs. She took off her jeans and tank top, took off her bra and panties, slipped into an oversize T-shirt. This wasn't so hard. Life wasn't so hard. Breathe. Drink water. Eat food. Maintain shelter from the elements. Simple.

She picked up the phone and dialed Cheryl's number. Got voicemail.

"In case you don't know yet," she said, "Blaze is pissed. Where were you? Call me."

She replaced the receiver. Easy. She lay down in the bed and pulled a sheet over her. On her back, she stared at the ceiling. No, life wasn't hard at all.

She waited for sleep. Wondered if it would come. That was what she needed right now. Not to think, not to try to make sense of anything that had happened, not even one small instant of her life, up to this moment in time. She looked at the windows, lit bright by afternoon sun. She should get up and pull the shades.

She closed her eyes. Afterimages swam on her eyelids, rectangles of window light.

She lay there, waiting for sleep.

A car rolled up the drive; a caliche rock popped loudly, caught by the edge of a tire and sent flying. Kit was on her feet in an instant, heart thumping, and halfway dressed before she realized it might only be Leila returning from work. The clock said it was late afternoon; it probably was

Leila, coming home after working the day shift. She'd left early, before Kit rose for breakfast: coffee and air.

The doorbell rang. That wouldn't be Leila.

She stepped into her jeans and headed downstairs. She stopped, ducked back into the room and grabbed her bag. Her bag with the gun. Down the stairs quickly, lightly, trying not to thump and give away her presence in the house, digging in the bag, and then she had it.

She forced her eye to the peephole, wanting whoever it was just to go away.

Luke.

She stepped back, flooded with anger. Tried to calm herself.

Holding the gun behind her back, she reached with her left hand to open the door.

"I came back for more punishment," he said. Kit couldn't tell if he was smiling. The right side of his mouth was swollen and bruised. He had a black eye. His right wrist was wrapped in an Ace bandage. He clutched an envelope with his left hand. But he didn't look threatening. Or even upset.

She stood there, blocking his entry.

"I know you think I'm a total asshole," he said, raising a hand like a cop stopping traffic. "Just please listen. Only for a minute."

She stepped aside and he walked past her and sat on the couch, putting the envelope on the coffee table, then cradling his wounded arm. "I—" he started. And then nothing. He looked around the room, soaking it in, perhaps remembering the last time he'd been there: with Jenny. He sighed and let himself sink back into the couch.

"Please." He motioned for Kit to join him. She kept her

back to him, closed the front door, and eased over to sit in the chair across from him.

He looked at her, his sandy eyebrows furrowed.

"What are you hiding?" he asked.

Kit stuffed the gun into the crack where the seat cushion met the chair back. She left her hand behind her, pretending to massage her lower back.

"Mental instability," Kit said, hoping it sounded deadpan. "That's kind of a strange question, don't you think?"

"Not at all," he said. He looked at her for a long moment.

She could see he didn't believe her.

"The other night," she said. "I don't know what happened."

"Apology accepted," he said. "I understand. You must be, I don't know, about half crazed. I know I am."

"Yeah."

"Now why don't you take that gun out from behind you and put it on the table here where we can both see it."

Kit brought it out slowly, and Luke watched as she put it carefully on the coffee table. Though she placed it down gently, the metal clattered against the glass, sounding unnaturally loud in the silence.

"Thank you," he said.

"I wasn't planning to, like, shoot you or anything. I didn't know it was you."

"Who'd you think it was?"

"No idea."

He looked at the gun. "Jenny?"

Kit nodded.

"She gave it to me that night we all had dinner."

"Did she say why?"

"Because I'd been attacked. And because some guy who used to hang out at the club had been murdered."

"Jake Weatherby?"

"That sounds right. I'm not sure. It didn't mean anything. Still doesn't."

"I wanted to tell you earlier," he said. "Maybe if I had, you wouldn't have seen fit to kick the living daylights outta me."

"I already said I was sorry. And I am."

"I believe you. No hard feelings. I was there for a reason."

"There's only one reason men go there. And it's not for the fabulous honey-dipped peanuts they serve at the bar."

"I was undercover," he said. "At least until the night Jenny introduced us. That kind of blew things, at least as far as you were concerned."

"Who were you investigating?"

A smile, or an attempt at one. He looked like he might cry.

"Jenny was onto this porn ring. Internet. Jake Weatherby? The dead guy?"

Kit waited.

"He hung out there sometimes. Biker dude. Sorry-assed scooter nasty. Wiry fella, small, stringy red hair."

"I'm drawing a blank," Kit said truthfully.

"We thought one of the customers at Blaze's might be involved, might be responsible even. The sergeant asked me to go in, see what I could find out."

He looked at her straight on with blue eyes that seemed even sharper in the daylight, with no window separating him from her. Either he was telling the truth or he was one jam-up liar. Kit smelled the lightest whiff of cologne, something earthy and fresh.

"That night we met, I pretended not to know you because I had to, or thought I had to. I didn't know if Jenny knew you worked there. She didn't talk much about you, but from what she'd said, I assumed that she didn't know. And I figured if you wanted her to know, you'd tell her."

"She thought I bartended," Kit said, "until she got the report about me getting assaulted. I didn't even want to report it. Wouldn't have. Blaze insisted."

"Madame Blaze. Quite the businesswoman."

"She was afraid if she didn't report it and it came out later, the Baptists would try to use it to get her license yanked. Not like they don't try several times a year as it is."

"I understand her fear. I'm scared to death of folks who refuse to ever dance or drink. Hell, you gotta let loose every once in a while. It's good for the soul." It probably was a smile he was trying, but she had busted his lip up pretty badly.

"I guess," was all Kit could say.

"This organization," Luke said, "if it even is one, the guy in charge, we thought—and now I know—he frequents Blaze's. But they're not just into run-of-the-mill porn. They're into the kiddie stuff. One of the suspects in the Weatherby case was a high-up in the organization, maybe even runs it. I was trying to meet him and get close to him, get hooked up in the ring so Jenny and I could bust them but good."

"So Jenny's murder—there are suspects?"

"Considering the timing, it could be that they were involved." He sighed.

"Does my father know?"

Luke shook his head. "Your dad and I haven't exactly bonded. He's not giving me anything; I'm not about to share with him."

"Smart," Kit said. "He'd only go beat them up."

"Must run in the family," he said, but this time he smiled with his eyes and left his mouth out of it. "Now I'm sorry," he said. "I shouldn't be joking about it."

"It's okay," Kit said, relieved that he *could* joke about it. She told him about Rusty, her suspicions concerning how Rusty had been hurt.

"Yeah, well, I still haven't figured out why Rusty is so high on your dad's list. It's almost like he needs so badly to solve this thing, for his own peace of mind, that he's latched onto Rusty and he's gonna do his damnedest to make the evidence fit, no matter how badly he's gotta bend it and squeeze it."

"You may find this hard to believe, but that's not like him."

"I know. He's got a fine rep. As a damn good lawman." Luke sighed. "He's lost a daughter, Kit. I know he's walking around like he's got it all under control, but he doesn't. Take a good look at him and you'll see it. He's walking around in the dark."

"But you think he's on the wrong track? As far as Rusty?"

"I'm not sure of anything. I mean, now you're telling me the guy split. Kind of sudden, don't you think?"

"You would, too, if my dad was on your case."

"The fact is, this investigation is still wide open. And that's not good."

"Why risk a capital murder charge when killing Jenny wouldn't stop the investigation?"

"I think she discovered something that scared the shit out of someone. Scared them so badly they thought she had to be done away with."

That hurt, to hear him say it that way.

He shifted forward to rest his arms on his thighs, as though the weight of his thoughts were too much for him, but winced in pain when he leaned on his injured arm. He pulled himself back up to sitting position.

He shook his head slowly; tears rimmed his eyes.

"I miss her," he said.

Kit sat silently. He had been at Blaze's to do a job. That was all. It was just one of those freaky things that she happened to be working there.

"I'm sorry," she said.

He wiped his eyes and stared at her.

"About your arm, too," she said. "I'm sorry."

"And my eye?" he said, half smiling. "And my ribs?"

"Everything," she said.

When he spoke, it was softly, kindly. "I already accepted your apology," he said. "Only thing I'm pissed about is how long it took for me to get to talk to you." He picked up the envelope and opened it. "I have some photos," he said. "I need you to take a look."

"It was in the report," Kit said. "His face was distorted. I couldn't tell you what he looked like, other than monstrous."

"Forget about him. Have you seen any of these guys at the club? Any of them hanging around?"

"Forget about him?" Kit shrugged. "I can't tell you how much I'd love to forget about him. I can't seem to do it."

"I mean just for the moment."

Kit took the photos, looked closely, began leafing through them. It was as if she were onstage, naked, staring at the faces. The images leered at her, though she knew their eyes had seen only the camera photographing them and the cop behind it. She took her time, examining features carefully. And then she tossed them back on the table.

"I don't rat," she said. "I don't tell on people. If Jenny told you anything about me, she should have told you that."

"She did," Luke said. "I'm not asking you to rat. Your sister, my fiancée, a woman both of us loved dearly, is dead. Murdered." He leaned toward her, his eyes intense. Angry. "I want whoever killed Jenny. Understand? I *want* them. You can tell me what you know or you can keep it to yourself. But I don't have much to go on here, and you might just have seen something at that club that could help me find who killed her. It's not like I've busted you with a damn dime bag of dope and I'm asking you to give up your dealer." He was in her face now. Up close. "It's not ratting. It's justice."

Kit picked up the photos and looked again. Mug shots. Each face looked menacing in its own particular way. Anyone would look menacing in a police photo. There was something about having those numbers under the chin, the dead giveaway that this person had been arrested.

"This one," she said. "He's a regular." It was the kid, the one she and Cheryl had dubbed Friedrich Nietzsche, freckle-faced Fred. He looked as young and innocent, even in his mug shot, as he did when he was at the club. Kit still wasn't sure he was of age.

Luke took the photo from her. He looked disappointed.

"Any dealings with him?"

"He shows up once or twice a week. I've never even seen him at the bar."

Luke slipped the photo into his shirt pocket, motioned for Kit to continue.

She stared at the photos, one by one, placing them face-down on the table as she went, as if she were dealing cards.

There. Maybe. She closed her eyes, looked again. Clean-cut. But those eyes.

She didn't know. She couldn't be sure. But, she thought, maybe.

The Tarantula.

What had Cheryl said. His name.

"This one," she said. "Maybe. I'm not sure. Ned. I think his name's Ned."

Luke took the photo from her. His lips curled into a smile.

"I was hoping you'd spot him," he said.

"He's the one you think did it?"

"Nothing certain. But he's the one I was trying to get next to."

"Can I see it again?" She wanted to be sure. He looked different, clean-shaven, his facial hair precision trimmed. She wasn't sure. "If it's him, who I think it is—but, please, I'm not sure—we call him the Tarantula," Kit said.

Luke looked at her questioningly.

"The other dancers and I," Kit said. "We make up nick-names for the regulars. He's all shaggy now. Hairy like a Tarantula."

"Did you have one for me?"

Kit felt her face go hot, knew she was blushing but didn't know why.

"Sweet," she said.

"Sweet?" Luke's eyes softened.

"What'd you think?"

"Maybe something reptilian?"

"Like snake in the grass?"

"Do you think Jenny would have fallen in love with a snake?" He looked at her with the honesty of a child.

"Not intentionally," Kit said quietly. "She made her share of mistakes, but I don't guess loving you was one of them."

"It wasn't," he said. "I promise you that." He took her hand; the bandage adding unnatural bulk to the shape of his palm. "If you need anything, Kit, if you need a friend, know that I'm your friend. Jenny would want that. And I want that. I'm here for you."

Kit didn't know what to say, much less what to think.

"Why Sweet?"

"We liked it that you were so respectful," she said. "It was kind of refreshing. Of course, we expected you to trap one of us in the hallway and try to save her wretched little soul. Usually that's what guys who act the way you did are up to."

"I got enough to do just taking care of my own," he said. "No time to salvage others'."

"Especially a stripper's, right?"

"A dancer's."

"That's kind," Kit said, hoping it sounded like a thank-you.

Luke shrugged, gave her an embarrassed smile.

"So this guy Ned," he said. "Know anything about him?"

"Don't you?"

"He won't even tell me what time it is."

"One of the girls at the club, she said he's a photographer. And more. He pays really well if you're willing to pose for him and let him put the pictures on the Web. He's got sites. She sort of indicated she could hook me up if I wanted to make some extra cash. I wasn't interested."

"Think you could get that way?"

Kit looked at him. No way.

And then she heard the words again, the words that came out of the mouth of the man who'd attacked her, right before she'd laid into him.

"The guy who mugged me," she said, "or tried to, in the parking lot. I thought he was about to rape me, or steal my bag. I thought it was about that. But he said something. He said, 'Better back off, bitch.'"

Luke looked at her, waiting.

"What if they were on to you, knew you were the heat?"

"That has nothing to do with you."

"Unless they knew I was Jenny's sister. Maybe they thought I was part of it. Giving Jenny information."

"It's a stretch." Luke shook his head. "How would they know?"

"You have to admit, the connections seem more than tenuous."

"The only ones who knew I was under were Jenny and the sergeant. It was strictly need-to-know."

"Things leak."

"I would trust Jenny with my life. And Sergeant Batista is a stand-up guy. He doesn't run his mouth. And how would they know you were Jenny's sister?"

But even as Luke said the words, Kit could see wheels turning.

"Easy enough to find out for the Internet savvy," she said.

"When do you work next?"

"I'm not even sure I'm going back at this point."

"Can you, though?" Luke looked at her hopefully. "Go back in?"

"Go back in?"

"I need someone who can get next to this guy," he said. "You can."

"Oh yeah." Kit tried a laugh, but it came out twisted. "Sure. I'll just jump into the porn thing. My goal in life." She felt her head going back and forth, gesturing a firm no.

"I'll make sure the photos never make it into cyberspace. We'll be on him before he uploads."

"You can't promise that."

"Look. I want this guy. He may hold the key to Jenny's murder. I'll be there, in the club, watching out for you." He looked at his bandaged arm. "Like you need it."

It was something she could do. Something real. Luke was looking at her, waiting. She remembered something Burt Simmons had said to her father one summer's evening out on the back porch. Wade had been lamenting a case they'd lost that afternoon in court. He was not used to hearing a jury foreman say not guilty. Burt had laughed at him. "Hell, Wade, if you looking for justice, it's on page 383 in the dictionary."

Maybe it could be about justice, instead of about her father going out with a lynch mob.

"You'll be there," she said.

"I'll be there."

Luke's assurance calmed her. He would look out for her.

She looked at the gun on the table between them. Luke eyes followed hers. She thought about the man in the elevator, how close she'd come to shooting him. And about her own state of mind, how she lived too close to obliteration to keep such a convenient tool in her possession.

"I'll take it if you want," Luke said. "I'm sure Jenny was only trying to make sure you'd be safe."

"I'd have to keep it in my locker anyway," Kit said. "I can't very well take it onstage."

"Guess not," he said.

When she didn't reply he stood and picked up the gun. He checked the safety and tucked it into his jeans.

"You don't need this thing lying around anyway," he said.

"I don't know about this," Kit said.

"I do," he said. "You don't need this. I've got your back."

"Not that," Kit said. "I seem to be having a rational moment here. They're so rare."

Luke smiled, then winced at the pain in his lip.

"Don't worry," he said. "I'll be there."

FOURTEEN

Her legs were rubbery, struggling to hold her weight as she stepped across the floor, hearing the music but unable to connect to it. Her arms felt like lead pipes, her joints were stiff, creaking, resisting any change of position. The smallest movements were a struggle. She knew what the Tin Man must've felt like, standing there rusted in the woods.

Luke sat in booth six, facing the center of the stage. His hands were in view as usual, but his smile was missing. Kit felt oddly unabashed dancing before him now, knowing he was there not to ogle, but to protect her.

When Cheryl emerged on the stage, Kit moved in.

"Where've you been?"

"Chill," Cheryl said. "Blaze already reamed my ass."

"You didn't call back," Kit said. "I was worried."

"I did this party," Cheryl said, her eyes going somnolent.

"The host got blasted and decided to take us all to Cancún. Private jet and everything."

Kit slipped into the swim so she wouldn't have to jump around much.

"It was awsome." Cheryl grabbed the pole with one hand and let her body circle slowly. "Fucking fabulous."

Cheryl looked like she might be in love. An addled brain, so much the better.

"I'm thinking of moving to Mexico," Cheryl said dreamily.

Kit stuck her index finger in her mouth, raised it before her, and held it there.

"What?" Cheryl said, half whining.

"Checking to see which way the wind is blowing."

"No," Cheryl said. "You should check it out. It's amazing there. Amazing."

"And all the tequila a virgin can drink."

"Ha-ha, very funny."

"You're lucky you still have a job," Kit said.

"Look who's talking."

The music went louder for just an instant and then back to its normal earsplitting volume, Blaze's signal to cut the crap onstage and get on with dancing. Kit moved away from Cheryl and wondered if what she was doing looked even remotely like dancing.

She tried a spin and almost fell, saw Luke's eyes narrow with concern as he watched her—*shake shake shake*—hear the horns now—and then there was the vertical slit of light as someone entered booth five, and Kit thought at first it was Ned, but it turned out not to be. Just another hairy guy. So drunk he missed the stool and fell against the window. She watched as his bearded cheek mashed against the Plexiglas and his face slid slowly downward. *Shake*. Where'd it go? She'd lost the music, couldn't hear anything but a long slow roar building from somewhere in the lower back section of her brain. Out of her mind. She had to be out of her mind, doing this. Kool. And the Gang. *Shake your booty*.

She did. She shook her booty and hoped Luke appreciated that she was doing it for the cause.

She danced back over next to Cheryl.

"Decided I'm interested," she whispered.

Cheryl segued from the pony to the jerk and looked at her, puzzled.

"The Internet thing," Kit said. "Can you hook me up?" She would just, by God, do it. If Luke thought it would lead to Jenny's killer. She didn't know if it would mean she could—what, get over it? It might be a start.

Cheryl's pink painted lips formed that O she made when surprised. "I'll ask," she said.

"You said the guy liked my look," Kit said. She didn't want to seem pushy, but she wanted in. She wanted to get in there and do it. She wanted to find Jenny's killer.

"I'll let you know," Cheryl said.

Kit couldn't be sure, but she thought Cheryl's tone held just a hint of hostility.

⁜

His voice was syrupy, the words dripping out of his mouth and sliding toward her slowly with the *a* sounds flat as a midwestern wheat field. In the corridor outside the bar, Kit stood shivering, thankful that the air-conditioning was on deep freeze so it would seem she was shivering from the cold and not because she was bugged-out nervous. She pulled her tiger-striped cape snug, wrapping herself in it.

Up close, Ned smelled of Aveda hair gel, all earthy and fresh. It surprised her how clean he smelled. And how quietly and gently he spoke, though there was unquestionably something slick about him. But outside the booths, standing there with his arms crossed and leaning against the flat black wall, talking business, he did not seem at all threatening. He seemed—Kit hesitated before admitting it—he seemed nice.

"The rate is a grand an hour," he was saying. "Cash. I prefer to start with a three-hour session, with paid breaks, of course. The product is all mine, in perpetuity, strictly for use on my sites. I won't license the images to any third parties."

"Sounds fair," Kit said. "When do we start?"

"You in a bind?"

"Going back to grad school," Kit said. "Tuition's a killer."

"Busy tomorrow?" Ned eyed her with those marble grays, only now they didn't seem at all cold. They seemed almost conspiratorial, in a fun kind of way. Like the eyes of a teenager about to make mischief of a harmless sort, play a prank, wrap a house in toilet paper or something.

"Oh," Kit said, taken by surprise. The guy worked fast.

Or maybe Luke was wrong and Ned knew she was Jenny's sister. A quiver of fear shot down her spine; she shivered.

"Cold?" Ned asked.

"It's freezing in here," Kit said, pulling her cape even tighter. "Tomorrow's good." She was supposed to work, but if she couldn't cover her shift she'd simply no-show; Cheryl seemed able to get away with it. She would take the passive-aggressive approach and hope Blaze would actually fire her.

Ned scribbled something on a small notepad he'd pulled from his shirt pocket. He tore off a sheet and handed it to her.

"I'll see you there around, say, one. That good?"

Kit nodded yes and headed back down the hallway. She could feel his eyes on her as she went.

She slipped into the dressing room and put the paper into her bag, in her locker. There was no bottle stashed behind the clothes. She was relieved. Strengthened. She walked over and stared at the month's schedule posted on the bulletin board, thinking she should at least make an effort to cover her shift. No sense pissing Blaze off if it wasn't absolutely necessary. And if Luke was right, that the porn crew was recruiting from right here in the club, who could say whether or not they were doing so with Blaze's knowledge, maybe even her consent.

FIFTEEN

She looked at herself in the mirror. Hot-pink wig, done in a pageboy, the bangs covering her eyebrows. She'd put on eyelashes, longish, but not extreme. She applied a shimmering pearl lipstick to match her eye shadow. Looked again. Was that her in the mirror, or cotton candy?

Ned's dressing room was plush, carpeted in thick beige pile, full of rounded, cushiony couches. A chrome clothes rack held everything from shining silver chaps (with matching cowgirl hat) to sheer black floor-length numbers. The colors leapt out at Kit: silver and black and pink and red and yellow, pale blues and fuchsias and lavenders, ochres and jades, hanging limp on plain wire hangers, waiting to be chosen, to be filled with flesh and made into a fantasy so some lonely guy spending a Wednesday night in a Motel 6 in St. Louis could get his rocks off.

Her sister was dead.

Out of nowhere, out of the recesses of her mind. She stepped back from the thought, watched it float through the center of her brain, like a stock quote scrolling across in bright green lights on a black background. It was a piece of information that she could not currently process. That was all. She felt nothing.

She could not let herself feel anything. Not now. If she allowed so much as one iota of emotion, she would lie down on that soft comfortable couch over there beneath the window and she would never get up again.

She took up a brush and splotched blush onto her cheeks. *You could always slit your wrists and smear blood in brilliant red stripes: across your forehead, down each cheekbone, across your chin, and maybe even a little something on your neck, just for good measure.*

War paint.

She settled for blush, brushed it across her face, following the contours of her cheekbones. She slipped on a bracelet, silver and slinky, stood and zipped up the knee-high white patent-leather boots Ned had asked her to wear. She looked down at her silver thong. The fabric—what little there was of it—looked like something approved by NASA for travel into deep space. She stepped into a white terry robe and cinched the belt around her waist.

Though she knew Luke was close, maybe even downstairs in the lobby, but if not, certainly in his car outside the building, she felt isolated. What good could he do out there? All she could be sure of was that if she didn't emerge from the shoot within four hours, he would come looking for her. What was it her father had said—you gotta go in there believing in your heart that you haven't got one damn thing in the world to lose.

The attitude came easily; it wasn't a big stretch. She looked herself over in the mirror one last time. If she'd been doing this for money she'd have called herself a whore. Top-dollar whore, but still.

The pert click of her boot heels against the concrete floor of the converted warehouse echoed hollowly as she left the dressing room. Most of the huge space of the seventeenth floor—all Ned's—was in shadow. But there in the far corner was the set. Photographic equipment gleamed under the light.

Ned would capture the artifice, convert the image of a lusting pink female body into digital bytes, save it on a cold, hard magnetic disk, and there it would reside, ready for distribution, ready to go anywhere in the world, at the click of a mouse. Ready to zip-zap at ever-so-many Mb per sec to display her body on the screen of a computer in . . . where? Zimbabwe? Azerbaijan? The former Yugoslavia, maybe? Was she ready for her close-up?

Ned turned to watch her approach, folded one fist onto his hip, and looked at her with unabashed male appreciation. Kit wished she could feel something. Anger even. Or reluctance to do this. Anything.

She stood, waiting.

"The robe?" Ned watched as Kit slipped out of it, tossing it onto a nearby chair. He let slip a moan of appreciation. "You've got a great body," he said.

"I work out," she said, trying to sound friendly, and walked to the edge of the stage. She thought briefly about going for perky, like that waitress at the Gypsy Wolf, be all bright and full of smiles and just, gosh, happy to be in the world, but that would be too big a reach.

She took up a place on the black leather chaise longue and looked at Ned, standing behind the tripod-mounted camera. He peered through the viewfinder, then walked over and moved her arms this way, her legs that. Kit watched him manipulate her limbs, but couldn't actually feel his touch. Her body was there on the couch; she existed entirely in her brain, and her brain seemed to have disconnected from everything outside it, even her heart. She was there, her very existence curled up in a snug little ball inside the soft wet orb in her head, and there was a man down there somewhere arranging her body into a position, posing her, his eyes calculating, gauging, as he looked and made decisions about where to put her hands, how to bend her legs, which angles might best create aesthetic satisfaction. He could have easily given verbal instructions, but it was apparent he wanted to take advantage of the opportunity to touch. Cheryl had warned her about that.

"Let's start there," he said, and returned to stand behind his camera. It was sleek and small, with a large lens sticking out like a metallic third eye, ogling her.

Kit half-closed her eyes, stared into the glass of the lens.

"Perfect," Ned whispered. "Just like that."

Kit wondered what he saw in her look, what message her eyes were sending. Because she wasn't trying to say anything at all.

He said move this way. He said turn that way. He said, oh, yes, that's it, just like that. Kit shifted on command, changing her positions, smiling, smirking, pouting, showing just the itty-bitty tip of her tongue, opening her mouth, closing her eyes, *and I will give you a big surprise.*

At some point Ned called a break. Kit got up from the chaise longue, which reminded her of a psychiatrist's couch—and of the fact that she hadn't called Dr. Wolfe—and wrapped herself in the robe. Ned's lighting man, a chubby young blond who wore his hair in short dreads and barely spoke during the shoot except to acknowledge Ned's instructions, brought them each a glass of iced tea. Ned took his and retreated to a desk in a far corner of the room, where he plugged the flashcard he'd removed from his camera into a desktop computer. His face glowed blue when the screen came up, and Kit could see he was smiling.

"Guess I did okay," she said to the lighting man. "I'm Kit, by the way."

"Rodney," he said. "Nice to meet you." All business.

"How long you been doing this?"

"Two years. Leaves time for school."

"Studying?"

"Graphic arts."

"Guess this is just the ticket then?" Kit's mouth curled into a smile, and Rodney ducked his head in an aw-shucks-ain't-that-funny gesture.

"You being ironic?" he asked.

"I was going for sarcasm."

"Oh." He took an unnaturally long sip from his glass of tea.

Kit stood, sipping also, marveling at her ability to bring conversation to a dead halt without even trying, especially, it seemed, when she was trying her best not to.

"I find irony to be tricky," she tried. "I don't think I can even define it, much less achieve it."

"Oh," he said.

"Do you photograph? As well as light?"

"Oh, yeah. I'm totally into that. I do some of Ned's stuff. He's really good. I've learned a lot from him."

"What kind of pictures?"

"Well, for Ned, you know, I shoot"—he waved a hand toward the stage—"this kind of stuff here. But for myself, I don't know. I've got a car series going. Old, decrepit, rusted-out cars. Find them in the weirdest places."

"So you're an artist."

"I guess. I mean I'm trying to be."

"I admire artists."

He looked at her, his hazel eyes appreciating the compliment.

"Yeah," he said. "But it's a tough gig. You got to love it."

"How'd you meet Ned?"

"Um." He looking around the cavernous room like the answer might be hiding somewhere in the shadows. "I don't think I even remember."

"Come on."

"No, really," he said. "I can't remember. Probably at some strip club somewhere." He glanced at her and blushed.

Kit smiled at him, hoping it looked real.

"So maybe I could see some of your work sometime," she said.

He looked awestruck. "My photos?"

"Yes. Your art."

Rodney shrugged an okay, his head nodding as though in time to a tune in his brain, his mouth pulled into a satisfied smile.

"Hold on," he said. "Or better yet, come with me."

Kit followed him to a large desk in the corner opposite the one where Ned sat, still clicking away on his computer. Rodney turned on a desk lamp and pulled a sheaf of photos from a portfolio on the desk. He handed them to Kit.

They had Ned's attention now. Kit saw him looking across the expanse of concrete, a less-than-happy expression on his face.

She pretended not to have noticed and stepped closer to the desk to put the photos under the light. Black-and-white. The first one was of a vehicle on its side in a woods somewhere, its underbelly exposed to the camera, revealing a rusted-out chassis, corroded pipes looking like petrified intestines. Rodney had framed the image nicely.

"You're good," she said. She slipped the print off the stack and laid it aside, and then her eye caught another set of prints on the desk, in shadow. But she saw. Color prints, these were.

The girl couldn't have been thirteen, or maybe she could be thirteen, but she looked about ten. She was naked. Posed much the way Ned had posed Kit at the start of their session. Her prepubescent body invited sex, but there was something in her eyes that might pass for innocence mixed with apprehension.

Kit tried to look at the photo in her hand, kept her head in position, but let her eyes go back to the photo on the desk. A child. A little girl. A shudder ran through her. Rodney didn't seem to notice. Kit forced her eyes back to the car photo. It was wrecked and burned out, its front caved in, the remains of a head-on collision.

Rodney moved next to her and looked over her shoulder.

"That one I found at the Maxwell Volunteer Fire Department. They park the wrecks outside and leave them there a few weeks so people can see. Like maybe it'll make folks think twice about how they drive."

"Think it helps?" Kit said, wondering what kind of life the child in the photo on Rodney's desk had in store for her, what highway she was on, and who the fuck had forgotten to post the speed limit.

Rodney shrugged, picked up a large manila envelope and tossed it carelessly back on the desk, covering the photo Kit had seen.

"So what do you think?" he asked.

Kit glanced at him, then back at the print.

"I like your work," she said, and set aside the photo of the wrecked car, trying to focus on the next one. She was saved from having to comment on it when Ned walked briskly from his desk to the stage, whistling something that sounded vaguely like "All Along the Watchtower."

"Let's get back to it," he called, giving Kit a thumbs-up as his voice echoed off concrete walls. "We're doing good work here. Looking fabulous."

She nodded, not wanting to go back to the stage.

"Hey," Rodney said, "you wanna maybe get a drink?" He was blushing; Kit could see it even in the shadows. "When we're finished?"

It was the last thing she wanted.

"Sure," she said. "You can bring the rest of your photos."

Rodney's smile seemed to hold more than simple relief at not being rebuffed. Kit told herself she was imagining things. They would go for a drink. She could handle one drink. For the cause. It didn't mean she'd have to go off on a bender. She needed to do this. She took a breath and ex-haled forcefully as she walked back over to the stage.

Under the lights, she disrobed and stood there awk-wardly, waiting for instructions from Ned.

"Phase two," he said. "Why don't you go ahead and lose those boots and the thong. We'll get down to business."

Kit sat on the couch to unzip the boots, tossed them out-side the circle of light that shone onto the stage. She stood and yanked lose the bows on either hip that held the thong in place. Tossed it over with the boots.

Stood there. Bathed in light. Naked but for the shiny sil-ver bracelet on her wrist. She found herself thinking of Eve, wondering if this was how Eve felt after she'd taken that bite of the apple. She caught Rodney staring, the look on his face less than professional. She stood there, a smile tug-ging at her lips, laughing inside at the absurdity of the situ-ation, dreaming of the Garden of Eden, the concept of it, the subversive nonsense written into the Bible by a bunch of misogynist scholars back there in the early anni Domini. Male scribes doing the bidding of the Levites, whose mis-sion it was to destroy the religion of the day: Goddess as the supreme creator. It just wouldn't do, having all these He-brews worshipping a female deity, hanging about the tem-ples engaging in sacred sex with the priestesses, uncaring that women owned property and were respected as thinkers and writers and creators. Maybe she should call Leila Jane and see about bringing home ribs for dinner.

Kit stood feeling the heat from the lights on her naked body as Ned and Rodney looked at her appraisingly. Rod-ney seemed to have managed the transition from ogler to photographer's assistant. She slid onto the couch, on her side, propped her head on her hand and looked at the glass and metal eye of the camera lens. Rodney came over with a light meter and held it inches from her face, from her belly, from her ribs beneath her breasts, pressing a button and paying close attention to the numbers flashing on the display.

Be sure you get the ribs, buddy. No irony intended. Kit laughed out loud and saw the disconcerted look on Ned's face and all she could think to say was "Oh, God, where *did* those fig leaves go?"

⌗

A cloud passed in front of the searing sun, casting weak shade over the asphalt. Kit cornered into Panchito's parking lot, following Rodney as he wheeled his red Ducatti to a stop in front of the bar. She parked and got out, saw Rodney remove his shining red helmet and lock it onto the matching bike without ever taking his eyes from her. She felt like an hors d'oeuvre, and Rodney was the famished guest at the cocktail party. At least he was being out-front. There was something refreshing about his lack of guile. But it didn't make her any more comfortable. She kept flashing on that photo. It sickened her. She took her time crossing the lot.

A crew of bikers rumbled in, revving their Harleys noisily before killing engines and putting down kickstands. They ambled into the bar, all black leather and headbands, skulls and crossbones on the backs of their vests, which most of them wore over fleshy bare chests and bellies that betrayed a fondness for Big Macs.

Kit pretended interest in the bikers as she approached Rodney, walking slowly until she saw Luke wheel his city car to a stop, parking well away from the cycles. He got out and strode toward the door, casually flipping his key chain shoulder high to bleep the vehicle locked as he walked away from it.

Rodney touched Kit's arm and she jumped, tried to cover her alarm with a laugh.

"Touchy, are we?" Rodney said.

"One of your regular hangouts?" Kit asked, nodding toward the bar, a rickety, run-down, single-story frame job that looked like it had once been someone's ranch-style house.

"Not really," he said.

"What do you want," Kit said flatly. "Not a great neighborhood, right?" She fell in next to Rodney as he headed for the entrance.

"It's just that it's the closest thing to the studio. I've only got an hour."

"Oh," Kit said, trying to sound disappointed even as she felt a wave of relief wash through her. An hour was good. An hour was perfect. She could get whatever information Rodney might have about Ned's business and then get the hell out of there.

Inside was what she expected: stale tobacco smell, industrial, beer-stained carpet, a pool table, and a couple of touch-screen video terminals offering card games and electronic slot machine action. The bar was wood-grain Formica, chipped along the front edges.

Rodney led the way toward a booth at the back. The red vinyl seats featured duct tape accents. Kit slid into the sticky bench seat.

A middle-aged waitress slouched over and nodded tiredly

when Rodney ordered a couple of Budweisers, then shuffled back toward the bar. Kit felt sad for her, wondering what had led her here.

"Bud okay?" Rodney shot a half smile across the table. "I should've asked. Just, I don't know. That's what I always drink."

"It's fine," Kit said. She felt dirty sitting there, almost expecting some weird virus or bacterium might crawl off the tabletop and burrow into the skin of her arms. "Bud's fine." She hoped she wouldn't retch.

The waitress put two red-white-and-blue-labeled bottles on the table between them. Rodney raised his to Kit, then seemed not to know what to say.

"To art," Kit said. She tapped her bottle against Rodney's and took a slow, tiny swallow of beer. It wasn't like she was drinking. She wasn't drinking. She was investigating. The stuff tasted awful, but delivered warmth to her body; she could feel it washing into her bloodstream. This was not good. She would take it in slow, tiny sips.

"Yeah to that." Rodney smiled goofily, affecting the demeanor of a stoned Cali surfer dude. "To what you said."

It took Kit a moment to realize he was kidding.

"I got some killer brownies, dude," he said, still with the accent.

It took her another moment to realize he wasn't kidding.

He sat there, staring at her or staring at nothing, she couldn't tell. She looked around the bar, at the late afternoon patrons, rough trade, most of them. Bikers shooting pool, a pair of painted-up prostitutes in micromini denim skirts and tube tops perched on bar stools, drinking B-52s and giggling together. There were the gainfully employed in the bar as well: a smattering of oil-stained mechanics, a few construction workers, and a duo of steroid addicts in paint-stained Carhartt overalls, all burly and muscled up. At the cash register end of the bar sat Luke, a bottle of Tecate in front of him, looking perhaps a little too clean-cut for such an establishment, too cute, even, with the wayward blond curl that kept falling onto his forehead.

A few stools down from Luke, leaning against the bar, was a real live wannabe disco king, slender the way a snake is slender, wearing tight polyester pants and a slinky print shirt unbuttoned to reveal a swatch of chest hair. He had on patent leather loafers with shiny, gold-tone buckles that looked like misplaced tie bars. Straight out of '79. He kept rubbing his nose and sniffing, his eyes pinballing from one corner of the bar to another. Wired up and wasted.

She tapped her bottle against the table, agitated. She had no interest in taking so much as another milliliter of the stuff. It was nowhere.

"This place is, ah . . ." Kit sought a word.

"They got good nachos," Rodney said, back to himself again. Or himself as much as Kit knew of him. At any rate he'd abandoned the stoner rib. "Should we get some?"

"Feel free," Kit said. "I'm not really hungry right now."

Rodney tossed off the idea and took a cyclopean swallow of beer.

"Did you bring your work?" Kit asked. Please, God, let him have brought some pictures.

"Left 'em out on the bike," he said. "Should I go get them?"

"Well, hey, Rodney," Kit said, sounding to herself like a seller of used cars trying to buddy up to a customer. "Why not, if you don't mind." Flash a smile, quick. "I'd like to see the rest of them." She shouldn't be getting sarcastic on this guy, she knew, but she'd spoken before she could stop herself. It didn't seem to matter. If he'd picked up on it, he wasn't showing it.

"My friends call me Rod," he said, and Kit didn't feel so smart-assed all of a sudden. She didn't like the look in his eyes.

"Okay then," she said. "Rod it is."

"Oh yeah," he said. "It sure is, baby." He stood up, at the edge of the booth, digging slowly in the pocket of his black denims for his keys, taking a little too long to find them and pull them out.

Kit picked up her Bud and drank, anything to allow her to avert her eyes from the spectacle Rod was evidently trying to create.

"Be right back," he said, and turned for the door.

When he was outside, Kit ventured a look at the bar. Luke cut his eyes over, quickly, and she could tell it was all he could do not to break out laughing. But he hadn't been able to see how Rod had looked at her. She ran a hand through her hair, surreptitiously giving him the finger as she did. He ducked his head. He'd deserved that, and they both knew it.

She scanned the bar again. It was unreal somehow. She felt as if she'd stumbled into an alternative universe—Sartre meets Homer Simpson. They were all, these afternoon barflies, simply ghosts. No one was really alive. She felt surrounded by violence; something very bad had happened in this place, probably more than once, and the energy from it was enveloping her, draining her of vitality. She wanted to scream. Maybe if she just cut loose, ran through the place screaming as loud as she could, maybe that would take it all out of her. She could leave it here, in this trash heap, leave all the fear and rage and grief right here in this hellhole, where it belonged, and go back out into world a changed human being. Halle-fuckin'-lujah! Praise the Lord and pass a tangerine.

An envelope slapped onto the table in front of her, jolting her back to herself. Rod slipped into the booth and took up his beer. She opened the envelope and slid out the prints. More cars. More rust. She perused the photos, nodding in what she hoped was an appreciative manner. Almost at the bottom of the stack, a print caught her attention. It was another car, an old Nova with only a gray primer coat for paint, up on jacks, parked in front of a veritable residential junkyard. The house behind it was tiny and square with peeling paint and a worn roof, broken windows boarded up from inside. But there in the background, next to the porch—though still in focus—was a guy on a motorcycle. No helmet, scraggy, shoulder-length light-colored hair. The photo was black-and-white, so she couldn't tell the exact shade. He was skinny, emaciated almost, wearing baggy jeans with ripped-out knees. A chain draped around from his back pocket to a front loop of his pants. He was staring at the car.

"Who's the guy?" she asked. His face seemed familiar. Had she seen him in the club?

Rod took the photo from her and stared.

"Nobody," he said quickly. "Just some guy who let me shoot his car. He said I could if he could be in the picture. Kinda weird."

Kit nodded. "Good shot," she said. "First one I've seen with a person in it."

"Yeah," Rod said. "I do girls all the time for work, you know. I don't put many people in my, uh, personal stuff."

"Your art."

"I guess."

"You should say it, Rod. It's art. Call it that."

"Yeah. Okay. My art."

"Give yourself permission, man. It's what you do."

He seemed heartened, gave her a sincere smile.

Kit took one more look at the photo, and scanned the remaining few beneath it. She was relieved that Rod seemed to have abandoned Romeo mode in favor of talking about his portfolio.

"So when's the show?" Kit asked.

"Huh?"

"You should have a show, you know. Get the stuff all mounted and hang it somewhere and invite people. See if you can sell something."

"I don't think I'm ready for that."

"The work is good," Kit said. "Get it all together, who knows?"

"Says you."

"I've been to a gallery or two. You could hold your own against most of what I've seen." It was true. The photos were good. Impressive, even.

"I don't know." Rod finished his beer, glanced at his watch. "Got time for another?"

"Better not," Kit said. "I have to head for work."

"Which is where?"

She didn't want to tell him, but she couldn't very well lie. He'd find out from Ned anyway.

"Blaze's," she said. "I dance."

"I figured," Rod said. "Ned gets a lot of his girls there. You know Cheryl?"

"Sure," Kit said.

"Yeah," Rod said. "Everyone knows Cheryl. Next time you see her, tell her to hurry up and fall in love with me, will you?"

Kit laughed. "No problem." She took a swallow of beer and was thankful she didn't drink these days and slammed the bottle against the table as she stood up. "Oops," she said. "Thanks for the beer and all."

"Hey," Rod said.

She turned back to him.

"If you want to, like, get in touch, Ned's got my number."

"Thanks," Kit said. "And let me know if you decide to mount a show. I'd like to see it."

When she turned again, Rod grabbed her wrist. She yanked and spun around quickly, but he had a firm grip and held tight. Kit stepped toward him, slacking the taut line that was their joined arms.

"I'll tell you what I'd like to mount," Rod whispered.

It took everything she had not to slam his empty fucking head. He had her by one wrist. But her feet were free. She was standing on them. She saw it unfold in her mind, even as she stood there stock-still, staring at him, waiting. She could twist, step to the side, wheel on the ball of her left foot and knock the shit out of him with a short roundhouse to the temple. Cross the bastard's eyes. Luke was still at the bar, though she didn't dare chance looking over at him. She stood there, waiting. Giving Rod a chance to do the right thing and let her go.

Glass shattered.

At the bar.

Kit felt Rod's grip slacken, and she slipped her arm free, following Rod's eyes to where Luke stood staring down at jagged shards of brown glass and a spreading puddle of beer and foam on the worn linoleum floor next to where he'd been sitting.

"Shit!" Luke said loudly, not even looking in Kit's direction. He raised his hands apologetically to the bartender. "Sorry, man."

She took another step away from Rod. Out of reach now. He seemed not to notice, focused as he was on Luke.

"Can I get another?" Luke said, still loudly, but calmly.

The bartender tugged at his Fu Manchu and grudgingly set another bottle in front of Luke.

The last thing Kit heard before she made it through the front door was Luke saying to the bartender, "Toss me a towel, man. I got it covered."

SIXTEEN

She went home. Not to Leila's, but to her own apartment downtown. The place was even smaller than she remembered it. A studio, the living area bare but for bookcases along one wall and an oriental carpet, a Bokhara in shades of mauve and light brown that she'd picked up second-hand after she made her first sale as a real estate agent. Real estate. Tangible. She'd sold a few houses.

She closed the door and threw the deadbolt and walked to the middle of the carpet. Sat down, folding her legs into the lotus position. She'd thought for a while there, when she first moved into this place, that she might make a go of trying to live normally, whatever that was. Make some kind of home for herself, hold a job, stay clean and relatively sober and maintain her relationship with Rusty. She'd thought for a while about all that. Tried it. Found herself unable to connect with any of it, except for being with

Rusty. And then he'd gone and pulled his big marriage stunt and left the picture. Boredom moved in, big-time.

She could still feel Rod's grip on her wrist. The asshole. He'd assumed he could pull rank on her, his rank coming from his strength. Me-Tarzan syndrome. Fucker. His hand on her wrist, forcing her to stay while he said things she didn't want to hear. A small, grimy, stupid moment that left her where she was now. Sitting on the carpet, enraged. Trying to clear her mind of it, trying to let it go. She couldn't.

She stood up and moved to the bookcase, but found herself unable to focus on the titles. Plato was there, she knew. And Aristotle and Socrates. All that alleged wisdom, but in the end they didn't know why they were here either, or how to deal with it. Epictetus, he had a good attitude: *While we exist, death is not present, and when death is present, we no longer exist.* Existence and Death could not cohabit, not even in those old appliance boxes you saw wedged up beneath the overpasses out on the freeway, the homes of the homeless. But the philosopher's argument hadn't accounted for death *lurking.* Hiding in shadows, luring Jenny from her car.

And, now that Jenny was gone, dogging Kit. Hanging in the recesses of her mind. It would be fine, wouldn't it, if Death would simply get the job over and done with. Stop peeking at her from behind the curtains. But all she wanted anymore, if she really wanted anything, was to go down fighting. Fuck whimpering.

"And just what the hell is that about?"

She heard someone speak, then realized it had been her, saying what she'd wanted to say to Rod, sitting there in Panchito's with her wrist in his grip, refusing to let her leave when, goddammit, she wanted to leave.

He'd been counting on her to act civilized and capitulate to his superior physical strength—he did have a grip. But she could have broken it, she could have, she was about to—

Her cell phone jerked her out of the fantasy.

"He'll probably never know how close he came to getting the shit kicked out of him."

Luke's voice.

She heard him chuckle.

"Are you okay?" Serious now.

"I think so," she said.

"How's your place? Any visitors?"

"How'd you know I was here?"

"I told you I'd have your back, Kit. I got you covered."

"That's reassuring?" She made it a question. Pointedly.

"It should be."

Silence then as he waited for a reply. She didn't have one.

"We should talk."

"Tomorrow, okay?" She didn't know why. It just came out. "I need some time."

"You'll call?"

"I'll call." She flipped her cell shut.

She climbed the steps to the sleep loft, stared at her unmade bed, a futon on the platform. Next to it, open facedown on the floor, yet another self-help book about how to improve some aspect of her personality and change her life. She'd been trying to do some work on herself, trying to get it together somehow, get to a point where she could go through a day without bugging out, through a night without dreams of being hunted. She'd been thinking about giving up drinking.

At least that part, now, since Jenny's death, she'd got to. The beer had done nothing for her. Only reminded her that she needed to stay clean, stay sober. Stay on track and find the bastard who killed her sister.

She picked up the book, stared at the pages. She didn't have to read. She remembered, at least, the gist of it. As far as she'd gotten anyway. *There is only now. Only this instant. Time is a creation of the human mind. The past and the future are nothing but creations of the human mind. They do not exist in reality.* She stared. The rape no longer existed. Nor did the assault in the parking lot. They were the past, and the past was only in her mind. Jenny does not exist. Words danced on the page.

She put the book back as she found it, the way she had left it the day she got the call from her father.

She would have to come back here at some point, try to resume her life, leave Leila Jane to find another roommate. Or maybe not. It wasn't bad, living at Leila's. The air was good, much better than the carbon monoxide–laced fumes of downtown, and it was certainly peaceful in the countryside. She felt like she should take something with her, something of her former life back to Leila Jane's house. But she couldn't think of anything she needed, really. Her favorite coffee mug? Leila had plenty. Maybe a book or two? She couldn't focus enough to read these days.

In the end she took only a framed picture from childhood: she and Jenny, tanned and standing in swimsuits next to a pond. From one of the Ranger picnics. She thought she remembered Burt Simmons snapping the photo. His wife, Sugar, had made prints and framed them, one for Kit and one for Jenny, and given them to them when Kit graduated high school. Such a thoughtful woman, Sugar was, and married to a walking contradiction of a husband. Burt could be the kindest fellow you'd ever want to meet. And he could be a killer. He was her godfather, in the non-Mafia sense of the word. But she had a feeling he would gladly step into the other godfather role as well. She had thought about calling him, that awful night. But she knew he wouldn't keep the secret from Wade. And she would die, simply die, if her father found out she'd been stupid enough to let herself get raped.

She put the photo in her black Crumpler bag, the one that no longer had a gun in it. Luke had been right to take it from her. She had no business with it. She wondered what she would have done earlier, when Rod grabbed her like that, if she'd still had the thing in her bag. She wanted to think she was above that, but still, she couldn't help imagining the look on Rod's face. The twerp. To think, she'd called him an artist.

She locked her front door and headed for her car. She'd got a spot on the street, half a block down. She was almost there, key out, when a voice stopped her midstride on the sidewalk.

"Kit."

She turned, ready to bolt.

Luke caught up to her at her car, took her arm. She jerked loose, then caught herself and leaned back against the hot metal of the door. She stayed that way for a moment, feeling the heat burn into her, melting the tension out of her muscles. Then it got too hot, began to scorch her skin, even through her jeans and T. She stepped away from the Mustang, stood facing Luke.

"What is it?" he asked. "What the hell's the matter?"

She couldn't talk. She stared past him.

"What's wrong?" Luke started to reach for her again, seemed to think better of it.

"You startled me," she said.

"Sorry."

"It's okay," she said. "It doesn't take much these days."

"So?"

"So what?"

"So tell me. What'd you see? And who was that wigger you were with at Panchito's?"

She felt so tired. Achingly tired. Exhausted on every possible level. "I told you I'd call tomorrow."

"I'm sorry. But we should talk about it now. While it's fresh."

"I didn't see much," Kit said. "A photo of a girl. She looked about ten. And it wasn't from the school play."

"The guy?"

"He works with Ned. Rodney. He prefers to be called Rod."

"That's it?"

"Look," Kit said. "I went in. I posed for them. There were no minors there, anywhere. Like there would be. But there was that one photo. So you're probably on to something if you're looking for child porn. But I'm afraid that's all I saw. We didn't exactly bond."

Luke's face betrayed his disappointment.

"And now how are you going to keep those photos of me off the Internet?"

"I'll need a day or so."

"So should I tell my legions of friends to rush home and log on to www.kitstits.com?"

"Come on."

"No, you come on. You said you'd block the shit. Now how're you going to do it?" She should have asked before. But the fact was she'd probably have gone in anyway. She wanted Jenny's killer, even if she didn't have a clue what she would do once she found out. If she ever did.

"Just a little time, Kit. I'm moving as fast as I can on this. I'm going over to visit my dad tomorrow. In Blanco. Maybe there's something."

Blanco. Sleepy little Blanco, dusty and flat, right down at the tail end of the Devil's Backbone, where they'd found Jenny's body.

"I'm getting a copy of the report," he added. "Crime scene. The details."

"Your dad?"

"It was his jurisdiction." He sighed. "Where they found the body."

The body. What was left of Jenny.

"I want to see it," Kit said. "The well. I want to see it."

"Kit."

"No. I want to. I have to. And you owe me."

They stood silently for a while; tiny clouds rolled one after the other past the late afternoon sun, casting long shadows that skittered across the pavement. Kit felt frightened at the prospect of visiting the site. She didn't know why she wanted to go there. She just did, that was all.

"Are you okay?" Luke asked finally. "Where you headed?"

"Home," she said. "To Leila's."

She wondered if she should tell him about Dr. Wolfe, about the break-in and the guy following her doctor.

But she had a feeling things were not as airtight at the police department as Luke seemed to think. She would keep her own counsel, for now at least, until she knew who she could trust.

If anyone.

SEVENTEEN

K it followed Luke up two concrete steps, almost slipping on the sandy grit that coated them as she glanced at the woodburnt sign hanging from the eaves of the plain board and batten building. BLANCO COUNTY SHERIFF. TOWN OFFICES. U.S. POST OFFICE. It was very Old West. In the center of the square sat a three-story limestone lump of a building that had once functioned as the county courthouse. Court had long ago been adjourned to a modern brick air-conditioned and carpeted building in a neighboring town.

Inside, the air was lukewarm, but at least cooler than outdoors. An annoying rattle came from a single window unit struggling to cool the room. Luke nodded at the postmaster and made a left through the door that led to his dad's offices.

Norvil Saner was built like a tractor, stubby and muscular, with wavy gray hair. He stood next to his desk, just hanging up the phone. He saw Luke, brushed a gray curl off his forehead, and opened his arms to embrace his son. The two of them hugged, pounding each other affectionately on the back.

"Hey, boy." Norvil's tenor twang filled the room. He stepped back, gave Luke a quick once-over, his eyes the same pale blue as Luke's, softening. "I know," he said somberly, "I know." He patted Luke's shoulder, and Kit saw that his eyes were moist. "You hanging tough, son?"

Luke nodded and turned to introduce Kit. She extended a hand and felt Norvil's warm, fleshy palm against her own, and then he reached out suddenly and wrapped her in a hug. She felt her body go tense and tried to make herself relax, return the hug.

"I'm so sorry for your loss," said Norvil. The sincerity in his voice had a lightening effect on Kit, but at the same time she was deeply saddened. Norvil would have been Jenny's father-in-law. They should have met, not here, but at Jenny's wedding.

"And I apologize for not being at the funeral," Norvil added. "I just got back from California yesterday. The thing was supposed to be a training seminar slash convention, but I'm thinkin' maybe it was a damn weeklong beer bust. Still not sure." He turned to Luke. "I tried to get a flight. I'm sorry, son."

He sat back on the edge of his desk, looked again at Kit. "Terrible thing. Terrible, awful thing." His eyes went to his spit-shined black boots. "I am so, so sorry for you."

Kit thanked him, wishing he would stop with the condolences. She didn't want any more condolences.

"We'd like to see—" she started, and felt herself choke up. She swallowed hard and continued. "Where the body was found."

She saw Norvil glance at Luke and Luke nodded ever so slightly.

"And I was hoping for a copy of the evidence list," Luke said. "Along with any reports."

Norvil walked to the bank of beige metal cabinets that lined the back wall.

"I just wish to God we had a good suspect," he said. He pulled open a drawer, thumbed through, yanked out a file. He opened the folder, closed it, and looked behind it, as though he expected to find something hiding there. He dug in the cabinet again. Sighed. Frowned. He ran a hand through his hair, trying again to push the bothersome curl back.

"Looks like it's been borrowed," he said. He looked at a single sheet of paper in the file. "Says here it was given over to the care, custody, and control of the Texas Rangers." He snapped the folder shut and slipped it back into its slot in the drawer, looked at Kit. "Your father has it. That's who signed it out anyway."

"No copy?" Luke's eyebrows raised with his question.

"Musta come by while I was away. I'll have to ask my secretary. She's the one signed off on it." He picked up the phone and punched in some numbers.

"Becky," Norvil barked into the phone. "You let Wade Metcalf take the paperwork on his daughter's murder? When did he come by? And why isn't the original still in the file cabinet?"

He said a few mmm-hmms into the phone.

"All right then. When you comin' back from lunch?" A pause, and then, "See you in twenty. Mmm-bye-bye." He hung up and shrugged. "She said Wade came by Monday and requested the file, said the Rangers were handling the investigation, which comes as no surprise to any of us, I'm sure. Evidently he was in too big a hurry to wait for copies to be made and assured Becky that he would return it intact." Norvil sat on the edge of his desk, turned his palms out to Luke and Kit, and shrugged. "So," he said.

"Can you get it back?" Luke's voice held an edge.

"Frankly, this kind of thing hasn't happened," Norvil said. "Least not since I been sheriff. Always before, Becky would only give out copies. But hell, just ask him. I'm sure he'd be happy to let you see it."

"I'm not." Luke cleared his throat. "He's been acting kind of proprietary in this thing."

"The man lost his daughter," Norvil said softly. "I hate to think what I'd do." He sighed deeply. "Anyway, he'll get the job done. I've known Wade Metcalf for more years than I'd like to say. The man's as persistent as a mosquito."

Kit thought to say, "Yeah, he makes you want to slap him, all right," but she held her tongue.

"I just wonder whether the suspect will come in breathing," Luke said.

Kit saw the look that passed between father and son.

"I wouldn't want to be taking wagers on that," Norvil said.

"I don't want a lynching," Luke said. "I want whoever did this to spend the rest of his life in a cage. Death is too easy."

"I happen to agree with you, son. Life in prison's a hell of a lot more punishment than a few minutes of terror while you're walking down that hallway so's the government can give you the big fix." Norvil took a sheet of paper out of the fax machine on his desk. "I'll draw y'all a map," he said. "Out to the site."

His desk chair let out a squeaky metallic complaint as he eased into it. He finished and handed the paper to Luke.

"I'll call you as soon as I have the file back."

"Good to see you," Luke said. He flicked a finger against the map Norvil had drawn. It made a loud snap in the silence. "Thanks for your help."

Norvil nodded and looked at Kit, and she could tell he was about to offer more sympathy. She waved a hand at Norvil and turned to leave, exiting quickly.

⁂

She stood next to Luke. Around them the rolling landscape of the Texas Hill Country, the Blanco River pale as the sky in the afternoon sun, running shallow over a limestone bed. Scrub oaks and junipers stood deep green against the dry blond grasses leaning under a gentle afternoon breeze.

The top of the well was nothing more than a circular concrete slab. Luke took hold of an edge and eased the cover aside, straining with its weight.

A deep hole in the ground. Hand dug, it looked like. Inlaid stone. Dried up. Dark. Empty and smelling of earth.

He took Kit's hand, and the two of them stood there, staring.

There was no sign that anything terrible had happened here.

⁂

Luke drove with one hand resting on top of the steering wheel, with the ease of someone who'd spent many an hour behind one, probably driving the unmarked squad they were in now. Kit shifted in the seat and her heel bumped against something hard and metallic tucked beneath it, just above the floorboard. She leaned down to look and discovered a shotgun snapped into a rack mounted beneath the seat.

"Ithaca," Luke said. "Full of double-aught buck."

Kit nodded as if, of course, she knew—wasn't her family in law enforcement?—but she found it both comforting and discomfiting, having a firearm that close to her. She felt the now familiar emptiness coming over her. She wanted to do something to break the somber mood in the car. And she wanted to talk about Jenny, share her experiences of her sister with Luke, and hear his memories. But she couldn't go there. She couldn't bear to put her pain into words. It would be, somehow, completely inadequate.

"You get along with your dad," she said.

"Pretty well," Luke said. "He's always been there for me."

"My father, "she said, and then wasn't sure how to finish the sentence.

Luke glanced over at her.

"He pawned his ring," she said finally.

"That pinkie thing?"

"Said he couldn't bear to be reminded of my mother and of Jenny. It's like he just wants to shut the memory of them out of his life."

"We each have our own ways of coping," Luke said quietly.

"You're kind," Kit said.

"I like to think I am," Luke said. "To folks who deserve it."

"Who deserves it?"

"I guess everybody, unless they do something to show they don't. Mean people, you know."

"Maybe they need it the most."

"Maybe they do."

"Do you think I'm mean?"

Luke laughed gently. "I think you throw a hell of a punch," he said. "You can be mean when you have to be. Or when you think you do." He paused. "But no, I don't think you're mean. I think you're angry."

"My father is mean."

"Maybe he is."

"No. He is. He shouldn't have pawned that ring. That was mean. To me."

"Maybe he wasn't thinking of you."

"He's been mean to me for as long as I can remember."

"Maybe it was just selfish."

"I saw it. The other day."

Luke raised his eyebrows.

"In Luckenbach. The café there. Some cowboy was wearing it. Said his girlfriend gave it to him."

"You sure it was his?"

"My mom had it made for him. It's one of a kind."

"Why's it so important to you?"

"If he didn't want it anymore, he should have offered it to me. My mother gave it to him. It should be in the family."

"You're not just after the diamonds?"

Kit looked at him sharply, but he was smiling.

"They're too tiny to be worth anything."

"I know," Luke said. "I saw it that night at dinner."

"Oh." Kit didn't want to think about that night. About how she'd felt toward Luke that night.

"You want to go look for him?"

"The cowboy?"

"Yeah," Luke said. "Luckenbach is hardly Houston. What is it, population thirty-seven or something?"

It wasn't like she had pressing business back in Austin. And she wanted the ring. Or maybe she just wanted to see the look on Wade's face when she showed up wearing it.

"You've got the time?" she asked.

"I'll make the time," he said.

⊞

Luke held open the squeaky screen door of The Café for Kit as they entered. She looked quickly around the dining room. Not a cowboy hat in sight. Instead, a smattering of tourists, plump, T-shirt-and-baseball-cap-wearing boomers and their families. She caught a young man staring at her from a table near the back. He looked quickly away and moved a hand up near his ear, blocking her view of his face. But she'd seen him. And she knew him. From where? He was familiar. She just couldn't place him.

She found a table and took a seat. Luke followed her over. At the table next to them, a family: mom, dad, a brother teasing his little sister, playing keep-away with a paper napkin. Kit watched for a moment, gave a toss of her head in their direction.

"That could have been you and Jenny in a few years," she said. "You two, a couple of rug rats. You could have a beer belly and she could make lists of household repairs that needed doing, tack them on the fridge for you to ignore."

He laughed sadly. "We could always have dropped them off with Aunt Kit, gone off for a picnic out in the country somewhere while you amused your niece and nephew."

"You're all right, Luke." Kit felt good, sort of, to be kidding about things. "I'm glad Jenny had you in her life."

He looked at her, straight on, earnest and thoughtful. "I'm glad she was in mine. I miss her."

Kit saw his eyes watering up, and reached across the table to squeeze his hand.

"Thank you," she said. "For taking me there."

"I wasn't sure I should," he said. "But I'm glad we went." He took a breath and let it come out in a sigh. Looked around the café. "No sign of your cowboy?"

"No," Kit said, and then the guy at the back table turned slightly and she realized where she'd seen him.

"What the hell is Friedrich Nietzsche doing in Luckenbach, Texas?"

"Excuse me?" Luke leaned toward her, his head cocked to one side.

"A customer," Kit said. "From Blaze's."

Luke scanned the room.

"The guy back there, with all the freckles," Kit said.

Luke barely nodded, then turned to look at the chalkboard menu next to the front door. Kit found herself regretting that she'd brought up the subject of her job.

"I pointed him out," she said. "From those photos you showed me."

Now Luke seemed interested. He glanced over again.

"What'd you call him?"

"Nietzsche," Kit said. "Fred."

"Another nickname."

"You had to be there," Kit said. "But he's in all the time."

"Ever see him with Ned?"

"No," Kit said. "But I don't hang in the bar. I go in, dance my shift, get the hell out."

"Ever see him anyplace else, other than the club?"

"Not till just now."

"Maybe it's just coincidence," Luke said. "But I'll check him out." He looked again at Fred, and Kit had the feeling he was memorizing features.

"So." Kit sighed. "No cowboy."

"Know what you're having?"

Kit shrugged and pretended to concentrate on the menu. She wished she'd kept her recognition of Fred to herself. She had run into customers outside the club on a few occasions, but when she had, the customers had seemed sort of subtly thrilled to see her, giving her knowing looks and the smiles to go with them. One had even approached her and asked her out.

The waitress came. Luke ordered huevos rancheros and Kit said make it two.

Midway through the meal, Fred and his friend, who also looked like twenty-one going on sixteen, paid their check and left. Kit couldn't be sure, but it seemed like Fred was trying to keep his face averted.

When Fred was gone, Luke put down his fork and looked around the café.

"He was here for breakfast?"

Kit thought first Luke was talking about Fred, but then she realized he meant the cowboy.

"We could come back," he said. "Early tomorrow morning. Maybe stay over in Fredericksburg. That's close enough, rather than drive all the way back to Austin."

Kit wondered briefly if he was coming on to her, but saw from the way he was looking at her that he wasn't. And that he knew she was trying to figure if he was.

"I don't have to be in the office until four tomorrow," he said.

"That's so weird," she said.

"No, I'm on evenings," Luke said.

"Not that." She shifted in her chair, straightened, but couldn't shake the uneasiness she'd felt at seeing someone from work—a customer—outside the confines of Blaze's. He hadn't even acknowledged recognizing her. Maybe he really hadn't seen her. But he'd looked right at her, and then seemed to want to hide his face.

"—don't want to go home," Luke was saying. "I want to go somewhere and pretend that everything's okay. Give myself a break, you know? I think you could use one, too."

He was right about that.

"There's a couple of really sweet bed and breakfasts there. We could go, have dinner, tool around town or something."

"Sounds good," Kit said.

She wondered why she never thought that way. Thought about just giving herself a break. She didn't know when she'd started taking every single moment so seriously, as if it were a matter of life and death. As though each simple decision necessarily involved momentous consideration because who could tell what the consequences might be. Yet if a butterfly flapping its wings on a cotton boll in West Texas could really set off a chain of events that wound up causing an earthquake in China, how on earth could she decide where to have dinner, or with whom, or whether to go out to a movie with some guy she didn't really know that well. A simple nod of her head could set up a chain of events that meant she wound up crouched under a bush in the middle of the night, having been fucked against her will.

And now just look how easily she'd gone and got herself all knotted up inside. In a matter of seconds. The butterfly effect: one thing leading to another. Chaos theory. She took a slow, quiet breath. Chaos. Wasn't that just it. She let the breath out softly, controlling precisely the rate of exhalation.

Luke took her hand. "Are you okay?"

She nodded. "I just, you know. That place."

He gave a squeeze and let go.

"Kit," he said, "take it easy. It doesn't matter to me. I already told you, I knew you didn't belong there the first time I saw you dancing."

"Do you like it?"

"What? Blaze's?"

"Yes. Going there."

"Let me put it this way," he said, grinning, "it's not the worst assignment I've ever drawn." His eyes were playful. "But no, to answer your question, I didn't like it. I'm just not the kind of guy who's into that stuff. Some are. Some aren't."

"What are you into?"

"Keeping it real," he said.

He wheeled the car to a stop in a small parking lot in front of a single-story stone and wood structure that looked to have been, long ago, part of someone's ranch. Kit waited in the car, listening to the bubble and gurgle of water in a stone fountain in the center of the courtyard. The water looked especially pure and refreshing, surrounded as it was by the limestone building and dry, dusty ground.

Luke emerged carrying a key and drove them to the end of the long, low building. Their room was at the very end.

They entered into a living area. Stone floors, plaster walls, done in rustic western; a small kitchenette off to the right; next to it a large bathroom with a thick, rough-hewn oak door; and inside, a footed tub.

"The bedroom's yours," Luke said. "They told me the couch is made up for sleeping. Just have to fold it out."

Kit entered, saw a four-poster bed, its mattress high up off the floor. A down comforter, cream-colored with a tiny floral print. The room was peaceful. She lay across the bed. The mattress was perfect: firm and soft at the same time. She let her eyes close. Heard Luke running some water out in the kitchen. Heard him slip off his holster and set his automatic on the kitchen bar, redo his belt. He was the only one in the world who knew where she was right now. Nobody could even begin to find her. She lay there, feeling safe for the first time since she didn't know when.

The sound of Luke's voice brought her from sleep.

"Kit?" Gentle.

Caring? Maybe.

She opened her eyes and saw him standing in the doorway, one shoulder posted against the doorframe.

"Hey," she said, her voice husky with sleep.

"Hey," he said. "Feel like some dinner?"

She glanced at the window. From behind the curtains, the hint of dusk peeked in.

"I made a reservation," he said. "We can walk. It's just down the road a ways."

Antique shops and restaurants lined the street. They strolled, among tourists. As they approached a large, open-fronted market, Kit picked up the scent of chili. She glanced at Luke—he'd smelled it, too, and it smelled delicious.

Inside the market, narrow aisles cut through islands of tables laden with cheeses, olives, sauces, dips, almost like a giant brunch buffet. Large crockery bowls full of salsas and hot sauces sat before trays of tortilla chips. Kit took a chip and dipped it into a black bean salsa, savoring the tang of its cilantro finish.

"Food heaven," said Luke, popping a cracker coated with a garlic and pepper goat cheese into his mouth. Kit smiled and looked away, trying to deny to herself that she wanted just then to kiss him. She headed for the large cauldrons of chili simmering near the back of the place, took a spoon and a small cup for tasting.

Luke followed her, and after a single taste of the chili, picked up three muslin bags of chili fixings.

"Got to have some of this," he said.

Standing in line to pay for their purchases, Kit felt her cheeks flush with something like embarrassment, only she wasn't feeling embarrassed. She was wondering if this was what it was like to be married, to go to the grocery store with your mate and select food for the week: the twenty-first century equivalent of hunting and gathering. Luke seemed completely at ease, gazing around at shelf after shelf of foodstuffs, looking as though he were trying to re-call whether he'd forgotten anything on his list.

They strolled out of the store, ambled past antique

shops, an ice cream parlor, a few clothing stores with boots and western shirts displayed in the front windows. Kit wished she were a tourist, like practically everyone else walking on these sidewalks. A tourist, taking a break from her life's routine. There was something to be said for a change of scenery.

The Plateau Café was originally a saloon, back in the days when cowboys rode in on horseback, tied their mounts to the hitching post out front, and strode inside for an evening of honky-tonk. A huge buffalo head was mounted on the wall above a large open fireplace. In the heat of summer the logs were in place, but were decorated with sprays of dried wildflowers and herbs. A dark wooden bar ran halfway down the opposite side of the restaurant. Kit wondered how many men had stood there, drinking whiskey, six-shooters strapped to the hips, how many saloon girls had plied their trade, flitting about the bar in tightly laced, floor-length silk or satin dresses, like goldfinches or blue-birds in summer plumage.

Their table was next to the fireplace. Kit took the chair that put her back to it, not wanting to have to look at the dead buffalo head on the wall. It was massive. Its eyes, though glass, seemed to hold an expression of deep sadness.

Luke ordered a margarita, straight up, no salt, poured with Patron, please, and questioned Kit with his eyes. She ordered seltzer with lime.

"Picky about your margaritas?"

"Selective," Luke said. "That crap they make in the machines? Hangover-flavored slushees. Give me real lime juice and top-shelf tequila or I'm not interested."

"Blaze is like that," Kit said. Whatever. He'd said he

didn't care about where she worked. She was glad she didn't have to waltz around the issue. "She drinks only the finest."

"The difference between me and her being that she can probably afford it."

"No doubt." Kit smiled. "The lady has got her act together."

"Think she's on to me?" Luke asked.

"About what?"

"Being a cop."

"She's legal," Kit said. "She's not afraid of the cops. She's afraid of the Baptists."

The waiter came with their drinks, placed them carefully on the table and disappeared quickly.

"Anyway," Kit said, "she's too busy counting money."

"What's it like?" Luke laughed at himself. "Working there? People are always asking me, when they find out I'm one, always saying, 'But what's it like being a cop?' It gets annoying. Do they do that to you? When they find out you dance?"

"I don't volunteer information," Kit said. "I pretty much keep to myself."

"Before I knew you were Jenny's sister, I kind of thought I might somehow help you get out of there."

"So we had you pegged," Kit said. "A savior."

"No. I was just there working."

"Just doing your job?" She grinned at him.

"You somehow seemed like you had something going on." He ducked his head. "Your eyes. Maybe that's what gave you away. I wanted to help you get out of there."

"I'm only doing what all the others there are doing. Making really good money while I still have the body to do it, and trying to decide what the hell to do with my life."

Luke nodded, silently urging her to continue.

"It's so screwy," Kit said. "you grow up in this world of fucking sexual repression, like, hey, let's all be eunuchs for the Kingdom of God, we'll get our reward in the great hereafter. But do it quick and make more babies so we'll have another generation of consumers, so they can grow up and pay their tithes, pay their taxes. But whatever you do, *don't enjoy it.*"

"You've done some thinking about this?" Luke smiled.

"Philosophy major," Kit said. "Go figure." She laughed, glad to turn the discussion away from what she did for a living. "You read some of that stuff, like the antisex bullshit from the Catholic Church? Like, St. Augustine? Whew. I mean talk about specious reasoning. It blows my mind. Way back when? Women who died while pregnant could not be laid out in the church since their unborn child hadn't been baptized. Not until the fetus was cut out of the womb—do you believe this shit?—could the mother-to-be's body be buried in a consecrated cemetery. I mean, what kind of fucked-up message is that?"

"You think they were trying to send a message?"

"I think it was all about control. And small-minded bureaucrats—for lack of a better word—getting all wrapped up in rule making so they could exert that control. Jesus."

"Somehow I doubt he would have approved."

"That's for sure."

"You think he'd approve of, say, Blaze's?"

"What?"

"Jesus. What do you think his take would be?"

"WWJD?"

"Yeah. What would Jesus do?"

"Let's face it. As far as Jesus's teachings go, Christianity

256

has blown it big-time. I don't think Jesus would want any wars fought on his behalf."

"You're begging the question."

He was right. That was exactly what she was doing.

"So what's it like?" Luke looked her in the eye. "Dancing up there."

"I stay inside my own head and don't think about it all that much."

"Does your boyfriend mind?"

"No boyfriend," Kit said. "I'm not seeing anyone." She could have added *since Rusty*. For some reason she didn't want to.

"A loner."

"It's just worked out that way." She hesitated. "I was raped," she said, surprised that the words came out so easily.

Luke winced.

"In college. I don't do so well with relationships."

"Jenny never mentioned—"

"She didn't know," Kit said. "I kept it to myself."

"Why?"

"Shame maybe? Embarrassment that I could be so stupid as to let myself get into that situation?"

Luke took her hands and, instead of a surge of distrust and apprehension, Kit felt warmth. He held on, exploring her fingertips, as though he were looking for some kind of clue there. To what, Kit didn't know.

"I'm glad you told me," he said.

"As long as we're being honest," Kit said, "I think maybe it had something to do with taking the job at Blaze's. Like by doing that I could make sense of the rape. Understand it somehow."

"There's no understanding that." Luke shook his head no, just barely, very slowly. "There is no understanding that *at all*. Ever."

Kit left her hands in his, though she was trying not to admit to herself the attraction she felt. He was looking into her eyes, his own holding the sadness of their shared loss. Kit managed a smile and took her hands slowly away, picked up a menu. He left his there on the table for a moment, looking empty, then picked up his menu and leaned back in his chair. But he only glanced at the single page of entrées before placing it back on the table and leaning toward her again, resting his square jaw on his folded hands.

"How'd it happen?"

"Stupidity," she said. "Mine. First date. I knew him from a class, but not very well."

"How's that stupid? How could you know?"

"I just feel like I should have."

"But you didn't want to prosecute."

"I didn't want anyone to know."

"You should have had his ass arrested. Fucking scumbag."

Kit could feel his anger, hard as stone.

"When I hear about things like that," he said, "I just get—I don't know— Busting someone like that makes all the bullshit seem worth it."

"You don't like your job?"

"Every time I take the witness stand I'm reminded that I could be doing a hell of a lot better job than whatever half-wit prosecutor is questioning me. And we're on the same side."

"I thought about law school," Kit said. "I did a little grad work. Got bored."

"That's where I'm headed," Luke said. "At least that was what we thought."

"Or maybe I got derailed. Can't remember. You and Jenny?"

"We weren't either one of us gonna stay in law enforcement forever."

"I don't know," Kit said. "I can't even pretend to know."

"You'll get past it, Kit. We'll both get past it." Kit nodded. But it was only a concept.

Her eye caught a figure coming in the front door of the Plateau.

It couldn't be. But it was.

The cowboy. He had a pleasant-looking blonde with him. Kit looked again.

Luke glanced over his shoulder, following Kit's gaze, but she touched his arm.

"Don't," she said. "It's him. I think." Luke turned back to her, watching her face intently. Kit took another look. "Yeah," she said. "It's him."

"Aren't we lucky, "Luke said, but something about the way he said it gave Kit pause.

"Are we?" she asked.

"If he didn't show up here, we were going to check out two other places. I did some asking this afternoon about where the locals go for dinner."

"And what if he hadn't been a local?"

"From the way you described him to me, he didn't exactly sound like a damyankee turista. He sounded like a working cowboy, and it doesn't take a detective to see that's what that fella there is. You sure it's him?"

"I think so."

Luke summoned the waiter and placed their order, and then pointed to the cowboy and his girlfriend, now seated at a table across the room, sipping margaritas.

"Could you deliver another round of drinks to that table," Luke said, "and tell them it's on me?" The waiter glanced over, penciled something on his order pad and gave them a whatever shrug.

Kit and Luke were halfway through their steaks when Kit saw the waiter deliver a round of drinks to the cowboy, and the cowboy's puzzled look when the waiter pointed toward Luke and her.

Luke left his dinner, walked to the cowboy's table, pulled a chair from a nearby empty table and offered it to Kit before sliding one over for himself.

"Luke and Kit," Luke said warmly. "Don't mean to intrude—" He turned to Kit.

"It's about the other day," Kit said. Now the cowboy looked thoroughly confused, his tan face crinkled with puzzlement. "Over in Luckenbach," Kit added. "You were having breakfast. With another guy. I asked you about a ring you were wearing?" Still no sign that the fellow knew what she was talking about. "A diamond pinkie ring. I asked you about it." Kit glanced at his hands.

No ring.

He shrugged, moved his hands to his lap, beneath the table.

Kit stared at him, at his eyes. He looked back at her, waiting. She closed her eyes and tried to see the face from the other morning, and opened her eyes and she was looking at him. Or was she? She realized she was squinting at him, trying to match him to her memory, and she felt a sudden and awful embarrassment. This couple must think she was mad. Maybe she was. Thoughts crowded in, pushing and shoving like children at the window of an ice cream truck that had just braked to a halt, and Kit sat, still staring, and at the edge of her vision saw Luke looking at her, worry on his face, and why was he worried, why were they all looking at her, waiting for her to make sense of this mess when they all knew she couldn't, no one could, and the cowboy took his hands back out from under the table and Kit thought the ring would be on his finger this time.

But it wasn't.

His hands were tanned and rough from the work he did. His nails were clean and nicely trimmed. Kit glanced up at the buffalo head, the sad eyes. Back to the cowboy. She cleared her throat.

"It belonged to my father," she said. "He pawned it." She looked at the girlfriend, who looked quickly at her menu, seeming completely uninterested and slightly miffed at the intrusion, and why couldn't she just look at Kit? Was she afraid of seeing a crazy person sitting at the table? But crazy people never thought they were crazy; that was part of their illness. They thought they were perfectly sane. And so, Kit reasoned, I can't be crazy, because I'm really way more than halfway convinced right now—sitting here in this room built where the buffalo once roamed but now their slaughtered heads hang on the wall—I am almost completely convinced that I am in the process of losing my mind. This was him. This was the man she had talked to in the café. This was the man who had been wearing her father's pawned ring.

And who gave a fuck? He wanted to keep it? He wanted

to hide it? Let him. Fuck it. She didn't need it. Wade hadn't thought of her, hadn't thought to ask if she wanted it. Why make a big deal out of it? *Because it was your mother's gift to your father* came the answer.

She looked again at the buffalo head. Had it spoken to her?

She looked at Luke. He sat patiently. He didn't seem to have heard anything. How had he found this guy? How had Luke known to come here tonight? Was it, as he claimed, the result of not-quite-blind luck? Or did Luke know things? Luke probably knew all kinds of things that she didn't know. She leaned back, tried to reframe the table. Okay. *Okay.* She reached up and ran a hand through her hair. She was here. This was real. She leaned forward again, looked directly at the cowboy.

"I really want to buy it from you," Kit said. She spoke clearly and firmly. That much she could tell. "It's important to me," she added.

The cowboy gave her a long, appraising look before leaning back in his chair.

"Miss," he said, "I wish I could help you, but I don't have the first idea what in Sam Hill you're talking about." He looked from her to Luke and back again, as though the two of them were a couple of wackos. "I don't have any ring, Don't wear 'em, and I have to say that I don't believe I've ever laid eyes on you in my life."

The girlfriend pretended to be engrossed in the menu.

"I'm afraid I can't help you," the cowboy said. "I think you must be mixing me up with someone else."

Kit wanted to say she wasn't, and they both knew it, but held her tongue. Luke dug in his back pocket, pulled out a business card.

"If your memory comes back all the sudden, give me a call, why don't you?" The cowboy looked at the card; his eyes widened only slightly, and only for an instant. He tossed the card on the table as though chucking it into a trash basket.

"I already said I can't help you." He raised his glass to his lips and took a purposeful sip of margarita, giving Luke a hard eye over the rim of his glass. "But thanks for the drinks."

Outside the restaurant, Kit stood looking up and down the street. The evening was still quite warm, and though most of the shops had closed, there was a good deal of window-shopping going on.

"That was him," she said to Luke.

"You didn't seem sure for a moment there," Luke said. "I'll walk over and get the car. If he leaves, try to get a tag number."

Kit stood outside the café, watching couples stroll hand in hand under antique street lamps. She felt like the wall-flower at a junior high school dance. Every time someone exited the café, she looked to see if it was the cowboy. Her senses felt alive, almost vibratory, in a way they hadn't for ages. She was tuned in, not fearfully so, but keenly aware of the goings-on around her. Seeing people walk down the same sidewalk she was standing on, their reality an everyday one, or a vacation one, or a night-on-the-town one. And though occurring on those very same streets, her reality was twice different. Her reality was a hunt. But she was now the hunter, instead of the hunted.

She heard that little voice in her head, the one that was always second-guessing her, the mean one: *Yeah, right bigtime detective, trying to recover an ugly-assed ring so you can stick it to your old man. Go for it, sweetheart. See if you can make Daddy cry.*

Maybe that was what she really wanted. Maybe she was, beneath the self-righteousness that she so tried to guard against and truly despised in herself, nothing more than a bully. Maybe she wanted nothing more in life than to hurt the man who'd hurt her so many times before.

Luke's car eased to a stop at the curb and he leaned across the front seat to open the door for Kit. She got in and he pulled down the street, shot an expert U-turn, and drove back past the Plateau, backing into a parking space down the block where they'd have a view of the front door. They sat in silence, both of them looking at the front of the restaurant.

"So," Kit said finally.

"I'm sorry," Luke said.

Kit looked at him, puzzled.

"That there's no coffee. Isn't this the part where we're supposed to drink coffee so we don't fall asleep waiting for our suspect to emerge? Have pithy conversation about our personal lives and how fucked-up the entire world is?"

"Except that I'm not a cop."

"Fake it." He winked.

"I thought we were only trying to get my dad's ring back."

"We are," Luke said. "And we'll keep trying. But that guy's wrong in there. My card shook him up and I want to know why."

"It would shake most people up, to be in the middle of dinner and have a cop come sit down at their table and start asking questions. Don't you think?"

"Not like that. Not like he was."

"I'd probably bug right out." Thinking that she already had.

"Why? Got something to hide?"

"Doesn't everyone?" She wondered what Luke had to hide.

"It could be anything. Maybe he boosts cars. Maybe he steals construction materials. Maybe smaller stuff. We can be pretty sure he goes to pawnshops, right? He bought your dad's ring."

"Now it's you begging the question. Anyway, he said his girlfriend did."

"Maybe he lied. He's one wrong son of a bitch. I can feel it."

"And does the court recognize feelings as probable cause?"

Luke laughed. "That's why we're sitting here," he said. "Waiting to see where he goes."

"As long as I'm in this," she said, "I guess there's some stuff you should know." She had to trust. She had to trust in someone. Something.

She told him about Dr. Wolfe, about the threatening calls and the office break-ins, watching his face carefully for some kind of reaction, some kind of clue that he might have been involved. Not that she really believed anymore that he might have been, but this much she knew from growing up around Wade and from helping Jenny study for her academy exams: The most important thing was to keep a completely open mind; don't let your personal expectations or prejudices cause you to rule *anyone* out. Only an alibi could cross someone off the suspect list. Maybe Luke was trying to charm his way out of being a suspect. Dragging her around on a wild goose chase, hoping to bond with her to the point that she'd never think he could possibly be involved. He'd certainly been on her list early on. It was only his undercover story that had relieved her of suspecting him.

No. That wasn't true. It was him. It was who he was. It was the fact that she knew now, was certain, that he'd loved Jenny and would never do anything to harm her.

"And you don't have any idea who it might be?" Luke kept his eyes on the café.

"My dad seemed pretty focused on Rusty."

"He had a reason?"

"You know Jenny's roommate?"

"Leila."

"She told my dad what Rusty had said to her after we broke up."

"Which was?"

"That the way to really hurt someone was to take away something they loved."

"That would sure as hell put him on my list of suspects."

"My dad chased him off. Beat him up bad. Wasn't that a brilliant investigative technique?"

"Maybe he wasn't trying to get Rusty to cop out. Maybe it was for something else."

"For what?"

"Dating his daughter?"

Kit scoffed. "No way. My dad doesn't particularly give a shit about me. We're just kind of stuck with each other."

"Some of these guys, the ones who've been in it for a while, they never upgraded their software, you know? They're still running version 1.0 when the programmers have written all the way to version 10.3.3." He straightened in his seat suddenly and cranked the engine.

"There they are," he said. "Wonder if my card gave him indigestion."

"Maybe I should just let it go," Kit said. "It's not that big a deal. I mean, what am I going to do with it but stick it away in some drawer somewhere?"

They watched as the cowboy held the door of a tan metallic pickup for his girlfriend and then walked around the back to enter the driver's side. Kit grabbed a pen from her bag and copied down the license plate number.

"Look at that," Luke said. "They got a parking place right in front." He faced Kit. "It's up to you."

"I don't know," she said. "I mean, I do want it back. But that guy, maybe I'm mistaken. Maybe it wasn't him."

"He's got my card. If it was him and he has a change of heart."

"I really thought it was him. And then when he denied it . . ." She didn't want to finish the sentence. It led straight into too many doubts.

"Let's just follow him awhile, see where he goes," Luke said. He pulled out.

"You could phone your office, call in the plate number."

Luke shook his head no.

"I'll run it myself tomorrow. No need to have it on the shift log. Dispatchers are the biggest gossips in the world."

"I could try to find the pawnshop."

"Almost impossible. You gonna go visit every pawnshop

in the county? And even with that, the guys who run them aren't the most cooperative folks you've ever met."

"I should forget about it."

"You don't have to if you don't want to. I'll run the tag tomorrow. We'll find out who this fellow is and persuade him to sell you his ring."

"It's a lot of trouble. For you."

"Maybe I just want to help you out."

"Or maybe you want to give Wade Metcalf a bit of a hard time?"

"The man has tried to cut me out of everything. Like the case was his and his alone."

"He probably thinks it is."

"Well, it's not." Luke smiled tightly. "I wouldn't mind helping you surprise him. When he sees you wearing that ring? Kodak moment. And who knows? I may get a whole new case out of this, 'cause I'll tell you what."

"Tell me what," Kit said.

"I doubt seriously if that cowboy is your basic law-abiding citizen."

Kit sat back and rested her head against the seat. She had a feeling that Luke wasn't telling her the whole story. But she was glad that she was with him, instead of facing another lonely night at Leila Jane's.

Luke kept his distance from the truck ahead of them as they cruised along the dark Hill Country highway, a two-lane blacktop. The afternoon nap and the meal conspired against Kit's eyelids. She felt them growing heavy against her will. She let them close, content to ride in silence.

"There he goes," Luke said.

Kit opened her eyes in time to see the truck's taillights

turning onto a farm-to-market road. Luke continued on the highway.

"Headed for Luckenbach," Luke said. "I'll run the tag tomorrow."

"Sounds good," Kit said, and let her eyes close again. It felt good just to sit there in the car, letting her eyes rest. They'd been irritated from all the crying she'd been doing, and she hadn't even realized it until now.

They'd been driving for a while, long enough that they should have been nearing Fredericksburg. Kit opened her eyes, expecting to see lights from the town. No sign of settlement anywhere. They were out in the countryside. She had a picture, suddenly, of a butterfly sitting on a cotton boll, flapping its wings.

Ever so slowly.

She didn't say anything. She couldn't name her fear, but it was there inside her, a growing apprehension surfacing from within, manifesting itself like a fever. Luke glanced over at her and returned his attention to the road.

A few miles later, he turned off the highway onto a ranch road.

"Where are we going?" Kit said.

"Just down the road a ways," Luke said. "It's early yet."

"I want to know where we're going."

"It's a secret." He gave her a quick smile and drove on in silence.

Kit's heart thudded against her breastbone, beating out warnings. She heard a voice in her head saying *Stay calm, just stay calm. You have to stay calm so you can think.*

You have to be able to think. Clearly. Or you won't stand a chance.

Luke wheeled to a sudden stop at the edge of the road and killed the ignition. He got out and walked around to her door, opened it. The landscape glowed under the soft light of a perfect half-moon. Scrubby pines and short, splayed cedar trees rose from pale soil dotted with clumps of grass.

Kit sat, frozen in place, her skin prickling with fear.

"Come on," he said. Kit heard impatience in his voice. She sat.

"Why are we here?" she asked.

"That's the big question, isn't it?" Luke laughed. "Come on." He offered his hand.

Better she should be on her feet. The car offered no safety, not out here. She flashed on the shotgun in its rack beneath her seat. She'd never be able to get to it, not with Luke so close.

She could run, but probably he'd catch her. All she knew was that she would fight. She would fight until one of them was unable to fight anymore. Her thoughts intertwined with her fear, got tangled up in it, knotted like two fishing lines snarled in deep water. How had this happened? She was stupid. That was all. Stupid.

Of course it had been Luke. Who else? And of course she could be that stupid. She'd been stupid that night. She'd been stupid all her life. Luke had killed Jenny and now he would kill her. The skills of the psychopath: Charm the victim. Lure the victim. Smile and say murder. Shit. Shit. Shit. Famous last words: Oh shit. Someone was screaming in her head, from beneath the cacophony of an orchestra tuning up, screaming and screaming.

And then, silence.

could drive, we'd come out here on our own. Since high school I guess it's been." He sighed. "After I went off to college, I got too busy to take an afternoon off for the swimming hole."

The owl hooted again. From somewhere way out on the highway, the tires of an eighteen-wheeler sang, whining high and sad-sounding as they rolled across concrete, friction the name of their tune.

The sounds of the truck faded into the distance, and there was stillness again.

Kit shifted on the hard ground. She heard the solitary plop of a frog breaking the shining surface of the still pond as it hopped into the water.

"I didn't know where we were going," she said. "And I didn't know why."

Luke turned to face her, his eyes gray in the moonlight.

"Oh my God," he said softly. "I'm sorry. I didn't mean to— I'm sorry."

"It happened at a lake," she said. "And now? After Jenny?" She couldn't talk. She couldn't tell him what she'd been thinking he was about to do.

He moved close to her and wrapped an arm around her shoulder, brushed her hair away from her eyes.

"I didn't mean to frighten you," he said.

They sat like that, with his arm around her, listening to the silence of the night. Sometimes they talked, of Jenny, of Wade, of the investigation. Sometimes they were quiet, simply absorbing the peacefulness of the warm night air. Minutes evaporated. His arm felt good on her shoulders, strong and comforting. Protecting her. She was safe. Hours disappeared.

She was in his arms and safe. She let her head fall gently against his shoulder, thinking to steal a moment of rest. He let his hand go to her waist, caressing her back as he did. He pulled her closer and she leaned into him, slipped her arms around his waist and let the scent of him pull her closer still. He moaned, only a whisper, but it said he wanted her and the ache inside her blossomed into pain. His hands were on her, and she pressed her lips against his neck and tasted the salt on his skin. He leaned to her, and they were kissing then, and kissing, his lips against hers and his strong arms pulling her closer until there was no closer and they grabbed frantically at clothes, tossing them aside, and then it was skin against skin, delirious touch, and Kit felt the grass soft beneath her as Luke raised himself, still kissing her. He held his body above her, pressed the tip of himself against her, against the ache, his eyes on hers, the connection of want, and Kit reached to guide him inside and they fucked urgently, desperately, until their cries went out into the night.

<hr>

He opened the door to their cottage and held it while Kit entered. She stepped inside and stood there.

Luke went to the kitchen, took a couple of glasses from the cabinet, and opened a bottle of wine. He poured one, turned to look at her.

"Wine?" he asked.

"No thanks." What had they done?

"A glass of water?"

"No," she said. "Nothing."

Kit stood, staring at an intricately woven Indian blanket hanging on the wall above the unlit woodstove.

Luke slugged back a swallow of wine and walked to the living room to open a window, though the air-conditioning was on. The sound of locusts, humming lazily in the trees outside, floated in. He went to the couch and sat, taking another large swallow of wine, sighing as he put the glass on the coffee table. He glanced over at her and looked away quickly.

Kit moved toward the bedroom. She stood a moment, wanting to tell him that he didn't have to sleep on the couch. What had they done? She wanted to say the words, and knew that he wanted her to.

"Good night," she said quietly.

He stood and began folding out the couch.

"Good night, Kit," he said.

She walked to the bedroom, knowing he was watching her, knowing he wanted to come with her. She thought about those times at the club, when Luke had sat watching her dance. She could do that now. She could turn around and walk back over, put on some music and take up a place in front of him. He could lie on the couch and watch her dance. For real. For him.

She could feel his eyes on her.

She played the scene out in her head, and in it Luke stopped her. He stood and came to her in the middle of the dance. Took her hands, shaking his head no, gently. And he said, "That's not how I want it." It was as if the more jaded she got, the more hardened she was by life, the more romantic and unrealistic, and sometimes horrifying, her fantasies became.

She turned at the door and gave him a nervous smile, and a look that said they were doing the right thing. They were doing the right thing after doing the wrong thing. Kit felt sickened by what had happened, disgusted with herself. She'd done some things, to be sure, but never anything approaching the wrong she'd done tonight.

She undressed and slipped between the sheets. The mean little voice in her head sat in the middle of her skull, all smug and vicious, calling her a fool. Again and again, *you fool, you fool, you fool.*

She had a craving suddenly for hard-boiled eggs. Or better, deviled eggs. Like Sugar Simmons used to make. The kind that set your tongue on fire and cooled it off all in the same moment. *You fool, you fool, you fool.* What have you done?

He was out there in the living room, lying on the couch. As though they were a married couple who'd had a huge fight that ended in cold silence and separate beds.

Wade was right. She was a Class A Fuckup.

EIGHTEEN

K it pulled into the driveway to see Leila Jane's pearl
white GMC pickup truck in its usual spot, backed in
with the tailgate only a few yards from the front porch
of the bungalow. Leila stood in the truck bed, holding one
of her boots poised to throw, peering at the bushes next to
the porch. She was still in her uniform trousers, but had removed her top, revealing a pink wife-beater undershirt.

Kit parked and opened her door.

"No!" Leila Jane's voice was a yell-whisper. "There's a
rattler."

Kit froze. The mere mention of snake sent a shiver
through her, as though one of the creatures had got up inside her spine through her tailbone and was trying to crawl
into her brain. She scanned the area, didn't see any snake.
She got out, slipped carefully around the front of her car,
and climbed up into the truck bed next to Leila.

"Where?" Kit still couldn't see the snake.

"By the porch," Leila replied. "I threw my other boot at it and now it's up there in the bushes somewhere."

"You didn't shoot it?"

"My gun's inside. I just came out, 'cause I left my newspaper in the truck. Little fucker scared the bejesus outta me. I jumped clean from the front porch into the back of the truck here." Leila waved her boot in the air. "Anyway, all it was doing was trying to eat a few June bugs. I'd rather just scare it off." She hurled her boot at the bushes, eyeing them suspiciously. No sign of movement.

"I think it's gone," she said.

"I'll go." Kit slipped down from the back of the truck and walked toward the porch, looking for movement on the ground beneath the bushes, stomping more than walking, hoping that if the snake was still there, her forceful footsteps would send it fleeing.

Leila Jane stared after her, and when Kit reached the front door and pulled open the screen, Leila jumped down from the truck and skipped quickly across the porch, practically pushing Kit through the door.

Kit went slowly upstairs, dropped her bag on the bed. Her sister's bed. She would not think about last night. She could either do a number on herself or she could press on. She turned to go back downstairs. She hadn't realized how wrung-out she was, but now fatigue settled on her, heavy and dense, like one of those lead aprons used for protection during the taking of X-rays. She would make a cup of tea. Come back up and get in bed. Try to sleep the day away.

When she got back downstairs, Leila was standing at the sink behind the bar that separated the kitchen from the living area, gnawing the last of the flesh from a curved white bone, her fingers barbecue-sauce red. Kit walked over and leaned on the faux granite countertop, eyeing the foil carry-out pan. Leila smacked her lips and tossed the bone into the trash basket under the sink, sucked the sauce from her fingers, and picked out another rib.

Kit stared at the takeout pan.

"What?" Leila said.

"Ribs," Kit said. "Food of the gods."

"Huh?"

"Breakfast?" Kit asked.

Leila nodded yes, her green eyes ringed by dark circles. "Deep nights are killing me. Want some? They're from the Salt Lick," she said.

Kit shook her head no. Make some tea. Put water in the kettle and make some tea. She didn't move.

Leila chewed contentedly, swallowed, letting out a tiny moan of happiness. "Why didn't you answer your cell?" She took another bite. "I tried to call."

"It never rang," Kit said. "I must've been in a no service zone."

"Where?"

"Out around Blanco." Kit watched Leila pick at a hangnail. "I went to the place. The well."

"Oh." Leila stopped eating, let the rib fall back into the foil container. "And?"

"I don't know," Kit said.

"What'd it look like?" Leila's tone suggested she didn't want to actually hear the answer.

"Like nothing," Kit said. "Like it was supposed to, I guess."

"What did you expect it to look like?" Leila asked quietly. She picked up her rib and went back to eating, but without much gusto.

"I don't know," Kit said. "I'm not sure what I was expecting."

"You should have told me. I'd have gone with you."

"I was okay."

"Someone called for you," Leila said. "Some guy. Caller ID said Private Caller. Would that be your, ah, shrink?"

"No, that wouldn't. My shrink is a woman."

Kit saw Leila watching her closely.

"And Blaze called, too. And *she* . . . said it was urgent."

Kit made an oh-please face.

"I feel like an answering service. Sure you don't want one?" Leila offered a rib.

"No thanks," Kit said. "What guy?"

"Some guy," Leila said testily. "Not exactly forthcoming. Said he'd call back."

Kit picked up the phone and dialed Dr. Wolfe, wishing Leila wouldn't stare at her. Leila sucked the last of the sauce from the rib she was working on.

When Dr. Wolfe's voicemail came on the line, Kit felt relief. She didn't really want to talk to the doctor right now. She didn't want to talk to anyone. But she felt obligated to call. She left her name and number.

Leila rinsed her hands and blotted them dry on a dish towel and let out a yawn.

"I'm going upstairs to get some sleep," she said. "God, I'll be happy to get off this godforsaken shift."

"Good night," Kit said.

"Good morning," said Leila.

Kit watched Leila trail up the stairs. She sat staring at the phone. Dr. Wolfe would call back, and then what? What to tell her? *I fucked my dead sister's fiancé?* Nice work. She waited until she heard Leila's bedroom door shut before going upstairs and falling into bed herself.

She lay there staring at the ceiling, and when sleep finally came, she drifted into it with relief.

Sunlight woke her, streaming in through a slit in the curtains. It couldn't even be midday yet. What had she slept, a couple of hours? She rolled onto her side, checked the clock. Not even two.

She went quietly downstairs to the kitchen, poured a glass of iced tea. The tiny red light on the answering machine was off, indicating no new messages. That wasn't like Dr. Wolfe. She was usually prompt about returning calls, and with the way they'd left things, Kit felt certain that if the doctor had gotten her message, she would have called back by now.

When Kit dialed, Dr. Wolfe's phone went immediately to voicemail. She left a second message and hung up, feeling deeply uneasy.

She sat at the kitchen bar and stared out the window. Pastures rolled toward the horizon. The horses were nowhere to be seen. Probably hiding somewhere in the shade, under the oak trees at the far side of the field.

Sometime later Leila Jane wandered downstairs, stretching and yawning. She looked at Kit's empty glass and poured herself a glass of tea, offering the pitcher to Kit, who shook it off.

"What's going on?" Leila asked. "You don't look so great."

"I'm worried," Kit said. "My doctor hasn't returned my call."

"You worried about her, or about you?"

"Can you, like, check at the department or something? See if anything's been reported?"

Leila crunched down on the ice cube in her mouth and let a chunk slip back into her glass.

"No problem," she said. "What's her name?"

"Emily Wolfe," Kit said.

"Hand me the phone." Leila hit the speed dial. She asked for dispatch and gave them the name and stood waiting, munching noisily on ice cubes. Kit stared at the bamboo wallpaper. It made the room seem crowded.

"Oh," she heard Leila say, concern in her tone. "What time? Uh-huh. And where is she now?"

Kit stood, wanting to grab the phone from Leila and hear for herself. Leila gave her a look as she was thanking the dispatcher and hanging up the phone.

"Well?" Kit said, impatient.

Leila was scribbling something on the notepad next to the phone.

"You were right to be concerned," she said, and stood there looking at Kit like she didn't want to say anything more.

"Tell me, for God's sake. Is she all right?"

"She's in the hospital. St. Martin's. She was mugged. Last night. Somewhere downtown."

"Is she—"

"She has a broken arm. And they're keeping her for observation, concerned about internal injuries."

Kit's knees went weak, and she eased onto the bar stool. "I don't believe this."

"Evidently she's been having some problems? There've been threats? Did you know about this, Kit? Why didn't you tell me? I might've been able to help."

"It wasn't like that," Kit said. "She made reports to the cops. It wasn't my business. It wasn't like I was trying to hide anything from you."

"She's in room 4768." Leila shrugged, clearly hurt. "I think I'll resume my nap. Until I have to go *on duty* tonight."

Kit watched her round the corner to the stairs, listened as Leila thumped heavily up, seeming to pound her anger into each step she took. The bedroom door closed with conviction.

The phone startled Kit. She picked it up and was saying hello when she realized she hadn't checked the caller ID.

"Kit!"

That voice. Shit. Blaze didn't wait for a reply before launching into a forceful plea for Kit to come to work as soon as she could get there. It was urgent. Absolutely urgent.

Kit hung up the phone, cursing herself for saying yes. She didn't know why she had. But Blaze would have to wait until Kit could get there. She had something to do.

Kit walked down the wide, shining corridor, pale green floor tiles gleaming with fresh wax. The hospital was less than a year old, and still had that new look to it, but already there was the sour hospital hallway smell, the stench of necrosis and illness steeped in antiseptic. She checked room numbers as she walked; slowed as she approached 4768. She eased up to the doorway, which was open wide. Tinny television sounds came from inside, a silky voice promising brighter colors, whiter whites.

She peered into the room. An old man lay semiupright in the far bed, which had been adjusted to recliner position. He stared at the ceiling-mounted television, an oxygen tube trailing from his nose to the wall. He didn't seem to notice Kit.

She stepped back into the hallway, checked the room number. She had it right. She looked down the hall, and that's when she saw the cop sitting outside the door of a room on the right, near the stairwell. He was reading a magazine.

He looked up as she approached, sized her up, and didn't seem alarmed. He watched as she walked past. She tried to seem casual as she glanced into the room, and then continued down the hallway as if that hadn't been her destination. She couldn't go in. She couldn't face Dr. Wolfe.

She was almost to the stairwell when she heard the cop call after her.

"Miss!"

His voice filled her with panic. She pushed through the heavy beige doors and ran down the stairs, gripping the railing and practically flinging herself down the steps. She reached ground level, breathing hard, her heart pounding, and was out of the stairwell and down the hall and out the front doors of the hospital. She loped down the wide concrete path toward the parking lot, slowed to a quick walk when she noticed people staring at her.

No one was following, that she could see anyway. She wound through the lot, taking a circuitous route to her car. Checked again to see if anyone was pursuing her.

Nothing.

She didn't know why she was fleeing.

NINETEEN

The music rattled her bones, thumped clean into her lungs, vibrating her ribs. Louder than ever, the music, or maybe it was fear thumping through her. It felt like it was seeping into her skin, flooding in with the heavy bass and Motown-style vocals. She looked at the windows, at the faces behind them. Laughed, caught herself, choked it back. What safer place to be than onstage in front of all these witnesses.

No one could touch her here.

Kit recognized the music, couldn't stand the band, the funky, hip-hoppy, fusion-happy Venjantz, laying down lyrics from somewhere beneath the beat, coming at her through a tunnel, *let's get the war on, let's get some hash, let's rock Iraq now, let's get some cash.* Who was writing this garbage? Squealing now, voices pitched Mickey Mouse high, *'cause we Ah-mer-eee-kah, the bootiful, so get your booty full, go get your booty now, don't give a hooty now, go get your bling, and sing Ah-mer-eee-kah, we kickin' ass . . .*

She stomped around the stage: strut, march, prance, anything. Anything at all. Whatever, just keep moving. Arms akimbo, flap them like wings, go on now, go right on. Aren't you the one who used to dream of flying?

A dancer climbed through the hole in the stage and Kit was outta there and down the ladder and into the dressing room. And there was Blaze.

Blaze, doing a dressage thing today, in jodhpurs and a tailored cream silk blouse, sporting riding boots of faultless brown leather, stood hip-cocked in the center of the room. Kit half expected her to produce a riding crop and slap it smartly against her boot.

Instead, Blaze greeted her with a red-lipsticked smile, folded her cell and tossed it onto the couch. From upstairs Kit heard creamed-coffee female voices soothing *back to life, back to reality . . .* Whatever. Just thank God the Venjantz tune was over.

"Thank you, thank you, thank you," Blaze said. "For coming in on such short notice." She ran a hand through her curls. "Took you awhile to get here?"

"I had an errand," Kit said. "Couldn't wait."

"And if you see Cheryl before I do? Tell her she's fired."

"I don't think so," Kit said.

"She's pushed me too hard," Blaze said. "I don't have time for any more of her bullshit. Just, if you see her, tell her there's no need to come back."

Kit felt something harden inside her, her body going defensive against Blaze's tone. God knew Blaze was a gentle soul by precisely nobody's standards, but something in her voice today sounded particularly unforgiving.

"She should hear it from you."

"Whatever fries your eel," Blaze said.

"I'll ask her to call."

"Please don't. If you even ever see her again. I have no need to talk to the little bitch." She turned at the door and winked at Kit, her perfect white teeth bared in a smile, her red hair flaring about her shoulders. "I *do* appreciate your coming in on such short notice."

"Sure," Kit said. She could walk out. Right now. Totally piss Blaze off. She thought of Dr. Wolfe, lying in a hospital bed. Better to stay here. Better to stay in public and around people until she heard from Luke. There it was again: What had she done?

Forget it. Just forget it. It happened, it's over, you can't change it, forget it. It won't ever happen again. Forget it.

Kit's cell phone rang from inside her locker. Maybe it was Luke. Maybe maybe maybe. She turned to get it, managed to dig it out and answer before it went to voicemail.

As Kit answered her phone, Blaze disappeared, closing the door softly behind her.

"I'm looking for Detective Saner," a voice said. Kit was about to tell whoever-it-was to bend over and look up his butt, and then realized she should chill out fast. Disavow any knowledge.

"Who?"

"Luke Saner."

"You've got the wrong—" The voice. It didn't make sense. But she was sure.

"Daddy?"

"Who's speaking?"

"Dad?"

"Kit?"

"Why would you call my number looking for Luke?"

"I must've dialed wrong," he drawled. "You wouldn't happen to know where he is, would you?"

"You don't even recognize when you dial my number?" Kit felt her face go hot with anger. "Oh, of course not. You hardly ever dial it, do you. I'd forgotten."

"Kit."

She should tell him she needed help. She should tell him everything. Now.

She couldn't.

"Kit."

"What."

"I need to reach him."

"Why?"

"I'm sorry, darlin'. I can't talk about it. Police business."

"Then dial fucking 911."

She heard her father take a deep breath, let it out with a low, almost whistling sound.

"Do you have his cell number?"

"I don't."

"I'll try to catch him at the office, then."

"It's something about Jenny."

Silence.

"I have a right to know."

"I need to talk to him. Do you know if he's working to-day?"

"No idea."

"All right then." Silence. "Kit?"

Tell him you need help.

"Sweetie. I can't go into it right now. I'll explain it all later."

She heard the click of her father disconnecting. Great. Yeah, she knew how it worked. If she'd grown up and become a cop like he'd wanted her to, like Jenny had, he would be telling her everything right now. But she had let him down; she had always let him down in everything she did. Asshole of the Century. She'd find out from Luke. Luke would call her soon and she would find out from him and he would help her. That was all.

She went to her locker to take out her snack. A banana. Two bananas. A blueberry smoothie. Things that went down easily and made their way into her system without causing trouble. At least she was feeling stronger now, her body responding to the lack of invasion by booze. She looked at the food. She couldn't eat.

⌗

If she'd had a watch, she would surely be eyeing it, counting down the seconds until her—no, Cheryl's—shift was done. Late afternoon and it was slow, maybe half the booths occupied. The music was slow, too, too slow for Kit's liking, but at least there were customers here. There would be witnesses if anyone tried for her. She lolled about the stage, letting her hips do most of the work, not even bothering to look at the windows.

But then something caught her eye, in booth seven. A hat. A black Stetson. Pulled low, and there was a mustache, that much she could see. She started to move toward the window, picking up the pace of her dance, trying not to appear interested.

As Kit approached, he tilted his head down, hiding his features behind the broad brim of the hat. He ducked around, slipped off the stool.

She saw the flash of a vertical line of light illuminate his bulky figure almost in silhouette before he slipped out the door.

She shivered, turned it into a shimmy for the benefit of those watching. Blaze would throw a hissy fit if she saw Kit bugging out onstage. So what. But she kept dancing, kept moving, trying to match the figure she'd just seen in booth seven with the one that had attacked her in the parking lot. He was big enough, that was certain. That was the only certainty. She hadn't seen enough. But whoever this guy was, he hadn't wanted her to get a good look at him. Or maybe he had.

She tried to stay with the music and tried to remember what she'd seen that night, and at the same time she didn't want to remember what she'd seen that night. Maybe—no, probably—the guy in the Stetson was just another customer, only here to ogle the dancers. Jenny was dead. Dr. Wolfe was in the hospital, a cop guarding her door. Luke was nowhere to be found.

She tried to stay with the music.

She sat in the bar, pretending to be calm and pretending to sip at a cranberry spritzer, waiting for Ezra to walk her to her car. Humiliating, not to be able to cross the lot to her Mustang without company, but the other women were all onstage dancing and she was not going out there alone. Not now.

Cheryl wasn't the only employee who'd decided to skip work today. It was really tight. Ezra was pulling triple duty:

taking money at the door, bouncing, and bar-backing. But the guy in the Stetson had spooked Kit; she would wait for Ezra, even though there was still plenty of daylight.

She took a sip of her spritzer. The drink, though she'd asked Ezra to water down the cranberry juice thoroughly, was still way too sweet. She slid it away, and just as she did, someone slipped onto the cowhide-covered bar stool next to her. It wasn't like the bar was crowded, either.

"I like the way you dance," a voice said. A very deep voice. Radio announcer deep. Resonant. A voice that was easy on the ear.

"The athleticism," he said. "I guess that's what gets me."

Kit looked over and nodded her thanks.

And almost fell off her barstool.

Friedrich Nietzsche extended a hand.

"Bryan," he said. Kit saw for the first time that he had dark brown eyes, very dark brown. His wavy hair was almost black, natural reddish highlights.

Kit reached for the drink she'd pushed away. Forced herself to take a sip. She didn't want it, but she wanted something to do. Her lip curled into a sneer as she forced down the sweetness. Worse than Budweiser. Way worse. Her tongue felt coated.

"Ugh," she said. "Can't deal with all that sweetness."

Bryan took her glass, held it up to the light shimmering from above the bar. He shook his head, set the glass back down in front of Kit.

"Fucking high-fructose corn syrup," he said, his tone that of a doctor diagnosing an illness that, while not serious, was nonetheless a nuisance that would have to be dealt with.

"Stuff's in everything. Barbecue sauce, spaghetti sauce, salad dressing. Everything."

She should get up and walk away. Who was this guy and why the hell was he talking to her? She should get up. She wasn't going anywhere without Ezra. Maintain. Talk to him as if everything is just wonderful. Gosh.

"You're with the food police?" Kit asked.

"Doesn't quench thirst, loaded with calories, tastes like crap. Hey! I'd like some of *that*! Put it in *everything*, please."

Kit stared at her drink.

"And graceful, too," Bryan said. "You're very graceful on stage."

"Thank you."

"Would you have dinner with me?"

Kit stared at her drink some more. She was frozen in place. Unable, even if she'd known what to say, to say anything. *Dinner and a movie, maybe?*

Then she heard her voice and felt her tongue pressed against the roof of her mouth and felt it drop and then her lips formed an O, maybe even as flawless as the O that Cheryl's lips were capable of forming. And the word that came out was perfect in its simplicity: "No."

No room for confusion, no need for definition or explanation or obligation or remorse.

She wondered if Luke would be upset that she'd declined the offer. Told herself she didn't care.

"Because it's against policy, right? You one of the straight ones?"

Kit looked again at the young man sitting next to her. And then past him as a cop entered the bar.

She looked again.

It was Leila, in uniform, her mouth drawn in a grim line.

Bryan was saying something but Kit couldn't hear it; she watched Leila approach.

"—dinner," Bryan said, his voice pleading. "I really think you're—"

Leila halted, standing behind them at the bar. Bryan turned; his face went ashen.

"You," Leila said. "Get lost."

Bryan started to say something, thought better of it. Glared at her.

"Yeah, whatever," he said finally. He spun off the stool with a flourish and made for the exit.

"You knew her," Leila said. "You must've known her."

"Who?"

"Cheryl."

"Cheryl who?"

"This woman Cheryl Akins." Leila's tone was all business.

"What about her?"

"She worked here. Cheryl Akins. White female, twenty-six years old. Did you know her?"

"Did I know her?" Kit heard Leila's words, but they weren't meaning anything.

And then they did: You *knew* her. The room went blue; the air between Kit and Leila pulsed electric blue. Then yellow, and then the colors swirled together, merging into a sickening yellowish green. Leila's voice was in there somewhere, saying words that made no sense. Kit sat, felt herself fall into it. It was on her skin, eating into her. She wanted to swim against it, pull herself back, but it engulfed her, sucked her down and down and down; she felt herself falling off the bar stool, falling, someone's arms catching her, and then there was only black.

And out of the black, inside the black, a voice.

"Kit?"

It was Jenny's voice, but not her voice as a young woman, not her grown voice. It was her voice as a child, a little girl. It was her voice coming in through Kit's bedroom door and Kit was still hurting from Wade's belt.

Jenny slipped in, followed her voice through the tiny opening in the doorway, and she came and stood next to Kit's bed, looking at Kit curled up against the wall in the corner. "Are you okay?"

Kit nodded yes, afraid if she spoke she'd start crying and frighten her sister. She wasn't sure she was okay.

"Kit?" Only now it wasn't Jenny's voice.

"Kit, wake up."

An insistent tapping at her face. Jenny hands on her cheeks, moving her head back and forth.

"Are you there?" It was Leila Jane's voice. Urgent. Concerned.

She held on to the image of Jenny, grasping at it helplessly as it slipped away.

"Kit. Open your eyes." Leila Jane, ordering her.

Jenny was gone. Kit forced her eyelids up. The bar loomed over her. Leila knelt next to her, Ezra next to Leila.

Kit felt Leila's arms slip under her own and Leila helped her sit up. She was on the floor. A good place to be when you didn't want to fall down anymore.

She didn't resist when Leila pressed her head down toward her knees. The yellow was still there, little pinpricks of it sparkling at the edges of her vision. Kit kept her head down until they faded away completely.

"Cheryl's dead?" Her voice sounded hollow, floating into the space between her upraised knees. She lifted her head slowly.

"They found her in her car," Leila said. "Beneath an overpass out on the loop."

Kit closed her eyes, trying to absorb Leila's words.

"Strangled, apparently," Leila said. "We'll know for certain when the autopsy comes back. But they're pretty sure."

Leila Jane stared at her.

"What's going on, Kit?"

"I don't know. I don't know what's going on." She pulled herself up, let Ezra, who looked stricken at the news of Cheryl's death, help her onto a stool. She looked at the bottles lined up there behind the bar, gleaming, sparkling under the lights. She wanted a drink.

She did not want a drink. She sat, numbly staring.

"Does Luke know about this? About Cheryl?"

"I tried to raise him on the radio," Leila said. "Technically he's off duty today, but someone saw him in the office earlier."

"He needs to know," Kit said.

"Kit," Leila said, "They need someone to ID the body. To be sure."

Kit looked at her, not immediately comprehending what Leila was saying.

"Can you come with me? I'll drive you over." Leila watched her closely, looking at her as if expecting her to faint again.

Kit turned to Ezra.

"Did you see a guy today, wearing a Stetson?"

"Yeah, I saw him," Ezra said.

"Ever seen him before?"

"Not that I recall. Why? He give you a hard time or something?"

"No," Kit said. "He was odd, that's all."

"I didn't notice," Ezra said. He placed his arms on the bar, leaning, his head bent, shaking it slowly back and forth. "Cheryl," he said. "Unbelievable."

"Kit." Leila put a hand on her shoulder. "They need you to do this."

"They?"

"Sergeant Batista is waiting for us at the morgue."

"Okay." Kit sucked in a breath and sighed it back out. "Let me go get changed."

"Can you walk?" Ezra moved next to her, took her arm gently as she stood up.

"I'm okay," Kit said. "Just give me a couple of minutes." She left them both standing in the bar and made her way toward the dressing room.

She wondered how long it would be before Leila realized she wasn't coming back.

TWENTY

The guard was still posted outside Dr. Wolfe's door. But it was a different cop, not the same guy as before. Kit wondered if the other one had left her description.

She walked slowly toward him, fighting the urge to turn and run. She walked, managed a tight smile as she approached. He had mouse brown hair clipped in a crew cut, short enough that the scalp shone through, a strong jaw, cold green eyes.

"I'm here to see Dr. Wolfe," she said.

The door to the room stood open behind him. She could see Dr. Wolfe lying on her side, her back to the door.

"Who are you?" He pulled a pen and small notepad from his shirt pocket.

"A friend," Kit said. "Emma Bovary."

"Spell that last name?"

She did. She saw Dr. Wolf turn at the sound of her voice.

"No visitors allowed," the cop said. "I'll let her know you were—"

"Please," Dr. Wolfe called. "She can come in."

The cop gave Kit a look.

"You got ID?"

"I left my bag in the car," Kit said. She didn't add *on purpose*.

"What's your date of birth?" He held his pen poised to write.

"March 15, 1979." *Whatever.*

"Please," Dr. Wolfe called weakly. "She's fine."

The cop tucked the pad into his pocket and shrugged.

"Go on ahead then." He sat back down in his chair. Picked up his magazine.

"Emma Bovary?" Dr. Wolfe's voice held pain, but she managed a smile. She shifted uncomfortably in the bed so she was facing Kit.

"Just popped into mind."

"Sit. Please."

"I can't stay long." Air whooshed out of the cushion vents when Kit perched on the turquoise-colored chair next to the bed. The cushion collapsed in slow motion until she could feel the chrome-plated ribs of the chair beneath her digging into her buttocks.

Dr. Wolfe turned herself slowly onto her back and rested her left arm in its cast across her stomach. Her face was drained of its usual coppery glow. She had a large black eye and a gash, stitched shut, above her left eyebrow. Her mouth was swollen on the left side.

Kit felt a wave of nausea as she took in the doctor's injuries. She moved the chair closer to the bed, leaned to whisper.

"A dancer I worked with," Kit said quietly, "the cops found her dead." Her voice sounded cold, mechanical. Was she speaking? "Strangled in her car."

Dr. Wolfe moved again, wincing.

"I can't see you anymore. You can't see me anymore," Kit said.

"That's not a solution."

"And what? This is? They're not done. They'll be back."

Dr. Wolfe sighed.

"Did you get a look?"

"Not really. One guy."

"Heavyset? Dark hair?"

"I don't know. Passersby scared him off. It was dark; it happened fast. I'm not good at this."

Kit could see him, the way she'd seen him in Blaze's parking lot that night. She could see him scuttling across the asphalt like some huge, misshapen crab.

"This guy"—Kit nodded at the door—"why's he—" She stood and walked to the door, kicked up the doorstop and listened to the hydraulic sigh as it eased shut. She returned to Dr. Wolfe's bedside.

"Did they say why they were putting a cop at your door?"

"Some sergeant or other ordered it. I don't know."

"Did you tell them you were seeing me? Fill them in on anything? What about your office? Did you tell them about that?"

"They said they'd put it all in the report."

"How reassuring. Could it have been the cowboy? The one you noticed before?"

"No hat."

300

"I'm sorry they did this to you." Kit shifted in the uncomfortable chair.

Dr. Wolfe reached out her hand, left it open and hanging off the edge of the bed. Kit took it, and Dr. Wolfe squeezed gently, affectionately.

"It's not your fault," she said.

"It happened because you're treating me."

"We don't know that."

"Maybe you don't know that, but I do. I'm sure of it."

"Do you know how the Eskimos hunt wolves?"

Kit shook her head no.

"They bury the handle of a knife in the ground, good and firm. And then they put a piece of bloody meat on the blade. And then they move away and wait."

"I can't put you at risk anymore," Kit said. "I won't."

"When the wolf smells the meat, he comes over and begins eating, and in the process he cuts his mouth. But he won't stop eating, the scent and taste of fresh blood keep him gnawing on the blade. He can't stop himself. It is in his nature to chew, to gnaw. So he does. Eventually he bleeds to death."

"My sister is dead. One of my coworkers is dead. You've been beaten up."

"If they force us apart, they'll have succeeded." Dr. Wolfe lay there, brushing the fingertips of her right hand across those protruding from her cast. "Tell me what's going on," she said. "Please."

Dr. Wolfe pulled herself up onto her pillows, so that she was almost sitting upright. "Talk to me."

Kit was silent. She could almost see the thoughts pinging around in her brain, as though they weren't hers, as though they'd somehow gotten inside her head but didn't really belong to her. They were someone else's thoughts, bouncing around in there and not connected to any of her own neurons.

"My mother used to read to us, at night, to Jenny and me." Kit felt warm suddenly, as though she'd stepped into a sauna. Silence hung in the room, dead air. Her breathing came short and shallow as she tried to contain her rage, deny her rage, pretend against her memory.

"He would come in. I can see him standing at the bedroom doorway, smiling, come to say good night. Sometimes I was half asleep by then, but I can hear his voice, saying how special I was to him, telling me how much he loved me. I don't remember exactly when things went sour between us."

It had been a gradual process, the disintegration of their relationship. Like molten metal, hardening as it cools.

"Metal fears fire," Kit said.

"I'm sorry?" Dr. Wolfe adjusted the bedsheet, folding it neatly across her midsection.

"The five elements. Interconnected. Metal fears fire. Fears being melted by it."

"Your father? Metal?"

Kit felt her head nodding yes, and then she heard someone whisper, "She knew."

Kit looked around to see who'd said it. Dr. Wolfe stared, waiting, and Kit realized the words had been her own. This thing that had been stalking her, hiding in the depths of her mind, lurking there, pounced. The flashbacks into a black hole of memory. She said the words, heard words spilling out of her, and now she felt tears leaking from her eyes and running down her face.

"I'm dead, you know. I'm next."

Someone held out a tissue, Dr. Wolfe was handing her a tissue.

"There's a cop right outside the door, Kit. You're safe here."

"Except that they're looking for me right now to identify Cheryl's body."

"They don't know you're in here. You're safe. Talk to me."

Kit swiped at her face with a tissue. Blew her nose and discovered a wastebasket next to the hospital bed.

"My mother knew," Kit said. "That was what she apologized for."

She saw her mother healthy then, before the disease began killing her. Standing in the kitchen that night, the night Kit came over to tell her she was dropping out of grad school, couldn't take the bullshit anymore, and her mother leaned back against the sink, the dishwasher humming and sloshing next to her, and Kit let go, told her how she couldn't stand it anymore, trying to live up to the expectations of a father who would never like or admire anything she did, a father who despised her, a father who simply didn't want her as his daughter, who didn't know her and didn't know how to know her, didn't even *want* to know her. So just by God fuck him and his stupid lawman sensibility and his holier-than-thou attitude and what made him think he knew what was best for her when he didn't know her at all. At all. Never would.

And her mother had stood there pensively, taking all Kit's anger without generating any in response. She stood there with sympathy in her eyes and finally, when Kit had finished spilling her ire into the warm kitchen air and onto her mother's shoulders, her mother had let go a quiet sigh.

"You think he's messed you up," she said.

Kit nodded. "He's been a big part of it."

"Yes," Karen said. Her mother said, "I'm sure that's true. Well." Another sigh. "You're lucky. You should see what he did to your sister."

Kit had stormed from the room, out the front door to her car and off into the night. Off to another club. Off to another fucked-up evening of drinking and drugging and not thinking about what she'd feel like in the morning. What did that mean, *what he'd done to her sister*? Wade and Jenny were double tight. She was his dream daughter. His pride and joy.

Kit looked at Dr. Wolfe. "I can feel it," she said. "I can feel it now, remember it, and everything is getting all mixed up. It's crazy, it's insane, I'm lying in bed next to Jenny and pretending to be asleep and hearing him whisper how much he loves her, how special she is to him and how wonderful it is that they can share these secrets and never tell anyone else in the world and it's just theirs, it's all theirs and nobody else's, and then one day it wasn't anymore, and I could see the way he looked at Jenny after that, but I can't tell you if the memories are real or if I'm making them up in this sick, twisted little mind of mine."

"You're not sick," Dr. Wolfe said. "Remember, Kit. You're suffering from trauma. From several distinct traumas, in fact."

"I went black," Kit said. "I had this blackout. The night your office was trashed? I don't know where I was."

Dr. Wolfe looked startled.

"No idea?"

"I took that medication. I don't remember what happened afterward."

"You had a reaction?"

"I don't know. I have no memory of that night. Nothing."

"Have you taken any since?"

Kit shook her head no.

"Good. Do you need something different? Valium, for a week or two?"

"It won't help." Kit buried her face in her hands and stayed that way for a long moment, until she could hold her head up again and look at Dr. Wolfe.

"I'm so scared," she said.

"Of what, Kit?" Dr. Wolfe's voice reached her as though coming through a long concrete tunnel, almost a whispering echo of itself.

Kit wanted to tell her. She couldn't tell her. She had to tell her.

"I'm scared I might have done it." She drew her legs up and rested her forehead on her knees. "The blackouts. I had them even before."

She was silent.

When she spoke again, her voice was quiet.

"She knew about it. She did nothing to stop it."

"Your mother."

"She knew what my father did. She knew about Jenny. What he did to her."

"Maybe she *did* do something, Kit. Maybe she tried but couldn't, in the end, do anything to stop it."

"If that were true, then she had nothing to apologize for."

"I doubt she saw it that way."

"I didn't do anything."

Dr. Wolfe was silent for a long moment. "You were a little girl. What could you have done?"

"I didn't know what to do."

"There wasn't anything, Kit. There was nothing you could have done."

"There should have been. There should have been some way to stop him."

"You're right. There should have been. But there wasn't."

But it didn't change anything. It didn't change the amazing, awful, dirty little secret that she'd been carrying all these years, knowing and not knowing, refusing to know, incapable of knowing, because to acknowledge it would have killed her. And it didn't change the fact that she had no memory of the night her sister was killed.

"I can't do this," she said. She stood quickly and bolted for the door.

The cop jumped to his feet when she yanked open the door; she heard Dr. Wolfe call after her, call her name, and then the cop's voice, shouting out, "Hold it!" but she was halfway down the first flight of stairs by then.

TWENTY-ONE

The acrid tang of barbecue whooshed out with Kit as she pushed open the heavy oak door of the Salt Lick BBQ carrying a large brown bag of takeout. Just like a normal person. She heard a circus ringmaster making introductions inside her head: *Ladeeees and gentlemen, the moment you've been waiting for: She walks, she talks, she crawls on her belly like a reptile! See the spectacular . . .*

Kit headed for her car. But she'd managed to order dinner, hadn't she? *She walks, she talks, she orders takeout for dinner!* She would get in her car and drive to her father's house. She could walk. She could talk. She could even ask questions. She would fucking *function*. What day was it? What time was it? It didn't matter. The sun was headed down, but the air wasn't cooling, and she would just go there as she had so many times before with Jenny and bring a late dinner and fucking confront him. She would go there. Dinner with

Dad. Dinner with Dad without Jenny. She had to *know*.

If she played nice, weren't confrontational, maybe he would tell her what he knew about Jenny's murder, give her something she could give Luke that would help Luke find the killer.

His silver Wrangler was parked in the drive. She halfway hoped some emergency would arise, something requiring the immediate and heroic assistance of the Texas Rangers, something that would take her father out on business. She pictured herself sitting alone at the table, gnawing on ribs. And then searching the house, searching every possible spot—for what she wasn't sure. Something to let her know that her memories were real.

He was in his easy chair, sipping on a Tecate, staring at a baseball game on TV.

"I wish they hadn't named the damn team after us," he said, trying a grin. "Those boys right there are nothing but an embarrassment."

"What's the score?" Kit asked, but only because she had to say something. Respond to Wade's friendly overture. She realized he'd said some numbers.

"What?" Like she couldn't believe the score.

"Ten-zip. You'd think by the time a guy got to the majors, he'd know how to handle a ball."

She flashed on the image of her father, that day at her softball practice, throwing like a girl.

"Yeah," she said. "You'd think."

Wade seemed not to remember it.

"Daddy," she said, hoping to sound casual, "did you ever reach Luke?"

"No," he said. "But it was nothing. Didn't pan out."

Right. Should she ask him about Cheryl? Even bring it up? She wished she'd been able to reach Luke earlier.

"What's that you got there?"

"I brought ribs," Kit said. "And chicken. There's fries and cole slaw, too."

"Let's get to it then."

"You want to watch the game while we eat?" Please say yes. Please, Daddy, please.

"I'll get the TV tables," Wade said.

They sat, the two of them, each behind a foldout oak tray, eating silently and staring at the TV. Kit couldn't remember the last time she'd watched a baseball game. She didn't even know her father was into it. Maybe he wasn't. Maybe he wanted an excuse not to actually sit and talk to her, a mere remnant of his family.

She managed to get down two ribs and a spoonful of cole slaw. She could barely swallow. She tried not to look as Wade shoveled food into his mouth, those huge front-loader-sized bites that pouched his cheeks out and brought nausea to Kit when she watched him eat. She didn't remember him eating that way when she was little. Nothing about him then had been repulsive.

She glanced at the clock above the mantel. Twenty whole minutes down. Eternity to go.

"It was a good funeral," Wade said. "As funeral's go."

"I guess," Kit said, surprised that he'd brought it up. "I wouldn't really know."

"You're young yet. I've been to my share already."

"I'm sure you have."

"Trust me," Wade said. "It was fine. It was what she deserved."

"I thought funerals were for the bereaved, or something like that. The ones who have to press on."

"Press on." Wade grunted. "How you doing, little girl? You holding up?"

"I guess," Kit said. She should bring it up; now was the moment. Tell him about Cheryl, get his take on it. And then ask him about Jenny, and why her mother had said that. Just open her mouth and talk.

A crack of the bat against the ball brought her up short.

She pretended interest in what was happening on the screen, heard one of the sportscasters say: "That's a double and two RBIs for Dash Stratton, the rookie out of Stanford, and it looks like that's gonna just about sink the Rangers tonight."

"Enough of this bull-dookie," Wade said. He grabbed the remote from his armrest and zapped the TV into darkness.

"I'll clean up," Kit said, rising to gather the plates.

When she returned from the kitchen, Wade had put the TV tables back in their rack and was kicked back in his easy chair, sock-footed, rubbing one foot with the other.

"New boots," he explained. "Not broke in yet and my feet are sure feeling it."

"What'd you get?" Kit asked.

"Full-quill ostrich," Wade said. "Not for work. Just dress up." He motioned toward the corner of the room and Kit saw a pair of gray boots, dimply ostrich skin topped off with a darker gray leather stitched with an intricate star pattern. Expensive.

"Nice," Kit said. *Too much*, she thought. Way too much. She curled up on the couch, trying to looked relaxed, trying to look like she was in no hurry to leave.

They sat in a silence punctuated by a series of quiet sighs coming from Wade.

"What is it, Daddy?"

"Aw, you know."

Kit nodded.

"I know, Daddy," she said. "You're disappointed in the Rangers, right? You really wanted them to win tonight?"

Wade couldn't help smiling, but then Kit saw his eyes were almost watery.

"I loved her so," he said.

"I know you did." She hoped he wasn't going to get maudlin on her. As much as she'd needed him to cry at her mother's funeral, and at Jenny's, right now she needed him not to. She just didn't want to go there.

He sighed again and shifted in his easy chair. She couldn't believe her father actually seemed to want to talk to her. Seemed to *need* to talk to her. She wanted to jump up and scream at him: Gosh, Dad, it's only been like, what—*a couple of decades or so?* Since we had a meaningful conversation? And now you expect me to hold your hand while you mourn for your daughter?

Slow down, just calm down now. Sit here and try to seem sympathetic.

But they took her from *me*, too, Dad, I'm hurting as badly as you, and aren't you the one who— Her mother's voice rang in her ears, echoing. Kit could see into the kitchen from right where she sat; she didn't even have to move to see her mother standing there, listening to Kit rant, all patient and quiet, but with pain in her eyes as she listened, wanting to help her daughter, and her mother's words: *You should have seen what he did to your sister,* and even if she hadn't seen it, she had *heard it*, hadn't she, and now here was her father all these years later, grief-stricken and wanting Kit to make it better. Fuck it, just fuck it all.

"Daddy," she said. Her voice sounded so matter-of-fact it stunned her. "What did you do to Jenny?"

He rocketed forward, bringing his recliner to attention.

"What?" His face went red with rage, his eyes narrowed on her, calculating. "What the *hell* are you talking about?"

"I know what you did," Kit said. "I know. I remembered. After all this time, I remembered. Those nights? You thought I was asleep? The secret places? I *remember*."

Wade slammed his recliner back, knit his fingers together, arms across his broad chest.

"I don't know what the hell you're talking about. Secret places? What's that supposed to mean? You're crazy."

"No, I'm not."

"Yes, you are. I don't know what you think might have maybe happened, but whatever it is, it didn't. You're making shit up in your head, girl."

"What'd you do to Jenny?"

Kit saw him controlling himself, saw him holding his breath and then exhaling slowly.

"I loved her."

"I know that. *How* did you love her, Dad? Like a daughter? Or what? What'd you do to her?"

He sat up again. Cornered. She could see it in his eyes. She thought that if there were an eject button on that stupid chair of his, he would have pushed it and sent himself into orbit, as far away from her as he could get. He closed his eyes, held them that way. His breathing slowed. He opened his eyes and looked at her, hard and cold. He had himself back. In control.

"What do you think I did to her," he spat, "in that messed-up little mind of yours?"

"I think you didn't love her the right way. I think it was a sickness."

His face changed; the anger disappeared. Kit kept her eyes on him, waiting.

"Kit," he said. "I never did *anything* to either one of you. I'm your father. I love you."

She heard the words and wanted desperately to believe him.

He rose from the chair and stood before her, all six foot two of him, towering, looking down at her. And then he sat down on the couch and took her in his arms and pulled her head to his chest, stroking her hair gently. He was her father.

"Where did you ever get such an idea?" he said quietly. "Are you taking something, Kit? Are you back on drugs? Are you taking something to make you crazy like this?"

"I'm not making this up. I know."

"Do you *really*, in your heart, think I'd ever do anything like that? I mean, think about it, for God's sake. I'm your father."

That's the point, she wanted to say, but she felt herself shrinking, going back in time, her mind imploding on itself and then, blossoming out of the rubble and dust, watered by her father's tears, a flower. And she was six again, and Daddy's little girl. And now, in this moment, Daddy loved her. Maybe he had all along.

"Kit," he whispered. "My baby." He pulled her tight to him. "It will be all right." A shudder ran through her, and then she was crying, sobbing like a child, and she was in her father's arms, feeling his strength, his protection. "There, there," he said. "There, there."

Everything would be all right.

But it wouldn't. It never could. Jenny was gone. A spasm shook her; she almost retched, caught herself, pulled back from him. His eyes, those hard blue eyes, staring into hers, trying to see something there.

"Mom said." Kit slumped back against the couch. Looked at him hard. "Daddy," she whispered, "if you've never ever told me the truth in your whole life, you have to do it now. You *have to*." She saw her plea reach him, take hold of him, fill his eyes with kindness.

And then the kindness seemed to jell, ever so slightly, turn into something a little less liquid, like molten steel. Her father's blue eyes. Metal fears fire.

Her father's eyes told her he thought she needed help, and would see to it that she got it.

Maybe she did. Maybe she was crazy. Maybe her mother never said that. Maybe none of it ever really happened.

"Daddy?"

"I loved Jenny, Kit. And I love you. I never did anything bad to either of you. I don't know how you could think that about me."

She looked at him. And if he were telling the truth, she didn't know it. And if he were lying, she didn't know that, either.

She didn't know him.

She didn't think she ever would.

"I have to go now," she said.

"Kit—"

The tone of her cell phone brought his words to a halt.

She stumbled over to where she'd left her bag, next to her father's new boots, and dug inside for the phone.

"What?" she answered.

"Kit. It's Luke." His voice urgent. "Can you meet me at the PD?"

"Okay," Kit said. She pressed the end button on her phone and slipped it back into her bag. "I have to go now, Dad. I'll call you tomorrow. We should talk some more. When I've had time to try to sort some things out."

Her father sat there on the couch, his eyes watching her.

She picked up her bag and moved toward the door.

"I'll call you tomorrow. I promise. I'm sorry, Daddy. I'm just all confused here."

He got up and followed her to the door, reached to hug her. She let him pull her to his chest. He ran a hand across her hair.

"It'll work out," he said. "We'll get through this." He put a fist under her chin, raised her face gently. "It's just you and me now, little girl. We'll just have figure out how to make things right."

She hurried to her car and cranked the engine, backed out of the driveway and onto the smooth white pavement.

And then in her rearview she saw the Wrangler's lights come on as Wade started his car.

He was following her. Why was he following her? She floored it; the Mustang's engine roared in response.

The Wrangler's headlights flared in Kit's rearview as Wade pulled onto the street behind her. She hit the intersection at the end of the road, slammed one foot on the gas, the other on the brake pedal, cut the wheel hard left, fishtailing through the intersection with minimal loss of speed, straightened the wheel, and gunned the engine again. Darkness behind her now as she headed full speed for the main road, and then Wade's headlights again as he made the turn in pursuit.

Kit drove all out, screaming down manicured residential streets until she was on the boulevard, blasted through three greens before she lost the lights and caught a red. She hit the brakes, scanned for cross traffic before busting the light in a headlong rush toward Austin police headquarters. The Wrangler was back there, gaining on her.

She hit traffic on Lamar, dodging expertly from lane to lane, slipping around vehicles, darting between them, squeezing past with mere inches to spare, alternately mashing the accelerator and brake pedal. Car horns blared angrily; the lights of the Wrangler disappeared into the glare of headlights behind her.

Traffic thinned, and she saw a set of headlights coming up fast behind her. And then the Wrangler was in her rearview. She caught another red light and had to stop for this one. Wade eased to a stop one car behind.

The light changed and she gunned it, and watched as the Wrangler made a right at the intersection.

Just like that, he was gone.

Kit felt foolish. He'd just been going somewhere, not following her. If he hadn't thought she was nuts before, surely he did now. She continued down the boulevard, driving with sanity now, wondering what Luke had that made it so urgent he see her, but glad they would be able to talk.

She wheeled into the parking lot and eased into a slot for visitors.

The vacuum whoosh of the front doors as she pushed through them startled her. She walked quickly to the front desk.

"Detective Saner," she said to the officer behind the counter. "He's expecting—"

Luke emerged briskly from a door to the left of the desk, his eyes filled with concern. She ran to him. He slipped an arm around her shoulder, hugging her to him.

"You're here." Low and urgent. "Come with me."

"Luke, what the hell is going on?"

"I'll need an affidavit from you," he said. "Come with me."

She walked next to him as he strode quickly through fluorescent-lit hallways, past staring uniformed officers, and into a large room full of shoulder-high cubicles. He led her through a maze toward his cubicle, in the far corner of the room. As they approached, Kit saw that one of the cubicles had bright yellow crime scene tape tacked across its entrance. A wide black ribbon was draped above the yellow tape.

Jenny's desk inside. Jenny's office, the chair where she'd sat and done paperwork, made phone calls, done all the little tasks her job entailed. The job that had gotten her killed.

Kit squeezed her eyes shut as she walked past the cubicle to the one where Luke was standing, waiting for her.

"We have to do this now," he said. "Are you all right?"

Kit managed a nod but in her head she heard *No! No, I'm not all right. Somebody tell me what's happening.* She entered, sat in a small wire-frame chair with a spare, gray-upholstered seat and back. She put her bag on the brown carpeted floor and folded her hands in her lap.

Luke took his chair, swiveled around to face her.

"The cowboy," Luke said. "His name is Harlan Dale Stamm, he works the ranch where the well is, where Jenny's body was found. Stamm is the one who discovered the body and called the sheriff's office."

Kit sat, trying to absorb what Luke was telling her. Trying to make sense of it.

"Kit," Luke said, "Stamm didn't get the ring from his girlfriend. I'm betting he found it when he found Jenny's body. He liked it. He decided to keep it."

Kit saw Luke looking at her, watching her, waiting.

"How did it get there?"

"I don't know," Luke said. "But I doubt it was left there on purpose."

She sat, stunned by the questions somersaulting in her brain.

"What, exactly, did your father say to you when you asked him about his ring?"

She could see Wade standing there on the back porch. She remembered how he'd held his hands out, inspecting them, when she asked what he'd done with it.

"He said he'd pawned it," Kit said. "Like I told you before. I wanted to ask him where. But I knew he wouldn't tell me."

"So he didn't say where. Did he say when?"

"He said that morning. The morning of the funeral. He couldn't stand the memories it brought to him. When he looked at it."

"I'll just bet he's got some memories," Luke said bitterly. "Did you ever see it, between the time of Jenny's death and the funeral? Did he ever wear it then, that you can remember?"

Kit tried to remember if Wade had been wearing the ring that night she went to his house and learned Jenny was dead. It was a blur.

"I just can't remember," she said. "If he was wearing it that night, I can't remember."

"And he got her into the ground the very next day," Luke said. "I remember thinking that was unusual, to have the funeral so fast."

"In some cultures it's the way it's done." Kit didn't know why she was trying to rationalize her father's actions.

"In some cultures, yeah but not his. It's usually three days later."

Nothing was making sense. Why couldn't she think. Kit sat mute, stunned almost unconscious.

"Kit," Luke said quietly, "whoever put Jenny's body in that well was wearing your father's ring. It fell off. Stamm found it when he found the body."

"It was him then. Maybe my father did exactly what he said. Pawned it. And Stamm's girlfriend bought it and gave it to him for his birthday, just like he said. Stamm is the one."

"But Wade told you he pawned it the morning of the funeral. If that's true, then he had it when she was killed. And if it's not true, then why would he lie about it?" Luke leaned toward her.

Rage brought her to her feet and she was stomping around in circles, trying to trample the fear, grind it into the floor.

"What the hell does it matter!" she screamed. "Jenny is dead! Cheryl is dead! Did you know that, Luke? Did you know Cheryl was murdered while you were coming up with all these grand fucking *theories* of what in God's name happened to my sister? My shrink is in the hospital and I'm sure she'd be dead, too, except some fools happened along and scared off the worthless motherfucking lowlife scumbag before he could goddamn murder her! What the hell does it—"

He was looking at her. He sat in his chair and looked, his eyes pained. He waited.

She stood, trembling silently. Slowed herself. Sat down. She sat down in the chair. Her lip hurt. She realized she had it clamped in her teeth. She let go. She expected to feel tears on her face. There were none.

"Kit?" Luke took her hands. She pulled them away.

She felt hands on her shoulders. They were hers. She was wrapped in a hug, hugging herself, her arms across her chest as if to protect her heart. She rocked slowly in the chair. Her hands fell to her lap.

"Kit," Luke said, "I need an affidavit. I need cause to arrest Harlan Stamm and question him."

"For what?"

"Theft of evidence." He sighed and leaned toward her. "And if he cops out, says he found the ring at the crime scene..." He let the sentence fall unfinished between them.

No. And no. And no and no and no. Kit felt her head shaking back and forth, methodically, denying the possibility. No. She felt her insides go hollow, simply disintegrate, leaving dead space inside her body. She knew she was still breathing, but she couldn't feel any air coming into her lungs or leaving them. She was suspended in a timeless vapor, her thoughts, her very body, experiencing a kind of light-speed petrifaction. She was stone.

What did stone fear?

Luke left the cubicle; he was gone before she realized he'd said something about going to get some paperwork.

She was alone. The office empty. She watched herself stand and walk across the aisle to Jenny's cubicle. Watched herself step carefully over the crime scene tape, under the black ribbon. Saw her hands reach for a desk drawer. And then another, full of files.

She thumbed through them, her fingers shaking like she had the DTs. Nothing. There was nothing about Weatherby or Ned or Bryan or any of them. She pushed the files back angrily, pressing them against the back of the drawer.

Saw something beneath, blue-black metal glinting, hiding at the back of the file drawer. She pulled the files forward, mashed them against the front of the drawer. There was a gun. A Colt .38 revolver. Wade had to have given Jenny that. Cops didn't carry revolvers anymore. It was an antique, for God's sake. Kit's hands reached for it; Kit's hands slipped the gun from beneath the files and closed the desk drawer and Kit's body slipped out over the yellow tape and under the black ribbon.

TWENTY-TWO

She stood in a small room, her right hand raised, and heard herself swear before God and Luke and the pasty-faced, jowly judge seated at the desk that the information contained in her affidavit was true. The judge signed some papers, and then Luke was hurrying her back through a maze of hallways to his cubicle.

"There's a holding cell downstairs if you'd like to rest. Best I can do."

"This is fine," Kit said. She sat down at his desk.

"You'll stay here then?"

"Where am I gonna go?"

"Saner?" The voice was deep and full of urgency. A dark-haired man stuck his head into the doorway at the front of the room. Luke leaned out of the cubicle.

"Right here, Sergeant."

"Let's roll."

"There's Sergeant Batista," Luke said. "I have to go." His voice held reluctance. "I'll call you as soon as we have him." He stood there, holding the arrest warrant rolled into a tube. "And try not to worry," he said. "Wade won't be coming for you."

"You don't believe that."

"Not here," Luke said, "so just stay here until I get back."

Kit glanced up at him, the phrase "grace under pressure" flitting around in her head. She leaned forward in the chair to watch Luke walk away.

The room fell silent but for the sounds of someone shuffling papers in a cubicle in the far corner of the room, and the hum of fluorescent lighting emanating from the ceiling. The faint grumble of flowing traffic filtered into the building from the streets outside. People drove past, going where they were going. Kit sat at the desk, folded her hands in front of her. They were hers. She looked at her arms and legs and torso. They were hers. She was here, inside this body. This was real.

None of it was real. This wasn't happening.

A detective walked by, briskly, but something passed through his eyes when he glanced at Kit. She'd seen it. Concern. The kind of look you give someone when you know they're in danger. This was real. This was happening.

She waited until the detective was gone before she stood up. She looked around the office. The paper shuffling stopped, and she heard someone on the phone, asking to speak to someone. She picked up her bag and walked to the office doorway.

The officer at the front desk was talking to a couple of angry civilians when she walked out the front door. Her car was still in the visitor's spot. She glanced around quickly and stepped over to it.

Inside the car, she pulled the revolver out of her bag and flipped open the cylinder: six copper-jacketed .38s nestled snug in their places. She clicked the cylinder back into place and tucked the gun next to her on the seat. She started the engine and pulled out of the lot.

She drove slowly, carefully, with the windows down, feeling the heated breeze as it flowed into the car. She drove, distanced from herself, watching the mundane possibilities roll through her brain, watching her own thoughts as they flowed through her head, one on the tail of another, all lined up and progressing in order, a parade of absurdity.

And then, in the rearview, she saw it and didn't want to see it. Didn't want to let herself see it. A Wrangler. Her father's? It was the right color. It was maintaining its distance, in the next lane. Nothing to stop it from pulling past her. Other cars passed, slipping from behind the Wrangler into her lane, and then easing back over to drive past her. She was driving slowly. She drove slower.

The Wrangler drove slower.

She sped up, only a little, but enough.

The Wrangler held its position. It had to be Wade. Looking after her? He must have followed her to police headquarters. He must know she'd been talking to Luke.

What the hell had she been thinking? When would she learn to trust herself? Maybe she'd been right, that night at the pond. She'd felt it then. And she felt it now. Luke had an answer for everything. It was too neat, the package too beautifully wrapped. When, and why, had she stopped suspecting him? She didn't know. Jenny had trusted him, had loved him, and look what had happened. Kit slapped herself, hard, savoring the sting on her face. *You stupid bitch*. She'd fucked him. She had let him fuck her. Her thoughts broke ranks then, ran screaming, stumbling over each other, knocking one another down like theater-goers in a fire, seeking the safety of exit, fleeing into the recesses of her brain.

⌗

Her apartment smelled of absence. Airless. Lifeless. No one lived here. She left the lights off, went to the kitchen, placed the revolver on the dusty counter. She opened the freezer, and there in the rectangle of light that stung her eyes was her old friend, the Grey Goose. The frosted glass bottle lay on its side, half full still of thick, icy liquid. She took it out and pressed it to her forehead, slid it back and forth, slowly, wiping away perspiration. She put the bottle on the kitchen counter and closed the freezer. She stared at the bottle, stared long enough that water condensed on the glass, began dripping down the sides.

She picked up the bottle and picked up the gun and walked to the living room. She sat on the carpet, facing the window. Put the bottle and gun on the carpet at her feet.

Luke had an answer for everything.

Her father had an answer for everything.

The coffin had been closed.

She picked up the gun, felt its heavy metal essence. She rubbed a thumb along the a groove in the cylinder. *Metal fears fire*. The gun was metal. Inside it was fire.

She placed the gun before her and picked up the bottle. Sweet relief? What the hell. She could go slowly; she could go quickly. But she would go. She would go where her mother had gone, where her sister had gone. She would prove to her father once and for all how much he really loved her.

The cork made a pop when she pulled it from the bottle. The glass was ice on her lips. The liquid was fire in her throat.

A sip. Just one. For courage.

She pushed the cork back into place. Put the bottle back on the carpet. It shone like ice in the city light spilling onto the carpet through the living room window. Warmth spread through her, traveling with her blood.

She would not have to run anymore. Not from anything. Not from Rusty, not from Luke, not from her father. Not from memory: of Jenny, of her mother, of her father's whispered words to her sister.

Not even from herself.

No one could touch her.

She picked up the gun and turned it around in her hands, slid her palm around the back of the grip and slipped her thumb inside the trigger guard. Felt the crisscross cut of the trigger against her thumb.

She raised the barrel to her forehead, her forehead cool from the icy bottle. She moved slowly, feeling the smooth rounded end of the barrel as she slid it down, between her eyebrows, over the bridge of her nose, and stopped at her lips. She opened her mouth and pressed the barrel in past her lips. She tasted metal. The front sight was rough against the roof of her mouth. She could do this. The pain could be over. The pain would be over.

She brought her other hand up, cupped it around the grip, twined her fingers together. She used her other thumb to steady her aim, pressing it against the smooth metal just above the trigger guard. She tilted back her head. Opened her mouth wide. Trajectory was important. She could do this.

Her thumb pressed against the trigger, testing. It was tight. It would take some pressure. She squeezed slowly, sensed the hammer rising. She had to do this. A little bit farther and it would be done. She had to. She squeezed slowly. *Please, God, let me do this one small thing.*

She squeezed harder.

She held the pressure. *Please, God.*

Something whispered in her head: No.

She felt a tear brim out of her eye, trickle down her cheek.

No.

She could not.

Slowly, ever so slowly, she eased her pressure on the trigger. The hammer came to rest. Metal on metal. Quiet as a butterfly.

TWENTY-THREE

The windows were dark. A weak light seeped out from behind the house, coming from the back porch. Kit parked in the drive, behind the Wrangler, blocking it where it sat. She got out, tucked Jenny's gun into the waistband of her jeans, pulled her shirt down over it. It felt hard and cold against her back.

She walked slowly past Wade's car to the front door. It was locked. She walked around the side of the house. The latch clicked metallically; hinges squeaked as she eased open the low wooden gate.

The yard was empty, the barn and garage dark. Kit stepped onto the deck. A cluster of moths fluttered around the porch light next to the sliding glass door. A couple of June bugs pinged their paper-shell bodies repeatedly against the kitchen window screen, their senses thrown into utter confusion by electricity.

Kit tried the door. It gave. She pulled the gun from her waist and slid open the door, stepped into the house almost reverently, as though entering a church. She closed the door behind her. The air-conditioning kicked on; air flowed from ceiling vents: whispered white noise. Light from the porch came through the kitchen window, spilling yellow onto the tile floor. Kit stood a moment, letting her eyes adjust to the shadows.

She stepped slowly into the living room, thankful for the silence afforded her steps by the carpet. She gripped the gun at her side.

She slipped down the hallway. Nothing. Only the sound of air flowing from the vents. She checked Jenny's room, crept past it to the one that had been hers.

From somewhere down the road, a dog barked.

Kit moved toward Wade's room, the room her mother had died in, wondering at how calm she was. How prepared she felt for this moment, being here, knowing that if she found him, one of them was going to die, and it didn't so much as make her heart flutter.

A sudden thump outside the window hit her ears and she pressed herself to the wall. What was he doing out there? And then she realized it was the air conditioner shutting off. The whir of air from the vents stopped, and the house was silent. She gripped the gun and walked back toward the kitchen, slipped through the door and onto the deck.

She felt the dry grass crunch softly under her shoes as she made her way toward the barn. The door was standing open. She hadn't noticed that before. She slipped into the darkness, stepped inside and to the right, pressing herself against the wall so as not to silhouette herself in the doorway.

She listened. A car pulled down the street, went past without slowing.

Silence. Not a sound. The barn was empty.

She felt weak suddenly, squatted there next to the wall, put her head down. Her pulse whooshed in her ears as blood returned to her head.

A locust started up out in the yard, humming on a tree branch. Others joined in, a chorus, chanting.

"Ain't life a fine, complicated mess?"

There was a click as the single overhead bulb came on, naked in its ceiling socket. Kit, crouched where she was, laughed, her eyes trained on his boots, then moving up that oak of a body. His pancake holster was strapped to his belt, holding his weapon snug against his side.

He stood there, on the opposite side of the door, just inside it, his hand still on the light switch. She stood and raised the gun at him. Held her aim.

Wade snorted, a kind of half laugh.

"Why." It wasn't a question, the way it came out. It was a statement: There could be no reason for what he'd done.

"I'm right here," he said. "Go ahead." He held his arms away from his sides, palms out to her, offering himself.

"Tell me why you did it." She wanted—needed—to know what her mother's words had meant. She wanted to know what had happened, all those years ago, when she'd kept her eyes closed and heard Wade talking to Jenny, heard the rustle of covers, the loving tones in his voice.

"You know," Wade said, "I'm just thankful your mother isn't around to see you. She didn't have to know about you getting up there and dancing naked. That would've just about killed her anyway, don't you think?"

"Fuck you."

"Oh, yeah, now there's an answer." He laughed, and it was an ugly laugh, a mean laugh. "I saw your photos," he said. "Out there on the goddamn World Wide Web. Made me proud to be your father."

"What did you do to her?" Kit felt her hands trembling, tried to steady them. "She was a little girl, Daddy. You had no right."

"She grew up," Wade said. "My little girl." He snapped his fingers. "Just like that. Gone."

"Why." Again. Kit couldn't stop from saying it.

"Why? She was a fine investigator, your little sister. She got too close. Things went straight to hell, to hell in a hand-basket."

This wasn't it. This wasn't what she'd come here for. Confusion roiled in her skull.

"What are you talking about?"

He looked at her with a loathing that turned her spine cold.

"I had to," he said. "There was no choice." His face clouded up, his lips twisted, he seemed to choke, and his eyes—Kit stared, disbelieving—her father was crying.

"I followed her," he said. "Waited in the lot while she went inside and picked out all the stuff for her goddamn wedding." Kit stood, afraid to move, afraid to breathe lest he stop talking.

"She opened her door and put a package in the backseat. When she was about to close her door, I rolled up next to her."

He wiped at his face, but more tears came, falling freely now.

"I startled her, but she was glad to see me. I asked her if she had time for dinner."

He glared at Kit.

She stood watching her father cry, listening as the story spilled forth.

Jenny got in his car. She gave him a sweet hug and a kiss on the cheek. She was bubbly and excited from picking out dinnerware.

She talked on about the choices she'd made, how she knew he'd approve. She'd picked out a pattern that was similar to the one he and Mom had; she remembered from childhood. The Wedgewood with the plums and cherries around the edges of the plates, the colors subtle. Kind of old-fashioned, she knew, but she liked that about it.

It wasn't until they went past the loop and exited onto the ranch road that she asked where he was taking her.

He told her he had a hankering for Mexican. He said he was taking her somewhere special. Someplace she hadn't been before. Kind of a hole-in-the-wall, but they had the best tamales in the world. It was a bit of a drive. Did she have time? Was her fiancé expecting her back soon?

But Wade knew Luke wouldn't be getting off work. He'd put in a call to make sure Luke was kept busy for the evening.

They were well out of the city and surrounded by darkness when he pulled to the side of the road. He told her it was a call of nature. He feigned embarrassment.

He pissed near the back tire of the car, zipped up, and pretended something caught his attention: something over in the low line of trees off the highway. He rapped on the rear fender of the car.

Jenny opened her door and leaned out.

He said there was something over there in the trees, pointing. He'd heard something. He would be right back.

She got out of the car and stood, watching as he loped toward the trees. He tucked himself in behind one, waited a moment.

And then he called to her. Said she should come have a look. She wouldn't believe it.

He watched her walk toward him. He was behind the tree.

She peered at the darkness.

He watched her walk toward him. The headlights from the car shone down the highway behind her. She stumbled once, caught herself.

He called out to her. Sounding like it was something funny he had to show her.

She followed his voice, walking away from the lights.

She was barely three feet away when he stepped out.

He shot from the hip.

He'd always been good at that.

She fell quickly.

She didn't even bleed much, so clean was his aim.

Dead into the heart.

He picked up her body and carried it to the car.

He put it in the trunk.

He drove then, for the longest while, feeling slightly confused and a little disoriented.

He remembered the well.

From years earlier. From an earlier case. When a little girl had fallen down it, out playing one afternoon with the ghosts of Indians. He'd been the one to be lowered down in a harness to scoop her into his arms and raise her to safety.

He'd been a hero that day.

He parked just off the road and got Jenny's body from the trunk. Still not much blood.

He carried her body, winding around scrub oak and brush, and laid it on the ground next to the well. He moved aside the heavy concrete cover. The one that had been put on a week or so after he saved the young girl, all those years ago.

He tried to drop the body gently, held her by the wrists and let go slowly.

The sound of his daughter's body hitting bottom did something to him. He shoved the cover back over the hole and he ran.

If it hadn't been for that sound, that fleshy thud of skin and bone hitting the unforgiving earth, he might have thought to check.

It was as though Jenny had reached back from the other side of death and grabbed the ring from his finger as her hand slipped through his.

The sound had panicked him. He hadn't thought to check.

He coughed and looked at Kit, his face soaked with tears, the front of his shirt damp with them.

"Kind of stupid," he said quietly, "don't you think?"

Kit fell to her knees, and he moved faster than she could have imagined, leapt at her, reaching for the gun. She staggered up, gripping the gun, but he had it, he had her hands in his, his big hands wrapped around hers, powerful as he ever was, and Kit felt herself go weak with fear and then go strong again, struggling against him, trying to twist the barrel of the gun free and stick it in his gut, but he was mighty, tensed against her, and she heard herself scream as he wrested the gun from her grip and turned it on her, his face bulging red with rage, twisted with hatred.

"Go ahead, Daddy, shoot me like you did Jenny!" Kit screamed, her words blasting against him, "Go on! Now!"

And a roar filled her head and then silence, she couldn't hear, she couldn't feel, she couldn't smell. She felt her knees buckle, struggled to stay standing. Heat filled her brain, and she watched her father's head explode into red and nothingness. Bits of bone stung her face. He stood, staring past her, wobbling ever so slightly. His hand went limp; the gun fell to the ground. Wade stood, but blood poured now from the wound that had been his forehead, running down over his blank eyes, bathing his face.

And then he fell, spinning like a boxer knocked blind by a punch he never saw coming, and landed hard on the ground. His body thudded onto dirt.

Kit stood, staring down at him, unthinking, unable to process what she was seeing. Her being went light. She was floating somewhere above the surface of the earth, hovering there, looking down from above, where Jenny would be. She could almost feel her sister's presence, there next to her, staring down at their father's lifeless body as blood pooled around his head.

"Kit."

The sound of Luke's voice brought her back, and she saw him holster his weapon and then his arms were around her and he was holding her to him, turning to take her eyes away from what she was seeing, and she let him do that, stand there holding her, because she was sure that if he let go, she might very simply disintegrate.

TWENTY-FOUR

Kit sat at graveside. Next to her, Luke. Leila Jane was there, and Rusty had resurfaced. Dr. Wolfe had a small yin-yang symbol on her cast, just above the wrist. Blaze and Ezra were present as well. A few Rangers were in attendance. Five or six. The old guard and hard core, Burt Simmons among them, who'd known Wade since he was inducted. Perhaps figuring to show solidarity. They pointedly refused to meet Kit's eyes, or Luke's.

The preacher said some words. Kit heard a chorus of amens. And then Luke took her arm and led her from the grave.

Blaze caught up to them as Luke was about to help Kit into the passenger seat. She took Kit by the shoulders, pulled her close, briefly, in something that felt almost like a hug. She stepped back, still holding Kit's shoulders.

"I knew something was going on," she said. "But I had

no idea what. I'm so sorry for you, Kit. This shouldn't have happened. Cheryl—" She stopped herself, blinking rapidly, cleared her throat. "I tried to get Cheryl to talk to me." She glanced at Luke, and seemed to pull back inside herself, brushing a hand across the lapel of her tailored black suit. "I should have gone to the cops." Again she looked at Luke.

"We were already there," Luke said. "It didn't seem to matter much."

"All I had was suspicion," Blaze said. "And you know me. I prefer a low profile."

"Of course," Kit said, looking at the suit, the perfectly done red hair, the lipstick to match. Even at a funeral Blaze was a knockout. A misguided knockout perhaps, but still.

"I wish you the best," Blaze said.

"You, too, Blaze."

"I'd better scoot. I've got a bunch of damn Baptists ready to raise hell over all this. Like I could have done some-thing." She turned and walked away quickly, down the row of parked cars to her Jag.

Luke watched her go, and then waited until Kit was in the front seat before closing the door.

He started the engine and drove. Kit didn't know where they were going, and it didn't much matter.

The Tavern was a plain wooden building perched on the spiny ridge, surrounded by sky. A small reddish sign with painted yellow letters proclaimed this the highest point along the Devil's Backbone. Out back were a few weather-worn cedar picnic tables dotted with tourists drinking beer.

Kit stood next to Luke, looking out over the valleys that stretched into the distance. They could see for miles.

"Did you see the way they wouldn't look at us?" she said.

Luke nodded.

"You think they'll come after you? Or me?"

"No doubt they want to," he said. "But they gotta know they'd be first on the list of suspects. We may even yet be able to pop Burt Simmons on the case. It's looking like Fred might cooperate."

Kit felt weak, thinking about her father. About what his buddies might do for him.

"The thing is, first on the list or not, they've got a big reach. I don't think they'd be scared to try something. They'd just have to be careful, that's all. And they know it."

"Do you think Cheryl knew?"

"I think she liked to party, and didn't much care who was throwing them."

Luke took her arm, led her to the table where they'd left their drinks. They sat in the August heat; Kit took a long slow sip of iced tea. She hadn't realized how thirsty she was.

"No," Luke said. "I mean it's possible she knew, but I doubt it. I mean yes, she knew about recruiting at the clubs; she was part of that. But the girls there were of age. Not like the ones they grabbed off the street. Arrest some sweet young thing, give her the option of facing the judge or facing the camera. Talk about your no-brainer."

He sipped his beer, staring out past her at the sky.

"Yeah," Luke continued, "if that stupid son of a bitch Weatherby hadn't decided to take a shot at blackmailing your old man, demanding money to keep his mouth shut about the operation, he'd still be breathing."

Kit saw Luke's eyes go soft with memory, and knew he was thinking that Jenny wouldn't have gotten the murder case, and wouldn't have done such a diligent job of investigating it. And would still be alive.

Luke sighed deeply. "And if Jenny and I hadn't told Wade so much about the case."

"You had no way of knowing," Kit said.

"I wanted to impress him," Luke said. "That night we had dinner? I wanted him to think his daughter was marrying some hotshot investigator who had it all together. Shit."

"Luke," she said, "don't blame yourself. Long and short of it? My father was a bastard."

She wondered how Jenny had lived with it, if Jenny even had any conscious awareness of it. How Jenny had managed to love and respect their father after what he'd done to her when she was little. Her mother's words rang in her ears: *You should have seen what he did to your sister.* She hadn't seen. But she'd heard. She'd heard and not understood and then found a way to forget about it. Pressed it back into the darkness in her brain until it went away. Or almost. Jenny must have been able to blot out the memory even more effectively than Kit had, for all those years. Jenny had even been able to trust Wade. Trust him enough to tell him she had a suspect in her latest murder case, a suspect named Ned, who frequented a place called Blaze's.

"How and why he got that way, we'll never know," she said. "But that's what he was."

"Yeah," Luke said, letting the word out long and slow. He sighed.

"I'm thinking of getting out of here. Moving to California."

"Think it's far enough away?"

"Not because I'm afraid of them."

"You've taken out a Texas Ranger, Luke. I'd keep an eye on the rearview if I were you."

"I've applied to some law schools. Who knows what'll happen with that. Meantime I'm thinking I'll get some kind of PI gig somewhere on the West Coast." He paused. Kit saw a hint of something in his eyes. Not fear, exactly, but something close. Vulnerability, maybe. "I think you should consider a change of scenery yourself."

"I don't know where I'd go."

"Look," he said, "we both need to get out of here, at least for a while. Until things cool down."

As clouded and confused as Kit's thoughts were, if she could even call the racket in her brain thought, she knew he was right about that.

"You can't stay here. I wouldn't feel right leaving you here."

"You don't owe me anything."

"I know I don't owe you." He shook his head emphatically. "But I'd kind of like to see you stay alive. And I don't think Texas is the best place for that in the immediate future."

He gave his head that tilt she had grown to like, but hadn't realized until this moment. "We've both got to get out of here," he said. "You know it. And I know it."

❖

Luke drove and the Hill Country rolled past the window: Kit watched the landscape unfold beneath the radiant yellow sun, so bright it was almost white, the deep green of the junipers and the pale green of the live oaks. At times the road edged close enough to the Blanco River that she could see its waters slipping pale blue across the smooth lime-stone riverbed. Who was it? Heraclitus, maybe? *You could not step twice into the same river, for other waters are ever flow-ing over you.*

There were no actors in the film she saw through the car window, there was no plot, there were no special effects. No tanks in flames or burning buildings or exploding airplanes, no muscle-bound hero running across the shallow waters of the river with a machine gun in hand. There was no villain lurking in the shadows.

Just the trees, and the sun, and the tall blond grasses bending gently in the breeze. Birdsong breaking the silence, calling to the seeds in the soil, inviting them to emerge into sunshine and rich, clean air. Inviting them to be washed pure when it rained, and to flourish.

Luke drove, and Kit didn't ask where they were going.

And she didn't recognize the spot where he pulled off the road, not until he got out of the car and motioned for her to follow as he headed for the path.

They trailed through the trees.

The afternoon was silent now, owls and locusts asleep in the bright of day.

Luke sat down at the edge of the pond, patted a spot next to him on the grass. She sat, feeling the sun warm on her shoulders.

"Promise me you'll get out of Texas," he said quietly.

"You're a good guy, Luke." The words came out pure; saying them felt like an affirmation of a belief she'd lost sight of since that night in the park.

He picked up a stone, flat and rounded, flung it sidearm at the pond. They watched the rock skip across the mirror surface, setting off a row of concentric ripples, one following the other, before it lost momentum and plunged down, disappearing.

It occurred to Kit that for the first time in a long, long time, she wanted to stay alive. More than that, she wanted to try living. Even with all its convoluted ups and downs. Her sister had managed it, coping with whatever private demons she'd had to deal with. Her sister's memory demanded that Kit try, that Kit press on.

"I will," she said finally. "I'll leave."

"I'm gonna hold you to it," he said.

The two of them sat, the water still once more.